THE WORLD'S CLASSICS

SHORT STORIES

AND

THE UNBEARABLE BASSINGTON

'SAKI' (Hector Hugh Munro) was born in Burma in 1870, the son of a senior officer in the British Imperial police, but his mother died when he was 2 and he was brought up in Devon by aunts, whom he hated. At 23 he followed his father into the Burmese police, but was soon invalided out with malaria. He became a foreign correspondent on the *Morning Post*, witnessing thrilling events in the Balkans and St Petersburg. Meanwhile he had begun publishing his brilliantly witty and often chilling short stories in the *Westminster Gazette* and other periodicals. In 1908 he settled in London as a full-time writer. At the outbreak of the Great War he enlisted enthusiastically as a private soldier and was killed at Beaumont-Hamel in November 1916.

JOHN CAREY is Merton Professor of English Literature at Oxford University. His books include critical studies of Donne, Milton, Thackeray, and Dickens. In *The Intellectuals and the Masses* (1992) he examines the hostility shown by Modernist writers and other 'highbrows' to popular culture and universal education.

THE WORLD'S CLASSICS

SAKI
Short Stories

AND

The Unbearable Bassington

Selected with an Introduction by
JOHN CAREY

Oxford   New York
OXFORD UNIVERSITY PRESS
1994

Oxford University Press, Walton Street, Oxford OX2 6DP
Oxford New York Toronto
Delhi Bombay Calcutta Madras Karachi
Kuala Lumpur Singapore Hong Kong Tokyo
Nairobi Dar es Salaam Cape Town
Melbourne Auckland Madrid
and associated companies in
Berlin Ibadan

Oxford is a trade mark of Oxford University Press

Editorial matter © John Carey 1994

First published as a World's Classics paperback 1994

British Library Cataloguing in Publication Data
Data available

Library of Congress Cataloging in Publication Data
Saki, 1870–1916.
[Short stories. Selections]
Short stories and The unbearable Bassington / Saki ; selected with
an introduction by John Carey.
p. cm.—(The World's classics)
Includes bibliographical references (p.   ).
I. Carey, John. II. Saki, 1870–1916. Unbearable Bassington.
1994. III. Title: Unbearable Bassington. IV. Series.
PR6025.U675A6 1994 823'.912—dc20 93–45276
ISBN 0–19–283169–0

1 3 5 7 9 10 8 6 4 2

Typeset by Best-set Typesetter Ltd., Hong Kong
Printed in Great Britain
by BPC Paperbacks Ltd.
Aylesbury, Bucks

CONTENTS

VIRTUALLY all Saki's stories are about encounters between the wild and the tame. Usually wildness is represented by animals: a bull, a boar, a hyena, or a tiger (if that is not too grand a name for the unfortunate old beast that dies of heart failure when Mrs Packletide lets fly at it with her rifle). Saki's favourite animals were wolves, perhaps because, unlike tigers, they had never been endowed with romantic nobility. They remained outcasts, their eyes gleaming with 'unspeakable ferocity' (as in 'The Story-Teller'), their howls expressing 'all the relentless hunger-fury of the wild' ('The Wolves of Cernogratz'). He once advised his beloved sister Ethel to get a wolf instead of a dog. It would, he pointed out, devour annoying children, and make shopping easier by scaring off other customers.

Apart from animals, Saki's main models of wildness were boys. Foremost among these, in that he has a whole novel devoted to him, is the sadist and charmer Comus Bassington, celebrated by his creator as 'one of those untamable young lords of misrule that frolic and chafe themselves through nursery and preparatory and public-school days'. The plausible young liar in 'Dusk' and the irrepressible practical joker in 'Adrian' belong to the same breed. Though less refined than Comus, they embody, as he does, the anarchy and danger that Saki always associated with boyhood.

In 'Gabriel-Ernest', the first story he wrote after deciding to become a full-time writer in 1909, his two symbols of wildness combine. Gabriel-Ernest is both a naked boy, alluringly wild and rude, and 'a large wolf, blackish in colour, with gleaming fangs and cruel, yellow eyes'. Like the wolf Saki recommended to his sister, Gabriel-Ernest eats children.

The tameness which these wild things disrupt in Saki's stories is for the most part simply humdrum home life—the routines of job and family and the dull social round, which are likened, in 'The Mapped Life', to the bedraggled fate of the captive animals on their concrete terraces at London Zoo. At the root of this soul-destroying respectability lies woman. It is she, according to Saki, who tames the wild, adventurous male, and condemns him to the meek roles of husband and bread-winner. Alaric Clyde in 'Cross Currents' is such a man. In the 'high waste places of the world' he has 'roamed and hunted and dreamed, death-dealing and gracious as some god of Hellas'. But Vanessa Pennington plans to entrap this godlike male and turn him into a tame husband—one of 'the legion of men who were once young and unfettered and now eat out their souls in dustbins'.

Vanessa is punished for this by disgrace, and a job on the kitchen staff of a London club. She is lucky. For the penalties Saki inflicts on bossy or presumptuous women tend to be more severe. Sylvia Seltoun in 'The Music on the Hill' pays with her life for enticing a confirmed bachelor into marriage and 'settling him down'. The climax of this story might stand as an emblem of Saki's central male myth. The wilful woman, now doomed and terrified, shrieks for help. The antlers of the great stag drive vindictively 'straight at her breast'. As she dies she hears a boy laughing—the 'brown and beautiful' boy 'with unutterably evil eyes' whom she had earlier seen scowl-ing at her from the undergrowth, and who, it is strongly implied, is Pan.

Saki seems to have been aware that he risked monotony by basing his stories so constantly on collisions between the wild and the tame. There is surely an element of self-mockery in 'The Stalled Ox', where the cow-painter Theophil Eshley hits on a winning formula with 'Ox in a Morning-room', and follows it up with 'Barbary Apes Wrecking a Boudoir'. But to be aware of a tendency is not the same as reversing it. Saki's stories continued to exploit the same set of favourite situations. He even repeated his 'Stalled Ox' joke about repetition in 'On Approval', where conjunctions of wildness and tameness such as 'Vultures attacking dying camel in Upper Berkeley Street' or 'Hyaenas asleep in Euston Station' form the stock-in-trade of the wily peasant artist Gebhard Knopfschrank.

That Saki recognized the formulaic element in his work, but could not or would not change it, suggests that it answered powerful imaginative needs. To judge from the biography written by his sister, who knew him better than any other mortal, there was an unusually close correlation between those needs and the circumstances of his early life. His real name was Hector Hugh Munro, and he was born on 18 December 1870 in Akyab, Burma, where his father Charles Augustus Munro was a senior officer in the British military police. When he was two he and his older siblings, Charlie and Ethel, were brought back to England by their mother, who was expecting another child. Soon after their arrival Mrs Munro met a runaway cow while walking in a Devon lane. A miscarriage and her death followed rapidly.

What bearing this tragedy had on her son's later preoccupation with animals that attack women we can only surmise— but it can hardly have been insignificant. Less speculative is the imprint left on him by the upbringing to which their mother's loss doomed the Munro children. Obliged to return to Burma, their father entrusted them to the care of his two spinster sisters, Aunt Charlotte ('Tom') and Aunt Augusta, who lived in a large, dark villa in the village of Pilton, near Barnstaple. According to Ethel, who is the sole authority for this part of Saki's life, the two aunts hated each other 'with a ferocity and intensity worthy of a bigger cause', and made the house miserable with their ceaseless bickering. Aunt Tom was unscrupulous, 'perhaps a reincarnation of Catherine of Russia'. Aunt Augusta, the dominant sister, was even worse, scoring poorly across the whole ethical spectrum: 'A woman of ungovernable temper, of fierce likes and dislikes, imperious, a moral coward, possessing no brains worth speaking of, and a primitive disposition. Naturally the last person who should have been in charge of children.' Such was Ethel's verdict, and it was one which, she assures us, Hector thoroughly endorsed.

It was partly from, and partly in reaction to, Aunt Augusta that the children learnt to keep a stiff upper lip and disguise their feelings—tendencies that underlie what is often referred to as the 'cruelty' of Saki's humour. Augusta had a peculiarly unpleasant smile—'the meaning smile', the children called it—with which she would greet any show of emotion. A keen disciplinarian, she 'positively used to enjoy whipping' Charlie, or so it seemed to Ethel. Being a girl, Ethel herself escaped this punishment, and so did Hector, who was a delicate child and, in his early years, not expected to live. But all the children were subjected to 'mental cruelty', and they 'longed for revenge often and intensely'.

Persecution drove them in on themselves. Forbidden to play with other children, they formed an unusually close comrade-ship against the outer world, seeking in animals the love that adults denied them. Cats, cocks, hens, tortoises, rabbits, doves, and guinea pigs were their pets and allies, also a retriever which the aunts kept chained in an outhouse and exercised (Ethel alleges) 'perhaps twice in the year'. Hector once owned 'a most intelligent Houdan cock' which got something wrong with its leg and had to be destroyed. The children believed a vet could have saved it, but the aunts would have considered that a sinful extravagance. Such lapses were not forgiven or forgotten. According to Ethel, Mrs De Ropp, the would-be destroyer of guinea pigs, who meets her bloody nemesis in 'Sredni Vashtar', and the aunt whom Nicholas torments in 'The Lumber Room', were both portraits of Aunt Augusta.

Hector had to put up with the aunts longer than Charlie, who went off to prep school at eight, and then to Charterhouse. Too frail for school, Hector stayed at home, having lessons with Ethel and her governesses, until he was twelve. Then he spent two years at Pencarwick School, Exmouth (where he was, Ethel says, 'very happy'), before graduating not to Charterhouse, to join Charlie, but to an inferior establishment, Bedford Grammar School. He stayed there only four terms, and his reports suggest that he did not exert himself. The children suspected that sending the brothers to different schools was a deliberate ploy, on the part of the aunts, to weaken their alliance, and it became an additional grievance.

Hector's real education began when he left school. Retiring early from the Burma police, the kindly and enlightened Colonel Munro rescued his now almost grown-up children from the aunts and took them off on an extended Continental tour, aimed at improving their foreign languages and widening their culture. From Etretat in Normandy they went to Dresden for a lengthy stay, then made an excursion into eastern Europe and returned via Berlin, Munich, Nuremberg, Prague, and Innsbruck (visiting, Ethel recalls, 'an immense number of picture galleries') to Davos, where they set up house for the winter, attending lectures and art classes. On their return to England, Colonel Munro bought a house in Devon not far from the aunts, and Hector studied with him there for two years, wintering, again, in Davos, where he and Ethel amused themselves with tobogganing and fancy-dress balls.

It is hard, nowadays, to read Ethel's gleeful accounts of the Davos holidays without some misgiving. She tells us of the 'wild games' and 'pillow fights' she and Hector enjoyed, and of how they would hide in their art teacher's bedroom and leap out at him, and of the 'wild scrimmages' that ensued, round and round the studio, before they would submit to lessons. When we reflect that Hector was, by this time, 21 or 22, and Ethel older, such behaviour seems wilfully retarded—and Ethel, indeed, concedes as much. Her brother, she adoringly records, 'had no intention of growing up'; he remained 'a Puck to the end of his life'.

A prime outlet for his Puckishness was practical jokes—a taste shared by Clovis Sangrail and by other jokers in the stories, such as Vera, the ironically named heroine of 'The Open Window'. Hector's own jokes, as Ethel recounts them, do not seem just innocent frolics. They look like expressions of hostility against certain types of people, or against society as a whole. At Davos in the winter of 1892, for example, Ethel tells us that Hector painted red and blue devils 'in all stages of intoxication' over the walls of the Hôtel des Îles, while she and others kept watch. This 'gorgeous hoax' was justified because the owners of the hotel were 'very pious' and 'mean', which Hector considered an 'unforgivable crime'.

The interest of this story lies, to a degree, in the social attitudes it reveals. Malicious damage, we learn, can be accepted as fun so long as the victims are foreigners and business people—a class Hector always despised—and so long as the perpetrators are high-spirited young English men and women of good family. But Ethel's celebration of Hector's eternal boyishness is also intriguing because it tempts us to think that this was her way of accommodating herself to, or keeping at bay, the recognition that her brother was homosexual.

Hector's homosexuality has been an accepted fact since A. J. Langguth's biography was published in 1981. Looking back it seems incredible that any reader of his fiction can ever have doubted it, or doubted that it was the most important influence on his creative life. His earliest stories recount the doings of a foppish young scapegrace called Reginald, who wears apricot ties and lilac waistcoats, and delivers sub-Wildean *bons mots*. The narrator of these tales, an older friend or cousin, referred to as 'the Other', evidently dotes on Reginald, and the homosexual nuances of their relationship are underlined by some of Reginald's escapades, as when he takes a group of choirboys to a woodland stream to bathe, and confiscates their clothes. When, at an early stage of Saki's writing career, the more resourceful and less narcissistic Clovis replaced Reginald as the central figure, the stories became more versatile and the creepy attendance of the Other could fortunately be dispensed with.

The beneficial effect of Clovis's wit and detachment on the narratives can be gauged by comparison with the self-indulgence that intrudes when Saki decides to do without him. In *The Unbearable Bassington* the giggling excitement with which we are almost allowed a peek at Comus in the bath-tub (at the end of Chapter 3) leaves an uncomfortable impression, and the caning scene (in Chapter 2) is pornography of a peculiarly blatant kind. If a young woman were substituted for the boy victim in this scene it would immediately become apparent that its level was that of the spanking mag. Such a substitution would, presumably, have spoiled the satisfactions the scene afforded its creator—satisfactions which, it seems, include the circumstance that it is to preserve himself from marriage to a young woman, the victim's sister, that Comus pays such vigorous attention to the male bottom. It is impossible to imagine Clovis being a party to anything so self-revealing.

Whether Ethel understood her brother's sexual nature is not clear. In her biography she talks of him 'chumming' with various young men in London and on his forays abroad, as if it were boyish comradeship with no sexual content. On the other hand, she destroyed most of his letters soon after receiving them, which suggests she knew there was something to hide. Caution was vital. The Oscar Wilde scandal was still fresh in the public mind. Active homosexuality was punishable by law, and homosexuals risked imprisonment or blackmail whenever they told their love. In dress and behaviour Hector was always careful to appear the model English gentleman, with no trace of dandyism or foppery. To casual observers he seemed devoid of sex, and this was the view of him Ethel stoutly encouraged. 'One subject he never wrote on', she declared, 'was sex, and I am certain if he had, he would have made fun of it. The only way to treat it.'

Another consideration which may have inclined Hector to conceal his homosexuality was fear of hurting or offending his father, whose care and generosity he seems to have repaid with strong affection. When she admits destroying Hector's letters, Ethel adds that it was to prevent their father seeing them. The Munros had been for generations a military family, loyal servants of empire, and a son might justifiably feel trepidation about owning up to tendencies that could bring such a clan into disrepute. Besides, Hector evidently found the family traditions of manliness and courage attractive. His story 'The Easter Egg', in which a young man's cowardice disgraces 'the stock he came from', rings poignantly in this respect. Like some other homosexual men of his era, Hector seems to have resented the popular assumption that homosexuals were cissies or 'nancy boys'. To compensate, he aspired to be more manly and courageous than the average, more dispassionate and buttoned-up, more staunchly conservative.

This personal adjustment helps to account for what some readers may find paradoxical about Saki's fiction, namely, the strict limits within which its rebelliousness operates. Despite its invocations of wildness and violence, it strongly underpins conservative precepts. Do-gooders and social workers are routinely mocked. The sympathy which, as a member of a persecuted minority, Saki might have been expected to extend to other victims of social injustice does not materialize. 'The Gala Programme' jocularly envisages suffragettes being torn to pieces by wild beasts, and refers facetiously to the death of Emily Davison, who had flung herself in front of the king's horse at the 1913 Derby.

Munro's choice of a pseudonym reflects the dual personality suggested by his fiction—the irresponsible pleasure-seeker on the one hand, and on the other the ramrod-backed, soldierly stoic, with a twisted smile uncommonly like Aunt Augusta's. He took the name 'Saki' from *The Rubáiyát of Omar Khayyám*, a set of twelfth-century Persian quatrains expressing sentimental fatalism which became immensely popular with the Victorians following Edward Fitzgerald's translation in 1859. In verses from the sequence that Munro copied into his commonplace book, Saki appears as a cup-bearer, whom the poet imagines joyously roaming through a moonlit garden, pouring wine for revellers 'star-scattered on the grass'. This is Saki the pleasure-lover. But Omar Khayyám also enjoins Saki to meet death unflinchingly:

> . . . when the angel of the darker drink
> At last shall find you by the river-brink,
>   And, offering his cup, invite your soul
> Forth to your lips to quaff, you shall not shrink.

This valiant repression of feeling represents Saki's other face, and the one Munro showed to the world.

His family tradition did not view writing stories as a feasible career, and Hector himself showed no inclination towards it in early manhood. In June 1893, the summer after the high jinks at the Hôtel des Îles in Davos, he set sail for Rangoon, his father having arranged for him to follow Charlie into the Burmese police. Hector's letters to Ethel from Burma are cheerful and robust, conveying a taste for adventure, pride in his smartness and uniform, and facetious affection for the natives. The opportunities for extending his pet-collection engage much of his spare time. He acquires a silver-grey squirrel and a tiger kitten, whose endearing combination of tameness and wildness, quite on the Saki model, yields endless amusement:

> I found the tiger-kitten quite wild; pretended it had never seen me before, so I had to go through the ceremony of introduction again. I soon made it tame again, and we have great games together. It has not learnt how to drink properly yet and immerses its nose in the milk, then it gets mad with the saucer and shakes it, which sends the milk over its paws, upon which it swears horribly . . . The kitten throws off the cat and assumes the tiger when it is fed; I have to throw it its food (generally the head of a chicken) and then bolt; it is making the day hideous with its growling now, as I gave it the head and the wing, and it is trying to eat both at once.

Unlike George Orwell, Hector did not resign from the Burmese police because he was sickened by the oppressive nature of British rule. His letters give no inkling of any worry on that count. It was, rather, his delicate health that cut short his police career. In his thirteen months in Burma he suffered seven attacks of fever, the last of which was diagnosed as malaria, and he arrived back in England near to death. But his father took him to Devon for a long recuperation and, ever generous, set him up in London on an allowance once he was fit again, so that he would have time to write. Even now Hector did not see fiction as his *métier*. He studied early Russian history in the British Museum Reading Room, and his first book, recounting *The Rise of the Russian Empire* up to the time of Peter the Great, was published in 1900.

Its subject might seem a million miles from the Saki stories, but it derives its thrills, just as they do, from the perpetual clash between savagery and civilization. An imaginative historian, Hector revels in the atrocities of old Russia, 'its gibbets, axes, impalements, and boiling cauldrons, its man-devouring hounds and blood-splashed bear-dens'. The future creator of the wolf-boy Gabriel-Ernest quivers with excitement at the incursions of the Mongols, 'those dusky wolf-eyed warriors, who teemed in the wide, arid plain land of Asia like rats on an old threshing-floor'. One affectation the critics picked on was Hector's use of unfamilar name-forms—*Moskva* for Moscow, the *Kreml* for the Kremlin. But this too prefigures Saki, who specialized in inventing improbable names for his characters. Ada Spelvexit, Lady Caroline Benaresq, the Reverend Poltimore Vardon—the purpose of such tongue-twisters is to create, though facetiously, an air of distinction. Like Munro's pretentious Russian forms, they upstage the reader by flaunting a familiarity he or she does not possess.

During this first spell as a writer in London, from 1896 to 1902, Hector became known, however, not for history but for political satire. He wrote a series of parodies of *Alice in Wonderland*, deriding government mismanagement of the Boer War, which were illustrated by the cartoonist Francis Carruthers Gould, and published in the *Westminster Gazette*, beginning on 25 July 1900. Their wit and effrontery gained eager readers and they appeared in book form in 1902 as *The Westminster Alice*. But by this time, although Hector had started sending the occasional short story to magazines, he seems to have realized that some more profitable use must be found for his pen, and he became a foreign correspondent on the *Morning Post*.

Like his keen and sympathetic critic Graham Greene, Saki gained immensely from working on a newspaper. It slimmed and sharpened his style, and plunged him among the murders and massacres and exotic scenarios that his Russian history had shown him thirsting for. It seems likely, too, that the freer atmosphere abroad allowed him to enjoy love affairs that would have been risky in London. We find him writing to Ethel, for example, about a '14 year old Polish kid' in Warsaw who sprays siphons of soda water between his shoulder blades on hot days.

But it is the conservative side of Saki that most appears in his journalism. He was sent first to the Balkans, where Bulgarian guerrillas were fighting for independence from Turkish rule. Saki showed no sympathy with their cause. He deplored rebellion on principle, and played down the importance of the uprising ('The turbulent persons are very few and the Government is alert'). This phlegmatic response amounted to an unspoken criticism of the hysteria and sensationalism of other correspondents. The radical journalist H. W. Nevinson, for example, who was one of Saki's colleagues in the British press corps, sent home graphic accounts of the ruthlessness of guerrilla warfare—the bodies left in the street to be eaten by dogs, the hunger and smallpox among the peasantry, the rape of women and desecration of churches by Turkish soldiers. Saki's only criticism of the Turks was that they had used Asiatic soldiers to quell the uprising, who were 'naturally more excitable, more ignorant, and more terrified of the unknown than their Western brothers'.

The innate superiority of Western troops was what Saki's conservative *Morning Post* readers would wish to be told about. But there is nothing to suggest he did not firmly believe it himself. His recommendation of corporal punishment as the likeliest means to quell political unrest would also have been welcome at many middle-class breakfast tables, while representing, so far as we can tell, his own sincere opinion, or at any rate the opinion of a personality that he found it congenial to adopt:

If a permanent beating tribunal, armed with sticks of appreciable thickness, was set up to chastise without mercy or favour all Bashi Bazouks [Turkish irregulars] and citizens guilty of breaking or attempting to break the peace, and if a general confiscation of weapons was carried into practice, both the desire and the means for disturbance would be restricted within manageable limits.

Though Saki's dispatches generally preserved a superior calm, there was no lack of excitement in the political events he was witnessing. On 10 June 1903, King Alexander of Serbia and his queen, Draga, were murdered by rebel army officers, who first dynamited their bedchambers and then shot them, throwing their bodies down into the street. Hector was in Sofia when he got the news, and rushed to Belgrade the same evening. His report to the *Morning Post* allows itself a moment of imaginative sympathy with the victims, and the studied reserve of its conclusion is worthy of Clovis:

But above all other reflections stands the horror of that final loneliness in the dark Palace, when amid the crashing uproar of forced-in doors the hunted couple sought in room after room for succour or safety and found only desertion and enemies.

'It was dreadful, was it not?' a Servian will ask you half-anxiously when going over the pitiful details.

And you can truthfully make answer, 'It was intensely dramatic.'

More dramatic still was the experience that awaited Munro in St Petersburg. He arrived there in September 1904 and witnessed, four months later, one of the most tragic events of twentieth-century Russian history, Father Gapon's march on the Winter Palace. By chance Ethel had joined him for a holiday, and her account of the 'perfect time' she had brims with undisguised excitement which cannot but seem callous in the circumstances.

On the fateful day, Sunday, 9 January, she and Hector hurried down to the Hôtel de France and wolfed their luncheons so that they would be sure of a ringside seat. Hector left Ethel in the smoking-room, with a view of the street leading to the Palace, while he and a Polish friend reconnoitred. They saw the huge crowd of peaceful demonstrators surge forwards towards the Palace, solemnly singing the Tsar's hymn 'God Save thy People'. Children ran about on its edges, and, at its head, rows of women had placed themselves in front of the reformist priest Father Gapon to protect him with their bodies. Before them, at the Narva Gate, files of infantry blocked the road, and a company of Cossacks, their sabres sparkling in the sunlight, was drawn up.

Suddenly the Cossacks charged. Men, women, and children fell on all sides, their skulls split by sabre cuts. With solemn resolution the demonstration reformed, and kept up its forward momentum. Then the Cossacks turned and cut their way back through the crowd. As they emerged, the infantry smartly opened ranks to let them through. Still the demonstrators advanced. When the leaders were about thirty yards from the soldiers a bugle was blown and volley after volley rang out. The firing continued as the unarmed demonstrators lay or kneeled on the ground or tried to run away, and the soldiers also fired into the courtyards of adjoining houses where fugitives had found refuge. Hector and his Polish friend were caught in one of these volleys. A bullet buried itself in the wall a foot away from Hector's head.

The next day, his *Morning Post* dispatch was headed 'Russia's Dark Day Came Yesterday'. He and Ethel had ridden round the city in a sleigh, viewing the corpses that still lay in the streets, and whenever they passed a patrol of Cossacks ('an evil looking lot, pronounced Mongolian type, with criminal faces', Ethel reported) Hector scowled meaningfully at them—to Ethel's alarm. All the same, his account of the massacre was distinctly more measured and conservative than most. He described the demonstrators as 'almost demented', and estimated the dead and wounded at 1,500—a considerably smaller figure than historians now accept. Significantly, when General Trepoff, Governor of St Petersburg, sent for foreign correspondents to rebuke them for their exaggerated reports, Hector was the only one not summoned. He assured readers of the *Morning Post* in October 1905 that General Trepoff's autocratic behaviour had saved St Petersburg from 'anything savouring of serious bloodshed'.

Hector's years as a journalist, like his tour of duty in Burma, fed his taste for wildness, and stored his mind with images that were to provide a constant resource, in his fiction, against the Mappin Terraces of the modern world. Typically, he had written to Ethel from Üsküb (present-day Skopje) in April 1903:

This is the most delightfully outlandish and primitive place I have ever dared to hope for . . . lovely rolling hills and huge snow-capped mountains, and storks nesting in large communities; everything wild and open and full of life.

When we read in *The Unbearable Bassington* of Tom Keriway, who has 'wandered through Hungarian horse-fairs' and 'hunted shy crafty beasts on lonely Balkan hillsides', we recognize the same wistful escapism that, more than any creed or moral value, remained for Saki the dearest thing in life.

His paper moved him from St Petersburg to Paris early in 1907, but his days as a reporter were numbered. Later that year his father died, leaving him enough money to quit journalism. He bought a cottage in the Surrey hills for Ethel, and took rooms himself at 97 Mortimer Street, near Oxford Circus. By 1909 he had settled down to the life of a full-time writer. He took meals at the Cocoa Tree Club, and did not venture much into society. His choice of privacy allowed him, we may suppose, to follow his own tastes in the matter of male companions. Ben Travers, then a young clerk with

Hector's publisher John Lane, recalled in conversation with A. J. Langguth, how Hector gave him lunch at the Cocoa Tree. It was a delightful occasion, and only later did Travers discover, from gossip around the office, that Hector had a reputation as a homosexual.

The years in London from 1909 to 1914 produced all Saki's best work. We have been considering it mainly in relation to his life. But to understand it more fully, we must put it in its cultural context. The years from 1880 to the outbreak of the First World War witnessed great changes in English culture and society. The Education Act of 1870 had produced for the first time a huge literate (or, as the intellectuals disdainfully called it, semi-literate) public. To cater for this, popular newspapers such as the *Daily Mail* and the *Daily Express* came into being. The advent of mass culture was accompanied by the growth of Socialism as a real political force. At the same time, the sheer number of people crammed into the available space was causing alarm. As the Spanish philosopher Ortega y Gasset observed in *The Revolt of the Masses*, the population of Europe had risen from 180 to 460 millions in the course of the nineteenth century. Everywhere seemed crowded, and the countryside was being eaten up by ugly suburbs that sprawled round all the major English towns.

Writers responded acutely to these conditions. The threat to the countryside gave impetus to a new ruralism, involving practitioners as different as Richard Jefferies, Thomas Hardy, and D. H. Lawrence. Saki's emphasis on the immemorial wisdom and mystery of country life, in stories like 'The Peace of Mowsle Barton' or 'The Cobweb', allies him with this trend, drawing on his Devon childhood (Ethel said a witch lived near their house in Devon and possessed 'uncanny powers', like the Mowsle Barton witches). The revival of a vague 'paganism', associated with the god Pan, was a feature of the new pastoral mode. Pan makes a personal appearance in Kenneth Grahame's *The Wind in the Willows* and E. M. Forster's first published story, *The Story of a Panic*, as well as in Saki's 'The Music on the Hill'. Pan's goatish associations gave him a particular appeal for exponents of sexual freedom, including homosexuals, who blamed Christianity for emasculating Western culture.

The adventure story (Wild West, frozen North, darkest Africa) was another form that flourished in the new conditions. The awareness that Europe had grown, as Comus Bassington laments, 'too civilized and too crowded' made people dream of wide open spaces and the law of the wild. Sigmund Freud's essay *Civilization and Its Discontents* translated this yearning into psychoanalytical terms, and the romantic wanderlust Saki voices was another expression of it. Lady Caroline's sneering reference to 'the suburbs' in *The Unbearable Bassington* (Chapter 10) belongs to an anti-suburban animus to be found in nearly all the Modernist and intellectual writers of the period—an animus that confidently identified suburbs as the site of philistinism, dullness, and narrow-minded bigotry. Suburbia was despised, too, because it housed those engaged in trade and business, pursuits which, aesthetes and intellectuals believed, spelt death to romance. Clovis Sangrail speaks for this prejudice when preaching against the typical suburban businessman who

married early and worked late, and lived, thousands upon thousands of him, in little villas outside big towns. He is buried by the thousand in Kensal Green and other large cemeteries; any romance that was ever in him was buried prematurely in shop and warehouse and office. Whenever I feel in the least tempted to be business-like or methodical or even decently industrious I go to Kensal Green and look at the graves of those who died in business.

The wish to feel aristocratic by comparison with other people such as businessmen, and to side, in fantasy, with the well-born, was another outcome of the heightened social consciousness that the revolt of the masses precipitated. That Saki's stories feature duchesses and baronesses, and take place in gracious surroundings, are not negligible elements in the reassurance they convey. The inimitable superiority of a trueborn lady is illustrated by 'The Schartz-Metterklume Method', where the genuine aristocrat Lady Carlotta is wild and free, speaks Russian, and keeps (or says she keeps) a leopard cub as pet—in all of which she resembles the emanci-

pated side of Saki, and differs from the *nouveaux riches*
Quabarls. The true aristocrat's redeeming kinship with wild
animals is re-emphasized in 'The Wolves of Cernogratz',
where it appears that even wolves can distinguish the well-
born from tradespeople.

We should not assume from all this, of course, that Saki's
stories were mainly read by aristocrats, or that he moved in
titled society himself. Like P. G. Wodehouse's Jeeves stories a
few years later, they were designed to take their readers across
a social barrier, offering an amused view of the exotics who
cavorted in the never-never land beyond. In this respect they
might be compared, too, to the boys' weeklies George Orwell
examined, which purveyed an outdated image of public-
school life for the benefit of poorer boys. Saki's stories are
similarly backward-looking. It has been noted that they
seldom mention the cinema or the telephone—features of
mass culture that were gaining ascendancy at the time.
Published mainly in the *Westminster Gazette* and the *Morning
Post*, they were designed to amuse a largely middle-class (and
suburban) readership with social representations that were
self-consciously nostalgic and unreal.

Though unreal, they could still embody social models and
aspirations, as fiction frequently does. The vital factor in
Saki's stories is his wit, and this may be seen as an effect of
and a reaction against the social movement identified by conservative commentators as the rise of the masses. Derived
from Oscar Wilde, its first practitioner, and eagerly imitated
by Evelyn Waugh, Saki-style wit is playful but no mere play-
thing. It speaks for definite social assumptions or pretensions.
It disowns vulgar emotionalism and mimics what it takes to be
the high, dry nonchalance of the well-bred. When Gabriel-
Ernest devours one of the Toop children (and Mrs Toop,
having eleven other children, is 'decently resigned to her
bereavement'), or when the Baroness in 'Esmé' calmly de-
scribes the screaming gipsy child 'firmly, and I expect painfully' held in the hyena's jaws, we can clearly pick up messages
about the exorbitant fertility of the lower classes and about
the sang-froid in the face of suffering that truly civilized
people preserve.

Saki's conservatism became more pronounced towards the end of his life, reinforcing itself with patriotism, militarism, and justified anxiety about Germany's war aims. In 1913 he published a novel, *When William Came*, which imagines Britain defeated and occupied by husky, efficient Prussians. Only the Boy Scouts, in Saki's fantasy, resist the conqueror. The novel features a foppish young Englishman, Percival Plarsey, almost indistinguishable from the cosseted and adored Reginald of Saki's early stories, who, Saki now gives us to understand, deserves to be 'kicked and pommelled' for his effeminacy, over-refinement, and general slackness. With the outbreak of war his scorn for such specimens redoubled. A *Morning Post* article denounces unwarlike youths, perfumed with eau-de-Cologne, who fritter away their time on art and culture while others are dying for their country:

It is inconceivable that these persons were ever boys, they have certainly not grown up into men; one cannot call them womanish—the women of our race are made of different stuff. They belong to no sex, and it seems a pity they should belong to any nation.

The wording of this suggests that Saki saw his own valour as somehow atoning for or justifying his homosexuality. At all events, he grasped the opportunity to prove himself in war with boisterous eagerness. 'I have always looked forward to the romance of a European war,' he rejoiced—voicing, as did thousands of others in 1914, the hope that warfare would put an end to an ignoble, aimless, tame existence of 'The Mapped Life' variety. At 43 he was past the usual age for active service, but he embraced his ordeal with almost religious fervour, turning down the chance of a commission, and putting on a common soldier's uniform with—as a friend said—the exaltation of a novice assuming a monastic habit.

He went to France with the 22nd Battalion of the Royal Fusiliers. His cheery letters to Ethel tell her how much he is enjoying his own fitness and efficiency. 'The fun and adventure of the whole thing and the good comradeship of some of one's companions make it jolly.' He planned, he told her, to farm in Siberia after the war: 'I could never settle down again to the tameness of London life.' The *angst* and torment that

we are so used to from the poets of the First World War are
largely excluded from his writing. He was still in high spirits
when he came home on leave in June 1915, cramming in as
many theatres and dinner parties as he could. 'Kill a good few
for me!' shouted Ethel, as she waved goodbye to him at
Victoria Station—'and', she adds, 'I believe he did—he was
never, though, to have the satisfaction of a bayonet charge,
which was his ambition'.

In August 1916 at Delville Wood he showed, a comrade
tells us, conspicuous courage under fire. Promoted by now
from corporal to lance-sergeant, he took over the command of
frightened and demoralized men whose officers had been
killed, calming and heartening them. In October he was struck
down by malaria and sent back to base. But he insisted,
though still far from fit, on rejoining the battalion before the
big assault on Beaumont-Hamel. The attack was launched in
the early hours of 13 November. By 4 a.m. on the morning of
the 14th some advance had been made, and the men of
Munro's company were resting during a lull in the battle.
Unwarily, a fusilier lit up. 'Put out that bloody cigarette,'
shouted Lance-Sergeant Munro. A German sniper, it seems,
aimed at the shout, not the light, and his bullet killed Saki.

'Simplify me when I'm dead,' wrote Keith Douglas, a casu-
alty of the Second World War. Accounts of Saki simplify him
because they separate out the components of a personality—
rebellious and conformist, romantic and conscience-stricken,
escapist and vengeful, flippant, boyish, adult—which in life
made up a single, complicated being. Saki, too, simplified
himself for the sake of his stories. From personal circumstances that might have bred resentment or introspection,
he evolved a brilliantly public comic medium, ranging in
tone from the genial ('The Story-Teller') to the vindictive
('The Sheep'), but always resilient, hard-edged, and on guard
against conventional pieties and benign cant.

NOTE ON THE TEXT

MOST of the stories in this selection were first published in the *Westminster Gazette* or the *Morning Post*. A few (e.g. 'Mrs Packletide's Tiger' and 'Filboid Studge') were published in the *Bystander*, and 'The Music on the Hill' was not published before its appearance in *The Chronicles of Clovis* (1912). In collecting his stories for publication in book form, Saki sometimes made minor alterations to the texts.

The order in which the stories appear in the book-length collections may have been left to the publisher, but it may have been Saki's choice. It does not always strictly follow the order of their original publication. 'Gabriel-Ernest', for example, was originally published in the *Westminster Gazette* on 29 May 1909, whereas 'The Soul of Laploshka', which appears after 'Gabriel-Ernest' in *Reginald in Russia* (1910), was originally published before it, on 8 May 1909, also in the *Westminster Gazette*. This rearrangement may reflect Saki's preference (supposing he was responsible for it) or it may represent the order in which the stories were written, as opposed to their original publication dates.

At all events, in this collection I have arranged the stories in the order in which they appear in the book-length collections, since there seems some chance that this may preserve Saki's own choice. I have also followed the texts Saki approved or emended for the book-length collections—i.e. *Reginald in Russia* (1910), *The Chronicles of Clovis* (1912), and *Beasts and Super-Beasts* (1914). Similarly, stories from the two posthumous collections, *The Toys of Peace* (1919) and *The Square Egg* (1924), follow the order of those collections. The text of *The Unbearable Bassington* is that of the first edition (1912).

SELECT BIBLIOGRAPHY

DRAKE, ROBERT, 'Saki: Some Problems and a Bibliography', in *English Fiction in Transition* (Lafayette, Ind., 1962), 6–26.

GREENE, GRAHAM, 'Introduction' to *The Best of Saki* (London: John Lane, 1950); reprinted as 'The Burden of Childhood' in *The Lost Childhood and Other Essays* (London: Eyre and Spottiswoode, 1951).

HARTLEY, L. P., 'Saki', *Bookman*, 71 (London) (Jan. 1927), 214–17.

LAMBERT, J. W., 'Jungle Boy in the Drawing Room', *Listener*, 55 (9 Feb. 1956), 211–12.

—— 'Introduction' to *The Bodley Head Saki* (London: The Bodley Head, 1963).

LANGGUTH, A. J., *Saki: A Life of Hector Hugh Munro* (London: Hamish Hamilton, 1981).

MUNRO, ETHEL, 'Biography of Saki', in *The Square Egg and Other Sketches* (London: John Lane, The Bodley Head, 1924).

PRITCHETT, V. S., 'The Performing Lynx', *New Statesman*, NS 53 (5 Jan. 1957), 18–19.

REYNOLDS, ROTHAY, 'Memoir' of Saki in *The Toys of Peace and Other Papers* (London: John Lane, The Bodley Head, 1919).

SHARPE, TOM, 'Introduction' to *The Best of Saki* (London: Pan Books Ltd., 1976).

SPEARS, GEORGE JAMES, *The Satire of Saki: A Study of the Satiric Art of Hector H. Munro* (New York: Exposition Press, 1963).

WAUGH, EVELYN, 'Introduction' to *The Unbearable Bassington* (London: Eyre and Spottiswoode, 1947).

A CHRONOLOGY OF SAKI

1870   18 December: Hector Hugh Munro born in Akyab, Burma, second son of Colonel Charles Augustus Munro of the Bengal Staff Corps, Inspector-General of Police in Burma, and Mary Munro (née Mercer).

1872   Family move to England. Mother dies in accident. Before returning to Burma, Colonel Munro takes villa in Pilton, near Barnstaple, for his children—Ethel Mary (b. April 1868), Charles Arthur (b. July 1869), and Hector—where they are brought up by their paternal grandmother, Lucy Jones Munro, and her spinster daughters Charlotte Maria and Augusta Georgina.

1882   Hector goes as boarder to Pencarwick School, Exmouth.

1885   September: Hector begins first of four terms at Bedford Grammar School.

1886   December: Hector leaves Bedford.

1887   Father retires and takes Ethel, Charlie, and Hector to Etretat, Normandy, then to Dresden for a 'lengthy stay'.

1888   Father takes Ethel and Hector on a cultural tour, visiting art galleries in Berlin, Munich, Nuremberg, Prague, and Innsbruck.

1888–9   The Munros settle at Davos (Hotel Belvedere) for the winter. Hector befriended by John Addington Symonds, well-known homosexual man of letters, resident at Davos.

1889   April: the Munros move to Schloss Salenstein on Lake Constance, where they stay with friends, then move back to Devon, where Colonel Munro takes a house at Heanton, near Barnstaple.

1889–91   Hector studies at home under his father's direction.

1892–3   The Munros winter in Davos.

1893   June: Hector leaves for Rangoon to take up post in Burmese police.

1894   August: resigns from police with malaria and sails home.

1896   Moves to London to earn living as writer: working in British Museum Reading Room.

1899   February: first of Hector's short stories to be published appears in St Paul's magazine.

1900   Publishes The Rise of the Russian Empire. 25 July: first of Hector's satirical parodies of Alice in Wonderland,

SHORT STORIES

GABRIEL-ERNEST

'THERE is a wild beast in your woods,' said the artist Cunningham, as he was being driven to the station. It was the only remark he had made during the drive, but as Van Cheele had talked incessantly his companion's silence had not been noticeable.

'A stray fox or two and some resident weasels. Nothing more formidable,' said Van Cheele. The artist said nothing.

'What did you mean about a wild beast?' said Van Cheele later, when they were on the platform.

'Nothing. My imagination. Here is the train,' said Cunningham.

That afternoon Van Cheele went for one of his frequent rambles through his woodland property. He had a stuffed bittern in his study, and knew the names of quite a number of wild flowers, so his aunt had possibly some justification in describing him as a great naturalist. At any rate, he was a great walker. It was his custom to take mental notes of everything he saw during his walks, not so much for the purpose of assisting contemporary science as to provide topics for conversation afterwards. When the bluebells began to show themselves in flower he made a point of informing every one of the fact; the season of the year might have warned his hearers of the likelihood of such an occurrence, but at least they felt that he was being absolutely frank with them.

What Van Cheele saw on this particular afternoon was, however, something far removed from his ordinary range of experience. On a shelf of smooth stone overhanging a deep pool in the hollow of an oak coppice a boy of about sixteen lay asprawl, drying his wet brown limbs luxuriously in the sun. His wet hair, parted by a recent dive, lay close to his head, and his light-brown eyes, so light that there was an almost tigerish gleam in them, were turned towards Van Cheele with a certain lazy watchfulness. It was an unexpected apparition, and Van Cheele found himself engaged in the novel process of thinking before he spoke. Where on earth could this wild-looking boy hail from? The miller's wife had lost a child some two months ago, supposed to have been swept away by the mill-race, but that had been a mere baby, not a half-grown lad.

'What are you doing there?' he demanded.

'Obviously, sunning myself,' replied the boy.

'Where do you live?'

'Here, in these woods.'

'You can't live in the woods,' said Van Cheele.

'They are very nice woods,' said the boy, with a touch of patronage in his voice.

'But where do you sleep at night?'

'I don't sleep at night; that's my busiest time.'

Van Cheele began to have an irritated feeling that he was grappling with a problem that was eluding him.

'What do you feed on?' he asked.

'Flesh,' said the boy, and he pronounced the word with slow relish, as though he were tasting it.

'Flesh! What flesh?'

'Since it interests you, rabbits, wild-fowl, hares, poultry, lambs in their season, children when I can get any; they're usually too well locked in at night, when I do most of my hunting. It's quite two months since I tasted child-flesh.'

Ignoring the chaffing nature of the last remark Van Cheele tried to draw the boy on the subject of possible poaching operations.

'You're talking rather through your hat when you speak of feeding on hares.' (Considering the nature of the boy's toilet the simile was hardly an apt one.) 'Our hillside hares aren't easily caught.'

'At night I hunt on four feet,' was the somewhat cryptic response.

'I suppose you mean that you hunt with a dog?' hazarded Van Cheele.

The boy rolled slowly over on to his back, and laughed a weird low laugh, that was pleasantly like a chuckle and disagreeably like a snarl.

'I don't fancy any dog would be very anxious for my company, especially at night.'

Van Cheele began to feel that there was something positively uncanny about the strange-eyed, strange-tongued youngster.

'I can't have you staying in these woods,' he declared authoritatively.

'I fancy you'd rather have me here than in your house,' said the boy.

The prospect of this wild, nude animal in Van Cheele's primly ordered house was certainly an alarming one.

'If you don't go I shall have to make you,' said Van Cheele.

The boy turned like a flash, plunged into the pool, and in a moment had flung his wet and glistening body half-way up the bank where Van Cheele was standing. In an otter the move-ment would not have been remarkable; in a boy Van Cheele found it sufficiently startling. His foot slipped as he made an involuntary backward movement, and he found himself almost prostrate on the slippery weed-grown bank, with those tigerish yellow eyes not very far from his own. Almost instinc-tively he half raised his hand to his throat. The boy laughed again, a laugh in which the snarl had nearly driven out the chuckle, and then, with another of his astonishing lightning movements, plunged out of view into a yielding tangle of weed and fern.

'What an extraordinary wild animal!' said Van Cheele as he picked himself up. And then he recalled Cunningham's remark, 'There is a wild beast in your woods.'

Walking slowly homeward, Van Cheele began to turn over in his mind various local occurrences which might be trace-able to the existence of this astonishing young savage.

Something had been thinning the game in the woods lately, poultry had been missing from the farms, hares were growing unaccountably scarcer, and complaints had reached him of lambs being carried off bodily from the hills. Was it possible that this wild boy was really hunting the countryside in com-pany with some clever poacher dog? He had spoken of hunt-ing 'four-footed' by night, but then, again, he had hinted strangely at no dog caring to come near him, 'especially at night'. It was certainly puzzling. And then, as Van Cheele ran his mind over the various depredations that had been commit-

ted during the last month or two, he came suddenly to a dead
stop, alike in his walk and his speculations. The child missing
from the mill two months ago—the accepted theory was that
it had tumbled into the mill-race and been swept away; but the
mother had always declared she had heard a shriek on the hill
side of the house, in the opposite direction from the water.
It was unthinkable, of course, but he wished that the boy
had not made that uncanny remark about child-flesh eaten
two months ago. Such dreadful things should not be said even
in fun.

Van Cheele, contrary to his usual wont, did not feel disposed to be communicative about his discovery in the wood.
His position as a parish councillor and justice of the peace
seemed somehow compromised by the fact that he was har-
bouring a personality of such doubtful repute on his property;
there was even a possibility that a heavy bill of damages for
raided lambs and poultry might be laid at his door. At dinner
that night he was quite unusually silent.

'Where's your voice gone to?' said his aunt. 'One would
think you had seen a wolf.'

Van Cheele, who was not familiar with the old saying,
thought the remark rather foolish; if he *had* seen a wolf on his
property his tongue would have been extraordinarily busy
with the subject.

At breakfast next morning Van Cheele was conscious that
his feeling of uneasiness regarding yesterday's episode had
not wholly disappeared, and he resolved to go by train to
the neighbouring cathedral town, hunt up Cunningham, and
learn from him what he had really seen that had prompted
the remark about a wild beast in the woods. With this resolution taken, his usual cheerfulness partially returned, and he
hummed a bright little melody as he sauntered to the morning-
room for his customary cigarette. As he entered the room the
melody made way abruptly for a pious invocation. Gracefully
asprawl on the ottoman, in an attitude of almost exaggerated
repose, was the boy of the woods. He was drier that when Van
Cheele had last seen him, but no other alteration was noticeable in his toilet.

'How dare you come here?' asked Van Cheele furiously.

'You told me I was not to stay in the woods,' said the boy calmly.

'But not to come here. Supposing my aunt should see you!'

And with a view to minimizing that catastrophe Van Cheele hastily obscured as much of his unwelcome guest as possible under the folds of a *Morning Post*. At that moment his aunt entered the room.

'This is a poor boy who has lost his way—and lost his memory. He doesn't know who he is or where he comes from,' explained Van Cheele desperately, glancing apprehensively at the waif's face to see whether he was going to add inconvenient candour to his other savage propensities.

Miss Van Cheele was enormously interested.

'Perhaps his underlinen is marked,' she suggested.

'He seems to have lost most of that, too,' said Van Cheele, making frantic little grabs at the *Morning Post* to keep it in its place.

A naked homeless child appealed to Miss Van Cheele as warmly as a stray kitten or derelict puppy would have done.

'We must do all we can for him,' she decided, and in a very short time a messenger, dispatched to the rectory, where a page-boy was kept, had returned with a suit of pantry clothes, and the necessary accessories of shirt, shoes, collar, etc. Clothed, clean, and groomed, the boy lost none of his uncanniness in Van Cheele's eyes, but his aunt found him sweet.

'We must call him something till we know who he really is,' she said. 'Gabriel-Ernest, I think; those are nice suitable names.'

Van Cheele agreed, but he privately doubted whether they were being grafted on to a nice suitable child. His misgivings were not diminished by the fact that his staid and elderly spaniel had bolted out of the house at the first incoming of the boy, and now obstinately remained shivering and yapping at the farther end of the orchard, while the canary, usually as vocally industrious as Van Cheele himself, had put itself on an allowance of frightened cheeps. More than ever he was resolved to consult Cunningham without loss of time.

As he drove off to the station his aunt was arranging that Gabriel-Ernest should help her to entertain the infant members of her Sunday-school class at tea that afternoon.

Cunningham was not at first disposed to be communicative.

'My mother died of some brain trouble,' he explained, 'so you will understand why I am averse to dwelling on anything of an impossibly fantastic nature that I may see or think that I have seen.'

'But what *did* you see?' persisted Van Cheele.

'What I thought I saw was something so extraordinary that no really sane man could dignify it with the credit of having actually happened. I was standing, the last evening I was with you, half-hidden in the hedgegrowth by the orchard gate, watching the dying glow of the sunset. Suddenly I became aware of a naked boy, a bather from some neighbouring pool, I took him to be, who was standing out on the bare hillside also watching the sunset. His pose was so suggestive of some wild faun of Pagan myth that I instantly wanted to engage him as a model, and in another moment I think I should have hailed him. But just then the sun dipped out of view, and all the orange and pink slid out of the landscape, leaving it cold and grey. And at the same moment an astounding thing happened—the boy vanished too!'

'What! vanished away into nothing?' asked Van Cheele excitedly.

'No; that is the dreadful part of it,' answered the artist; 'on the open hillside where the boy had been standing a second ago, stood a large wolf, blackish in colour, with gleaming fangs and cruel, yellow eyes. You may think—'

But Van Cheele did not stop for anything as futile as thought. Already he was tearing at top speed towards the station. He dismissed the idea of a telegram. 'Gabriel-Ernest is a werewolf' was a hopelessly inadequate effort at conveying the situation, and his aunt would think it was a code message to which he had omitted to give her the key. His one hope was that he might reach home before sundown. The cab which he chartered at the other end of the railway journey bore him with what seemed exasperating slowness along the country roads, which were pink and mauve with the flush of the sinking sun. His aunt was putting away some unfinished jams and cake when he arrived.

'Where is Gabriel-Ernest?' he almost screamed.

'He is taking the little Toop child home,' said his aunt. 'It was getting so late, I thought it wasn't safe to let it go back alone. What a lovely sunset, isn't it?'

But Van Cheele, although not oblivious of the glow in the western sky, did not stay to discuss its beauties. At a speed for which he was scarcely geared he raced along the narrow lane that led to the home of the Toops. On one side ran the swift current of the mill-stream, on the other rose the stretch of bare hillside. A dwindling rim of red sun showed still on the skyline, and the next turning must bring him in view of the ill-assorted couple he was pursuing. Then the colour went suddenly out of things, and a grey light settled itself with a quick shiver over the landscape. Van Cheele heard a shrill wail of fear, and stopped running.

Nothing was ever seen again of the Toop child or Gabriel-Ernest, but the latter's discarded garments were found lying in the road, so it was assumed that the child had fallen into the water, and that the boy had stripped and jumped in, in a vain endeavour to save it. Van Cheele and some workmen who were near by at the time testified to having heard a child scream loudly just near the spot where the clothes were found. Mrs Toop, who had eleven other children, was decently resigned to her bereavement, but Miss Van Cheele sincerely mourned her lost foundling. It was on her initiative that a memorial brass was put up in the parish church to 'Gabriel-Ernest, an unknown boy, who bravely sacrificed his life for another'.

Van Cheele gave way to his aunt in most things, but he flatly refused to subscribe to the Gabriel-Ernest memorial.

THE SOUL OF LAPLOSHKA

LAPLOSHKA was one of the meanest men I have ever met, and quite one of the most entertaining. He said horrid things about other people in such a charming way that one forgave him for the equally horrid things he said about oneself behind one's back. Hating anything in the way of ill-natured gossip ourselves, we are always grateful to those who do it for us and do it well. And Laploshka did it really well.

Naturally Laploshka had a large circle of acquaintances, and as he exercised some care in their selection it followed that an appreciable proportion were men whose bank balances enabled them to acquiesce indulgently in his rather one-sided views on hospitality. Thus, although possessed of only moderate means, he was able to live comfortably within his income, and still more comfortably within those of various tolerantly disposed associates.

But towards the poor or to those of the same limited resources as himself his attitude was one of watchful anxiety; he seemed to be haunted by a besetting fear lest some fraction of a shilling or franc, or whatever the prevailing coinage might be, should be diverted from his pocket or service into that of a hard-up companion. A two-franc cigar would be cheerfully offered to a wealthy patron, on the principle of doing evil that good may come, but I have known him indulge in agonies of perjury rather than admit the incriminating possession of a copper coin when change was needed to tip a waiter. The coin would have been duly returned at the earliest opportunity— he would have taken means to ensure against forgetfulness on the part of the borrower—but accidents might happen, and even the temporary estrangement from his penny or sou was a calamity to be avoided.

The knowledge of this amiable weakness offered a perpetual temptation to play upon Laploshka's fears of involuntary generosity. To offer him a lift in a cab and pretend not to have enough money to pay the fare, to fluster him with a request for a sixpence when his hand was full of silver just received in change, these were a few of the petty torments that ingenuity prompted as occasion afforded. To do justice to Laploshka's resourcefulness it must be admitted that he always emerged somehow or other from the most embarrassing dilemma without in any way compromising his reputation for saying 'No'. But the gods send opportunities at some time to most men, and mine came one evening when Laploshka and I were supping together in a cheap boulevard restaurant. (Except when he was the bidden guest of some one with an irreproachable income, Laploshka was wont to curb his appetite for high living; on such fortunate occasions he let it go on an easy snaffle.) At the conclusion of the meal a somewhat urgent message called me away, and without heeding my companion's agitated protest, I called back cruelly, 'Pay my share; I'll settle with you tomorrow.' Early on the morrow Laploshka hunted me down by instinct as I walked along a side street that I hardly ever frequented. He had the air of a man who had not slept.

'You owe me two francs from last night,' was his breathless greeting.

I spoke evasively of the situation in Portugal, where more trouble seemed brewing. But Laploshka listened with the abstraction of the deaf adder, and quickly returned to the subject of the two francs.

'I'm afraid I must owe it to you,' I said lightly and brutally. 'I haven't a sou in the world,' and I added mendaciously, 'I'm going away for six months or perhaps longer.'

Laploshka said nothing, but his eyes bulged a little and his cheeks took on the mottled hues of an ethnographical map of the Balkan Peninsula. That same day, at sundown, he died. 'Failure of the heart's action' was the doctor's verdict; but I, who knew better, knew that he had died of grief.

There arose the problem of what to do with his two francs. To have killed Laploshka was one thing; to have kept his beloved money would have argued a callousness of feeling of which I am not capable. The ordinary solution, of giving it to the poor, would by no means fit the present situation, for nothing would have distressed the dead man more than such a misuse of his property. On the other hand, the bestowal of two francs on the rich was an operation which called for some tact. An easy way out of the difficulty seemed, however, to present itself the following Sunday, as I was wedged into the cosmopolitan crowd which filled the side-aisle of one of the most popular Paris churches. A collecting-bag, for 'the poor of Monsieur le Curé', was buffeting its tortuous way across the seemingly impenetrable human sea, and a German in front of me, who evidently did not wish his appreciation of the magnificent music to be marred by a suggestion of payment, made audible criticisms to his companion on the claims of the said charity.

'They do not want money,' he said; 'they have too much money. They have no poor. They are all pampered.'

If that were really the case my way seemed clear. I dropped Laploshka's two francs into the bag with a murmured blessing on the rich of Monsieur le Curé.

Some three weeks later chance had taken me to Vienna, and I sat one evening regaling myself in a humble but excellent little Gasthaus up in the Währinger quarter. The appointments were primitive, but the Schnitzel, the beer, and the cheese could not have been improved on. Good cheer brought good custom, and with the exception of one small table near the door every place was occupied. Half-way through my meal I happened to glance in the direction of that empty seat, and saw that it was no longer empty. Poring over the bill of fare with the absorbed scrutiny of one who seeks the cheapest among the cheap was Laploshka. Once he looked across at me, with a comprehensive glance at my repast, as though to say, 'It is my two francs you are eating,' and then looked swiftly away. Evidently the poor of Monsieur le Curé had been genuine poor. The Schnitzel turned to leather in my mouth, the beer seemed tepid; I left the Emmenthaler untasted. My one idea was to get away from the room, away from the table where *that* was seated; and as I fled I felt Laploshka's reproachful eyes watching the amount that I gave to the piccolo—out of his two francs. I lunched next day at an expensive restaurant which I felt sure that the living Laploshka would never have entered on his own account, and I hoped that the dead Laploshka would observe the same barriers. I was not mistaken, but as I came out I found him miserably studying the bill of fare stuck up on the portals. Then he slowly made his way over to a milk-hall. For the first time in my experience I missed the charm and gaiety of Vienna life.

After that, in Paris or London or wherever I happened to be, I continued to see a good deal of Laploshka. If I had a seat in a box at a theatre I was always conscious of his eyes furtively watching me from the dim recesses of the gallery. As I turned into my club on a rainy afternoon I would see him taking inadequate shelter in a doorway opposite. Even if I indulged in the modest luxury of a penny chair in the Park he generally confronted me from one of the free benches, never staring at me, but always elaborately conscious of my presence. My friends began to comment on my changed looks, and advised me to leave off heaps of things. I should have liked to have left off Laploshka.

On a certain Sunday—it was probably Easter, for the crush was worse than ever—I was again wedged into the crowd listening to the music in the fashionable Paris church, and again the collection-bag was buffeting its way across the human sea. An English lady behind me was making ineffectual efforts to convey a coin into the still distant bag, so I took the money at her request and helped it forward to its destination. It was a two-franc piece. A swift inspiration came to me, and I merely dropped my own sou into the bag and slid the silver coin into my pocket. I had withdrawn Laploshka's two francs from the poor, who should never have had that legacy. As I backed away from the crowd I heard a woman's voice say, 'I don't believe he put my money in the bag. There are swarms of people in Paris like that!' But my mind was lighter than it had been for a long time.

The delicate mission of bestowing the retrieved sum on the deserving rich still confronted me. Again I trusted to the inspiration of accident, and again fortune favoured me. A shower drove me, two days later, into one of the historic churches on the left bank of the Seine, and there I found, peering at the old wood-carvings, the Baron R., one of the wealthiest and most shabbily dressed men in Paris. It was now or never. Putting a strong American inflection into the French which I usually talked with an unmistakable British accent, I catechized the Baron as to the date of the church's building, its dimensions, and other details which an American tourist would be certain to want to know. Having acquired such information as the Baron was able to impart on short notice, I solemnly placed the two-franc piece in his hand, with the

hearty assurance that it was 'pour vous', and turned to go.
The Baron was slightly taken aback, but accepted the situation with a good grace. Walking over to a small box fixed
in the wall, he dropped Laploshka's two francs into the
slot. Over the box was the inscription, 'Pour les pauvres de
M. le Curé.'

That evening, at the crowded corner by the Café de la Paix,
I caught a fleeting glimpse of Laploshka. He smiled, slightly
raised his hat, and vanished. I never saw him again. After all,
the money had been *given* to the deserving rich, and the soul
of Laploshka was at peace.

THE BAG

'THE Major is coming in to tea,' said Mrs Hoopington to her
niece. 'He's just gone round to the stables with his horse. Be
as bright and lively as you can; the poor man's got a fit of
the glooms.'

Major Pallaby was a victim of circumstances, over which he
had no control, and of his temper, over which he had very
little. He had taken on the Mastership of the Pexdale Hounds
in succession to a highly popular man who had fallen foul of
his committee, and the Major found himself confronted with
the overt hostility of at least half the hunt, while his lack of
tact and amiability had done much to alienate the remainder.
Hence subscriptions were beginning to fall off, foxes grew
provokingly scarcer, and wire obtruded itself with increasing
frequency. The Major could plead reasonable excuse for his fit
of the glooms.

In ranging herself as a partisan on the side of Major Pallaby
Mrs Hoopington had been largely influenced by the fact that
she had made up her mind to marry him at an early date.
Against his notorious bad temper she set his three thousand
a year, and his prospective succession to a baronetcy gave a
casting vote in his favour. The Major's plans on the subject of
matrimony were not at present in such an advanced stage as
Mrs Hoopington's, but he was beginning to find his way over

to Hoopington Hall with a frequency that was already being commented on.

'He had a wretchedly thin field out again yesterday,' said Mrs Hoopington. 'Why you didn't bring one or two hunting men down with you, instead of that stupid Russian boy, I can't think.'

'Vladimir isn't stupid,' protested her niece; 'he's one of the most amusing boys I ever met. Just compare him for a moment with some of your heavy hunting men—'

'Anyhow, my dear Norah, he can't ride.'

'Russians never can; but he shoots.'

'Yes; and what does he shoot? Yesterday he brought home a woodpecker in his game-bag.'

'But he'd shot three pheasants and some rabbits as well.'

'That's no excuse for including a woodpecker in his game-bag.'

'Foreigners go in for mixed bags more than we do. A Grand Duke pots a vulture just as seriously as we should stalk a bustard. Anyhow, I've explained to Vladimir that certain birds are beneath his dignity as a sportsman. And as he's only nineteen, of course, his dignity is a sure thing to appeal to.'

Mrs Hoopington sniffed. Most people with whom Vladimir came in contact found his high spirits infectious, but his present hostess was guaranteed immune against infection of that sort.

'I hear him coming in now,' she observed. 'I shall go and get ready for tea. We're going to have it here in the hall. Entertain the Major if he comes in before I'm down, and, above all, be bright.'

Norah was dependent on her aunt's good graces for many little things that made life worth living, and she was conscious of a feeling of discomfiture because the Russian youth whom she had brought down as a welcome element of change in the country-house routine was not making a good impression. That young gentleman, however, was supremely unconscious of any shortcomings, and burst into the hall, tired, and less sprucely groomed than usual, but distinctly radiant. His game-bag looked comfortably full.

'Guess what I have shot,' he demanded.

'Pheasants, wood-pigeons, rabbits,' hazarded Norah.

'No; a large beast; I don't know what you call it in English. Brown, with a darkish tail.' Norah changed colour.

'Does it live in a tree and eat nuts?' she asked, hoping that the use of the adjective 'large' might be an exaggeration.

Vladimir laughed.

'Oh, no; not a *biyelka*.'

'Does it swim and eat fish?' asked Norah, with a fervent prayer in her heart that it might turn out to be an otter.

'No,' said Vladimir, busy with the straps of his game-bag; 'it lives in the woods, and eats rabbits and chickens.'

Norah sat down suddenly, and hid her face in her hands.

'Merciful Heaven!' she wailed; 'he's shot a fox!'

Vladimir looked up at her in consternation. In a torrent of agitated words she tried to explain the horror of the situation. The boy understood nothing, but was thoroughly alarmed.

'Hide it, hide it!' said Norah frantically, pointing to the still unopened bag. 'My aunt and the Major will be here in a moment. Throw it on the top of that chest; they won't see it there.'

Vladimir swung the bag with fair aim; but the strap caught in its flight on the outstanding point of an antler fixed in the wall, and the bag, with its terrible burden, remained suspended just above the alcove where tea would presently be laid. At that moment Mrs Hoopington and the Major entered the hall.

'The Major is going to draw our covers tomorrow,' announced the lady, with a certain heavy satisfaction. 'Smithers is confident that we'll be able to show him some sport; he swears he's seen a fox in the nut copse three times this week.'

'I'm sure I hope so; I hope so,' said the Major moodily. 'I must break this sequence of blank days. One hears so often that a fox has settled down as a tenant for life in certain covers, and then when you go to turn him out there isn't a trace of him. I'm certain a fox was shot or trapped in Lady Widden's woods the very day before we drew them.'

'Major, if any one tried that game on in my woods they'd get short shrift,' said Mrs Hoopington.

Norah found her way mechanically to the tea-table and made her fingers frantically busy in rearranging the parsley round the sandwich dish. On one side of her loomed the morose countenance of the Major, on the other she was conscious of the scared, miserable eyes of Vladimir. And above it all hung *that*. She dared not raise her eyes above the level of the tea-table, and she almost expected to see a spot of accusing vulpine blood drip down and stain the whiteness of the cloth. Her aunt's manner signalled to her the repeated message to 'be bright'; for the present she was fully occupied in keeping her teeth from chattering.

'What did you shoot today?' asked Mrs Hoopington suddenly of the unusually silent Vladimir.

'Nothing—nothing worth speaking of,' said the boy.

Norah's heart, which had stood still for a space, made up for lost time with a most disturbing bound.

'I wish you'd find something that was worth speaking about,' said the hostess; 'every one seems to have lost their tongues.'

'When did Smithers last see that fox?' said the Major.

'Yesterday morning; a fine dog-fox, with a dark brush,' confided Mrs Hoopington.

'Aha, we'll have a good gallop after that brush tomorrow,' said the Major, with a transient gleam of good humour. And then gloomy silence settled again round the tea-table, a silence broken only by despondent munchings and the occasional feverish rattle of a teaspoon in its saucer. A diversion was at last afforded by Mrs Hoopington's fox-terrier, which had jumped on to a vacant chair, the better to survey the delicacies of the table, and was now sniffing in an upward direction at something apparently more interesting than cold tea-cake.

'What is exciting him?' asked his mistress, as the dog suddenly broke into short, angry barks, with a running accompaniment of tremulous whines.

'Why,' she continued, 'it's your game-bag, Vladimir! What *have* you got in it?'

'By Gad,' said the Major, who was now standing up; 'there's a pretty warm scent!'

And then a simultaneous idea flashed on himself and Mrs Hoopington. Their faces flushed to distinct but harmonious tones of purple, and with one accusing voice they screamed, 'You've shot the fox!'

Norah tried hastily to palliate Vladimir's misdeed in their eyes, but it is doubtful whether they heard her. The Major's fury clothed and reclothed itself in words as frantically as a woman up in town for one day's shopping tries on a succession of garments. He reviled and railed at fate and the general scheme of things, he pitied himself with a strong, deep pity too poignant for tears, he condemned every one with whom he had ever come in contact to endless and abnormal punishments. In fact, he conveyed the impression that if a destroying angel had been lent to him for a week it would have had very little time for private study. In the lulls of his outcry could be heard the querulous monotone of Mrs Hoopington and the sharp staccato barking of the fox-terrier. Vladimir, who did not understand a tithe of what was being said, sat fondling a cigarette and repeating under his breath from time to time a vigorous English adjective which he had long ago taken affectionately into his vocabulary. His mind strayed back to the youth in the old Russian folk-tale who shot an enchanted bird with dramatic results. Meanwhile, the Major, roaming round the hall like an imprisoned cyclone, had caught sight of and joyfully pounced on the telephone apparatus, and lost no time in ringing up the hunt secretary and announcing his resignation of the Mastership. A servant had by this time brought his horse round to the door, and in a few seconds Mrs Hoopington's shrill monotone had the field to itself. But after the Major's display her best efforts at vocal violence missed their full effect; it was as though one had come straight out from a Wagner opera into a rather tame thunderstorm. Realizing, perhaps, that her tirades were something of an anticlimax, Mrs Hoopington broke suddenly into some rather necessary tears and marched out of the room, leaving behind her a silence almost as terrible as the turmoil which had preceded it.

'What shall I do with—*that*?' asked Vladimir at last.

'Bury it,' said Norah.

'Just plain burial?' said Vladimir, rather relieved. He had almost expected that some of the local clergy would have insisted on being present, or that a salute might have to be fired over the grave.

And thus it came to pass that in the dusk of a November evening the Russian boy, murmuring a few of the prayers of his Church for luck, gave hasty but decent burial to a large polecat under the lilac trees at Hoopington.

CROSS CURRENTS

VANESSA PENNINGTON had a husband who was poor, with few extenuating circumstances, and an admirer who, though comfortably rich, was cumbered with a sense of honour. His wealth made him welcome in Vanessa's eyes, but his code of what was right impelled him to go away and forget her, or at the most to think of her in the intervals of doing a great many other things. And although Alaric Clyde loved Vanessa, and thought he should always go on loving her, he gradually and unconsciously allowed himself to be wooed and won by a more alluring mistress; he fancied that his continued shunning of the haunts of men was a self-imposed exile, but his heart was caught in the spell of the Wilderness, and the Wilderness was kind and beautiful to him. When one is young and strong and unfettered the wild earth can be very kind and very beautiful. Witness the legion of men who were once young and unfettered and now eat out their souls in dustbins, because, having erstwhile known and loved the Wilderness, they broke from her thrall and turned aside into beaten paths.

In the high waste places of the world Clyde roamed and hunted and dreamed, death-dealing and gracious as some god of Hellas, moving with his horses and servants and four-footed camp followers from one dwelling ground to another, a welcome guest among wild primitive village folk and no-mads, a friend and slayer of the fleet, shy beasts around him.

By the shores of misty upland lakes he shot the wild fowl
that had winged their way to him across half the old world;
beyond Bokhara he watched the wild Aryan horsemen at their
gambols; watched, too, in some dim-lit tea-house one of those
beautiful uncouth dances that one can never wholly forget; or,
making a wide cast down to the valley of the Tigris, swam and
rolled in its snow-cooled racing waters. Vanessa, meanwhile,
in a Bayswater back street, was making out the weekly laundry list, attending bargain sales, and, in her more adventurous
moments, trying new ways of cooking whiting. Occasionally
she went to bridge parties, where, if the play was not illumi-
nating, at least one learned a great deal about the private life
of some of the Royal and Imperial Houses. Vanessa, in a way,
was glad that Clyde had done the proper thing. She had a
strong natural bias towards respectability, though she would
have preferred to have been respectable in smarter surroundings, where her example would have done more good. To be
beyond reproach was one thing, but it would have been nicer
to have been nearer to the Park.

And then of a sudden her regard for respectability and
Clyde's sense of what was right were thrown on the scrapheap
of unnecessary things. They had been useful and highly important in their time, but the death of Vanessa's husband made
them of no immediate moment.

The news of the altered condition of things followed Clyde
with leisurely persistence from one place of call to another,
and at last ran him to a standstill somewhere in the Orenburg
Steppe. He would have found it exceedingly difficult to
analyse his feelings on receipt of the tidings. The Fates had
unexpectedly (and perhaps just a little officiously) removed an
obstacle from his path. He supposed he was overjoyed, but he
missed the feeling of elation which he had experienced some
four months ago when he had bagged a snow-leopard with a
lucky shot after a day's fruitless stalking. Of course he would
go back and ask Vanessa to marry him, but he was determined
on enforcing a condition: on no account would he desert his
newer love. Vanessa would have to agree to come out into the
Wilderness with him.

The lady hailed the return of her lover with even more relief

than had been occasioned by his departure. The death of John
Pennington had left his widow in circumstances which were
more straitened than ever, and the Park had receded even
from her note-paper, where it had long been retained as a
courtesy title on the principle that addresses are given to us to
conceal our whereabouts. Certainly she was more independent now than heretofore, but independence, which means so
much to many women, was of little account to Vanessa, who
came under the heading of the mere female. She made little
ado about accepting Clyde's condition, and announced herself
ready to follow him to the end of the world; as the world was
round she nourished a complacent idea that in the ordinary
course of things one would find oneself in the neighbourhood
of Hyde Park Corner sooner or later no matter how far afield
one wandered.

East of Budapest her complacency began to filter away, and
when she saw her husband treating the Black Sea with a
familiarity which she had never been able to assume towards
the English Channel, misgivings began to crowd in upon her.
Adventures which would have presented an amusing and enticing aspect to a better-bred woman aroused in Vanessa only
the twin sensations of fright and discomfort. Flies bit her,
and she was persuaded that it was only sheer boredom that
prevented camels from doing the same. Clyde did his best, and
a very good best it was, to infuse something of the banquet
into their prolonged desert picnics, but even snow-cooled
Heidsieck lost its flavour when you were convinced that the
dusky cupbearer who served it with such reverent elegance
was only waiting a convenient opportunity to cut your throat.
It was useless for Clyde to give Yussuf a character for devotion such as is rarely found in any Western servant. Vanessa
was well enough educated to know that all dusky-skinned
people take human life as unconcernedly as Bayswater folk
take singing lessons.

And with a growing irritation and querulousness on her
part came a further disenchantment, born of the inability of
husband and wife to find a common ground of interest. The
habits and migrations of the sand grouse, the folklore and
customs of Tartars and Turkomans, the points of a Cossack

pony—these were matters which evoked only a bored in-difference in Vanessa. On the other hand, Clyde was not thrilled on being informed that the Queen of Spain detested mauve, or that a certain Royal duchess, for whose tastes he was never likely to be called on to cater, nursed a violent but perfectly respectable passion for beef olives.

Vanessa began to arrive at the conclusion that a husband who added a roving disposition to a settled income was a mixed blessing. It was one thing to go to the end of the world; it was quite another thing to make oneself at home there. Even respectability seemed to lose some of its virtue when one practised it in a tent.

Bored and disillusioned with the drift of her new life, Vanessa was undisguisedly glad when distraction offered itself in the person of Mr Dobrinton, a chance acquaintance whom they had first run against in the primitive hostelry of a be-nighted Caucasian town. Dobrinton was elaborately British, in deference perhaps to the memory of his mother, who was said to have derived part of her origin from an English gov-erness who had come to Lemberg a long way back in the last century. If you had called him Dobrinski when off his guard he would probably have responded readily enough; holding, no doubt, that the end crowns all, he had taken a slight liberty with the family patronymic. To look at, Mr Dobrinton was not a very attractive specimen of masculine humanity, but in Vanessa's eyes he was a link with that civilization which Clyde seemed so ready to ignore and forgo. He could sing 'Yip-I-Addy' and spoke of several duchesses as if he knew them—in his more inspired moments almost as if they knew him. He even pointed out blemishes in the cuisine or cellar depart-ments of some of the more august London restaurants, a species of Higher Criticism which was listened to by Vanessa in awestricken admiration. And, above all, he sympathized, at first discreetly, afterwards with more latitude, with her fretful discontent at Clyde's nomadic instincts. Business connected with oil-wells had brought Dobrinton to the neighbourhood of Baku; the pleasure of appealing to an appreciative female audience induced him to deflect his return journey so as to coincide a good deal with his new acquaintances' line of march. And while Clyde trafficked with Persian horse-dealers or hunted the wild grey pigs in their lairs and added to his notes on Central Asian game-fowl, Dobrinton and the lady discussed the ethics of desert respectability from points of view that showed a daily tendency to converge. And one evening Clyde dined alone, reading between the courses a long letter from Vanessa, justifying her action in flitting to more civilized lands with a more congenial companion.

It was distinctly evil luck for Vanessa, who really was thoroughly respectable at heart, that she and her lover should run into the hands of Kurdish brigands on the first day of their flight. To be mewed up in a squalid Kurdish village in close companionship with a man who was only your husband by adoption, and to have the attention of all Europe drawn to your plight, was about the least respectable thing that could happen. And there were international complications, which made things worse. 'English lady and her husband, of foreign nationality, held by Kurdish brigands who demand ransom' had been the report of the nearest Consul. Although Dobrinton was British at heart, the other portions of him belonged to the Habsburgs, and though the Habsburgs took no great pride or pleasure in this particular unit of their wide and varied possessions, and would gladly have exchanged him for some interesting bird or mammal for the Schoenbrunn Park, the code of international dignity demanded that they should display a decent solicitude for his restoration. And while the Foreign Offices of the two countries were taking the usual steps to secure the release of their respective subjects a further horrible complication ensued. Clyde, following on the track of the fugitives, not with any special desire to over-take them, but with a dim feeling that it was expected of him, fell into the hands of the same community of brigands. Diplomacy, while anxious to do its best for a lady in misfor-tune, showed signs of becoming restive at this expansion of its task; as a frivolous young gentleman in Downing Street remarked, 'Any husband of Mrs Dobrinton's we shall be glad to extricate, but let us know how many there are of them.' For a woman who valued respectability Vanessa really had no luck.

Meanwhile the situation of the captives was not free from embarrassment. When Clyde explained to the Kurdish headmen the nature of his relationship with the runaway couple they were gravely sympathetic, but vetoed any idea of summary vengeance, since the Habsburgs would be sure to insist on the delivery of Dobrinton alive, and in a reasonably undamaged condition. They did not object to Clyde administering a beating to his rival for half an hour every Monday and Thursday, but Dobrinton turned such a sickly green when he heard of this arrangement that the chief was obliged to withdraw the concession.

And so, in the cramped quarters of a mountain hut, the ill-assorted trio watched the insufferable hours crawl slowly by. Dobrinton was too frightened to be conversational, Vanessa was too mortified to open her lips, and Clyde was moodily silent. The little Lemberg *négociant* plucked up heart once to give a quavering rendering of 'Yip-I-Addy', but when he reached the statement 'home was never like this' Vanessa tearfully begged him to stop. And silence fastened itself with growing insistence on the three captives who were so tragically herded together; thrice a day they drew near to one another to swallow the meal that had been prepared for them, like desert beasts meeting in mute suspended hostility at the drinking-pool, and then drew back to resume the vigil of waiting.

Clyde was less carefully watched than the others. 'Jealousy will keep him to the woman's side,' thought his Kurdish captors. They did not know that his wilder, truer love was calling to him with a hundred voices from beyond the village bounds. And one evening, finding that he was not getting the attention to which he was entitled, Clyde slipped away down the mountain side and resumed his study of Central Asian game-fowl. The remaining captives were guarded henceforth with greater rigour, but Dobrinton at any rate scarcely regretted Clyde's departure.

The long arm, or perhaps one might better say the long purse, of diplomacy at last effected the release of the prisoners, but the Habsburgs were never to enjoy the guerdon of their outlay. On the quay of the little Black Sea Port, where the rescued pair came once more into contact with civilization, Dobrinton was bitten by a dog which was assumed to be mad, though it may only have been indiscriminating. The victim did not wait for symptoms of rabies to declare themselves, but died forthwith of fright, and Vanessa made the homeward journey alone, conscious somehow of a sense of slightly restored respectability. Clyde, in the intervals of correcting the proofs of his book on the game-fowl of Central Asia, found time to press a divorce suit through the Courts, and as soon as possible hied him away to the congenial solitudes of the Gobi Desert to collect material for a work on the fauna of that region. Vanessa, by virtue perhaps of her earlier intimacy with the cooking rites of the whiting, obtained a place on the kitchen staff of a West End Club. It was not brilliant, but at least it was within two minutes of the Park.

ESMÉ

'ALL hunting stories are the same,' said Clovis; 'just as all Turf stories are the same, and all—'

'My hunting story isn't a bit like any you've ever heard,' said the Baroness. 'It happened quite a while ago, when I was about twenty-three. I wasn't living apart from my husband then; you see, neither of us could afford to make the other a separate allowance. In spite of everything that proverbs may say, poverty keeps together more homes than it breaks up. But we always hunted with different packs. All this has nothing to do with the story.'

'We haven't arrived at the meet yet. I suppose there was a meet,' said Clovis.

'Of course there was a meet,' said the Baroness; 'all the usual crowd were there, especially Constance Broddle. Constance is one of those strapping florid girls that go so well with autumn scenery or Christmas decorations in church. "I feel a presentiment that something dreadful is going to happen," she said to me; "am I looking pale?"

'She was looking about as pale as a beetroot that has suddenly heard bad news.

'"You're looking nicer than usual," I said, "but that's so easy for you." Before she had got the right bearings of this remark we had settled down to business; hounds had found a fox lying out in some gorse-bushes.'

'I knew it,' said Clovis; 'in every fox-hunting story that I've ever heard there's been a fox and some gorse-bushes.'

'Constance and I were well mounted,' continued the Baroness serenely, 'and we had no difficulty in keeping ourselves in the first flight, thought it was a fairly stiff run. Towards the finish, however, we must have held rather too independent a line, for we lost the hounds, and found ourselves plodding aimlessly along miles away from anywhere. It was fairly exasperating, and my temper was beginning to let itself go by inches, when on pushing our way through an accommodating hedge we were gladdened by the sight of hounds in full cry in a hollow just beneath us.

'"There they go," cried Constance, and then added in a gasp, "In Heaven's name, what are they hunting?"

'It was certainly no mortal fox. It stood more than twice as high, had a short, ugly head, and an enormous thick neck.

'"It's a hyaena," I cried; "it must have escaped from Lord Pabham's Park."

'At that moment the hunted beast turned and faced its pursuers, and the hounds (there were only about six couple of them) stood round in a half-circle and looked foolish. Evidently they had broken away from the rest of the pack on the trail of this alien scent, and were not quite sure how to treat their quarry now they had got him.

'The hyaena hailed our approach with unmistakable relief and demonstrations of friendliness. It had probably been accustomed to uniform kindness from humans, while its first experience of a pack of hounds had left a bad impression. The hounds looked more than ever embarrassed as their quarry paraded its sudden intimacy with us, and the faint toot of a horn in the distance was seized on as a welcome signal for unobtrusive departure. Constance and I and the hyaena were left alone in the gathering twilight.

' "What are we to do?" asked Constance.

' "What a person you are for questions," I said.

' "Well, we can't stay here all night with a hyaena," she retorted.

' "I don't know what your ideas of comfort are," I said; "but I shouldn't think of staying here all night even without a hyaena. My home may be an unhappy one, but at least it has hot and cold water laid on, and domestic service, and other conveniences which we shouldn't find here. We had better make for that ridge of trees to the right; I imagine the Crowley road is just beyond."

'We trotted off slowly along a faintly marked cart-track, with the beast following cheerfully at our heels.

' "What on earth are we to do with the hyaena?" came the inevitable question.

' "What does one generally do with hyaenas?" I asked crossly.

' "I've never had anything to do with one before," said Constance.

' "Well, neither have I. If we even knew its sex we might give it a name. Perhaps we might call it Esmé. That would do in either case."

'There was still sufficient daylight for us to distinguish wayside objects, and our listless spirits gave an upward perk as we came upon a small half-naked gipsy brat picking blackberries from a low-growing bush. The sudden apparition of two horsewomen and a hyaena set it off crying, and in any case we should scarcely have gleaned any useful geographical information from that source; but there was a probability that we might strike a gipsy encampment somewhere along our route. We rode on hopefully but uneventfully for another mile or so.

' "I wonder what the child was doing there," said Constance presently.

' "Picking blackberries. Obviously."

' "I don't like the way it cried," pursued Constance; "somehow its wail keeps ringing in my ears."

'I did not chide Constance for her morbid fancies; as a matter of fact the same sensation, of being pursued by a persistent fretful wail, had been forcing itself on my rather

over-tired nerves. For company's sake I hullooed to Esmé, who
had lagged somewhat behind. With a few springy bounds he
drew up level, and then shot past us.

'The wailing accompaniment was explained. The gipsy
child was firmly, and I expect painfully, held in his jaws.

' "Merciful Heaven!" screamed Constance, "what on earth
shall we do? What are we to do?"

'I am perfectly certain that at the Last Judgment Constance
will ask more questions than any of the examining Seraphs.

' "Can't we do something?" she persisted tearfully, as Esmé
cantered easily along in front of our tired horses.

'Personally I was doing everything that occurred to me at
the moment. I stormed and scolded and coaxed in English and
French and gamekeeper language; I made absurd, ineffectual
cuts in the air with my thongless hunting-crop; I hurled my
sandwich case at the brute; in fact, I really don't know what
more I could have done. And still we lumbered on through the
deepening dusk, with that dark uncouth shape lumbering
ahead of us, and a drone of lugubrious music floating in our
ears. Suddenly Esmé bounded aside into some thick bushes,
where we could not follow; the wail rose to a shriek and then
stopped altogether. This part of the story I always hurry over,
because it is really rather horrible. When the beast joined us
again, after an absence of a few minutes, there was an air of
patient understanding about him, as though he knew that he
had done something of which we disapproved, but which he
felt to be thoroughly justifiable.

' "How can you let that ravening beast trot by your side?"
asked Constance. She was looking more than ever like an
albino beetroot.

' "In the first place, I can't prevent it," I said; "and in the
second place, whatever else he may be, I doubt if he's ravening
at the present moment."

'Constance shuddered. "Do you think the poor little thing
suffered much?" came another of her futile questions.

' "The indications were all that way," I said; "on the other
hand, of course, it may have been crying from sheer temper.
Children sometimes do."

'It was nearly pitch-dark when we emerged suddenly into

the high road. A flash of lights and the whir of a motor went past us at the same moment at uncomfortably close quarters. A thud and a sharp screeching yell followed a second later. The car drew up, and when I had ridden back to the spot I found a young man bending over a dark motionless mass lying by the roadside.

' "You have killed my Esmé," I exclaimed bitterly.

' "I'm so awfully sorry," said the young man; "I keep dogs myself, so I know what you must feel about it. I'll do anything I can in reparation."

' "Please bury him at once," I said; "that much I think I may ask of you."

' "Bring the spade, William," he called to the chauffeur. Evidently hasty roadside interments were contingencies that had been provided against.

'The digging of a sufficiently large grave took some little time. "I say, what a magnificent fellow," said the motorist as the corpse was rolled over into the trench. "I'm afraid he must have been rather a valuable animal."

' "He took second in the puppy class at Birmingham last year," I said resolutely.

'Constance snorted loudly.

' "Don't cry, dear," I said brokenly; "it was all over in a moment. He couldn't have suffered much."

' "Look here," said the young fellow desperately, "you simply must let me do something by way of reparation."

'I refused sweetly, but as he persisted I let him have my address.

'Of course, we kept our own counsel as to the earlier episodes of the evening. Lord Pabham never advertised the loss of his hyaena; when a strictly fruit-eating animal strayed from his park a year or two previously he was called upon to give compensation in eleven cases of sheep-worrying and practically to re-stock his neighbours' poultry-yards, and an escaped hyaena would have mounted up to something on the scale of a Government grant. The gipsies were equally unobtrusive over their missing offspring; I don't suppose in large encampments they really know to a child or two how many they've got.'

The Baroness paused reflectively, and then continued:

'There was a sequel to the adventure, though. I got through the post a charming little diamond brooch, with the name Esmé set in a sprig of rosemary. Incidentally, too, I lost the friendship of Constance Broddle. You see, when I sold the brooch I quite properly refused to give her any share of the proceeds. I pointed out that the Esmé part of the affair was my own invention, and the hyaena part of it belonged to Lord Pabham, if it really was his hyaena, of which, of course, I've no proof.'

TOBERMORY

IT was a chill, rain-washed afternoon of a late August day, that indefinite season when partridges are still in security or cold storage, and there is nothing to hunt—unless one is bounded on the north by the Bristol Channel, in which case one may lawfully gallop after fat red stags. Lady Blemley's house-party was not bounded on the north by the Bristol Channel, hence there was a full gathering of her guests round the tea-table on this particular afternoon. And, in spite of the blankness of the season and the triteness of the occasion, there was no trace in the company of that fatigued restlessness which means a dread of the pianola and a subdued hankering for auction bridge. The undisguised open-mouthed attention of the entire party was fixed on the homely negative personality of Mr Cornelius Appin. Of all her guests, he was the one who had come to Lady Blemley with the vaguest reputation. Some one had said he was 'clever', and he had got his invitation in the moderate expectation, on the part of his hostess, that some portion at least of his cleverness would be contributed to the general entertainment. Until tea-time that day she had been unable to discover in what direction, if any, his cleverness lay. He was neither a wit nor a croquet champion, a hypnotic force nor a begetter of amateur theatricals. Neither did his exterior suggest the sort of man in whom women are willing to pardon a generous measure of mental deficiency. He had subsided into mere Mr Appin, and the Cornelius seemed a piece of transparent baptismal bluff. And now he was claiming to have launched on the world a discovery beside which the invention of gunpowder, of the printing-press, and of steam locomotion were inconsiderable trifles. Science had made bewildering strides in many directions during recent decades, but this thing seemed to belong to the domain of miracle rather than to scientific achievement.

'And do you really ask us to believe,' Sir Wilfrid was saying, 'that you have discovered a means for instructing animals in the art of human speech, and that dear old Tobermory has proved your first successful pupil?'

'It is a problem at which I have worked for the last seventeen years,' said Mr Appin, 'but only during the last eight or nine months have I been rewarded with glimmerings of success. Of course I have experimented with thousands of animals, but latterly only with cats, those wonderful creatures which have assimilated themselves so marvellously with our civilization while retaining all their highly developed feral instincts. Here and there among cats one comes across an outstanding superior intellect, just as one does among the ruck of human beings, and when I made the acquaintance of Tobermory a week ago I saw at once that I was in contact with a "Beyond-cat" of extraordinary intelligence. I had gone far along the road to success in recent experiments; with Tobermory, as you call him, I have reached the goal.'

Mr Appin concluded his remarkable statement in a voice which he strove to divest of a triumphant inflection. No one said 'Rats', though Clovis's lips moved in a monosyllabic contortion which probably invoked those rodents of disbelief.

'And do you mean to say,' asked Miss Resker, after a slight pause, 'that you have taught Tobermory to say and understand easy sentences of one syllable?'

'My dear Miss Resker,' said the wonder-worker patiently, 'one teaches little children and savages and backward adults in that piecemeal fashion; when one has once solved the problem of making a beginning with an animal of highly developed intelligence one has no need for those halting methods. Tobermory can speak our language with perfect correctness.'

This time Clovis very distinctly said, 'Beyond-rats!' Sir Wilfrid was more polite, but equally sceptical.

'Hadn't we better have the cat in and judge for ourselves?' suggested Lady Blemley.

Sir Wilfrid went in search of the animal, and the company settled themselves down to the languid expectation of witnessing some more or less adroit drawing-room ventriloquism.

In a minute Sir Wilfrid was back in the room, his face white beneath its tan and his eyes dilated with excitement.

'By Gad, it's true!'

His agitation was unmistakably genuine, and his hearers started forward in a thrill of awakened interest.

Collapsing into an armchair he continued breathlessly: 'I found him dozing in the smoking-room and called out to him to come for his tea. He blinked at me in his usual way, and I said, "Come on, Toby; don't keep us waiting"; and, by Gad! he drawled out in a most horribly natural voice that he'd come when he dashed well pleased! I nearly jumped out of my skin!'

Appin had preached to absolutely incredulous hearers; Sir Wilfrid's statement carried instant conviction. A Babel-like chorus of startled exclamation arose, amid which the scientist sat mutely enjoying the first fruit of his stupendous discovery.

In the midst of the clamour Tobermory entered the room and made his way with velvet tread and studied unconcern across to the group seated round the tea-table.

A sudden hush of awkwardness and constraint fell on the company. Somehow there seemed an element of embarrassment in addressing on equal terms a domestic cat of acknowledged dental ability.

'Will you have some milk, Tobermory?' asked Lady Blemley in a rather strained voice.

'I don't mind if I do,' was the response, couched in a tone of even indifference. A shiver of suppressed excitement went through the listeners, and Lady Blemley might be excused for pouring out the saucerful of milk rather unsteadily.

'I'm afraid I've spilt a good deal of it,' she said apologetically.

'After all, it's not my Axminster,' was Tobermory's rejoinder.

Another silence fell on the group, and then Miss Resker, in her best district-visitor manner, asked if the human language had been difficult to learn. Tobermory looked squarely at her for a moment and then fixed his gaze serenely on the middle distance. It was obvious that boring questions lay outside his scheme of life.

'What do you think of human intelligence?' asked Mavis Pellington lamely.

'Of whose intelligence in particular?' asked Tobermory coldly.

'Oh, well, mine for instance,' said Mavis, with a feeble laugh.

'You put me in an embarrassing position,' said Tobermory, whose tone and attitude certainly did not suggest a shred of embarrassment. 'When your inclusion in this house-party was suggested Sir Wilfrid protested that you were the most brainless woman of his acquaintance, and that there was a wide distinction between hospitality and the care of the feeble-minded. Lady Blemley replied that your lack of brain-power was the precise quality which had earned you your invitation, as you were the only person she could think of who might be idiotic enough to buy their old car. You know, the one the call "The Envy of Sisyphus", because it goes quite nicely up-hill if you push it.'

Lady Blemley's protestations would have had greater effect if she had not casually suggested to Mavis only that morning that the car in question would be just the thing for her down at her Devonshire home.

Major Barfield plunged in heavily to effect a diversion.

'How about your carryings-on with the tortoise-shell puss up at the stables, eh?'

The moment he had said it every one realized the blunder.

'One does not usually discuss these matters in public,' said Tobermory frigidly. 'From a slight observation of your ways since you've been in this house I should imagine you'd find it inconvenient if I were to shift the conversation on to your own little affairs.'

The panic which ensued was not confined to the Major.

'Would you like to go and see if cook has got your dinner

ready?' suggested Lady Blemley hurriedly, affecting to ignore the fact that it wanted at least two hours to Tobermory's dinner-time.

'Thanks,' said Tobermory, 'not quite so soon after my tea. I don't want to die of indigestion.'

'Cats have nine lives, you know,' said Sir Wilfrid heartily.

'Possibly,' answered Tobermory; 'but only one liver.'

'Adelaide!' said Mrs Cornett, 'do you mean to encourage that cat to go out and gossip about us in the servants' hall?'

The panic had indeed become general. A narrow ornamental balustrade ran in front of most of the bedroom windows at the Towers, and it was recalled with dismay that this had formed a favourite promenade for Tobermory at all hours, whence he could watch the pigeons—and heaven knew what else besides. If he intended to become reminiscent in his present outspoken strain the effect would be something more than disconcerting. Mrs Cornett, who spent much time at her toilet table, and whose complexion was reputed to be of a nomadic though punctual disposition, looked as ill at ease as the Major. Miss Scrawen, who wrote fiercely sensuous poetry and led a blameless life, merely displayed irritation; if you are methodical and virtuous in private you don't necessarily want every one to know it. Bertie van Tahn, who was so depraved at seventeen that he had long ago given up trying to be any worse, turned a dull shade of gardenia white, but he did not commit the error of dashing out of the room like Odo Finsberry, a young gentleman who was understood to be reading for the Church and who was possibly disturbed at the thought of scandals he might hear concerning other people. Clovis had the presence of mind to maintain a composed exterior; privately he was calculating how long it would take to procure a box of fancy mice through the agency of the *Exchange and Mart* as a species of hush-money.

Even in a delicate situation like the present, Agnes Resker could not endure to remain too long in the background.

'Why did I ever come down here?' she asked dramatically.

Tobermory immediately accepted the opening.

'Judging by what you said to Mrs Cornett on the croquet-lawn yesterday, you were out for food. You described the

Blemleys as the dullest people to stay with that you knew, but said they were clever enough to employ a first-rate cook; otherwise they'd find it difficult to get any one to come down a second time.'

'There's not a word of truth in it! I appeal to Mrs Cornett—' exclaimed the discomfited Agnes.

'Mrs Cornett repeated your remark afterwards to Bertie van Tahn,' continued Tobermory, 'and said, "That woman is a regular Hunger Marcher; she'd go anywhere for four square meals a day," and Bertie van Tahn said—'

At this point the chronicle mercifully ceased. Tobermory had caught a glimpse of the big yellow Tom from the Rectory working his way through the shrubbery towards the stable wing. In a flash he had vanished through the open French window.

With the disappearance of his too brilliant pupil Cornelius Appin found himself beset by a hurricane of bitter upbraiding, anxious inquiry, and frightened entreaty. The responsibility for the situation lay with him, and he must prevent matters from becoming worse. Could Tobermory impart his dangerous gift to other cats? was the first question he had to answer. It was possible, he replied, that he might have initiated his intimate friend the stable puss into his new accomplishment, but it was unlikely that his teaching could have taken a wider range as yet.

'Then,' said Mrs Cornett, 'Tobermory may be a valuable cat and a great pet; but I'm sure you'll agree, Adelaide, that both he and the stable cat must be done away with without delay.'

'You don't suppose I've enjoyed the last quarter of an hour, do you?' said Lady Blemley bitterly. 'My husband and I are very fond of Tobermory—at least, we were before this horrible accomplishment was infused into him; but now, of course, the only thing is to have him destroyed as soon as possible.'

'We can put some strychnine in the scraps he always gets at dinner-time,' said Sir Wilfrid, 'and I will go and drown the stable cat myself. The coachman will be very sore at losing his pet, but I'll say a very catching form of mange has broken out in both cats and we're afraid of its spreading to the kennels.'

'But my great discovery!' expostulated Mr Appin; 'after all my years of research and experiment—'

'You can go and experiment on the short-horns at the farm, who are under proper control,' said Mrs Cornett, 'or the elephants at the Zoological Gardens. They're said to be highly intelligent, and they have this recommendation, that they don't come creeping about our bedrooms and under chairs, and so forth.'

An archangel ecstatically proclaiming the Millennium, and then finding that it clashed unpardonably with Henley and would have to be indefinitely postponed, could hardly have felt more crestfallen than Cornelius Appin at the reception of his wonderful achievement. Public opinion, however, was against him—in fact, had the general voice been consulted on the subject it is probable that a strong minority vote would have been in favour of including him in the strychnine diet.

Defective train arrangements and a nervous desire to see matters brought to a finish prevented an immediate dispersal of the party, but dinner that evening was not a social success. Sir Wilfrid had had rather a trying time with the stable cat and subsequently with the coachman. Agnes Resker ostentatiously limited her repast to a morsel of dry toast, which she bit as though it were a personal enemy; while Mavis Pellington maintained a vindictive silence throughout the meal. Lady Blemley kept up a flow of what she hoped was conversation, but her attention was fixed on the doorway. A plateful of carefully dosed fish scraps was in readiness on the sideboard, but sweets and savoury and dessert went their way, and no Tobermory appeared either in the dining-room or kitchen.

The sepulchral dinner was cheerful compared with the subsequent vigil in the smoking-room. Eating and drinking had at least supplied a distraction and cloak to the prevailing embarrassment. Bridge was out of the question in the general tension of nerves and tempers, and after Odo Finsberry had given a lugubrious rendering of 'Mélisande in the Wood' to a frigid audience, music was tacitly avoided. At eleven the servants went to bed, announcing that the small window in the pantry had been left open as usual for Tobermory's private use. The guests read steadily through the current batch of magazines, and fell back gradually on the 'Badminton Library' and bound volumes of *Punch*. Lady Blemley made periodic visits to the pantry, returning each time with an expression of listless depression which forestalled questioning.

At two o'clock Clovis broke the dominating silence.

'He won't turn up tonight. He's probably in the local newspaper office at the present moment, dictating the first instalment of his reminiscences. Lady What's-her-name's book won't be in it. It will be the event of the day.'

Having made this contribution to the general cheerfulness, Clovis went to bed. At long intervals the various members of the house-party followed his example.

The servants taking round the early tea made a uniform announcement in reply to a uniform question. Tobermory had not returned.

Breakfast was, if anything, a more unpleasant function than dinner had been, but before its conclusion the situation was relieved. Tobermory's corpse was brought in from the shrubbery, where a gardener had just discovered it. From the bites on his throat and the yellow fur which coated his claws it was evident that he had fallen in unequal combat with the big Tom from the Rectory.

By midday most of the guests had quitted the Towers, and after lunch Lady Blemley had sufficiently recovered her spirits to write an extremely nasty letter to the Rectory about the loss of her valuable pet.

Tobermory had been Appin's one successful pupil, and he was destined to have no successor. A few weeks later an elephant in the Dresden Zoological Garden, which had shown no previous signs of irritability, broke loose and killed an Englishman who had apparently been teasing it. The victim's name was variously reported in the papers as Oppin and Eppelin, but his front name was faithfully rendered Cornelius.

'If he was trying German irregular verbs on the poor beast,' said Clovis, 'he deserved all he got.'

MRS PACKLETIDE'S TIGER

IT was Mrs Packletide's pleasure and intention that she should shoot a tiger. Not that the lust to kill had suddenly descended on her, or that she felt that she would leave India safer and more wholesome than she had found it, with one fraction less of wild beast per million of inhabitants. The compelling motive for her sudden deviation towards the footsteps of Nimrod was the fact that Loona Bimberton had recently been carried eleven miles in an aeroplane by an Algerian aviator, and talked of nothing else; only a personally procured tiger-skin and a heavy harvest of Press photographs could successfully counter that sort of thing. Mrs Packletide had already arranged in her mind the lunch she would give at her house in Curzon Street, ostensibly in Loona Bimberton's honour, with a tiger-skin rug occupying most of the foreground and all of the conversation. She had also already designed in her mind the tiger-claw brooch that she was going to give Loona Bimberton on her next birthday. In a world that is supposed to be chiefly swayed by hunger and by love Mrs Packletide was an exception; her movements and motives were largely governed by dislike of Loona Bimberton.

Circumstances proved propitious. Mrs Packletide had offered a thousand rupees for the opportunity of shooting a tiger without overmuch risk or exertion, and it so happened that a neighbouring village could boast of being the favoured rendezvous of an animal of respectable antecedents, which had been driven by the increasing infirmities of age to abandon game-killing and confine its appetite to the smaller domestic animals. The prospect of earning the thousand rupees had stimulated the sporting and commercial instinct of the villagers; children were posted night and day on the outskirts of the local jungle to head the tiger back in the unlikely event of his attempting to roam away to fresh hunting-grounds, and the cheaper kinds of goats were left about with elaborate carelessness to keep him satisfied with his present quarters. The one great anxiety was lest he should die of old age before the date appointed for the memsahib's shoot.

Mothers carrying their babies home through the jungle after the day's work in the fields hushed their singing lest they might curtail the restful sleep of the venerable herd-robber.

The great night duly arrived, moonlit and cloudless. A platform had been constructed in a comfortable and conveniently placed tree, and thereon crouched Mrs Packletide and her paid companion, Miss Mebbin. A goat, gifted with a particularly persistent bleat, such as even a partially deaf tiger might be reasonably expected to hear on a still night, was tethered at the correct distance. With an accurately sighted rifle and a thumb-nail pack of patience cards the sportswoman awaited the coming of the quarry.

'I suppose we are in some danger?' said Miss Mebbin.

She was not actually nervous about the wild beast, but she had a morbid dread of performing an atom more service than she had been paid for.

'Nonsense,' said Mrs. Packletide; 'it's a very old tiger. It couldn't spring up here even if it wanted to.'

'If it's an old tiger I think you ought to get it cheaper. A thousand rupees is a lot of money.'

Louisa Mebbin adopted a protective elder-sister attitude towards money in general, irrespective of nationality or denomination. Her energetic intervention had saved many a rouble from dissipating itself in tips in some Moscow hotel, and francs and centimes clung to her instinctively under circumstances which would have driven them headlong from less sympathetic hands. Her speculations as to the market depreciation of tiger remnants were cut short by the appearance on the scene of the animal itself. As soon as it caught sight of the tethered goat it lay flat on the earth, seemingly less from a desire to take advantage of all available cover than for the purpose of snatching a short rest before commencing the grand attack.

'I believe it's ill,' said Louisa Mebbin, loudly in Hindustani, for the benefit of the village headman, who was in ambush in a neighbouring tree.

'Hush!' said Mrs Packletide, and at that moment the tiger commenced ambling towards his victim.

'Now, now!' urged Miss Mebbin with some excitement; 'if

he doesn't touch the goat we needn't pay for it.' (The bait was an extra.)

The rifle flashed out with a loud report, and the great tawny beast sprang to one side and then rolled over in the stillness of death. In a moment a crowd of excited natives had swarmed on to the scene, and their shouting speedily carried the glad news to the village, where a thumping of tom-toms took up the chorus of triumph. And their triumph and rejoicing found a ready echo in the heart of Mrs Packletide; already that luncheon-party in Curzon Street seemed immeasurably nearer.

It was Louisa Mebbin who drew attention to the fact that the goat was in death-throes from a mortal bullet-wound, while no trace of the rifle's deadly work could be found on the tiger. Evidently the wrong animal had been hit, and the beast of prey had succumbed to heart-failure, caused by the sudden report of the rifle, accelerated by senile decay. Mrs Packletide was pardonably annoyed at the discovery; but, at any rate, she was the possessor of a dead tiger, and the villagers, anxious for their thousand rupees, gladly connived at the fiction that she had shot the beast. And Miss Mebbin was a paid companion. Therefore did Mrs Packletide face the cameras with a light heart, and her pictured fame reached from the pages of the *Texas Weekly Snapshot* to the illustrated Monday supplement of the *Novoe Vremya*. As for Loona Bimberton, she refused to look at an illustrated paper for weeks, and her letter of thanks for the gift of a tiger-claw brooch was a model of repressed emotions. The luncheon-party she declined; there are limits beyond which repressed emotions become dangerous.

From Curzon Street the tiger-skin rug travelled down to the Manor House, and was duly inspected and admired by the county, and it seemed a fitting and appropriate thing when Mrs Packletide went to the County Costume Ball in the character of Diana. She refused to fall in, however, with Clovis's tempting suggestion of a primeval dance party, at which every one should wear the skins of beasts they had recently slain. 'I should be in rather a Baby Bunting condition,' confessed Clovis, 'with a miserable rabbit-skin or two to wrap up in, but then,' he added, with a rather malicious glance at Diana's proportions, 'my figure is quite as good as that Russian dancing boy's.'

'How amused every one would be if they knew what really happened,' said Louisa Mebbin a few days after the ball.

'What do you mean?' asked Mrs Packletide quickly.

'How you shot the goat and frightened the tiger to death,' said Miss Mebbin, with her disagreeably pleasant laugh.

'No one would believe it,' said Mrs Packletide, her face changing colour as rapidly as though it were going through a book of patterns before post-time.

'Loona Bimberton would,' said Miss Mebbin. Mrs Packletide's face settled on an unbecoming shade of greenish white.

'You surely wouldn't give me away?' she asked.

'I've seen a week-end cottage near Dorking that I should rather like to buy,' said Miss Mebbin with seeming irrelevance. 'Six hundred and eighty, freehold. Quite a bargain, only I don't happen to have the money.'

Louisa Mebbin's pretty week-end cottage, christened by her 'Les Fauves', and gay in summer-time with its garden borders of tiger-lilies, is the wonder and admiration of her friends.

'It is a marvel how Louisa manages to do it,' is the general verdict.

Mrs Packletide indulges in no more big-game shooting.

'The incidental expenses are so heavy,' she confides to inquiring friends.

THE UNREST-CURE

ON the rack in the railway carriage immediately opposite Clovis was a solidly wrought travelling bag, with a carefully written label, on which was inscribed, 'J. P. Huddle, The Warren, Tilfield, near Slowborough'. Immediately below the rack sat the human embodiment of the label, a solid, sedate individual, sedately dressed, sedately conversational. Even without his conversation (which was addressed to a friend seated by his side, and touched chiefly on such topics as the backwardness of Roman hyacinths and the prevalence of measles at the Rectory), one could have gauged fairly accurately the temperament and mental outlook of the travelling bag's owner. But he seemed unwilling to leave anything to the imagination of a casual observer, and his talk grew presently personal and introspective.

'I don't know how it is,' he told his friend, 'I'm not much over forty, but I seem to have settled down into a deep groove of elderly middle-age. My sister shows the same tendency. We like everything to be exactly in its accustomed place; we like things to happen exactly at their appointed times; we like everything to be usual, orderly, punctual, methodical, to a hair's breadth, to a minute. It distresses and upsets us if it is not so. For instance, to take a very trifling matter, a thrush has built its nest year after year in the catkin-tree on the lawn; this year, for no obvious reason, it is building in the ivy on the garden wall. We have said very little about it, but I think we both feel that the change is unnecessary, and just a little irritating.'

'Perhaps,' said the friend, 'it is a different thrush.'

'We have suspected that,' said J. P. Huddle, 'and I think it gives us even more cause for annoyance. We don't feel that we want a change of thrush at our time of life; and yet, as I have said, we have scarcely reached an age when these things should make themselves seriously felt.'

'What you want,' said the friend, 'is an Unrest-cure.'

'An Unrest-cure? I've never heard of such a thing.'

'You've heard of Rest-cures for people who've broken down under stress of too much worry and strenuous living; well, you're suffering from overmuch repose and placidity, and you need the opposite kind of treatment.'

'But where would one go for such a thing?'

'Well, you might stand as an Orange candidate for Kilkenny, or do a course of district visiting in one of the Apache quarters of Paris, or give lectures in Berlin to prove that most of Wagner's music was written by Gambetta; and there's always the interior of Morocco to travel in. But, to be really effective, the Unrest-cure ought to be tried in the home. How you would do it I haven't the faintest idea.'

It was at this point in the conversation that Clovis became galvanized into alert attention. After all, his two days' visit to an elderly relative at Slowborough did not promise much excitement. Before the train had stopped he had decorated his sinister shirt-cuff with the inscription, 'J. P. Huddle, The Warren, Tilfield, near Slowborough'.

Two mornings later Mr Huddle broke in on his sister's privacy as she sat reading *Country Life* in the morning room. It was her day and hour and place for reading *Country Life*, and the intrusion was absolutely irregular; but he bore in his hand a telegram, and in that household telegrams were recognized as happening by the hand of God. This particular telegram partook of the nature of a thunderbolt. 'Bishop examining confirmation class in neighbourhood unable stay rectory on account measles invokes your hospitality sending secretary arrange.'

'I scarcely know the Bishop; I've only spoken to him once,' exclaimed J. P. Huddle, with the exculpating air of one who realizes too late the indiscretion of speaking to strange Bishops. Miss Huddle was the first to rally; she disliked thunderbolts as fervently as her brother did, but the womanly instinct in her told her that thunderbolts must be fed.

'We can curry the cold duck,' she said. It was not the appointed day for curry, but the little orange envelope involved a certain departure from rule and custom. Her brother said nothing, but his eyes thanked her for being brave.

'A young gentleman to see you,' announced the parlour-maid.

'The secretary!' murmured the Huddles in unison; they instantly stiffened into a demeanour which proclaimed that, though they held all strangers to be guilty, they were willing to hear anything they might have to say in their defence. The young gentleman, who came into the room with a certain elegant haughtiness, was not at all Huddle's idea of a bishop's secretary; he had not supposed that the episcopal establishment could have afforded such an expensively upholstered article when there were so many other claims on its resources. The face was fleetingly familiar; if he had bestowed more attention on the fellow-traveller sitting opposite him in the railway carriage two days before he might have recognized Clovis in his present visitor.

'You are the Bishop's secretary?' asked Huddle, becoming consciously deferential.

'His confidential secretary,' answered Clovis. 'You may call me Stanislaus; my other name doesn't matter. The Bishop and Colonel Alberti may be here to lunch. I shall be here in any case.'

It sounded rather like the programme of a Royal visit.

'The Bishop is examining a confirmation class in the neighbourhood, isn't he?' asked Miss Huddle.

'Ostensibly,' was the dark reply, followed by a request for a large-scale map of the locality.

Clovis was still immersed in a seemingly profound study of the map when another telegram arrived. It was addressed to 'Prince Stanislaus, care of Huddle, The Warren, etc.' Clovis glanced at the contents and announced: 'The Bishop and Alberti won't be here till late in the afternoon.' Then he returned to his scrutiny of the map.

The luncheon was not a very festive function. The princely secretary ate and drank with fair appetite, but severely discouraged conversation. At the finish of the meal he broke suddenly into a radiant smile, thanked his hostess for a charming repast, and kissed her hand with deferential rapture. Miss Huddle was unable to decide in her mind whether the action savoured of Louis Quatorzian courtliness or the reprehensible Roman attitude towards the Sabine women. It was not her day for having a headache, but she felt that the circumstances excused her, and retired to her room to have as much headache as was possible before the Bishop's arrival. Clovis, having asked the way to the nearest telegraph office, disappeared presently down the carriage drive. Mr Huddle met him in the hall some two hours later, and asked when the Bishop would arrive.

'He is in the library with Alberti,' was the reply.

'But why wasn't I told? I never knew he had come!' exclaimed Huddle.

'No one knows he is here,' said Clovis; 'the quieter we can keep matters the better. And on no account disturb him in the library. Those are his orders.'

'But what is all this mystery about? And who is Alberti? And isn't the Bishop going to have tea?'

'The Bishop is out for blood, not tea.'

'Blood!' gasped Huddle, who did not find that the thunderbolt improved on acquaintance.

'Tonight is going to be a great night in the history of Christendom,' said Clovis. 'We are going to massacre every Jew in the neighbourhood.'

'To massacre the Jews!' said Huddle indignantly. 'Do you mean to tell me there's a general rising against them?'

'No, it's the Bishop's own idea. He's in there arranging all the details now.'

'But—the Bishop is such a tolerant, humane man.'

'That is precisely what will heighten the effect of his action. The sensation will be enormous.'

That at least Huddle could believe.

'He will be hanged!' he exclaimed with conviction.

'A motor is waiting to carry him to the coast, where a steam yacht is in readiness.'

'But there aren't thirty Jews in the whole neighbourhood,' protested Huddle, whose brain, under the repeated shocks of the day, was operating with the uncertainty of a telegraph wire during earthquake disturbances.

'We have twenty-six on our list,' said Clovis, referring to a bundle of notes. 'We shall be able to deal with them all the more thoroughly.'

'Do you mean to tell me that you are meditating violence against a man like Sir Leon Birberry,' stammered Huddle; 'he's one of the most respected men in the country.'

'He's down on our list,' said Clovis carelessly; 'after all, we've got men we can trust to do our job, so we shan't have to rely on local assistance. And we've got some Boy-scouts helping us as auxiliaries.'

'Boy-scouts!'

'Yes; when they understood there was real killing to be done they were even keener than the men.'

'This thing will be a blot on the Twentieth Century!'

'And your house will be the blotting-pad. Have you realized that half the papers of Europe and the United States will publish pictures of it? By the way, I've sent some photographs of you and your sister, that I found in the library, to the *Matin* and *Die Woche*; I hope you don't mind. Also a sketch of the staircase; most of the killing will probably be done on the staircase.'

The emotions that were surging in J. P. Huddle's brain were almost too intense to be disclosed in speech, but he managed to gasp out: 'There aren't any Jews in this house.'

'Not at present,' said Clovis.

'I shall go to the police,' shouted Huddle with sudden energy.

'In the shrubbery,' said Clovis, 'are posted ten men, who have orders to fire on any one who leaves the house without my signal of permission. Another armed picquet is in ambush near the front gate. The Boy-scouts watch the back premises.'

At this moment the cheerful hoot of a motor-horn was heard from the drive. Huddle rushed to the hall door with the feeling of a man half-awakened from a nightmare, and beheld Sir Leon Birberry, who had driven himself over in his car. 'I got your telegram,' he said; 'what's up?'

Telegram? It seemed to be a day of telegrams.

'Come here at once. Urgent. James Huddle,' was the purport of the message displayed before Huddle's bewildered eyes.

'I see it all!' he exclaimed suddenly in a voice shaken with agitation, and with a look of agony in the direction of the shrubbery he hauled the astonished Birberry into the house. Tea had just been laid in the hall, but the now thoroughly panic-stricken Huddle dragged his protesting guest upstairs, and in a few minutes' time the entire household had been summoned to that region of momentary safety. Clovis alone graced the tea-table with his presence; the fanatics in the library were evidently too immersed in their monstrous machinations to dally with the solace of teacup and hot toast.

Once the youth rose, in answer to the summons of the front-door bell, and admitted Mr Paul Isaacs, shoemaker and parish councillor, who had also received a pressing invitation to The Warren. With an atrocious assumption of courtesy, which a Borgia could hardly have outdone, the secretary escorted this new captive of his net to the head of the stairway, where his involuntary host awaited him.

And then ensued a long ghastly vigil of watching and waiting. Once or twice Clovis left the house to stroll across to the shrubbery, returning always to the library, for the purpose evidently of making a brief report. Once he took in the letters from the evening postman, and brought them to the top of the stairs with punctilious politeness. After his next absence he came half-way up the stairs to make an announcement.

'The Boy-scouts mistook my signal, and have killed the postman. I've had very little practice in this sort of thing, you see. Another time I shall do better.'

The housemaid, who was engaged to be married to the evening postman, gave way to clamorous grief.

'Remember that your mistress has a headache,' said J. P. Huddle. (Miss Huddle's headache was worse.)

Clovis hastened downstairs, and after a short visit to the library returned with another message:

'The Bishop is sorry to hear that Miss Huddle has a headache. He is issuing orders that as far as possible no firearms shall be used near the house; any killing that is necessary on the premises will be done with cold steel. The Bishop does not see why a man should not be a gentleman as well as a Christian.'

That was the last they saw of Clovis; it was nearly seven o'clock, and his elderly relative liked him to dress for dinner. But, though he had left them for ever, the lurking suggestion of his presence haunted the lower regions of the house during the long hours of the wakeful night, and every creak of the stairway, every rustle of wind through the shrubbery, was fraught with horrible meaning. At about seven next morning the gardener's boy and the early postman finally convinced the watches that the Twentieth Century was still unblotted.

'I don't suppose,' mused Clovis, as an early train bore him townwards, 'that they will be in the least grateful for the Unrest-cure.'

SREDNI VASHTAR

CONRADIN was ten years old, and the doctor had pronounced his professional opinion that the boy would not live another five years. The doctor was silky and effete, and counted for little, but his opinion was endorsed by Mrs De Ropp, who counted for nearly everything. Mrs De Ropp was Conradin's cousin and guardian, and in his eyes she represented those three-fifths of the world that are necessary and disagreeable and real; the other two-fifths, in perpetual antagonism to the foregoing, were summed up in himself and his imagination. One of these days Conradin supposed he would succumb to the mastering pressure of wearisome necessary things—such as illnesses and coddling restrictions and drawn-out dullness. Without his imagination, which was rampant under the spur of loneliness, he would have succumbed long ago.

Mrs De Ropp would never, in her honestest moments, have confessed to herself that she disliked Conradin, though she might have been dimly aware that thwarting him 'for his good' was a duty which she did not find particularly irksome. Conradin hated her with a desperate sincerity which he was perfectly able to mask. Such few pleasures as he could contrive for himself gained an added relish from the likelihood that they would be displeasing to his guardian, and from the realm of his imagination she was locked out—an unclean thing, which should find no entrance.

In the dull, cheerless garden, overlooked by so many windows that were ready to open with a message not to do this or that, or a reminder that medicines were due, he found little attraction. The few fruit-trees that it contained were set jealously apart from his plucking, as though they were rare specimens of their kind blooming in an arid waste; it would probably have been difficult to find a market-gardener who would have offered ten shillings for their entire yearly produce. In a forgotten corner, however, almost hidden behind a dismal shrubbery, was a disused tool-shed of respectable proportions, and within its walls Conradin found a haven, something that took on the varying aspects of a playroom and a cathedral. He had peopled it with a legion of familiar phantoms, evoked partly from fragments of history and partly from his own brain, but it also boasted two inmates of flesh and blood. In one corner lived a ragged-plumaged Houdan hen, on which the boy lavished an affection that had scarcely another outlet. Further back in the gloom stood a large hutch, divided into two compartments, one of which was fronted with close iron bars. This was the abode of a large polecat-ferret, which a friendly butcher-boy had once smuggled, cage and all, into its present quarters, in exchange for a long-secreted hoard of small silver. Conradin was dreadfully afraid of the lithe, sharp-fanged beast, but it was his most treasured possession. Its very presence in the tool-shed was a secret and fearful joy, to be kept scrupulously from the knowledge of the Woman, as he privately dubbed his cousin. And one day, out of Heaven knows what material, he spun the beast a wonderful name, and from that moment it grew into a god and a religion. The Woman indulged in religion once a week at a church near by, and took Conradin with her, but to him the church service was an alien rite in the House of Rimmon. Every Thursday, in the dim and musty silence of the tool-shed, he worshipped with mystic and elaborate ceremonial before the wooden hutch where dwelt Sredni Vashtar, the great ferret. Red flowers in their season and scarlet berries in the winter-time were offered at his shrine, for he was a god who laid some special stress on the fierce impatient side of things, as opposed to the Woman's religion, which, as far as Conradin could observe, went to great lengths in the contrary direction. And on great festivals powdered nutmeg was strewn in front of his hutch, an important feature of the offering being that the nutmeg had to be stolen. These festivals were of irregular occurrence, and were chiefly appointed to celebrate some passing event. On one occasion, when Mrs De Ropp suffered from acute toothache for three days, Conradin kept up the festival during the entire three days, and almost succeeded in persuading himself that Sredni Vashtar was personally responsible for the toothache. If the malady had lasted for another day the supply of nutmeg would have given out.

The Houdan hen was never drawn into the cult of Sredni Vashtar. Conradin had long ago settled that she was an Anabaptist. He did not pretend to have the remotest knowledge as to what an Anabaptist was, but he privately hoped that it was dashing and not very respectable. Mrs De Ropp was the ground plan on which he based and detested all respectability.

After a while Conradin's absorption in the tool-shed began to attract the notice of his guardian. 'It is not good for him to be pottering down there in all weathers,' she promptly decided, and at breakfast one morning she announced that the Houdan hen had been sold and taken away overnight. With her short-sighted eyes she peered at Conradin, waiting for an outbreak of rage and sorrow, which she was ready to rebuke with a flow of excellent precepts and reasoning. But Conradin said nothing: there was nothing to be said. Something perhaps in his white set face gave her a momentary qualm, for at tea that afternoon there was toast on the table, a delicacy which she usually banned on the ground that it was bad for him; also because the making of it 'gave trouble', a deadly offence in the middle-class feminine eye.

'I thought you liked toast,' she exclaimed, with an injured air, observing that he did not touch it.

'Sometimes,' said Conradin.

In the shed that evening there was an innovation in the worship of the hutch-god. Conradin had been wont to chant his praises, tonight he asked a boon.

'Do one thing for me, Sredni Vashtar.'

The thing was not specified. As Sredni Vashtar was a god he must be supposed to know. And choking back a sob as he looked at that other empty corner, Conradin went back to the world he so hated.

And every night, in the welcome darkness of his bedroom,

and every evening in the dusk of the tool-shed, Conradin's bitter litany went up: 'Do one thing for me, Sredni Vashtar.'

Mrs De Ropp noticed that the visits to the shed did not cease, and one day she made a further journey of inspection. 'What are you keeping in that locked hutch?' she asked. 'I believe it's guinea-pigs. I'll have them all cleared away.'

Conradin shut his lips tight, but the Woman ransacked his bedroom till she found the carefully hidden key, and forthwith marched down to the shed to complete her discovery. It was a cold afternoon, and Conradin had been bidden to keep to the house. From the furthest window of the dining-room the door of the shed could just be seen beyond the corner of the shrubbery, and there Conradin stationed himself. He saw the Woman enter, and then he imagined her opening the door of the sacred hutch and peering down with her short-sighted eyes into the thick straw bed where his god lay hidden. Perhaps she would prod at the straw in her clumsy impatience. And Conradin fervently breathed his prayer for the last time. But he knew as he prayed that he did not believe. He knew that the Woman would come out presently with that pursed smile he loathed so well on her face, and that in an hour or two the gardener would carry away his wonderful god, a god no longer, but a simple brown ferret in a hutch. And he knew that the Woman would triumph always as she triumphed now, and that he would grow ever more sickly under her pestering and domineering and superior wisdom, till one day nothing would matter much more with him, and the doctor would be proved right. And in the sting and misery of his defeat, he began to chant loudly and defiantly the hymn of his threatened idol:

Sredni Vashtar went forth,
His thoughts were red thoughts and his teeth were white.
His enemies called for peace, but he brought them death.
Sredni Vashtar the Beautiful.

And then of a sudden he stopped his chanting and drew closer to the window-pane. The door of the shed still stood ajar as it had been left, and the minutes were slipping by. They were long minutes, but they slipped by nevertheless. He watched the starlings running and flying in little parties across the lawn; he counted them over and over again, with one eye always on that swinging door. A sour-faced maid came in to lay the table for tea, and still Conradin stood and waited and watched. Hope had crept by inches into his heart, and now a look of triumph began to blaze in his eyes that had only known the wistful patience of defeat. Under his breath, with a furtive exultation, he began once again the pæan of victory and devastation. And presently his eyes were rewarded: out through that doorway came a long, low, yellow-and-brown beast, with eyes a-blink at the waning daylight, and dark wet stains around the fur of jaws and throat. Conradin dropped on his knees. The great polecat-ferret made its way down to a small brook at the foot of the garden, drank for a moment, then crossed a little plank bridge and was lost to sight in the bushes. Such was the passing of Sredni Vashtar.

'Tea is ready,' said the sour-faced maid; 'where is the mistress?'

'She went down to the shed some time ago,' said Conradin.

And while the maid went to summon her mistress to tea, Conradin fished a toasting-fork out of the sideboard drawer and proceeded to toast himself a piece of bread. And during the toasting of it and the buttering of it with much butter and the slow enjoyment of eating it, Conradin listened to the noises and silences which fell in quick spasms beyond the dining-room door. The loud foolish screaming of the maid, the answering chorus of wondering ejaculations from the kitchen region, the scuttering footsteps and hurried embassies for outside help, and then, after a lull, the scared sobbings and the shuffling tread of those who bore a heavy burden into the house.

'Whoever will break it to the poor child? I couldn't for the life of me!' exclaimed a shrill voice. And while they debated the matter among themselves, Conradin made himself another piece of toast.

ADRIAN
A CHAPTER IN ACCLIMATIZATION

His baptismal register spoke of him pessimistically as John Henry, but he had left that behind with the other maladies of infancy, and his friends knew him under the front-name of Adrian. His mother lived in Bethnal Green, which was not altogether his fault; one can discourage too much history in one's family, but one cannot always prevent geography. And, after all, the Bethnal Green habit has this virtue—that it is seldom transmitted to the next generation. Adrian lived in a roomlet which came under the auspicious constellation of W.

How he lived was to a great extent a mystery even to himself; his struggle for existence probably coincided in many material details with the rather dramatic accounts he gave of it to sympathetic acquaintances. All that is definitely known is that he now and then emerged from the struggle to dine at the Ritz or Carlton, correctly garbed and with a correctly critical appetite. On these occasions he was usually the guest of Lucas Croyden, an amiable worldling, who had three thousand a year and a taste for introducing impossible people to irreproachable cookery. Like most men who combine three thousand a year with an uncertain digestion, Lucas was a Socialist, and he argued that you cannot hope to elevate the masses until you have brought plovers' eggs into their lives and taught them to appreciate the difference between coupe Jacques and Macédoine de fruits. His friends pointed out that it was a doubtful kindness to initiate a boy from behind a drapery counter into the blessedness of the higher catering, to which Lucas invariably replied that all kindnesses were doubtful. Which was perhaps true.

It was after one of his Adrian evenings that Lucas met his aunt, Mrs Mebberley, at a fashionable teashop, where the lamp of family life is still kept burning and you meet relatives who might otherwise have slipped your memory.

'Who was that good-looking boy who was dining with you last night?' she asked. 'He looked much too nice to be thrown away upon you.'

Susan Mebberley was a charming woman, but she was also an aunt.

'Who are his people?' she continued, when the protégé's name (revised version) had been given her.

'His mother lives at Beth—'

Lucas checked himself on the threshold of what was perhaps a social indiscretion.

'Beth? Where is it? It sounds like Asia Minor. Is she mixed up with Consular people?'

'Oh, no. Her work lies among the poor.'

This was a side-slip into truth. The mother of Adrian was employed in a laundry.

'I see,' said Mrs Mebberley, 'mission work of some sort. And meanwhile the boy has no one to look after him. It's obviously my duty to see that he doesn't come to harm. Bring him to call on me.'

'My dear Aunt Susan,' expostulated Lucas, 'I really know very little about him. He may not be at all nice, you know, on further acquaintance.'

'He has delightful hair and a weak mouth. I shall take him with me to Homburg or Cairo.'

'It's the maddest thing I ever heard of,' said Lucas angrily.

'Well, there is a strong strain of madness in our family. If you haven't noticed it yourself all your friends must have.'

'One is so dreadfully under everybody's eyes at Homburg. At least you might give him a preliminary trial at Etretat.'

'And be surrounded by Americans trying to talk French? No, thank you. I love Americans, but not when they try to talk French. What a blessing it is that they never try to talk English. Tomorrow at five you can bring your young friend to call on me.'

And Lucas, realizing that Susan Mebberley was a woman as well as an aunt, saw that she would have to be allowed to have her own way.

Adrian was duly carried abroad under the Mebberley wing; but as a reluctant concession to sanity Homburg and other inconveniently fashionable resorts were given a wide berth, and the Mebberley establishment planted itself down in the best hotel at Dohledorf, an Alpine townlet somewhere at the back of the Engadine. It was the usual kind of resort, with the usual type of visitors, that one finds over the greater part of Switzerland during the summer season, but to Adrian it was all unusual. The mountain air, the certainty of regular and abundant meals, and in particular the social atmosphere, affected him much as the indiscriminating fervour of a forcing-house might affect a weed that had strayed within its limits. He had been brought up in a world where breakages were regarded as crimes and expiated as such; it was something new and altogether exhilarating to find that you were considered rather amusing if you smashed things in the right manner and at the recognized hours. Susan Mebberley had expressed the intention of showing Adrian a bit of the world; the particular bit of the world represented by Dohledorf began to be shown a good deal of Adrian.

Lucas got occasional glimpses of the Alpine sojourn, not from his aunt or Adrian, but from the industrious pen of Clovis, who was also moving as a satellite in the Mebberley constellation.

'The entertainment which Susan got up last night ended in disaster. I thought it would. The Grobmayer child, a particularly loathsome five-year-old, had appeared as "Bubbles" during the early part of the evening, and been put to bed during the interval. Adrian watched his opportunity and kidnapped it when the nurse was downstairs, and introduced it during the second half of the entertainment, thinly disguised as a performing pig. It certainly *looked* very like a pig, and grunted and slobbered just like the real article; no one knew exactly what it was, but every one said it was awfully clever, especially the Grobmayers. At the third curtain Adrian pinched it too hard, and it yelled "Marmar"! I am supposed to be good at descriptions, but don't ask me to describe the sayings and doings of the Grobmayers at that moment; it was like one of the angrier Psalms set to Strauss's music. We have moved to an hotel higher up the valley.'

Clovis's next letter arrived five days later, and was written from the Hotel Steinbock.

'We left the Hotel Victoria this morning. It was fairly comfortable and quiet—at least there was an air of repose about it when we arrived. Before we had been in residence twenty-four hours most of the repose had vanished "like a dutiful bream", as Adrian expressed it. However, nothing unduly outrageous happened till last night, when Adrian had a fit of insomnia and amused himself by unscrewing and transposing all the bedroom numbers on his floor. He transferred the bathroom label to the adjoining bedroom door, which happened to be that of Frau Hofrath Schilling, and this morning from seven o'clock onwards the old lady had a stream of involuntary visitors; she was too horrified and scandalized it seems to get up and lock her door. The would-be bathers flew back in confusion to their rooms, and, of course, the change of numbers led them astray again, and the corridor gradually filled with panic-stricken, scantily robed humans, dashing wildly about like rabbits in a ferret-infested warren. It took nearly an hour before the guests were all sorted into their respective rooms, and the Frau Hofrath's condition was still causing some anxiety when we left. Susan is beginning to look a little worried. She can't very well turn the boy adrift, as he hasn't got any money, and she can't send him to his people as she doesn't know where they are. Adrian says his mother moves about a good deal and he's lost her address. Probably, if the truth were known, he's had a row at home. So many boys nowadays seem to think that quarrelling with one's family is a recognized occupation.'

Lucas's next communication from the travellers took the form of a telegram from Mrs Mebberley herself. It was sent 'reply prepaid', and consisted of a single sentence: 'In Heaven's name, where is Beth?'

THE EASTER EGG

IT was distinctly hard lines for Lady Barbara, who came of good fighting stock, and was one of the bravest women of her generation, that her son should be so undisguisedly a coward. Whatever good qualities Lester Slaggby may have possessed, and he was in some respects charming, courage could certainly never be imputed to him. As a child he had suffered from childish timidity, as a boy from unboyish funk, and as a youth he had exchanged unreasoning fears for others which were more formidable from the fact of having a carefully-thought-out basis. He was frankly afraid of animals, nervous with firearms, and never crossed the Channel without mentally comparing the numerical proportion of life belts to passengers. On horseback he seemed to require as many hands as a Hindu god, at least four for clutching the reins, and two more for patting the horse soothingly on the neck. Lady Barbara no longer pretended not to see her son's prevailing weakness; with her usual courage she faced the knowledge of it squarely, and, mother-like, loved him none the less.

Continental travel, anywhere away from the great tourist tracks, was a favoured hobby with Lady Barbara, and Lester joined her as often as possible. Eastertide usually found her at Knobaltheim, an upland township in one of those small princedoms that make inconspicuous freckles on the map of Central Europe.

A long-standing acquaintanceship with the reigning family made her a personage of due importance in the eyes of her old friend the Burgomaster, and she was anxiously consulted by that worthy on the momentous occasion when the Prince made known his intention of coming in person to open a sanatorium outside the town. All the usual items in a programme of welcome, some of them fatuous and commonplace, others quaint and charming, had been arranged for, but the Burgomaster hoped that the resourceful English lady might have something new and tasteful to suggest in the way of loyal greeting. The Prince was known to the outside world, if at all, as an old-fashioned reactionary, combating modern progress, as it were, with a wooden sword; to his own people he was known as a kindly old gentleman with a certain endearing stateliness which had nothing of standoffishness about it. Knobaltheim was anxious to do its best. Lady Barbara discussed the matter with Lester and one or two acquaintances in her little hotel, but ideas were difficult to come by.

'Might I suggest something to the gnädige Frau?' asked a

sallow high-cheek-boned lady to whom the Englishwoman had spoken once or twice, and whom she had set down in her mind as probably a Southern Slav.

'Might I suggest something for the Reception Fest?' she went on, with a certain shy eagerness. 'Our little child here, our baby, we will dress him in little white coat, with small wings, as an Easter angel, and he will carry a large white Easter egg, and inside shall be a basket of plover eggs, of which the Prince is so fond, and he shall give it to his Highness as Easter offering. It is so pretty an idea; we have seen it done once in Styria.'

Lady Barbara looked dubiously at the proposed Easter angel, a fair, wooden-faced child of about four years old. She had noticed it the day before in the hotel, and wondered rather how such a tow-headed child could belong to such a dark-visaged couple as the woman and her husband; probably, she thought, an adopted baby, especially as the couple were not young.

'Of course Gnädige Frau will escort the little child up to the Prince,' pursued the woman; 'but he will be quite good, and do as he is told.'

'We haf some pluffers' eggs shall come fresh from Wien,' said the husband.

The small child and Lady Barbara seemed equally unenthusiastic about the pretty idea; Lester was openly discouraging, but when the Burgomaster heard of it he was enchanted. The combination of sentiment and plovers' eggs appealed strongly to his Teutonic mind.

On the eventful day the Easter angel, really quite prettily and quaintly dressed, was a centre of kindly interest to the gala crowd marshalled to receive his Highness. The mother was unobtrusive and less fussy than most parents would have been under the circumstances, merely stipulating that she should place the Easter egg herself in the arms that had been carefully schooled how to hold the precious burden. Then Lady Barbara moved forward, the child marching stolidly and with grim determination at her side. It had been promised cakes and sweeties galore if it gave the egg well and truly to the kind old gentleman who was waiting to receive it. Lester had tried to convey to it privately that horrible smackings would attend any failure in its share of the proceedings, but it is doubtful if his German caused more than an immediate distress. Lady Barbara had thoughtfully provided herself with an emergency supply of chocolate sweetmeats; children may sometimes be time-servers, but they do not encourage long accounts. As they approached nearer to the princely daïs Lady Barbara stood discreetly aside, and the stolid-faced infant walked forward alone, with staggering but steadfast gait, encouraged by a murmur of elderly approval. Lester, standing in the front row of the onlookers, turned to scan the crowd for the beaming faces of the happy parents. In a side-road which led to the railway station he saw a cab; entering the cab with every appearance of furtive haste were the dark-visaged couple who had been so plausibly eager for the 'pretty idea'. The sharpened instinct of cowardice lit up the situation to him in one swift flash. The blood roared and surged to his head as though thousands of floodgates had been opened in his veins and arteries, and his brain was the common sluice in which all the torrents met. He saw nothing but a blur around him. Then the blood ebbed away in quick waves, till his very heart seemed drained and empty, and he stood nervelessly, help-lessly, dumbly watching the child, bearing its accursed burden with slow, relentless steps nearer and nearer to the group that waited sheep-like to receive him. A fascinated curiosity compelled Lester to turn his head towards the fugitives; the cab had started at hot pace in the direction of the station.

The next moment Lester was running, running faster than any of those present had ever seen a man run, and—he was not running away. For that stray fraction of his life some unwonted impulse beset him, some hint of the stock he came from, and he ran unflinchingly towards danger. He stooped and clutched at the Easter egg as one tries to scoop up the ball in Rugby football. What he meant to do with it he had not considered, the thing was to get it. But the child had been promised cakes and sweetmeats if it safely gave the egg into the hands of the kindly old gentleman; it uttered no scream, but it held to its charge with limpet grip. Lester sank to his knees, tugging savagely at the tightly clasped burden, and angry cries rose from the scandalized onlookers. A questioning, threatening ring formed round him, then shrank back in recoil as he shrieked out one hideous word. Lady Barbara heard the word and saw the crowd race away like scattered sheep, saw the Prince forcibly hustled away by his attendants; also she saw her son lying prone in an agony of overmastering terror, his spasm of daring shattered by the child's unexpected resistance, still clutching frantically, as though for safety, at that white-satin gew-gaw, unable to crawl even from its deadly neighbourhood, able only to scream and scream and scream. In her brain she was dimly conscious of balancing, or striving to balance, the abject shame which had him now in thrall against the one compelling act of courage which had flung him grandly and madly on to the point of danger. It was only for the fraction of a minute that she stood watching the two entangled figures, the infant with its woodenly obstinate face and body tense with dogged resistance, and the boy limp and already nearly dead with a terror that almost stifled his screams; and over them the long gala streamers flapping gaily in the sunshine. She never forgot the scene; but then, it was the last she ever saw.

Lady Barbara carries her scarred face with its sightless eyes as bravely as ever in the world, but at Eastertide her friends are careful to keep from her ears any mention of the children's Easter symbol.

FILBOID STUDGE, THE STORY OF A MOUSE THAT HELPED

'I WANT to marry your daughter,' said Mark Spayley with faltering eagerness. 'I am only an artist with an income of two hundred a year, and she is the daughter of an enormously wealthy man, so I suppose you will think my offer a piece of presumption.'

Duncan Dullamy, the great company inflator, showed no outward sign of displeasure. As a matter of fact, he was secretly relieved at the prospect of finding even a two-hundred-a-year husband for his daughter Leonore. A crisis was rapidly rushing upon him, from which he knew he would emerge with neither money nor credit; all his recent ventures had fallen flat, and flattest of all had gone the wonderful new breakfast food, Pipenta, on the advertisement of which he had sunk such huge sums. It could scarcely be called a drug in the market; people bought drugs, but no one bought Pipenta.

'Would you marry Leonore if she were a poor man's daughter?' asked the man of phantom wealth.

'Yes,' said Mark, wisely avoiding the error of over-protestation. And to his astonishment Leonore's father not only gave his consent, but suggested a fairly early date for the wedding.

'I wish I could show my gratitude in some way,' said Mark with genuine emotion. 'I'm afraid it's rather like the mouse proposing to help the lion.'

'Get people to buy that beastly muck,' said Dullamy, nodding savagely at a poster of the despised Pipenta, 'and you'll have done more than any of my agents have been able to accomplish.'

'It wants a better name,' said Mark reflectively, 'and something distinctive in the poster line. Anyway, I'll have a shot at it.'

Three weeks later the world was advised of the coming of a new breakfast food, heralded under the resounding name of 'Filboid Studge'. Spayley put forth no pictures of massive babies springing up with fungus-like rapidity under its forcing influence, or of representatives of the leading nations of the world scrambling with fatuous eagerness for its possession. One huge sombre poster depicted the Damned in Hell suffering a new torment from their inability to get at the Filboid Studge which elegant young fiends held in transparent bowls just beyond their reach. The scene was rendered even more gruesome by a subtle suggestion of the features of leading men and women of the day in the portrayal of the Lost Souls; prominent individuals of both political parties, Society hostesses, well-known dramatic authors and novelists, and distinguished aeroplanists were dimly recognizable in that doomed throng; noted lights of the musical-comedy stage flickered wanly in the shades of the Inferno, smiling still from force of habit, but with the fearsome smiling rage of baffled effort. The poster bore no fulsome allusions to the merits of the new breakfast food, but a single grim statement ran in bold letters along its base: 'They cannot buy it now.'

Spayley had grasped the fact that people will do things from a sense of duty which they would never attempt as a pleasure. There are thousands of respectable middle-class men who, if you found them unexpectedly in a Turkish bath, would explain in all sincerity that a doctor had ordered them to take Turkish baths; if you told them in return that you went there because you liked it, they would stare in pained wonder at the frivolity of your motive. In the same way, whenever a massacre of Armenians is reported from Asia Minor, every one assumes that it has been carried out 'under orders' from somewhere or another; no one seems to think that there are people who might *like* to kill their neighbours now and then.

And so it was with the new breakfast food. No one would have eaten Filboid Studge as a pleasure, but the grim austerity of its advertisement drove housewives in shoals to the grocers' shops to clamour for an immediate supply. In small kitchens solemn pig-tailed daughters helped depressed mothers to perform the primitive ritual of its preparation. On the breakfast-tables of cheerless parlours it was partaken of in silence. Once the womenfolk discovered that it was thoroughly unpalatable, their zeal in forcing it on their households knew no bounds. 'You haven't eaten your Filboid Studge!' would be screamed at the appetiteless clerk as he hurried weariedly from the breakfast-table, and his evening meal would be prefaced by a warmed-up mess which would be explained as 'your Filboid Studge that you didn't eat this morning'. Those strange fanatics who ostentatiously mortify themselves, inwardly and outwardly, with health biscuits and health garments, battened aggressively on the new food. Earnest spectacled young men devoured it on the steps of the National Liberal Club. A bishop who did not believe in a future state preached against the poster, and a peer's daughter died from eating too much of the compound. A further advertisement was obtained when an infantry regiment mutinied and shot its officers rather than eat the nauseous mess; fortunately, Lord Birrell of

Blatherstone, who was War Minister at the moment, saved the situation by his happy epigram, that 'Discipline to be effective must be optional.'

Filboid Studge had become a household word, but Dullamy wisely realized that it was not necessarily the last word in breakfast dietary; its supremacy would be challenged as soon as some yet more unpalatable food should be put on the market. There might even be a reaction in favour of something tasty and appetizing, and the Puritan austerity of the moment might be banished from domestic cookery. At an opportune moment, therefore, he sold out his interests in the article which had brought him in colossal wealth at a critical juncture, and placed his financial reputation beyond the reach of cavil. As for Leonore, who was now an heiress on a far greater scale than ever before, he naturally found her something a vast deal higher in the husband market than a two-hundred-a-year poster designer. Mark Spayley, the brainmouse who had helped the financial lion with such untoward effect, was left to curse the day he produced the wonder-working poster.

'After all,' said Clovis, meeting him shortly afterwards at his club, 'you have this doubtful consolation, that 'tis not in mortals to countermand success.'

THE MUSIC ON THE HILL

SYLVIA SELTOUN ate her breakfast in the morning-room at Yessney with a pleasant sense of ultimate victory, such as a fervent Ironside might have permitted himself on the morrow of Worcester fight. She was scarcely pugnacious by temperament, but belonged to that more successful class of fighters who are pugnacious by circumstance. Fate had willed that her life should be occupied with a series of small struggles, usually with the odds slightly against her, and usually she had just managed to come through winning. And now she felt that she had brought her hardest and certainly her most important struggle to a successful issue. To have married Mortimer Seltoun, 'Dead Mortimer' as his more intimate enemies called him, in the teeth of the cold hostility of his family, and in spite of his unaffected indifference to women, was indeed an achievement that had needed some determination and adroitness to carry through; yesterday she had brought her victory to its concluding stage by wrenching her husband away from Town and its group of satellite watering-places and 'settling him down', in the vocabulary of her kind, in this remote wood-girt manor farm which was his country house.

'You will never get Mortimer to go,' his mother had said carpingly, 'but if he once goes he'll stay; Yessney throws almost as much a spell over him as Town does. One can understand what holds him to Town, but Yessney—' and the dowager had shrugged her shoulders.

There was a sombre almost savage wildness about Yessney that was certainly not likely to appeal to town-bred tastes, and Sylvia, notwithstanding her name, was accustomed to nothing much more sylvan than 'leafy Kensington'. She looked on the country as something excellent and wholesome in its way, which was apt to become troublesome if you encouraged it overmuch. Distrust of town-life had been a new thing with her, born of her marriage with Mortimer, and she had watched with satisfaction the gradual fading of what she called 'the Jermyn-Street-look' in his eyes as the woods and heather of Yessney had closed in on them yesternight. Her will-power and strategy had prevailed; Mortimer would stay.

Outside the morning-room windows was a triangular slope of turf, which the indulgent might call a lawn, and beyond its low hedge of neglected fuchsia bushes a steeper slope of heather and bracken dropped down into cavernous combes overgrown with oak and yew. In its wild open savagery there seemed a stealthy linking of the joy of life with the terror of unseen things. Sylvia smiled complacently as she gazed with a School-of-Art appreciation at the landscape, and then of a sudden she almost shuddered.

'It is very wild,' she said to Mortimer, who had joined her; 'one could almost think that in such a place the worship of Pan had never quite died out.'

'The worship of Pan never has died out,' said Mortimer. 'Other newer gods have drawn aside his votaries from time to time, but he is the Nature-God to whom all must come back at last. He has been called the Father of all the Gods, but most of his children have been stillborn.'

Sylvia was religious in an honest, vaguely devotional kind of way, and did not like to hear her beliefs spoken of as mere aftergrowths, but it was at least something new and hopeful to hear Dead Mortimer speak with such energy and conviction on any subject.

'You don't really believe in Pan?' she asked incredulously.

'I've been a fool in most things,' said Mortimer quietly, 'but I'm not such a fool as not to believe in Pan when I'm down here. And if you're wise you won't disbelieve in him too boastfully while you're in his country.'

It was not till a week later, when Sylvia had exhausted the attractions of the woodland walks round Yessney, that she ventured on a tour of inspection of the farm buildings. A farmyard suggested in her mind a scene of cheerful bustle, with churns and flails and smiling dairymaids, and teams of horses drinking knee-deep in duck-crowded ponds. As she wandered among the gaunt grey buildings of Yessney manor farm her first impression was one of crushing stillness and desolation, as though she had happened on some lone deserted homestead long given over to owls and cobwebs; then came a sense of furtive watchful hostility, the same shadow of unseen things that seemed to lurk in the wooded combes and coppices. From behind heavy doors and shuttered windows came the restless stamp of hoof or rasp of chain halter, and at times a muffled bellow from some stalled beast. From a distant corner a shaggy dog watched her with intent unfriendly eyes; as she drew near it slipped quietly into its kennel, and slipped out again as noiselessly when she had passed by. A few hens, questing for food under a rick, stole away under a gate at her approach. Sylvia felt that if she had come across any human beings in this wilderness of barn and byre they would have fled wraith-like from her gaze. At last, turning a corner quickly, she came upon a living thing that did not fly from her. Astretch in a pool of mud was an enormous sow, gigantic beyond the town-woman's wildest computation of swine-flesh, and speedily alert to resent and if necessary repel the unwonted intrusion. It was Sylvia's turn to make an unobtrusive retreat. As she threaded her way past rickyards and cowsheds and long blank walls, she started suddenly at a strange sound—the echo of a boy's laughter, golden and equivocal. Jan, the only boy employed on the farm, a tow-headed, wizen-faced yokel, was visibly at work on a potato clearing half-way up the nearest hill-side, and Mortimer, when questioned, knew of no other probable or possible begetter of the hidden mockery that had ambushed Sylvia's retreat. The memory of that untraceable echo was added to her other impressions of a furtive sinister 'something' that hung around Yessney.

Of Mortimer she saw very little; farm and woods and trout-streams seemed to swallow him up from dawn till dusk. Once, following the direction she had seen him take in the morning, she came to an open space in a nut copse, further shut in by huge yew trees, in the centre of which stood a stone pedestal surmounted by a small bronze figure of a youthful Pan. It was a beautiful piece of workmanship, but her attention was chiefly held by the fact that a newly cut bunch of grapes had been placed as an offering at its feet. Grapes were none too plentiful at the manor house, and Sylvia snatched the bunch angrily from the pedestal. Contemptuous annoyance dominated her thoughts as she strolled slowly homeward, and then gave way to a sharp feeling of something that was very near fright; across a thick tangle of undergrowth a boy's face was scowling at her, brown and beautiful, with unutterably evil eyes. It was a lonely pathway, all pathways round Yessney were lonely for the matter of that, and she sped forward without waiting to give a closer scrutiny to this sudden apparition. It was not till she had reached the house that she discovered that she had dropped the bunch of grapes in her flight.

'I saw a youth in the wood today,' she told Mortimer that evening, 'brown-faced and rather handsome, but a scoundrel to look at. A gipsy lad, I suppose.'

'A reasonable theory,' said Mortimer, 'only there aren't any gipsies in these parts at present.'

'Then who was he?' asked Sylvia, and as Mortimer

appeared to have no theory of his own, she passed on to recount her finding of the votive offering.

'I suppose it was your doing,' she observed; 'it's a harmless piece of lunacy, but people would think you dreadfully silly if they knew of it.'

'Did you meddle with it in any way?' asked Mortimer.

'I—I threw the grapes away. It seemed so silly,' said Sylvia, watching Mortimer's impassive face for a sign of annoyance.

'I don't think you were wise to do that,' he said reflectively. 'I've heard it said that the Wood Gods are rather horrible to those who molest them.'

'Horrible perhaps to those that believe in them, but you see I don't,' retorted Sylvia.

'All the same,' said Mortimer in his even, dispassionate tone, 'I should avoid the woods and orchards if I were you, and give a wide berth to the horned beasts on the farm.'

It was all nonsense, of course, but in that lonely wood-girt spot nonsense seemed able to rear a bastard brood of uneasiness.

'Mortimer,' said Sylvia suddenly, 'I think we will go back to Town some time soon.'

Her victory had not been so complete as she had supposed; it had carried her on to ground that she was already anxious to quit.

'I don't think you will ever go back to Town,' said Mortimer. He seemed to be paraphrasing his mother's prediction as to himself.

Sylvia noted with dissatisfaction and some self-contempt that the course of her next afternoon's ramble took her instinctively clear of the network of woods. As to the horned cattle, Mortimer's warning was scarcely needed, for she had always regarded them as of doubtful neutrality at the best: her imagination unsexed the most matronly dairy cows and turned them into bulls liable to 'see red' at any moment. The ram who fed in the narrow paddock below the orchards she had adjudged, after ample and cautious probation, to be of docile temper; today, however, she decided to leave his docility untested, for the usually tranquil beast was roaming with every sign of restlessness from corner to corner of his meadow. A low, fitful piping, as of some reedy flute, was coming from the depth of a neighbouring copse, and there seemed to be some subtle connection between the animal's restless pacing and the wild music from the wood. Sylvia turned her steps in an upward direction and climbed the heather-clad slopes that stretched in rolling shoulders high above Yessney. She had left the piping notes behind her, but across the wooded combes at her feet the wind brought her another kind of music, the straining bay of hounds in full chase. Yessney was just on the outskirts of the Devon-and-Somerset country, and the hunted deer sometimes came that way. Sylvia could presently see a dark body, breasting hill after hill, and sinking again and again out of sight as he crossed the combes, while behind him steadily swelled that relentless chorus, and she grew tense with the excited sympathy that one feels for any hunted thing in whose capture one is not directly interested. And at last he broke through the outermost line of oak scrub and fern and stood panting in the open, a fat September stag carrying a well-furnished head. His obvious course was to drop down to the brown pools of Undercombe, and thence make his way towards the red deer's favoured sanctuary, the sea. To Sylvia's surprise, however, he turned his head to the upland slope and came lumbering resolutely onward over the heather. 'It will be dreadful,' she thought, 'the hounds will pull him down under my very eyes.' But the music of the pack seemed to have died away for a moment, and in its place she heard again that wild piping, which rose now on this side, now on that, as though urging the failing stag to a final effort. Sylvia stood well aside from his path, half hidden in a thick growth of whortle bushes, and watched him swing stiffly upward, his flanks dark with sweat, the coarse hair on his neck showing light by contrast. The pipe music shrilled suddenly around her, seeming to come from the bushes at her very feet, and at the same moment the great beast slewed round and bore directly down upon her. In an instant her pity for the hunted animal was changed to wild terror at her own danger; the thick heather roots mocked her scrambling efforts at flight, and she looked frantically downward for a glimpse of oncoming hounds. The huge antler spikes were within a few yards of her, and in a flash of numbing fear she remembered Mortimer's warning, to beware of horned beasts on the farm. And then with a quick throb of joy she saw that she was not alone; a human figure stood a few paces aside, knee-deep in the whortle bushes.

'Drive it off!' she shrieked. But the figure made no answering movement.

The antlers drove straight at her breast, the acrid smell of the hunted animal was in her nostrils, but her eyes were filled with the horror of something she saw other than her oncoming death. And in her ears rang the echo of a boy's laughter, golden and equivocal.

THE PEACE OF MOWSLE BARTON

CREFTON LOCKYER sat at his ease, an ease alike of body and soul, in the little patch of ground, half-orchard and half-garden, that abutted on the farmyard at Mowsle Barton. After the stress and noise of long years of city life, the repose and peace of the hill-begirt homestead struck on his senses with an almost dramatic intensity. Time and space seemed to lose their meaning and their abruptness; the minutes slid away into hours, and the meadows and fallows sloped away into middle distance, softly and imperceptibly. Wild weeds of the hedgerow straggled into the flower-garden, and wallflowers and garden bushes made counter-raids into farmyard and lane. Sleepy-looking hens and solemn preoccupied ducks were equally at home in yard, orchard, or roadway; nothing seemed to belong definitely to anywhere; even the gates were not necessarily to be found on their hinges. And over the whole scene brooded the sense of a peace that had almost a quality of magic in it. In the afternoon you felt that it had always been afternoon, and must always remain afternoon; in the twilight you knew that it could never have been anything else but twilight. Crefton Lockyer sat at his ease in the rustic seat beneath an old medlar tree, and decided that here was the life-anchorage that his mind had so fondly pictured and that latterly his tired and jarred senses had so often pined for. He would make a permanent lodging-place among these simple friendly people, gradually increasing the modest comforts with which he would like to surround himself, but falling in as much as possible with their manner of living.

As he slowly matured this resolution in his mind an elderly woman came hobbling with uncertain gait through the orchard. He recognized her as a member of the farm household, the mother or possibly the mother-in-law of Mrs Spurfield, his present landlady, and hastily formulated some pleasant remark to make to her. She forestalled him.

'There's a bit of writing chalked up on the door over yonder. What is it?'

She spoke in a dull impersonal manner, as though the question had been on her lips for years and had best be got rid of. Her eyes, however, looked impatiently over Crefton's head at the door of a small barn which formed the outpost of a straggling line of farm buildings.

'Martha Pillamon is an old witch' was the announcement that met Crefton's inquiring scrutiny, and he hesitated a moment before giving the statement wider publicity. For all he knew to the contrary, it might be Martha herself to whom he was speaking. It was possible that Mrs Spurfield's maiden name had been Pillamon. And the gaunt, withered old dame at his side might certainly fulfil local conditions as to the outward aspect of a witch.

'It's something about some one called Martha Pillamon,' he explained cautiously.

'What does it say?'

'It's very disrespectful,' said Crefton; 'it says she's a witch. Such things ought not to be written up.'

'It's true, every word of it,' said his listener with considerable satisfaction, adding as a special descriptive note of her own, 'the old toad.'

And as she hobbled away through the farmyard she shrilled out in her cracked voice, 'Martha Pillamon is an old witch!'

'Did you hear what she said?' mumbled a weak, angry voice somewhere behind Crefton's shoulder. Turning hastily, he beheld another old crone, thin and yellow and wrinkled, and evidently in a high state of displeasure. Obviously this was Martha Pillamon in person. The orchard seemed to be a favourite promenade for the aged women of the neighbourhood.

' 'Tis lies, 'tis sinful lies,' the weak voice went on. ' 'Tis Betsy Croot is the old witch. She an' her daughter, the dirty rat. I'll put a spell on 'em, the old nuisances.'

As she limped slowly away her eye caught the chalk inscription on the barn door.

'What's written up there?' she demanded, wheeling round on Crefton.

'Vote for Soarker,' he responded, with the craven boldness of the practised peacemaker.

The old woman grunted, and her mutterings and her faded red shawl lost themselves gradually among the tree-trunks. Crefton rose presently and made his way towards the farmhouse. Somehow a good deal of the peace seemed to have slipped out of the atmosphere.

The cheery bustle of tea-time in the old farm kitchen, which Crefton had found so agreeable on previous afternoons, seemed to have soured today into a certain uneasy melancholy. There was a dull, dragging silence around the board, and the tea itself, when Crefton came to taste it, was a flat, lukewarm concoction that would have driven the spirit of revelry out of a carnival.

'It's no use complaining of the tea,' said Mrs Spurfield hastily, as her guest stared with an air of polite inquiry at his cup. 'The kettle won't boil, that's the truth of it.'

Crefton turned to the hearth, where an unusually fierce fire was banked up under a big black kettle, which sent a thin wreath of steam from its spout, but seemed otherwise to ignore the action of the roaring blaze beneath it.

'It's been there more than an hour, an' boil it won't,' said Mrs Spurfield adding, by way of complete explanation, 'we're bewitched.'

'It's Martha Pillamon as has done it,' chimed in the old mother; 'I'll be even with the old toad. I'll put a spell on her.'

'It must boil in time,' protested Crefton, ignoring the suggestions of foul influences. 'Perhaps the coal is damp.'

'It won't boil in time for supper, nor for breakfast tomorrow morning, not if you was to keep the fire a-going all night for it,' said Mrs Spurfield. And it didn't. The household subsisted on fried and baked dishes, and a neighbour obligingly brewed tea and sent it across in a moderately warm condition.

'I suppose you'll be leaving us now that things has turned up uncomfortable,' Mrs Spurfield observed at breakfast; 'there are folks as deserts one as soon as trouble comes.'

Crefton hurriedly disclaimed any immediate change of plans; he observed, however, to himself that the earlier heartiness of manner had in a large measure deserted the household. Suspicious looks, sulky silences, or sharp speeches had become the order of the day. As for the old mother, she sat about the kitchen or the garden all day, murmuring threats and spells against Martha Pillamon. There was something alike terrifying and piteous in the spectacle of these frail old morsels of humanity consecrating their last flickering energies to the task of making each other wretched. Hatred seemed to be the one faculty which had survived in undiminished vigour and intensity where all else was dropping into ordered and symmetrical decay. And the uncanny part of it was that some horrid unwholesome power seemed to be distilled from their spite and their cursings. No amount of sceptical explanation could remove the undoubted fact that neither kettle nor saucepan would come to boiling-point over the hottest fire. Crefton clung as long as possible to the theory of some defect in the coals, but a wood fire gave the same result, and when a small spirit-lamp kettle, which he ordered out by carrier, showed the same obstinate refusal to allow its contents to boil he felt that he had come suddenly into contact with some unguessed-at and very evil aspect of hidden forces. Miles away, down through an opening in the hills, he could catch glimpses of a road where motor-cars sometimes passed, and yet here, so little removed from the arteries of the latest civilization, was a bat-haunted old homestead, where something unmistakably like witchcraft seemed to hold a very practical sway.

Passing out through the farm garden on his way to the lanes

beyond, where he hoped to recapture the comfortable sense of peacefulness that was so lacking around house and hearth—especially hearth—Crefton came across the old mother, sitting mumbling to herself in the seat beneath the medlar tree. 'Let un sink as swims, let un sink as swims,' she was repeating over and over again, as a child repeats a half-learned lesson. And now and then she would break off into a shrill laugh, with a note of malice in it that was not pleasant to hear. Crefton was glad when he found himself out of earshot, in the quiet and seclusion of the deep overgrown lanes that seemed to lead away to nowhere; one, narrower and deeper than the rest, attracted his footsteps, and he was almost annoyed when he found that it really did act as a miniature roadway to a human dwelling. A forlorn-looking cottage with a scrap of ill-tended cabbage garden and a few aged apple trees stood at an angle where a swift-flowing stream widened out for a space into a decent-sized pond before hurrying away again through the willows that had checked its course. Crefton leaned against a tree-trunk and looked across the swirling eddies of the pond at the humble little homestead opposite him; the only sign of life came from a small procession of dingy-looking ducks that marched in single file down to the water's edge. There is always something rather taking in the way a duck changes itself in an instant from a slow, clumsy waddler of the earth to a graceful, buoyant swimmer of the waters, and Crefton waited with a certain arrested attention to watch the leader of the file launch itself on to the surface of the pond. He was aware at the same time of a curious warning instinct that something strange and unpleasant was about to happen. The duck flung itself confidently forward into the water, and rolled immediately under the surface. Its head appeared for a moment and went under again, leaving a train of bubbles in its wake, while wings and legs churned the water in a helpless swirl of flapping and kicking. The bird was obviously drowning. Crefton thought at first that it had caught itself in some weeds, or was being attacked from below by a pike or water-rat. But no blood floated to the surface, and the wildly bobbing body made the circuit of the pond current without hindrance from any entanglement. A second duck had by this time launched itself into the pond, and a second struggling body rolled and twisted under the surface. There was something peculiarly piteous in the sight of the gasping beaks that showed now and again above the water, as though in terrified protest at this treachery of a trusted and familiar element. Crefton gazed with something like horror as a third duck poised itself on the bank and splashed in, to share the fate of the other two. He felt almost relieved when the remainder of the flock, taking tardy alarm from the commotion of the slowly drowning bodies, drew themselves up with tense outstretched necks, and sidled away from the scene of danger, quacking a deep note of disquietude as they went. At the same moment Crefton became aware that he was not the only human witness of the scene; a bent and withered old woman, whom he recognized at once as Martha Pillamon, of sinister reputation, had limped down the cottage path to the water's edge, and was gazing fixedly at the gruesome whirligig of dying birds that went in horrible procession round the pool. Presently her voice rang out in a shrill note of quavering rage:

' 'Tis Betsy, Croot adone it, the old rat. I'll put a spell on her, see if I don't.'

Crefton slipped quietly away, uncertain whether or no the old woman had noticed his presence. Even before she had proclaimed the guiltiness of Betsy Croot, the latter's muttered incantation 'Let un sink as swims' had flashed uncomfortably across his mind. But it was the final threat of a retaliatory spell which crowded his mind with misgiving to the exclusion of all other thoughts or fancies. His reasoning powers could no longer afford to dismiss these old-wives' threats as empty bickerings. The household at Mowsle Barton lay under the displeasure of a vindictive old woman who seemed able to materialize her personal spites in a very practical fashion, and there was no saying what form her revenge for three drowned ducks might not take. As a member of the household Crefton might find himself involved in some general and highly disagreeable visitation of Martha Pillamon's wrath. Of course he knew that he was giving way to absurd fancies, but the behaviour of the spirit-lamp kettle and the subsequent scene at the pond had considerably unnerved him. And the vagueness of his alarm added to its terrors; when once you have taken the Impossible into your calculations its possibilities become practically limitless.

Crefton rose at his usual early hour the next morning, after one of the least restful nights he had spent at the farm. His sharpened senses quickly detected that subtle atmosphere of things-being-not-altogether well that hangs over a stricken household. The cows had been milked, but they stood huddled about in the yard, waiting impatiently to be driven out afield, and the poultry kept up an importunate querulous reminder of deferred feeding-time; the yard pump, which usually made discordant music at frequent intervals during the early morning, was today ominously silent. In the house itself there was a coming and going of scuttering footsteps, a rushing and dying away of hurried voices, and long, uneasy stillnesses. Crefton finished his dressing and made his way to the head of a narrow staircase. He could hear a dull, complaining voice, a voice into which an awed hush had crept, and recognized the speaker as Mrs Spurfield.

'He'll go away, for sure,' the voice was saying; 'there are those as runs away from one as soon as real misfortune shows itself.'

Crefton felt that he probably was one of 'those', and that there were moments when it was advisable to be true to type.

He crept back to his room, collected and packed his few belongings, placed the money due for his lodgings on a table, and made his way out by a back door into the yard. A mob of poultry surged expectantly towards him; shaking off their interested attentions he hurried along under cover of cowstall, piggery, and hayricks till he reached the lane at the back of the farm. A few minutes' walk, which only the burden of his portmanteaux restrained from developing into an undisguised run, brought him to a main road, where the early carrier soon overtook him and sped him onward to the neighbouring town. At a bend of the road he caught a last glimpse of the farm; the old gabled roofs and thatched barns, the straggling orchard, and the medlar tree, with its wooden seat, stood out with an almost spectral clearness in the early morning light, and over it all brooded that air of magic possession which Crefton had once mistaken for peace.

The bustle and roar of Paddington Station smote on his ears with a welcome protective greeting.

'Very bad for our nerves, all this rush and hurry,' said a fellow-traveller; 'give me the peace and quiet of the country.'

Crefton mentally surrendered his share of the desired commodity. A crowded, brilliantly over-lighted music-hall, where an exuberant rendering of '1812' was being given by a strenuous orchestra, came nearest to his ideal of a nerve sedative.

THE SHE-WOLF

LEONARD BILSITER was one of those people who have failed to find this world attractive or interesting, and who have sought compensation in an 'unseen world' of their own experience or imagination—or invention. Children do that sort of thing successfully, but children are content to convince themselves, and do not vulgarize their beliefs by trying to convince other people. Leonard Bilsiter's beliefs were for 'the few', that is to say, any one who would listen to him.

His dabblings in the unseen might not have carried him beyond the customary platitudes of the drawing-room visionary if accident had not reinforced his stock-in-trade of mystical lore. In company with a friend, who was interested in a Ural mining concern, he had made a trip across Eastern Europe at a moment when the great Russian railway strike was developing from a threat to a reality; its outbreak caught him on the return journey, somewhere on the further side of Perm, and it was while waiting for a couple of days at a wayside station in a state of suspended locomotion that he made the acquaintance of a dealer in harness and metalware, who profitably whiled away the tedium of the long halt by initiating his English travelling companion in a fragmentary system of folklore that he had picked up from Trans-Baikal traders and natives. Leonard returned to his home circle garrulous about his Russian strike experiences, but oppressively reticent about certain dark mysteries, which he alluded to under the resounding title of Siberian Magic. The reticence wore off in a week or two under the influence of an entire lack of general curiosity, and Leonard began to make more detailed allusions to the enormous powers which this new esoteric force, to use his own description of it, conferred on the initiated few who knew how to wield it. His aunt, Cecilia Hoops, who loved sensation perhaps rather better than she loved the truth, gave him as clamorous an advertisement as any one could wish for by retailing an account of how he had turned a vegetable marrow into a wood-pigeon before her very eyes. As a manifestation of the possession of supernatural powers, the story was discounted in some quarters by the respect accorded to Mrs Hoops' powers of imagination.

However divided opinion might be on the question of Leonard's status as a wonder-worker or a charlatan, he certainly arrived at Mary Hampton's house-party with a reputation for pre-eminence in one or other of those professions, and he was not disposed to shun such publicity as might fall to his share. Esoteric forces and unusual powers figured largely in whatever conversation he or his aunt had a share in, and his own performances, past and potential, were the subject of mysterious hints and dark avowals.

'I wish you would turn me into a wolf, Mr Bilsiter,' said his hostess at luncheon the day after his arrival.

'My dear Mary,' said Colonel Hampton, 'I never knew you had a craving in that direction.'

'A she-wolf, of course,' continued Mrs Hampton; 'it would be too confusing to change one's sex as well as one's species at a moment's notice.'

'I don't think one should jest on these subjects,' said Leonard.

'I'm not jesting, I'm quite serious, I assure you. Only don't do it today; we have only eight available bridge players, and it would break up one of our tables. Tomorrow we shall be a larger party. Tomorrow night, after dinner—'

'In our present imperfect understanding of these hidden forces I think one should approach them with humbleness rather than mockery,' observed Leonard, with such severity that the subject was forthwith dropped.

Clovis Sangrail had sat unusually silent during the discussion on the possibilities of Siberian magic; after lunch he side-tracked Lord Pabham into the comparative seclusion of the billiard-room and delivered himself of a searching question.

'Have you such a thing as a she-wolf in your collection of wild animals? A she-wolf of moderately good temper?'

Lord Pabham considered. 'There is Louisa,' he said, 'a rather fine specimen of the timber-wolf. I got her two years ago in exchange for some Arctic foxes. Most of my animals get to be fairly tame before they've been with me very long; I think I can say Louisa has an angelic temper, as she-wolves go. Why do you ask?'

'I was wondering whether you would lend her to me for tomorrow night,' said Clovis, with the careless solicitude of one who borrows a collar stud or a tennis racquet.

'Tomorrow night?'

'Yes, wolves are nocturnal animals, so the late hours won't hurt her,' said Clovis, with the air of one who has taken everything into consideration; 'one of your men could bring her over from Pabham Park after dusk, and with a little help he ought to be able to smuggle her into the conservatory at the same moment that Mary Hampton makes an unobtrusive exit.'

Lord Pabham stared at Clovis for a moment in pardonable bewilderment; then his face broke into a wrinkled network of laughter.

'Oh, that's your game, is it? You are going to do a little Siberian magic on your own account. And is Mrs Hampton willing to be a fellow-conspirator?'

'Mary is pledged to see me through with it, if you will guarantee Louisa's temper.'

'I'll answer for Louisa,' said Lord Pabham.

By the following day the house-party had swollen to larger proportions, and Bilsiter's instinct for self-advertisement expanded duly under the stimulant of an increased audience. At dinner that evening he held forth at length on the subject of unseen forces and untested powers, and his flow of impressive eloquence continued unabated while coffee was being served in the drawing-room preparatory to a general migration to the card-room. His aunt ensured a respectful hearing for his utterances, but her sensation-loving soul hankered after something more dramatic than mere vocal demonstration.

'Won't you do something to *convince* them of your powers, Leonard?' she pleaded. 'Change something into another shape. He can, you know, if he only chooses to,' she informed the company.

'Oh, do,' said Mavis Pellington earnestly, and her request was echoed by nearly every one present. Even those who were not open to conviction were perfectly willing to be entertained by an exhibition of amateur conjuring.

Leonard felt that something tangible was expected of him.

'Has any one present,' he asked, 'got a three-penny bit or some small object of no particular value——?'

'You're surely not going to make coins disappear, or something primitive of that sort?' said Clovis contemptuously.

'I think it very unkind of you not to carry out my suggestion of turning me into a wolf,' said Mary Hampton, as she crossed over to the conservatory to give her macaws their usual tribute from the dessert dishes.

'I have already warned you of the danger of treating these powers in a mocking spirit,' said Leonard solemnly.

'I don't believe you can do it,' laughed Mary provocatively from the conservatory; 'I dare you to do it if you can. I defy you to turn me into a wolf.'

As she said this she was lost to view behind a clump of azaleas.

'Mrs Hampton——' began Leonard with increased solemnity, but he got no further. A breath of chill air seemed to rush across the room, and at the same time the macaws broke forth into ear-splitting screams.

'What on earth is the matter with those confounded birds, Mary?' exclaimed Colonel Hampton; at the same moment an even more piercing scream from Mavis Pellington stampeded the entire company from their seats. In various attitudes of helpless horror or instinctive defence they confronted the evil-looking grey beast that was peering at them from amid a setting of fern and azalea.

Mrs Hoops was the first to recover from the general chaos of fright and bewilderment.

'Leonard!' she screamed shrilly to her nephew, 'turn it back into Mrs Hampton at once! It may fly at us at any moment. Turn it back!'

'I—I don't know how to,' faltered Leonard, who looked more scared and horrified than any one.

'What!' shouted Colonel Hampton, 'you've taken the abominable liberty of turning my wife into a wolf, and now you stand there calmly and say you can't turn her back again!'

To do strict justice to Leonard, calmness was not a distinguishing feature of his attitude at the moment.

'I assure you I didn't turn Mrs Hampton into a wolf; nothing was farther from my intentions,' he protested.

'Then where is she, and how came that animal into the conservatory?' demanded the Colonel.

'Of course we must accept your assurance that you didn't turn Mrs Hampton into a wolf,' said Clovis politely, 'but you will agree that appearances are against you.'

'Are we to have all these recriminations with that beast standing there ready to tear us to pieces?' wailed Mavis indignantly.

'Lord Pabham, you know a good deal about wild beasts—' suggested Colonel Hampton.

'The wild beasts that I have been accustomed to,' said Lord Pabham, 'have come with proper credentials from well-known dealers, or have been bred in my own menagerie. I've never before been confronted with an animal that walks unconcernedly out of an azalea bush, leaving a charming and popular hostess unaccounted for. As far as one can judge from *outward* characteristics,' he continued, 'it has the appearance of a well-grown female of the North American timber-wolf, a variety of the common species *canis lupus.*'

'Oh, never mind its Latin name,' screamed Mavis, as the beast came a step or two further into the room; 'can't you entice it away with food, and shut it up where it can't do any harm?'

'If it is really Mrs Hampton, who has just had a very good dinner, I don't suppose food will appeal to it very strongly,' said Clovis.

'Leonard,' beseeched Mrs Hoops tearfully, 'even if this *is* none of your doing can't you use your great powers to turn this dreadful beast into something harmless before it bites us all—a rabbit or something?'

'I don't suppose Colonel Hampton would care to have his wife turned into a succession of fancy animals as though we were playing a round game with her,' interposed Clovis.

'I absolutely forbid it,' thundered the Colonel.

'Most wolves that I've had anything to do with have been inordinately fond of sugar,' said Lord Pabham; 'if you like I'll try the effect on this one.'

He took a piece of sugar from the saucer of his coffee cup and flung it to the expectant Louisa, who snapped it in mid-air. There was a sigh of relief from the company; a wolf that ate sugar when it might at the least have been employed in tearing macaws to pieces had already shed some of its terrors. The sigh deepened to a gasp of thanksgiving when Lord Pabham decoyed the animal out of the room by a pretended largesse of further sugar. There was an instant rush to the vacated conservatory. There was no trace of Mrs Hampton except the plate containing the macaws' supper.

'The door is locked on the inside!' exclaimed Clovis, who had deftly turned the key as he affected to test it.

Every one turned towards Bilsiter.

'If you haven't turned my wife into a wolf,' said Colonel Hampton, 'will you kindly explain where she has disappeared to, since she obviously could not have gone through a locked door? I will not press you for an explanation of how a North American timber-wolf suddenly appeared in the conservatory, but I think I have some right to inquire what has become of Mrs Hampton.'

Bilsiter's reiterated disclaimer was met with a general murmur of impatient disbelief.

'I refuse to stay another hour under this roof,' declared Mavis Pellington.

'If our hostess has really vanished out of human form,' said

Mrs Hoops, 'none of the ladies of the party can very well remain. I absolutely decline to be chaperoned by a wolf!'

'It's a she-wolf,' said Clovis soothingly.

The correct etiquette to be observed under the unusual circumstances received no further elucidation. The sudden entry of Mary Hampton deprived the discussion of its immediate interest.

'Some one has mesmerized me,' she exclaimed crossly; 'I found myself in the game larder, of all places, being fed with sugar by Lord Pabham. I hate being mesmerized, and the doctor has forbidden me to touch sugar.'

The situation was explained to her, as far as it permitted of anything that could be called explanation.

'Then you *really* did turn me into a wolf, Mr Bilsiter?' she exclaimed excitedly.

But Leonard had burned the boat in which he might now have embarked on a sea of glory. He could only shake his head feebly.

'It was I who took that liberty,' said Clovis; 'you see, I happen to have lived for a couple of years in North-eastern Russia, and I have more than a tourist's acquaintance with the magic craft of that region. One does not care to speak about these strange powers, but once in a way, when one hears a lot of nonsense being talked about them, one is tempted to show what Siberian magic can accomplish in the hands of some one who really understands it. I yielded to that temptation. May I have some brandy? the effort has left me rather faint.'

If Leonard Bilsiter could at that moment have transformed Clovis into a cockroach and then have stepped on him he would gladly have performed both operations.

LAURA

'You are not really dying, are you?' asked Amanda.

'I have the doctor's permission to live till Tuesday,' said Laura.

'But today is Saturday; this is serious!' gasped Amanda.

'I don't know about it being serious; it is certainly Saturday,' said Laura.

'Death is always serious,' said Amanda.

'I never said I was going to die. I am presumably going to leave off being Laura, but I shall go on being something. An animal of some kind, I suppose. You see, when one hasn't been very good in the life one has just lived, one reincarnates in some lower organism. And I haven't been very good, when one comes to think of it. I've been petty and mean and vindictive and all that sort of thing when circumstances have seemed to warrant it.'

'Circumstances never warrant that sort of thing,' said Amanda hastily.

'If you don't mind my saying so,' observed Laura, 'Egbert is a circumstance that would warrant any amount of that sort of thing. You're married to him—that's different; you've sworn to love, honour, and endure him: I haven't.'

'I don't see what's wrong with Egbert,' protested Amanda.

'Oh, I dare say the wrongness has been on my part,' admitted Laura dispassionately; 'he has merely been the extenuating circumstance. He made a thin, peevish kind of fuss, for instance, when I took the collie puppies from the farm out for a run the other day.'

'They chased his young broods of speckled Sussex and drove two sitting hens off their nests, besides running all over the flower beds. You know how devoted he is to his poultry and garden.'

'Anyhow, he needn't have gone on about it for the entire evening and then have said, "Let's say no more about it" just when I was beginning to enjoy the discussion. That's where one of my petty vindictive revenges came in,' added Laura with an unrepentant chuckle; 'I turned the entire family of speckled Sussex into his seedling shed the day after the puppy episode.'

'How could you?' exclaimed Amanda.

'It came quite easy,' said Laura; 'two of the hens pretended to be laying at the time, but I was firm.'

'And we thought it was an accident!'

'You see,' resumed Laura, 'I really *have* some grounds for

supposing that my next incarnation will be in a lower organism. I shall be an animal of some kind. On the other hand, I haven't been a bad sort in my way, so I think I may count on being a nice animal, some thing elegant and lively, with a love of fun. An otter, perhaps.'

'I can't imagine you as an otter,' said Amanda.

'Well, I don't suppose you can imagine me as an angel, if it comes to that,' said Laura.

Amanda was silent. She couldn't.

'Personally I think an otter life would be rather enjoyable,' continued Laura; 'salmon to eat all the year around, and the satisfaction of being able to fetch the trout in their own homes without having to wait for hours till they condescend to rise to the fly you've been dangling before them; and an elegant svelte figure—'

'Think of the otter hounds,' interposed Amanda; 'how dreadful to be hunted and harried and finally worried to death!'

'Rather fun with half the neighbourhood looking on, and anyhow not worse than this Saturday-to-Tuesday business of dying by inches; and then I should go on into something else. If I had been a moderately good otter I suppose I should get back into human shape of some sort; probably something rather primitive—a little brown, unclothed Nubian boy, I should think.'

'I wish you would be serious,' sighed Amanda; 'you really ought to be if you're only going to live till Tuesday.'

As a matter of fact Laura died on Monday.

'So dreadfully upsetting,' Amanda complained to her uncle-in-law, Sir Lulworth Quayne. 'I've asked quite a lot of people down for golf and fishing, and the rhododendrons are just looking their best.'

'Laura always was inconsiderate,' said Sir Lulworth; 'she was born during Goodwood week, with an Ambassador staying in the house who hated babies.'

'She had the maddest kind of ideas,' said Amanda; 'do you know if there was any insanity in her family?'

'Insanity? No, I never heard of any. Her father lives in West Kensington, but I believe he's sane on all other subjects.'

'She had an idea that she was going to be reincarnated as an otter,' said Amanda.

'One meets with those ideas of reincarnation so frequently, even in the West,' said Sir Lulworth, 'that one can hardly set them down as being mad. And Laura was such an unaccountable person in this life that I should not like to lay down definite rules as to what she might be doing in an after state.'

'You think she really might have passed into some animal form?' asked Amanda. She was one of those who shape their opinions rather readily from the standpoint of those around them.

Just then Egbert entered the breakfast-room, wearing an air of bereavement that Laura's demise would have been insufficient, in itself, to account for.

'Four of my speckled Sussex have been killed,' he exclaimed; 'the very four that were to go to the show on Friday. One of them was dragged away and eaten right in the middle of that new carnation bed that I've been to such trouble and expense over. My best flower bed and my best fowls singled out for destruction; it almost seems as if the brute that did the deed had special knowledge how to be as devastating as possible in a short space of time.'

'Was it a fox, do you think?' asked Amanda.

'Sounds more like a polecat,' said Sir Lulworth.

'No,' said Egbert, 'there were marks of webbed feet all over the place, and we followed the tracks down to the stream at the bottom of the garden; evidently an otter.'

Amanda looked quickly and furtively across at Sir Lulworth.

Egbert was too agitated to eat any breakfast, and went out to superintend the strengthening of the poultry yard defences.

'I think she might at least have waited till the funeral was over,' said Amanda in a scandalized voice.

'It's her own funeral, you know,' said Sir Lulworth; 'it's a nice point in etiquette how far one ought to show respect to one's own mortal remains.'

Disregard for mortuary convention was carried to further lengths next day; during the absence of the family at the funeral ceremony the remaining survivors of the speckled

Sussex were massacred. The marauder's line of retreat seemed to have embraced most of the flower beds on the lawn, but the strawberry beds in the lower garden had also suffered.

'I shall get the otter hounds to come here at the earliest possible moment,' said Egbert savagely.

'On no account! You can't dream of such a thing!' exclaimed Amanda. 'I mean, it wouldn't do, so soon after a funeral in the house.'

'It's a case of necessity,' said Egbert; 'once an otter takes to that sort of thing it won't stop.'

'Perhaps it will go elsewhere now that there are no more fowls left,' suggested Amanda.

'One would think you wanted to shield the beast,' said Egbert.

'There's been so little water in the stream lately,' objected Amanda; 'it seems hardly sporting to hunt an animal when it has so little chance of taking refuge anywhere.'

'Good gracious!' fumed Egbert, 'I'm not thinking about sport. I want to have the animal killed as soon as possible.'

Even Amanda's opposition weakened when, during church time on the following Sunday, the otter made its way into the house, raided half a salmon from the larder and worried it into scaly fragments on the Persian rug in Egbert's studio.

'We shall have it hiding under our beds and biting pieces out of our feet before long,' said Egbert, and from what Amanda knew of this particular otter she felt that the possibility was not a remote one.

On the evening preceding the day fixed for the hunt Amanda spent a solitary hour walking by the banks of the stream, making what she imagined to be hound noises. It was charitably supposed by those who overhead her performance, that she was practising for farmyard imitations at the forthcoming village entertainment.

It was her friend and neighbour, Aurora Burret, who brought her news of the day's sport.

'Pity you weren't out; we had quite a good day. We found it at once, in the pool just below your garden.'

'Did you—kill?' asked Amanda.

'Rather. A fine she-otter. Your husband got rather badly bitten in trying to "tail it". Poor beast, I felt quite sorry for it, it had such a human look in its eyes when it was killed. You'll call me silly, but do you know who the look reminded me of? My dear woman, what is the matter?'

When Amanda had recovered to a certain extent from her attack of nervous prostration Egbert took her to the Nile Valley to recuperate. Change of scene speedily brought about the desired recovery of health and mental balance. The escapades of an adventurous otter in search of a variation of diet were viewed in their proper light. Amanda's normally placid temperament reasserted itself. Even a hurricane of shouted curses, coming from her husband's dressing-room, in her husband's voice, but hardly in his usual vocabulary, failed to disturb her serenity as she made a leisurely toilet one evening in a Cairo hotel.

'What is the matter? What has happened?' she asked in amused curiosity.

'The little beast has thrown all my clean shirts into the bath! Wait till I catch you, you little—'

'What little beast?' asked Amanda, suppressing a desire to laugh; Egbert's language was so hopelessly inadequate to express his outraged feelings.

'A little beast of a naked brown Nubian boy,' spluttered Egbert.

And now Amanda is seriously ill.

THE BOAR-PIG

'THERE is a back way on to the lawn,' said Mrs Philidore Stossen to her daughter, 'through a small grass paddock and then through a walled fruit garden full of gooseberry bushes. I went all over the place last year when the family were away. There is a door that opens from the fruit garden into a shrubbery, and once we emerge from there we can mingle with the guests as if we had come in by the ordinary way. It's much safer than going in by the front entrance and running the risk of coming bang up against the hostess; that would be so awkward when she doesn't happen to have invited us.'

'Isn't it a lot of trouble to take for getting admittance to a garden party?'

'To a garden party, yes; to *the* garden party of the season, certainly not. Every one of any consequence in the county, with the exception of ourselves, has been asked to meet the Princess, and it would be far more troublesome to invent explanations as to why we weren't there than to get in by a roundabout way. I stopped Mrs Cuvering in the road yesterday and talked very pointedly about the Princess. If she didn't choose to take the hint and send me an invitation it's not my fault, is it? Here we are: we just cut across the grass and through that little gate into the garden.'

Mrs Stossen and her daughter, suitably arrayed for a county garden party function with an infusion of Almanack de Gotha, sailed through the narrow grass paddock and the ensuing gooseberry garden with the air of state barges making an unofficial progress along a rural trout stream. There was a certain amount of furtive haste mingled with the stateliness of their advance as though hostile searchlights might be turned on them at any moment; and, as a matter of fact, they were not unobserved. Matilda Cuvering, with the alert eyes of thirteen years and the added advantage of an exalted position in the branches of a medlar tree, had enjoyed a good view of the Stossen flanking movement and had foreseen exactly where it would break down in execution.

'They'll find the door locked, and they'll jolly well have to go back the way they came,' she remarked to herself. 'Serves them right for not coming in by the proper entrance. What a pity Tarquin Superbus isn't loose in the paddock. After all, as every one else is enjoying themselves, I don't see why Tarquin shouldn't have an afternoon out.'

Matilda was of an age when thought is action; she slid down from the branches of the medlar tree, and when she clambered back again, Tarquin, the huge white Yorkshire boar-pig, had exchanged the narrow limits of his sty for the wider range of the grass paddock. The discomfited Stossen expedition, returning in recriminatory but otherwise orderly retreat from the unyielding obstacle of the locked door, came to a sudden halt at the gate dividing the paddock from the gooseberry garden.

'What a villainous-looking animal,' exclaimed Mrs Stossen; 'it wasn't there when we came in.'

'It's there now, anyhow,' said her daughter. 'What on earth are we to do? I wish we had never come.'

The boar-pig had drawn nearer to the gate for a closer inspection of the human intruders, and stood champing his jaws and blinking his small red eyes in a manner that was doubtless intended to be disconcerting, and, as far as the Stossens were concerned, thoroughly achieved that result.

'Shoo! Hish! Hish! Shoo!' cried the ladies in chorus.

'If they think they're going to drive him away by reciting lists of the kings of Israel and Judah they're laying themselves out for disappointment,' observed Matilda from her seat in the medlar tree. As she made the observation aloud Mrs Stossen became for the first time aware of her presence. A moment or two earlier she would have been anything but pleased at the discovery that the garden was not as deserted as it looked, but now she hailed the fact of the child's presence on the scene with absolute relief.

'Little girl, can you find some one to drive away—' she began hopefully.

'*Comment? Comprends pas,*' was the response.

'Oh, are you French? *Êtes vous française?*'

'*Pas de tous. 'Suis anglaise.*'

'Then why not talk English? I want to know if—'

'*Permettez-moi expliquer.* You see, I'm rather under a cloud,' said Matilda. 'I'm staying with my aunt, and I was told I must behave particularly well today, as lots of people were coming for a garden party, and I was told to imitate Claude, that's my young cousin, who never does anything wrong except by accident, and then is always apologetic about it. It seems they thought I ate too much raspberry trifle at lunch, and they said Claude never eats too much raspberry trifle. Well, Claude always goes to sleep for half an hour after lunch, because he's told to, and I waited till he was asleep, and tied his hands and started forcible feeding with a whole bucketful of raspberry trifle that they were keeping for the garden party.

Lots of it went on to his sailor-suit and some of it on to the bed, but a good deal went down Claude's throat, and they can't say again that he has never been known to eat too much raspberry trifle. That is why I am not allowed to go to the party, and as an additional punishment I must speak French all the afternoon. I've had to tell you all this in English, as there were words like "forcible feeding" that I didn't know the French for; of course I could have invented them, but if I had said *nourriture obligatoire* you wouldn't have had the least idea what I was talking about. *Mais maintenant, nous parlons français.*'

'Oh, very well, *très bien*,' said Mrs Stossen reluctantly; in moments of flurry such French as she knew was not under very good control. '*Là, à l'autre côté de la porte, est un cochon—*'

'*Un cochon? Ah, le petit charmant!*' exclaimed Matilda with enthusiasm.

'*Mais non, pas du tout petit, et pas du tout charmant; un bête féroce—*'

'*Une bête*,' corrected Matilda, 'a pig is masculine as long as you call it a pig, but if you lose your temper with it and call it a ferocious beast it becomes one of us at once. French is a dreadfully unsexing language.'

'For goodness' sake let us talk English then,' said Mrs Stossen. 'Is there any way out of this garden except through the paddock where the pig is?'

'I always go over the wall, by way of the plum tree,' said Matilda.

'Dressed as we are we could hardly do that,' said Mrs Stossen; it was difficult to imagine her doing it in any costume.

'Do you think you could go and get some one who would drive the pig away?' asked Miss Stossen.

'I promised my aunt I would stay here till five o'clock; it's not four yet.'

'I am sure, under the circumstances, your aunt would permit—'

'My conscience would not permit,' said Matilda with cold dignity.

'We can't stay here till five o'clock,' exclaimed Mrs Stossen with growing exasperation.

'Shall I recite to you to make the time pass quicker?' asked Matilda obligingly, ' "Belinda, the little Breadwinner", is considered my best piece, or, perhaps, it ought to be something in French. Henri Quatre's address to his soldiers is the only thing I really know in that language.'

'If you will go and fetch some one to drive that animal away I will give you something to buy yourself a nice present,' said Mrs Stossen.

Matilda came several inches lower down the medlar tree.

'That is the most practical suggestion you have made yet for getting out of the garden,' she remarked cheerfully; 'Claude and I are collecting money for the Children's Fresh Air Fund, and we are seeing which of us can collect the biggest sum.'

'I shall be very glad to contribute half a crown, very glad indeed,' said Mrs Stossen, digging that coin out of the depths of a receptacle which formed a detached outwork of her toilet.

'Claude is a long way ahead of me at present,' continued Matilda, taking no notice of the suggested offering; 'you see, he's only eleven, and has golden hair, and those are enormous advantages when you're on the collecting job. Only the other day a Russian lady gave him ten shillings. Russians understand the art of giving far better than we do. I expect Claude will net quite twenty-five shillings this afternoon; he'll have the field to himself, and he'll be able to do the pale, fragile, not-long-for-this-world business to perfection after his raspberry trifle experience. Yes, he'll be *quite* two pounds ahead of me by now.'

With much probing and plucking and many regretful murmurs the beleaguered ladies managed to produce seven-and-sixpence between them.

'I am afraid this is all we've got,' said Mrs Stossen.

Matilda showed no sign of coming down either to the earth or to their figure.

'I could not do violence to my conscience for anything less than ten shillings,' she announced stiffly.

Mother and daughter muttered certain remarks under their breath, in which the word 'beast' was prominent, and probably had no reference to Tarquin.

'I find I *have* got another half-crown,' said Mrs Stossen in a shaking voice; 'here you are. Now please fetch some one quickly.'

Matilda slipped down from the tree, took possession of the donation, and proceeded to pick up a handful of over-ripe medlars from the grass at her feet. Then she climbed over the gate and addressed herself affectionately to the boar-pig.

'Come, Tarquin, dear old boy; you know you can't resist medlars when they're rotten and squashy.'

Tarquin couldn't. By dint of throwing the fruit in front of him at judicious intervals Matilda decoyed him back to his sty, while the delivered captives hurried across the paddock.

'Well, I never! The little minx!' exclaimed Mrs Stossen when she was safely on the high road. 'The animal wasn't savage at all, and as for the ten shillings, I don't believe the Fresh Air Fund will see a penny of it!'

There she was unwarrantably harsh in her judgment. If you examine the books of the fund you will find the acknowledgment: 'Collected by Miss Matilda Cuvering, 2s. 6d.'

THE BROGUE

THE hunting season had come to an end, and the Mullets had not succeeded in selling the Brogue. There had been a kind of tradition in the family for the past three or four years, a sort of fatalistic hope, that the Brogue would find a purchaser before the hunting was over; but seasons came and went without anything happening to justify such ill-founded optimism. The animal had been named Berserker in the earlier stages of its career; it had been rechristened the Brogue later on, in recognition of the fact that, once acquired, it was extremely difficult to get rid of. The unkinder wits of the neighbourhood had been known to suggest that the first letter of its name was superfluous. The Brogue had been variously described in sale catalogues as a light-weight hunter, a lady's hack, and, more simply, but still with a touch of imagination, as a useful brown gelding, standing 15.1. Toby Mullet had ridden him for four seasons with the West Wessex; you can ride almost any sort of horse with the West Wessex as long as it is an animal that knows the country. The Brogue knew the country intimately, having personally created most of the gaps that were to be met with in banks and hedges for many miles round. His manners and characteristics were not ideal in the hunting field, but he was probably rather safer to ride to hounds than he was as a hack on country roads. According to the Mullet family, he was not really road-shy, but there were one or two objects of dislike that brought on sudden attacks of what Toby called swerving sickness. Motors and cycles he treated with tolerant disregard, but pigs, wheelbarrows, piles of stones by the roadside, perambulators in a village street, gates painted too aggressively white, and sometimes, but not always, the newer kind of beehives, turned him aside from his tracks in vivid imitation of the zigzag course of forked lightning. If a pheasant rose noisily from the other side of a hedgerow the Brogue would spring into the air at the same moment, but this may have been due to a desire to be companionable. The Mullet family contradicted the widely prevalent report that the horse was a confirmed crib-biter.

It was about the third week in May that Mrs Mullet, relict of the late Sylvester Mullet, and mother of Toby and a bunch of daughters, assailed Clovis Sangrail on the outskirts of the village with a breathless catalogue of local happenings.

'You know our new neighbour, Mr Penricarde?' she vociferated; 'awfully rich, owns tin mines in Cornwall, middle-aged and rather quiet. He's taken the Red House on a long lease and spent a lot of money on alterations and improvements. Well, Toby's sold him the Brogue!'

Clovis spent a moment or two in assimilating the astonishing news; then he broke out into unstinted congratulation. If he had belonged to a more emotional race he would probably have kissed Mrs Mullet.

'How wonderful lucky to have pulled it off at last! Now you can buy a decent animal. I've always said that Toby was clever. Ever so many congratulations.'

'Don't congratulate me. It's the most unfortunate thing that could have happened!' said Mrs Mullet dramatically.

Clovis stared at her in amazement.

'Mr Penricarde,' said Mrs Mullet, sinking her voice to what she imagined to be an impressive whisper, though it rather resembled a hoarse, excited squeak, 'Mr Penricarde has just begun to pay attentions to Jessie. Slight at first, but now unmistakable. I was a fool not to have seen it sooner. Yesterday, at the Rectory garden party, he asked her what her favourite flowers were, and she told him carnations, and today a whole stack of carnations has arrived, clove and malmaison and lovely dark red ones, regular exhibition blooms, and a box of chocolates that he must have got on purpose from London. And he's asked her to go round the links with him tomorrow. And now, just at this critical moment, Toby has sold him that animal. It's a calamity!'

'But you've been trying to get the horse off your hands for years,' said Clovis.

'I've got a houseful of daughters,' said Mrs Mullet, 'and I've been trying—well, not to get them off my hands, of course, but a husband or two wouldn't be amiss among the lot of them; there are six of them, you know.'

'I don't know,' said Clovis, 'I've never counted, but I expect you're right as to the number; mothers generally know these things.'

'And now,' continued Mrs Mullet, in her tragic whisper, 'when there's a rich husband-in-prospect imminent on the horizon Toby goes and sells him that miserable animal. It will probably kill him if he tries to ride it; anyway it will kill any affection he might have felt towards any member of our family. What is to be done? We can't very well ask to have the horse back; you see, we praised it up like anything when we thought there was a chance of his buying it, and said it was just the animal to suit him.'

'Couldn't you steal it out of his stable and send it to grass at some farm miles away?' suggested Clovis. 'Write "Votes for Women" on the stable door, and the thing would pass for a Suffragette outrage. No one who knew the horse could possibly suspect you of wanting to get it back again.'

'Every newspaper in the country would ring with the affair,' said Mrs Mullet; 'can't you imagine the headline, "Valuable

Hunter Stolen by Suffragettes"? The police would scour the countryside till they found the animal.'

'Well, Jessie must try and get it back from Penricarde on the plea that it's an old favourite. She can say it was only sold because the stable had to be pulled down under the terms of an old repairing lease, and that now it has been arranged that the stable is to stand for a couple of years longer.'

'It sounds a queer proceeding to ask for a horse back when you've just sold him,' said Mrs Mullet, 'but something must be done, and done at once. The man is not used to horses, and I believe I told him it was as quiet as a lamb. After all, lambs go kicking and twisting about as if they were demented, don't they?'

'The lamb has an entirely unmerited character for sedateness,' agreed Clovis.

Jessie came back from the golf links next day in a state of mingled elation and concern.

'It's all right about the proposal,' she announced, 'he came out with it at the sixth hole. I said I must have time to think it over. I accepted him at the seventh.'

'My dear,' said her mother, 'I think a little more maidenly reserve and hesitation would have been advisable, as you've known him so short a time. You might have waited till the ninth hole.'

'The seventh is a very long hole,' said Jessie; 'besides, the tension was putting us both off our game. By the time we'd got to the ninth hole we'd settled lots of things. The honeymoon is to be spent in Corsica, with perhaps a flying visit to Naples if we feel like it, and a week in London to wind up with. Two of his nieces are to be asked to be bridesmaids, so with our lot there will be seven, which is rather a lucky number. You are to wear your pearl grey, with any amount of Honiton lace jabbed into it. By the way, he's coming over this evening to ask your consent to the whole affair. So far all's well, but about the Brogue it's a different matter. I told him the legend about the stable, and how keen we were about buying the horse back, but he seems equally keen on keeping it. He said he must have horse exercise now that he's living in the country, and he's going to start riding tomorrow. He's ridden a few times in the Row on an animal that was accustomed to carry octogenarians and people undergoing rest cures, and that's about all his experience in the saddle—oh, and he rode a pony once in Norfolk, when he was fifteen and the pony twenty-four; and tomorrow he's going to ride the Brogue! I shall be a widow before I'm married, and I do so want to see what Corsica's like; it looks so silly on the map.'

Clovis was sent for in haste, and the developments of the situation put before him.

'Nobody can ride that animal with any safety,' said Mrs Mullet, 'except Toby, and he knows by long experience what it is going to shy at, and manages to swerve at the same time.'

'I did hint to Mr Penricarde—to Vincent, I should say—that the Brogue didn't like white gates,' said Jessie.

'White gates!' exclaimed Mrs Mullet; 'did you mention what effect a pig has on him? He'll have to go past Lockyer's farm to get to the high road, and there's sure to be a pig or two grunting about in the lane.'

'He's taken rather a dislike to turkeys lately,' said Toby.

'It's obvious that Penricarde mustn't be allowed to go out on that animal,' said Clovis, 'at least not till Jessie has married him, and tired of him. I tell you what: ask him to a picnic tomorrow, starting at an early hour; he's not the sort to go out for a ride before breakfast. The day after I'll get the rector to drive him over to Crowleigh before lunch, to see the new cottage hospital they're building there. The Brogue will be standing idle in the stable and Toby can offer to exercise it; then it can pick up a stone or something of the sort and go conveniently lame. If you hurry on the wedding a bit the lameness fiction can be kept up till the ceremony is safely over.'

Mrs Mullet belonged to an emotional race, and she kissed Clovis.

It was nobody's fault that the rain came down in torrents the next morning, making a picnic a fantastic impossibility. It was also nobody's fault, but sheer ill-luck, that the weather cleared up sufficiently in the afternoon to tempt Mr Penricarde to make his first essay with the Brogue. They did

not get as far as the pigs at Lockyer's farm; the rectory gate
was painted a dull unobtrusive green, but it had been white a
year or two ago, and the Brogue never forgot that he had been
in the habit of making a violent curtsey, a back-pedal and a
swerve at this particular point of the road. Subsequently, there
being apparently no further call on his services, he broke his
way into the rectory orchard, where he found a hen turkey in
a coop; later visitors to the orchard found the coop almost
intact, but very little left of the turkey.

Mr Penricarde, a little stunned and shaken, and suffering from a bruised knee and some minor damages, good-
naturedly ascribed the accident to his own inexperience with
horses and country roads, and allowed Jessie to nurse him
back into complete recovery and golf-fitness within something
less than a week.

In the list of wedding presents which the local newspaper
published a fortnight or so later appeared the following item:

'Brown saddle-horse, "The Brogue", bridegroom's gift to
bride.'

'Which shows,' said Toby Mullet, 'that he knew nothing.'

'Or else,' said Clovis, 'that he has a very pleasing wit.'

THE OPEN WINDOW

'My aunt will be down presently, Mr Nuttel,' said a very self-
possessed young lady of fifteen; 'in the meantime you must try
and put up with me.'

Framton Nuttel endeavoured to say the correct something
which should duly flatter the niece of the moment without
unduly discounting the aunt that was to come. Privately he
doubted more than ever whether these formal visits on a
succession of total strangers would do much towards helping
the nerve cure which he was supposed to be undergoing.

'I know how it will be,' his sister had said when he was
preparing to migrate to this rural retreat; 'you will bury yourself down there and not speak to a living soul, and your nerves
will be worse than ever from moping. I shall just give you

letters of introduction to all the people I know there. Some of them, as far as I can remember, were quite nice.'

Framton wondered whether Mrs Sappleton, the lady to whom he was presenting one of the letters of introduction, came into the nice division.

'Do you know many of the people round here?' asked the niece, when she judged that they had had sufficient silent communion.

'Hardly a soul,' said Framton. 'My sister was staying here, at the rectory, you know, some four years ago, and she gave me letters of introduction to some of the people here.'

He made the last statement in a tone of distinct regret.

'Then you know practically nothing about my aunt?' pursued the self-possessed young lady.

'Only her name and address,' admitted the caller. He was wondering whether Mrs Sappleton was in the married or widowed state. An undefinable something about the room seemed to suggest masculine habitation.

'Her great tragedy happened just three years ago,' said the child; 'that would be since your sister's time.'

'Her tragedy?' asked Framton; somehow in this restful country spot tragedies seemed out of place.

'You may wonder why we keep that window wide open on an October afternoon,' said the niece, indicating a large French window that opened on to a lawn.

'It is quite warm for the time of the year,' said Framton; 'but has that window got anything to do with the tragedy?'

'Out through that window, three years ago to a day, her husband and her two young brothers went off for their day's shooting. They never came back. In crossing the moor to their favourite snipe-shooting ground they were all three engulfed in a treacherous piece of bog. It had been that dreadful wet summer, you know, and places that were safe in other years gave way suddenly without warning. Their bodies were never recovered. That was the dreadful part of it.' Here the child's voice lost its self-possessed note and became falteringly human. 'Poor aunt always thinks that they will come back some day, they and the little brown spaniel that was lost with them, and walk in at that window just as they used to do. That is why the window is kept open every evening till it is quite dusk. Poor dear aunt, she has often told me how they went out, her husband with his white waterproof coat over his arm, and Ronnie, her youngest brother, singing, "Bertie, why do you bound?" as he always did to tease her, because she said it got on her nerves. Do you know, sometimes on still, quiet evenings like this, I almost get a creepy feeling that they will all walk in through that window—'

She broke off with a little shudder. It was a relief to Framton when the aunt bustled into the room with a whirl of apologies for being late in making her appearance.

'I hope Vera has been amusing you?' she said.

'She has been very interesting,' said Framton.

'I hope you don't mind the open window,' said Mrs Sappleton briskly; 'my husband and brothers will be home directly from shooting, and they always come in this way. They've been out for snipe in the marshes today, so they'll make a fine mess over my poor carpets. So like you men-folk, isn't it?'

She rattled on cheerfully about the shooting and the scarcity of birds, and the prospects for duck in the winter. To Framton, it was all purely horrible. He made a desperate but only partially successful effort to turn the talk on to a less ghastly topic; he was conscious that his hostess was giving him only a fragment of her attention, and her eyes were constantly straying past him to the open window and the lawn beyond. It was certainly an unfortunate coincidence that he should have paid his visit on this tragic anniversary.

'The doctors agree in ordering me complete rest, an absence of mental excitement, and avoidance of anything in the nature of violent physical exercise,' announced Framton, who laboured under the tolerably wide-spread delusion that total strangers and chance acquaintances are hungry for the least detail of one's ailments and infirmities, their cause and cure. 'On the matter of diet they are not so much in agreement,' he continued.

'No?' said Mrs Sappleton, in a voice which only replaced a yawn at the last moment. Then she suddenly brightened into alert attention—but not to what Framton was saying.

'Here they are at last!' she cried. 'Just in time for tea, and don't they look as if they were muddy up to the eyes!'

Framton shivered slightly and turned towards the niece with a look intended to convey sympathetic comprehension. The child was staring out through the open window with dazed horror in her eyes. In a chill shock of nameless fear Framton swung round in his seat and looked in the same direction.

In the deepening twilight three figures were walking across the lawn towards the window; they all carried guns under their arms, and one of them was additionally burdened with a white coat hung over his shoulders. A tired brown spaniel kept close at their heels. Noiselessly they neared the house, and then a hoarse young voice chanted out of the dusk: 'I said, Bertie, why do you bound?'

Framton grabbed wildly at his stick and hat; the hall-door, the gravel-drive, and the front gate were dimly noted stages in his headlong retreat. A cyclist coming along the road had to run into the hedge to avoid imminent collision.

'Here we are, my dear,' said the bearer of the white mackintosh, coming in through the window; 'fairly muddy, but most of it's dry. Who was that who bolted out as we came up?'

'A most extraordinary man, a Mr Nuttel,' said Mrs Sappleton; 'could only talk about his illnesses, and dashed off without a word of good-bye or apology when you arrived. One would think he had seen a ghost.'

'I expect it was the spaniel,' said the niece calmly; 'he told me he had a horror of dogs. He was once hunted into a cemetery somewhere on the banks of the Ganges by a pack of pariah dogs, and had to spend the night in a newly dug grave with the creatures snarling and grinning and foaming just above him. Enough to make any one lose their nerve.'

Romance at short notice was her speciality.

THE COBWEB

THE farmhouse kitchen probably stood where it did as a matter of accident or haphazard choice; yet its situation might have been planned by a master-strategist in farmhouse architecture. Dairy and poultry-yard, and herb garden, and all the busy places of the farm seemed to lead by easy access into its wide flagged haven, where there was room for everything and where muddy boots left traces that were easily swept away. And yet, for all that it stood so well in the centre of human bustle, its long, latticed window, with the wide window-seat, built into an embrasure beyond the huge fireplace, looked out on a wild spreading view of hill and heather and wooded combe. The window nook made almost a little room in itself, quite the pleasantest room in the farm as far as situation and capabilities went. Young Mrs Ladbruk, whose husband had just come into the farm by way of inheritance, cast covetous eyes on this snug corner, and her fingers itched to make it bright and cozy with chintz curtains and bowls of flowers, and a shelf or two of old china. The musty farm parlour, looking out to a prim, cheerless garden imprisoned within high, blank walls, was not a room that lent itself readily either to comfort or decoration.

'When we are more settled I shall work wonders in the way of making the kitchen habitable,' said the young woman to her occasional visitors. There was an unspoken wish in those words, a wish which was unconfessed as well as unspoken. Emma Ladbruk was the mistress of the farm; jointly with her husband she might have her say, and to a certain extent her way, in ordering its affairs. But she was not mistress of the kitchen.

On one of the shelves of an old dresser, in company with chipped sauce-boats, pewter jugs, cheese-graters, and paid bills, rested a worn and ragged Bible, on whose front page was the record, in faded ink, of a baptism dated ninety-four years ago. 'Martha Crale' was the name written on that yellow page. The yellow, wrinkled old dame who hobbled and muttered about the kitchen, looking like a dead autumn leaf

which the winter winds still pushed hither and thither, had
once been Martha Crale; for seventy odd years she had been
Martha Mountjoy. For longer than any one could remember
she had pattered to and fro between oven and wash-house and
dairy, and out to chicken-run and garden, grumbling and
muttering and scolding, but working unceasingly. Emma
Ladbruk, of whose coming she took as little notice as she
would of a bee wandering in at a window on a summer's day,
used at first to watch her with a kind of frightened curiosity.
She was so old and so much a part of the place, it was difficult
to think of her exactly as a living thing. Old Shep, the white-
nozzled, stiff-limbed collie, waiting for his time to die, seemed
almost more human than the withered, dried-up old woman.
He had been a riotous, roystering puppy, mad with the joy of
life, when she was already a tottering, hobbling dame; now he
was just a blind, breathing carcase, nothing more, and she still
worked with frail energy, still swept and baked and washed,
fetched and carried. If there were something in these wise old
dogs that did not perish utterly with death, Emma used to
think to herself, what generations of ghost-dogs there must be
out on those hills, that Martha had reared and fed and tended
and spoken a last good-bye word to in that old kitchen. And
what memories she must have of human generations that had
passed away in her time. It was difficult for any one, let alone
a stranger like Emma, to get her to talk of the days that had
been; her shrill, quavering speech was of doors that had
been left unfastened, pails that had got mislaid, calves whose
feeding-time was overdue, and the various little faults and
lapses that chequer a farmhouse routine. Now and again,
when election time came round, she would unstore her recollections of the old names round which the fight had waged in
the days gone by. There had been a Palmerston, that had been
a name down Tiverton way; Tiverton was not a far journey as
the crow flies, but to Martha it was almost a foreign country.
Later there had been Northcotes and Aclands, and many other
newer names that she had forgotten; the names changed, but
it was always Libruls and Toories, Yellows and Blues. And
they always quarrelled and shouted as to who was right and

who was wrong. The one they quarrelled about most was a fine old gentleman with an angry face—she had seen his picture on the walls. She had seen it on the floor too, with a rotten apple squashed over it, for the farm had changed its politics from time to time. Martha had never been on one side or the other; none of 'they' had ever done the farm a stroke of good. Such was her sweeping verdict, given with all a peasant's distrust of the outside world.

When the half-frightened curiosity had somewhat faded away, Emma Ladbruk was uncomfortably conscious of another feeling towards the old woman. She was a quaint old tradition, lingering about the place, she was part and parcel of the farm itself, she was something at once pathetic and picturesque—but she was dreadfully in the way. Emma had come to the farm full of plans for little reforms and improvements, in part the result of training in the newest ways and methods, in part the outcome of her own ideas and fancies. Reforms in the kitchen region, if those deaf ears could have been induced to give them even a hearing, would have met with short shrift and scornful rejection, and the kitchen region spread over the zone of dairy and market business and half the work of the household. Emma, with the latest science of dead-poultry dressing at her fingertips, sat by, an unheeded watcher, while old Martha trussed the chickens for the market-stall as she had trussed them for nearly fourscore years—all leg and no breast. And the hundred hints anent effective cleaning and labour-lightening and the things that make for wholesomeness which the young woman was ready to impart or to put into action dropped away into nothingness before that wan, muttering, unheeding presence. Above all, the coveted window corner, that was to be a dainty, cheerful oasis in the gaunt old kitchen, stood now choked and lumbered with a litter of odds and ends that Emma, for all her nominal authority, would not have dared or cared to displace; over them seemed to be spun the protection of something that was like a human cobweb. Decidedly Martha was in the way. It would have been an unworthy meanness to have wished to see the span of that brave old life shortened by a few paltry months, but as the days sped by Emma was conscious that the wish was there, disowned though it might be, lurking at the back of her mind.

She felt the meanness of the wish come over her with a qualm of self-reproach one day when she came into the kitchen and found an unaccustomed state of things in that usually busy quarter. Old Martha was not working. A basket of corn was on the floor by her side, and out in the yard the poultry were beginning to clamour a protest of overdue feeding-time. But Martha sat huddled in a shrunken bunch on the window seat, looking out with her dim old eyes as though she saw something stranger than the autumn landscape.

'Is anything the matter, Martha?' asked the young woman.

''Tis death, 'tis death a-coming,' answered the quavering voice; 'I knew 'twere coming. I knew it. 'Tweren't for nothing that old Shep's been howling all morning. An' last night I heard the screech-owl give the death-cry, and there were something white as run across the yard yesterday; 'tweren't a cat nor a stoat, 'twere something. The fowls knew 'twere something; they all drew off to one side. Ay, there's been warnings. I knew it were a-coming.'

The young woman's eyes clouded with pity. The old thing sitting there so white and shrunken had once been a merry, noisy child, playing about in lanes and hay-lofts and farm-house garrets; that had been eighty odd years ago, and now she was just a frail old body cowering under the approaching chill of the death that was coming at last to take her. It was not probable that much could be done for her, but Emma hastened away to get assistance and counsel. Her husband, she knew, was down at a tree-felling some little distance off, but she might find some other intelligent soul who knew the old woman better than she did. The farm, she soon found out, had that faculty common to farmyards of swallowing up and losing its human population. The poultry followed her in interested fashion, and swine grunted interrogations at her from behind the bars of their sties, but barnyard and rickyard, orchard and stables and dairy, gave no reward to her search. Then, as she retraced her steps towards the kitchen, she came suddenly on her cousin, young Mr Jim, as every one called him, who divided his time between amateur horse-dealing, rabbit-shooting, and flirting with the farm maids.

'I'm afraid old Martha is dying,' said Emma. Jim was not the sort of person to whom one had to break news gently.

'Nonsense,' he said; 'Martha means to live to a hundred. She told me so, and she'll do it.'

'She may be actually dying at this moment, or it may just be the beginning of the break-up', persisted Emma, with a feeling of contempt for the slowness and dullness of the young man.

A grin spread over his good-natured features.

'It don't look like it,' he said, nodding towards the yard. Emma turned to catch the meaning of his remark. Old Martha stood in the middle of a mob of poultry scattering handfuls of grain around her. The turkey-cock, with the bronzed sheen of his feathers and the purple-red of his wattles, the game-cock with the glowing metallic lustre of his Eastern plumage, the hens, with their ochres and buffs and umbers and their scarlet combs, and the drakes, with their bottle-green heads, made a medley of rich colour, in the centre of which the old woman looked like a withered stalk standing amid the riotous growth of gaily-hued flowers. But she threw the grain deftly amid the wilderness of beaks, and her quavering voice carried as far as the two people who were watching her. She was still harping on the theme of death coming to the farm.

'I knew 'twere a-coming. There's been signs an' warnings.'

'Who's dead, then, old Mother?' called out the young man.

' 'Tis young Mister Ladbruk,' she shrilled back; 'they've just a-carried his body in. Run out of the way of a tree that was coming down an' ran hisself on to an iron post. Dead when they picked un up. Ay, I knew 'twere coming.'

And she turned to fling a handful of barley at a belated group of guinea-fowl that came racing toward her.

The farm was a family property, and passed to the rabbit-shooting cousin as the next-of-kin. Emma Ladbruk drifted out of its history as a bee that had wandered in at an open window might flit its way out again. On a cold grey morning she stood waiting with her boxes already stowed in the farm cart, till the last of the market produce should be ready, for the train she was to catch was of less importance than the chickens and butter and eggs that were to be offered for sale. From where she stood she could see an angle of the long latticed window that was to have been cozy with curtains and gay with bowls of flowers. Into her mind came the thought that for months, perhaps for years, long after she had been utterly forgotten, a white, unheeding face would be seen peering out through those latticed panes, and a weak muttering voice would be heard quavering up and down those flagged passages. She made her way to a narrow barred casement that opened into the farm larder. Old Martha was standing at a table trussing a pair of chickens for the market stall as she had trussed them for nearly fourscore years.

THE SCHARTZ-METTERKLUME METHOD

LADY CARLOTTA stepped out on to the platform of the small wayside station and took a turn or two up and down its uninteresting length, to kill time till the train should be pleased to proceed on its way. Then, in the roadway beyond, she saw a horse struggling with a more than ample load, and a carter of the sort that seems to bear a sullen hatred against the animal that helps him to earn a living. Lady Carlotta promptly betook her to the roadway, and put rather a different complexion on the struggle. Certain of her acquaintances were wont to give her plentiful admonition as to the undesirability of interfering on behalf of a distressed animal, such interference being 'none of her business'. Only once had she put the doctrine of non-interference into practice, when one of its most eloquent exponents had been besieged for nearly three hours in a small and extremely uncomfortable may-tree by an angry boar-pig, while Lady Carlotta, on the other side of the fence, had proceeded with the water-colour sketch she was engaged on, and refused to interfere between the boar and his prisoner. It is to be feared that she lost the friendship of the ultimately rescued lady. On this occasion she merely lost the train, which gave way to the first sign of impatience it had shown throughout the journey, and steamed off without her. She bore the desertion with philosophical indifference; her friends and relations were thoroughly well used to the fact of her luggage arriving without her. She wired a vague non-committal message to her destination to say that she was coming on 'by another train'. Before she had time to think what her next move might be she was confronted by an imposingly attired lady, who seemed to be taking a prolonged mental inventory of her clothes and looks.

'You must be Miss Hope, the governess I've come to meet,' said the apparition, in a tone that admitted of very little argument.

'Very well, if I must I must,' said Lady Carlotta to herself with dangerous meekness.

'I am Mrs Quabarl,' continued the lady; 'and where, pray, is your luggage?'

'It's gone astray,' said the alleged governess, falling in with the excellent rule of life that the absent are always to blame; the luggage had, in point of fact, behaved with perfect correctitude. 'I've just telegraphed about it,' she added, with a nearer approach to truth.

'How provoking,' said Mrs Quabarl; 'these railway companies are so careless. However, my maid can lend you things for the night,' and she led the way to her car.

During the drive to the Quabarl mansion Lady Carlotta was impressively introduced to the nature of the charge that had been thrust upon her; she learned that Claude and Wilfrid were delicate, sensitive young people, that Irene had the artistic temperament highly developed, and that Viola was something or other else of a mould equally common-place among children of that class and type in the twentieth century.

'I wish them not only to be *taught*,' said Mrs Quabarl, 'but *interested* in what they learn. In their history lessons, for instance, you must try to make them feel that they are being introduced to the life-stories of men and women who really lived, not merely committing a mass of names and dates to memory. French, of course, I shall expect you to talk at mealtimes several days in the week.'

'I shall talk French four days of the week and Russian in the remaining three.'

'Russian? My dear Miss Hope, no one in the house speaks or understands Russian.'

'That will not embarrass me in the least,' said Lady Carlotta coldly.

Mrs Quabarl, to use a colloquial expression, was knocked off her perch. She was one of those imperfectly self-assured individuals who are magnificent and autocratic as long as they are not seriously opposed. The least show of unexpected resistance goes a long way towards rendering them cowed and apologetic. When the new governess failed to express wondering admiration of the large newly purchased and expensive car, and lightly alluded to the superior advantages of one or two makes which had just been put on the market, the discomfiture of her patroness became almost abject. Her feelings were those which might have animated a general of ancient warfaring days, on beholding his heaviest battle-elephant ignominiously driven off the field by slingers and javelin throwers.

At dinner that evening, although reinforced by her husband, who usually duplicated her opinions and lent her moral support generally, Mrs Quabarl regained none of her lost ground. The governess not only helped herself well and truly to wine, but held forth with considerable show of critical knowledge on various vintage matters, concerning which the Quabarls were in no wise able to pose as authorities. Previous governesses had limited their conversation on the wine topic to a respectful and doubtless sincere expression of a preference for water. When this one went as far as to recommend a wine firm in whose hands you could not go very far wrong Mrs Quabarl thought it time to turn the conversation into more usual channels.

'We got very satisfactory references about you from Canon Teep,' she observed; 'a very estimable man, I should think.'

'Drinks like a fish and beats his wife, otherwise a very lovable character,' said the governess imperturbably.

'My *dear* Miss Hope! I trust you are exaggerating,' exclaimed the Quabarls in unison.

'One must in justice admit that there is some provocation,' continued the romancer. 'Mrs Teep is quite the most irritating bridge-player that I have ever sat down with; her leads and declarations would condone a certain amount of brutality in her partner, but to souse her with the contents of the only soda-water syphon in the house on a Sunday afternoon, when one couldn't get another, argues an indifference to the comfort of others which I cannot altogether overlook. You may think me hasty in my judgments, but it was practically on account of the syphon incident that I left.'

'We will talk of this some other time,' said Mrs Quabarl hastily.

'I shall never allude to it again,' said the governess with decision.

Mr Quabarl made a welcome diversion by asking what studies the new instructress proposed to inaugurate on the morrow.

'History to begin with,' she informed him.

'Ah, history,' he observed sagely; 'now in teaching them history you must take care to interest them in what they learn. You must make them feel that they are being introduced to the life-stories of men and women who really lived—'

'I've told her all that,' interposed Mrs Quabarl.

'I teach history on the Schartz-Metterklume method,' said the governess loftily.

'Ah, yes,' said her listeners, thinking it expedient to assume an acquaintance at least with the name.

'What are you children doing out here?' demanded Mrs Quabarl the next morning, on finding Irene sitting rather glumly at the head of the stairs, while her sister was perched in an attitude of depressed discomfort on the window-seat behind her, with a wolf-skin rug almost covering her.

'We are having a history lesson,' came the unexpected reply. 'I am supposed to be Rome, and Viola up there is the she-wolf; not a real wolf, but the figure of one that the Romans used to set store by—I forget why. Claude and Wilfrid have gone to fetch the shabby women.'

'The shabby women?'

'Yes, they've got to carry them off. They didn't want to, but

Miss Hope got one of father's fives-bats and said she'd give them a number nine spanking if they didn't, so they've gone to do it.'

A loud, angry screaming from the direction of the lawn drew Mrs Quabarl thither in hot haste, fearful lest the threatened castigation might even now be in process of infliction. The outcry, however, came principally from the two small daughters of the lodge-keeper, who were being hauled and pushed towards the house by the panting and dishevelled Claude and Wilfrid, whose task was rendered even more arduous by the incessant, if not very effectual, attacks of the captured maidens' small brother. The governess, fives-bat in hand, sat negligently on the stone balustrade, presiding over the scene with the cold impartiality of a Goddess of Battle. A furious and repeated chorus of 'I'll tell muvver' rose from the lodge children, but the lodge-mother, who was hard of hearing, was for the moment immersed in the preoccupation of her washtub. After an apprehensive glance in the direction of the lodge (the good woman was gifted with the highly militant temper which is sometimes the privilege of deafness) Mrs Quabarl flew indignantly to the rescue of the struggling captives.

'Wilfrid! Claude! Let those children go at once. Miss Hope, what on earth is the meaning of this scene?'

'Early Roman history; the Sabine women, don't you know? It's the Schartz-Metterklume method to make children understand history by acting it themselves; fixes it in their memory, you know. Of course, if, thanks to your interference, your boys go through life thinking that the Sabine women ultimately escaped, I really cannot be held responsible.'

'You may be very clever and modern, Miss Hope,' said Mrs Quabarl firmly, 'but I should like you to leave here by the next train. Your luggage will be sent after you as soon as it arrives.'

'I'm not certain exactly where I shall be for the next few days,' said the dismissed instructress of youth; 'you might keep my luggage till I wire my address. There are only a couple of trunks and some golf-clubs and a leopard cub.'

'A leopard cub!' gasped Mrs Quabarl. Even in her depar-

ture this extraordinary person seemed destined to leave a trail
of embarrassment behind her.

'Well, it's rather left off being a cub; it's more than half-
grown, you know. A fowl every day and a rabbit on Sundays
is what it usually gets. Raw beef makes it too excitable. Don't
trouble about getting the car for me, I'm rather inclined for
a walk.'

And Lady Carlotta strode out of the Quabarl horizon.

The advent of the genuine Miss Hope, who had made a
mistake as to the day on which she was due to arrive, caused
a turmoil which that good lady was quite unused to inspiring.
Obviously the Quabarl family had been woefully befooled,
but a certain amount of relief came with the knowledge.

'How tiresome for you, dear Carlotta,' said her hostess,
when the overdue guest ultimately arrived; 'how very tiresome
losing your train and having to stop overnight in a strange
place.'

'Oh, dear, no,' said Lady Carlotta; 'not at all tiresome—
for me.'

DUSK

NORMAN GORTSBY sat on a bench in the Park, with his back
to a strip of bush-planted sward, fenced by the park railings,
and the Row fronting him across a wide stretch of carriage
drive. Hyde Park Corner, with its rattle and hoot of traffic, lay
immediately to his right. It was some thirty minutes past six
on an early March evening, and dusk had fallen heavily over
the scene, dusk mitigated by some faint moonlight and many
street lamps. There was a wide emptiness over road and
sidewalk, and yet there were many unconsidered figures
moving silently through the half-light or dotted unobtrusively
on bench and chair, scarcely to be distinguished from the
shadowed gloom in which they sat.

The scene pleased Gortsby and harmonized with his present
mood. Dusk, to his mind, was the hour of the defeated. Men
and women, who had fought and lost, who hid their fallen

fortunes and dead hopes as far as possible from the scrutiny of
the curious, came forth in this hour of gloaming, when their
shabby clothes and bowed shoulders and unhappy eyes might
pass unnoticed, or, at any rate, unrecognized.

> A king that is conquered must see strange looks,
> So bitter a thing is the heart of man.

The wanderers in the dusk did not choose to have strange
looks fasten on them, therefore they came out in this bat-
fashion, taking their pleasure sadly in a pleasure-ground that
had emptied of its rightful occupants. Beyond the sheltering
screen of bushes and palings came a realm of brilliant lights
and noisy, rushing traffic. A blazing, many-tiered stretch of
windows shone through the dusk and almost dispersed it,
marking the haunts of those other people, who held their own
in life's struggle, or at any rate had not had to admit failure.
So Gortsby's imagination pictured things as he sat on his
bench in the almost deserted walk. He was in the mood to
count himself among the defeated. Money troubles did not
press on him; had he so wished he could have strolled into the
thoroughfares of light and noise, and taken his place among
the jostling ranks of those who enjoyed prosperity or strug-
gled for it. He had failed in a more subtle ambition, and for
the moment he was heart sore and disillusionized, and not
disinclined to take a certain cynical pleasure in observing and
labelling his fellow wanderers as they went their ways in the
dark stretches between the lamp-lights.

On the bench by his side sat an elderly gentleman with a
drooping air of defiance that was probably the remaining
vestige of self-respect in an individual who had ceased to defy
successfully anybody or anything. His clothes could scarcely
be called shabby, at least they passed muster in the half-light,
but one's imagination could not have pictured the wearer
embarking on the purchase of a half-crown box of chocolates
or laying out ninepence on a carnation buttonhole. He belonged unmistakably to that forlorn orchestra to whose piping
no one dances; he was one of the world's lamenters who
induces no responsive weeping. As he rose to go Gortsby
imagined him returning to a home circle where he was

snubbed and of no account, or to some bleak lodging where his ability to pay a weekly bill was the beginning and end of the interest he inspired. His retreating figure vanished slowly into the shadows, and his place on the bench was taken almost immediately by a young man, fairly well dressed but scarcely more cheerful of mien than his predecessor. As if to emphasize the fact that the world went badly with him the new-comer unburdened himself of an angry and very audible expletive as he flung himself into the seat.

'You don't seem in a very good temper,' said Gortsby, judging that he was expected to take due notice of the demonstration.

The young man turned to him with a look of disarming frankness which put him instantly on his guard.

'You wouldn't be in a good temper if you were in the fix I'm in,' he said; 'I've done the silliest thing I've ever done in my life.'

'Yes?' said Gortsby dispassionately.

'Came up this afternoon, meaning to stay at the Patagonian Hotel in Berkshire Square,' continued the young man; 'when I got there I found it had been pulled down some weeks ago and a cinema theatre run up on the site. The taxi driver recommended me to another hotel some way off and I went there. I just sent a letter to my people, giving them the address, and then I went out to buy some soap—I'd forgotten to pack any and I hate using hotel soap. Then I strolled about a bit, had a drink at a bar and looked at the shops, and when I came to turn my steps back to the hotel I suddenly realized that I didn't remember its name or even what street it was in. There's a nice predicament for a fellow who hasn't any friends or connections in London! Of course I can wire to my people for the address, but they won't have got my letter till to-morrow; meantime I'm without any money, came out with about a shilling on me, which went in buying the soap and getting the drink, and here I am, wandering about with twopence in my pocket and nowhere to go for the night.'

There was an eloquent pause after the story had been told. 'I suppose you think I've spun you rather an impossible yarn,' said the young man presently, with a suggestion of resentment in his voice.

'Not at all impossible,' said Gortsby judicially; 'I remember doing exactly the same thing once in a foreign capital, and on that occasion there were two of us, which made it more remarkable. Luckily we remembered that the hotel was on a sort of canal, and when we struck the canal we were able to find our way back to the hotel.'

The youth brightened at the reminiscence. 'In a foreign city I wouldn't mind so much,' he said; 'one could go to one's Consul and get the requisite help from him. Here in one's own land one is far more derelict if one gets into a fix. Unless I can find some decent chap to swallow my story and lend me some money I seem likely to spend the night on the Embankment. I'm glad, anyhow, that you don't think the story outrageously improbable.'

He threw a good deal of warmth into the last remark, as though perhaps to indicate his hope that Gortsby did not fall far short of the requisite decency.

'Of course,' said Gortsby slowly, 'the weak point of your story is that you can't produce the soap.'

The young man sat forward hurriedly, felt rapidly in the pockets of his overcoat, and then jumped to his feet.

'I must have lost it,' he muttered angrily.

'To lose an hotel and a cake of soap on one afternoon suggests wilful carelessness,' said Gortsby, but the young man scarcely waited to hear the end of the remark. He flitted away down the path, his head held high, with an air of somewhat jaded jauntiness.

'It was a pity,' mused Gortsby; 'the going out to get one's own soap was the one convincing touch in the whole story, and yet it was just that little detail that brought him to grief. If he had had the brilliant forethought to provide himself with a cake of soap, wrapped and sealed with all the solicitude of the chemist's counter, he would have been a genius in his particular line. In his particular line genius certainly consists of an infinite capacity for taking precautions.'

With that reflection Gortsby rose to go; as he did so an exclamation of concern escaped him. Lying on the ground by the side of the bench was a small oval packet, wrapped and sealed with the solicitude of a chemist's counter. It could be nothing else but a cake of soap, and it had evidently fallen out of the youth's overcoat pocket when he flung himself down on the seat. In another moment Gortsby was scudding along the dusk-shrouded path in anxious quest for a youthful figure in a light overcoat. He had nearly given up the search when he caught sight of the object of his pursuit standing irresolutely on the border of the carriage drive, evidently uncertain whether to strike across the Park or make for the bustling pavements of Knightsbridge. He turned round sharply with an air of defensive hostility when he found Gortsby hailing him.

'The important witness to the genuineness of your story has turned up,' said Gortsby, holding out the cake of soap; 'it must have slid out of your overcoat pocket when you sat down on the seat. I saw it on the ground after you left. You must excuse my disbelief, but appearances were really rather against you, and now, as I appealed to the testimony of the soap I think I ought to abide by its verdict. If the loan of a sovereign is any good to you—'

The young man hastily removed all doubt on the subject by pocketing the coin.

'Here is my card with my address,' continued Gortsby; 'any day this week will do for returning the money, and here is the soap—don't lose it again; it's been a good friend to you.'

'Lucky thing your finding it,' said the youth, and then, with a catch in his voice, he blurted out a word or two of thanks and fled headlong in the direction of Knightsbridge.

'Poor boy, he as nearly as possible broke down,' said Gortsby to himself. 'I don't wonder either; the relief from his quandary must have been acute. It's a lesson to me not to be too clever in judging by circumstances.'

As Gortsby retraced his steps past the seat where the little drama had taken place he saw an elderly gentleman poking and peering beneath it and on all sides of it, and recognized his earlier fellow occupant.

'Have you lost anything, sir?' he asked.

'Yes, sir, a cake of soap.'

THE STALLED OX

THEOPHIL ESHLEY was an artist by profession, a cattle painter by force of environment. It is not to be supposed that he lived on a ranch or a dairy farm, in an atmosphere pervaded with horn and hoof, milking-stool, and branding-iron. His home was in a park-like, villa-dotted district that only just escaped the reproach of being suburban. On one side of his garden there abutted a small, picturesque meadow, in which an enterprising neighbour pastured some small picturesque cows of the Channel Island persuasion. At noonday in summertime the cows stood knee-deep in tall meadow-grass under the shade of a group of walnut trees, with the sunlight falling in dappled patches on their mouse-sleek coats. Eshley had conceived and executed a dainty picture of two reposeful milch-cows in a setting of walnut tree and meadow-grass and filtered sunbeam, and the Royal Academy had duly exposed the same on the walls of its Summer Exhibition. The Royal Academy encourages orderly, methodical habits in its children. Eshley had painted a successful and acceptable picture of cattle drowsing picturesquely under walnut trees, and as he had begun, so, of necessity, he went on. His 'Noontide Peace', a study of two dun cows under a walnut tree, was followed by 'A Mid-day Sanctuary', a study of a walnut tree, with two dun cows under it. In due succession there came 'Where the Gad-Flies Cease from Troubling', 'The Haven of the Herd', and 'A Dream in Dairyland', studies of walnut trees and dun cows. His two attempts to break away from his own tradition were signal failures: 'Turtle Doves Alarmed by Sparrow-hawk' and 'Wolves on the Roman Campagna' came back to his studio in the guise of abominable heresies, and Eshley climbed back into grace and the public gaze with 'A Shaded Nook Where Drowsy Milkers Dream'.

On a fine afternoon in late autumn he was putting some finishing touches to a study of meadow weeds when his neighbour, Adela Pingsford, assailed the outer door of his studio with loud peremptory knockings.

'There is an ox in my garden,' she announced, in explanation of the tempestuous intrusion.

'An ox,' said Eshley blankly, and rather fatuously; 'what kind of ox?'

'Oh, I don't know what kind,' snapped the lady. 'A common or garden ox, to use the slang expression. It is the garden part of it that I object to. My garden has just been put straight for the winter, and an ox roaming about in it won't improve matters. Besides, there are the chrysanthemums just coming into flower.'

'How did it get into the garden?' asked Eshley.

'I imagine it came in by the gate,' said the lady impatiently; 'it couldn't have climbed the walls, and I don't suppose any one dropped it from an aeroplane as a Bovril advertisement. The immediately important question is not how it got in, but how to get it out.'

'Won't it go?' said Eshley.

'If it was anxious to go,' said Adela Pingsford rather angrily, 'I should not have come here to chat with you about it. I'm practically all alone; the housemaid is having her afternoon out and the cook is lying down with an attack of neuralgia. Anything that I may have learned at school or in after life about how to remove a large ox from a small garden seems to have escaped from my memory now. All I could think of was that you were a near neighbour and a cattle painter, presumably more or less familiar with the subjects that you painted, and that you might be of some slight assistance. Possibly I was mistaken.'

'I paint dairy cows, certainly,' admitted Eshley, 'but I cannot claim to have had any experience in rounding up stray oxen. I've seen it done on a cinema film, of course, but there were always horses and lots of other accessories; besides, one never knows how much of those pictures are faked.'

Adela Pingsford said nothing, but led the way to her garden. It was normally a fair-sized garden, but it looked small in comparison with the ox, a huge mottled brute, dull red about the head and shoulders, passing to dirty white on the flanks and hind-quarters, with shaggy ears and large blood-shot eyes. It bore about as much resemblance to the dainty paddock heifers that Eshley was accustomed to paint as the chief of a Kurdish nomad clan would to a Japanese tea-shop girl. Eshley stood very near the gate while he studied the animal's appearance and demeanour. Adela Pingsford continued to say nothing.

'It's eating a chrysanthemum,' said Eshley at last, when the silence had become unbearable.

'How observant you are,' said Adela bitterly. 'You seem to notice everything. As a matter of fact, it has got six chrysanthemums in its mouth at the present moment.'

The necessity for doing something was becoming imperative. Eshley took a step or two in the direction of the animal, clapped his hands, and made noises of the 'Hish' and 'Shoo' variety. If the ox heard them it gave no outward indication of the fact.

'If any hens should ever stray into my garden,' said Adela, 'I should certainly send for you to frighten them out. You "shoo" beautifully. Meanwhile, do you mind trying to drive that ox away? That is a *Mademoiselle Louise Bichot* that he's begun on now,' she added in icy calm, as a glowing orange head was crushed into the huge munching mouth.

'Since you have been so frank about the variety of the chrysanthemum,' said Eshley, 'I don't mind telling you that this is an Ayrshire ox.'

The icy calm broke down; Adela Pingsford used language that sent the artist instinctively a few feet nearer to the ox. He picked up a pea-stick and flung it with some determination against the animal's mottled flanks. The operation of mashing *Mademoiselle Louise Bichot* into a petal salad was suspended for a long moment, while the ox gazed with concentrated inquiry at the stick-thrower. Adela gazed with equal concentration and more obvious hostility at the same focus. As the beast neither lowered its head nor stamped its feet Eshley ventured on another javelin exercise with another pea-stick. The ox seemed to realize at once that it was to go; it gave a hurried final pluck at the bed where the chrysanthemums had been, and strode swiftly up the garden. Eshley ran to head it towards the gate, but only succeeded in quickening its pace from a walk to a lumbering trot. With an air of inquiry, but with no real hesitation, it crossed the tiny strip of turf that the charitable called the croquet lawn, and pushed its way through the open French window into the morning-room. Some chrysanthemums and other autumn herbage stood about the room in vases, and the animal resumed its browsing operations; all the same, Eshley fancied that the beginnings of a hunted look had come into its eyes, a look that counselled respect. He discontinued his attempt to interfere with its choice of surroundings.

'Mr Eshley,' said Adela in a shaking voice, 'I asked you to drive that beast out of my garden, but I did not ask you to drive it into my house. If I must have it anywhere on the premises I prefer the garden to the morning-room.'

'Cattle drives are not in my line,' said Eshley; 'if I remember I told you so at the outset.'

'I quite agree,' retorted the lady, 'painting pretty pictures of pretty little cows is what you're suited for. Perhaps you'd like to do a nice sketch of that ox making itself at home in my morning-room?'

This time it seemed as if the worm had turned; Eshley began striding away.

'Where are you going?' screamed Adela.

'To fetch implements,' was the answer.

'Implements? I won't have you use a lasso. The room will be wrecked if there's a struggle.'

But the artist marched out of the garden. In a couple of minutes he returned, laden with easel, sketching-stool, and painting materials.

'Do you mean to say that you're going to sit quietly down and paint that brute while it's destroying my morning-room?' gasped Adela.

'It was your suggestion,' said Eshley, setting his canvas in position.

'I forbid it; I absolutely forbid it!' stormed Adela.

'I don't see what standing you have in the matter,' said the artist; 'you can hardly pretend that it's your ox, even by adoption.'

'You seem to forget that it's in my morning-room, eating my flowers,' came the raging retort.

'You seem to forget that the cook has neuralgia,' said Eshley; 'she may be just dozing off into a merciful sleep and your outcry will waken her. Consideration for others should be the guiding principle of people in our station of life.'

'The man is mad!' exclaimed Adela tragically. A moment later it was Adela herself who appeared to go mad. The ox had finished the vase-flowers and the cover of *Israel Kalisch*, and appeared to be thinking of leaving its rather restricted quarters. Eshley noticed its restlessness and promptly flung it some bunches of Virginia creeper leaves as an inducement to continue the sitting.

'I forget how the proverb runs,' he observed; 'something about "better a dinner of herbs than a stalled ox where hate is". We seem to have all the ingredients for the proverb ready to hand.'

'I shall go to the Public Library and get them to telephone for the police,' announced Adela, and, raging audibly, she departed.

Some minutes later the ox, awakening probably to the suspicion that oil cake and chopped mangold was waiting for it in some appointed byre, stepped with much precaution out of the morning-room, stared with grave inquiry at the no longer obtrusive and pea-stick-throwing human, and then lumbered heavily but swiftly out of the garden. Eshley packed up his tools and followed the animal's example and 'Larkdene' was left to neuralgia and the cook.

The episode was the turning-point in Eshley's artistic career. His remarkable picture, 'Ox in a Morning-room, Late Autumn', was one of the sensations and successes of the next Paris Salon, and when it was subsequently exhibited at Munich it was bought by the Bavarian Government, in the teeth of the spirited bidding of three meat-extract firms. From that moment his success was continuous and assured, and the Royal Academy was thankful, two years later, to give a conspicuous position on its walls to his large canvas 'Barbary Apes Wrecking a Boudoir'.

Eshley presented Adela Pingsford with a new copy of *Israel Kalisch*, and a couple of finely flowering plants of *Madame André Blusset*, but nothing in the nature of a real reconciliation has taken place between them.

THE STORY-TELLER

IT was a hot afternoon, and the railway carriage was correspondingly sultry, and the next stop was at Templecombe, nearly an hour ahead. The occupants of the carriage were a small girl, and a smaller girl, and a small boy. An aunt belonging to the children occupied one corner seat, and the further corner seat on the opposite side was occupied by a bachelor who was a stranger to their party, but the small girls and the small boy emphatically occupied the compartment. Both the aunt and the children were conversational in a limited, persistent way, reminding one of the attentions of a housefly that refused to be discouraged. Most of the aunt's remarks seemed to begin with 'Don't', and nearly all of the children's remarks began with 'Why?' The bachelor said nothing out loud.

'Don't, Cyril, don't,' exclaimed the aunt, as the small boy began smacking the cushions of the seat, producing a cloud of dust at each blow.

'Come and look out of the window,' she added.

The child moved reluctantly to the window. 'Why are those sheep being driven out of that field?' he asked.

'I expect they are being driven to another field where there is more grass,' said the aunt weakly.

'But there is lots of grass in that field,' protested the boy; 'there's nothing else but grass there. Aunt, there's lots of grass in that field.'

'Perhaps the grass in the other field is better,' suggested the aunt fatuously.

'Why is it better?' came the swift, inevitable question.

'Oh, look at those cows!' exclaimed the aunt. Nearly every field along the line had contained cows or bullocks, but she spoke as though she were drawing attention to a rarity.

'Why is the grass in the other field better?' persisted Cyril.

The frown on the bachelor's face was deepening to a scowl. He was a hard, unsympathetic man, the aunt decided in her mind. She was utterly unable to come to any satisfactory decision about the grass in the other field.

The smaller girl created a diversion by beginning to recite

'On the Road to Mandalay'. She only knew the first line, but she put her limited knowledge to the fullest possible use. She repeated the line over and over again in a dreamy but resolute and very audible voice; it seemed to the bachelor as though some one had had a bet with her that she could not repeat the line aloud two thousand times without stopping. Whoever it was who had made the wager was likely to lose his bet.

'Come over here and listen to a story,' said the aunt, when the bachelor had looked twice at her and once at the communication cord.

The children moved listlessly towards the aunt's end of the carriage. Evidently her reputation as a story-teller did not rank high in their estimation.

In a low, confidential voice, interrupted at frequent intervals by loud, petulant questions from her listeners, she began an unenterprising and deplorably uninteresting story about a little girl who was good, and made friends with every one on account of her goodness, and was finally saved from a mad bull by a number of rescuers who admired her moral character.

'Wouldn't they have saved her if she hadn't been good?' demanded the bigger of the small girls. It was exactly the question that the bachelor had wanted to ask.

'Well, yes,' admitted the aunt lamely, 'but I don't think they would have run quite so fast to her help if they had not liked her so much.'

'It's the stupidest story I've ever heard,' said the bigger of the small girls, with immense conviction.

'I didn't listen after the first bit, it was so stupid,' said Cyril.

The smaller girl made no actual comment on the story, but she had long ago recommenced a murmured repetition of her favourite line.

'You don't seem to be a success as a story-teller,' said the bachelor suddenly from his corner.

The aunt bristled in instant defence at this unexpected attack.

'It's a very difficult thing to tell stories that children can both understand and appreciate,' she said stiffly.

'I don't agree with you,' said the bachelor.

'Perhaps *you* would like to tell them a story,' was the aunt's retort.

'Tell us a story,' demanded the bigger of the small girls.

'Once upon a time,' began the bachelor, 'there was a little girl called Bertha, who was extraordinarily good.'

The children's momentarily-aroused interest began at once to flicker; all stories seemed dreadfully alike, no matter who told them.

'She did all that she was told, she was always truthful, she kept her clothes clean, ate milk puddings as though they were jam tarts, learned her lessons perfectly, and was polite in her manners.'

'Was she pretty?' asked the bigger of the small girls.

'Not as pretty as any of you,' said the bachelor, 'but she was horribly good.'

There was a wave of reaction in favour of the story; the word horrible in connection with goodness was a novelty that commended itself. It seemed to introduce a ring of truth that was absent from the aunt's tales of infant life.

'She was so good,' continued the bachelor, 'that she won several medals for goodness, which she always wore, pinned on to her dress. There was a medal for obedience, another medal for punctuality, and a third for good behaviour. They were large metal medals and they clicked against one another as she walked. No other child in the town where she lived had as many as three medals, so everybody knew that she must be an extra good child.'

'Horribly good,' quoted Cyril.

'Everybody talked about her goodness, and the Prince of the country got to hear about it, and he said that as she was so very good she might be allowed once a week to walk in his park, which was just outside the town. It was a beautiful park, and no children were ever allowed in it, so it was a great honour for Bertha to be allowed to go there.'

'Were there any sheep in the park?' demanded Cyril.

'No,' said the bachelor, 'there were no sheep.'

'Why weren't there any sheep?' came the inevitable question arising out of that answer.

The aunt permitted herself a smile, which might almost have been described as a grin.

'There were no sheep in the park,' said the bachelor, 'because the Prince's mother had once had a dream that her son would either be killed by a sheep or else by a clock falling on him. For that reason the Prince never kept a sheep in his park or a clock in his palace.'

The aunt suppressed a gasp of admiration.

'Was the Prince killed by a sheep or by a clock?' asked Cyril.

'He is still alive, so we can't tell whether the dream will come true,' said the bachelor unconcernedly; 'anyway, there were no sheep in the park, but there were lots of little pigs running all over the place.'

'What colour were they?'

'Black with white faces, white with black spots, black all over, grey with white patches, and some were white all over.'

The story-teller paused to let a full idea of the park's treasures sink into the children's imaginations; then he resumed:

'Bertha was rather sorry to find that there were no flowers in the park. She had promised her aunts, with tears in her eyes, that she would not pick any of the kind Prince's flowers, and she had meant to keep her promise, so of course it made her feel silly to find that there were no flowers to pick.'

'Why weren't there any flowers?'

'Because the pigs had eaten them all,' said the bachelor promptly. 'The gardeners had told the Prince that you couldn't have pigs and flowers, so he decided to have pigs and no flowers.'

There was a murmur of approval at the excellence of the Prince's decision; so many people would have decided the other way.

'There were lots of other delightful things in the park. There were ponds with gold and blue and green fish in them, and trees with beautiful parrots that said clever things at a moment's notice, and humming birds that hummed all the popular tunes of the day. Bertha walked up and down and enjoyed herself immensely, and thought to herself: "If I were not so extraordinarily good I should not have been allowed to come into this beautiful park and enjoy all that there is to be seen in it," and her three medals clinked against one another as she walked and helped to remind her how very good she really was. Just then an enormous wolf came prowling into the park to see if it could catch a fat little pig for its supper.'

'What colour was it?' asked the children, amid an immediate quickening of interest.

'Mud-colour all over, with a black tongue and pale grey eyes that gleamed with unspeakable ferocity. The first thing that it saw in the park was Bertha; her pinafore was so spotlessly white and clean that it could be seen from a great distance. Bertha saw the wolf and saw that it was stealing towards her, and she began to wish that she had never been allowed to come into the park. She ran as hard as she could, and the wolf came after her with huge leaps and bounds. She managed to reach a shrubbery of myrtle bushes and she hid herself in one of the thickest of the bushes. The wolf came sniffing among the branches, its black tongue lolling out of its mouth and its pale grey eyes glaring with rage. Bertha was terribly frightened, and thought to herself: "If I had not been so extraordinarily good I should have been safe in the town at this moment." However, the scent of the myrtle was so strong that the wolf could not sniff out where Bertha was hiding, and the bushes were so thick that he might have hunted about in them for a long time without catching sight of her, so he thought he might as well go off and catch a little pig instead. Bertha was trembling very much at having the wolf prowling and sniffing so near her, and as she trembled the medal for obedience clinked against the medals for good conduct and punctuality. The wolf was just moving away when he heard the sound of the medals clinking and stopped to listen; they clinked again in a bush quite near him. He dashed into the bush, his pale grey eyes gleaming with ferocity and triumph, and dragged Bertha out and devoured her to the last morsel. All that was left of her were her shoes, bits of clothing, and the three medals for goodness.'

'Were any of the little pigs killed?'

'No, they all escaped.'

'The story began badly,' said the smaller of the small girls, 'but it had a beautiful ending.'

'It is the most beautiful story that I ever heard,' said the bigger of the small girls, with immense decision.

'It is the *only* beautiful story I have ever heard,' said Cyril.

A dissentient opinion came from the aunt.

'A most improper story to tell young children! You have undermined the effect of years of careful teaching.'

'At any rate,' said the bachelor, collecting his belongings preparatory to leaving the carriage, 'I kept them quiet for ten minutes, which was more than you were able to do.'

'Unhappy woman!' he observed to himself as he walked down the platform of Templecombe station; 'for the next six months or so those children will assail her in public with demands for an improper story!'

THE NAME-DAY

ADVENTURES, according to the proverb, are to the adventurous. Quite as often they are to the non-adventurous, to the retiring, to the constitutionally timid. John James Abbleway had been endowed by Nature with the sort of disposition that instinctively avoids Carlist intrigues, slum crusades, the tracking of wounded wild beasts, and the moving of hostile amendments at political meetings. If a mad dog or a Mad Mullah had come his way he would have surrendered the way without hesitation. At school he had unwillingly acquired a thorough knowledge of the German tongue out of deference to the plainly expressed wishes of a foreign-languages master, who, though he taught modern subjects, employed old-fashioned methods in driving his lessons home. It was this enforced familiarity with an important commercial language which thrust Abbleway in later years into strange lands where adventures were less easy to guard against than in the ordered atmosphere of an English country town. The firm that he worked for saw fit to send him one day on a prosaic business errand to the far city of Vienna, and, having sent him there, continued to keep him there, still engaged in humdrum affairs of commerce, but with the possibilities of romance and adventure, or even misadventure, jostling at his elbow. After two and a half years of exile, however, John James Abbleway had embarked on only one hazardous undertaking, and that was of a nature which would assuredly have overtaken him sooner or later if he had been leading a sheltered, stay-at-home existence at Dorking or Huntingdon. He fell placidly in love with a placidly lovable English girl, the sister of one of his commercial colleagues, who was improving her mind by a short trip to foreign parts, and in due course he was formally accepted as the young man she was engaged to. The further step by which she was to become Mrs John Abbleway was to take place a twelvemonth hence in a town in the English midlands, by which time the firm that employed John James would have no further need for his presence in the Austrian capital.

It was early in April, two months after the installation of Abbleway as the young man Miss Penning was engaged to, when he received a letter from her, written from Venice. She was still peregrinating under the wing of her brother, and as the latter's business arrangements would take him across to Fiume for a day or two, she had conceived the idea that it would be rather jolly if John could obtain leave of absence and run down to the Adriatic coast to meet them. She had looked up the route on the map, and the journey did not appear likely to be expensive. Between the lines of her communication there lay a hint that if he really cared for her—

Abbleway obtained leave of absence and added a journey to Fiume to his life's adventures. He left Vienna on a cold, cheerless day. The flower shops were full of spring blooms, and the weekly organs of illustrated humour were full of spring topics, but the skies were heavy with clouds that looked like cotton-wool that has been kept over long in a shop window.

'Snow comes,' said the train official to the station officials; and they agreed that snow was about to come. And it came, rapidly, plenteously. The train had not been more than an hour on its journey when the cotton-wool clouds commenced tu dissolve in a blinding downpour of snowflakes. The forest trees on either side of the line were speedily coated with a heavy white mantle, the telegraph wires became thick glistening ropes, the line itself was buried more and more completely under a carpeting of snow, through which the not very powerful engine ploughed its way with increasing difficulty. The Vienna–Fiume line is scarcely the best equipped of the Austrian State railways, and Abbleway began to have serious fears for a breakdown. The train had slowed down to a painful and precarious crawl and presently came to a halt at a spot where the drifting snow had accumulated in a formidable barrier. The engine made a special effort and broke through the obstruction, but in the course of another twenty minutes it was again held up. The process of breaking through was renewed and the train doggedly resumed its way, encountering and surmounting fresh hindrances at frequent intervals. After a standstill of unusually long duration in a particularly deep drift the compartment in which Abbleway was sitting gave a huge jerk and a lurch, and then seemed to remain stationary; it undoubtedly was not moving, and yet he could hear the puffing of the engine and the slow rumbling and jolting of wheels. The puffing and rumbling grew fainter, as though it were dying away through the agency of intervening distance. Abbleway suddenly gave vent to an exclamation of scandalized alarm, opened the window, and peered out into the snowstorm. The flakes perched on his eyelashes and blurred his vision, but he saw enough to help him to realize what had happened. The engine had made a mighty plunge through the drift and had gone merrily forward, lightened of the load of its rear carriage, whose coupling had snapped under the strain. Abbleway was alone, or almost alone, with a derelict railway waggon, in the heart of some Styrian or Croatian forest. In the third-class compartment next to his own he remembered to have seen a peasant woman, who had entered the train at a small wayside station. 'With the exception of that woman,' he exclaimed dramatically to himself, 'the nearest living beings are probably a pack of wolves.'

Before making his way to the third-class compartment to acquaint his fellow-traveller with the extent of the disaster

Abbleway hurriedly pondered the question of the woman's nationality. He had acquired a smattering of Slavonic tongues during his residence in Vienna, and felt competent to grapple with several racial possibilities.

'If she is Croat or Serb or Bosniak I shall be able to make her understand,' he promised himself. 'If she is Magyar, heaven help me! We shall have to converse entirely by signs.'

He entered the carriage and made his momentous announcement in the best approach to Croat speech that he could achieve.

'The train has broken away and left us!'

The woman shook her head with a movement that might be intended to convey resignation to the will of heaven, but probably meant noncomprehension. Abbleway repeated his information with variations of Slavonic tongues and generous displays of pantomime.

'Ah,' said the woman at last in German dialect, 'the train has gone? We are left. Ah, so.'

She seemed about as much interested as though Abbleway had told her the result of the municipal elections in Amsterdam.

'They will find out at some station, and when the line is clear of snow they will send an engine. It happens that way sometimes.'

'We may be here all night!' exclaimed Abbleway.

The woman looked as though she thought it possible.

'Are there wolves in these parts?' asked Abbleway hurriedly.

'Many,' said the woman; 'just outside this forest my aunt was devoured three years ago, as she was coming home from market. The horse and a young pig that was in the cart were eaten too. The horse was a very old one, but it was a beautiful young pig, oh, so fat. I cried when I heard that it was taken. They spare nothing.'

'They may attack us here,' said Abbleway tremulously; 'they could easily break in, these carriages are like matchwood. We may both be devoured.'

'You, perhaps,' said the woman calmly; 'not me.'

'Why not you?' demanded Abbleway.

'It is the day of Saint Mariä Kleophä, my name-day. She would not allow me to be eaten by wolves on her day. Such a thing could not be thought of. You, yes, but not me.'

Abbleway changed the subject.

'It is only afternoon now; if we are to be left here till morning we shall be starving.'

'I have here some good eatables,' said the woman tranquilly; 'on my festival day it is natural that I should have provision with me. I have five good blood-sausages; in the town shops they cost twenty-five heller each. Things are dear in the town shops.'

'I will give you fifty heller apiece for a couple of them,' said Abbleway with some enthusiasm.

'In a railway accident things become very dear,' said the woman; 'these blood-sausages are four kronen apiece.'

'Four kronen!' exclaimed Abbleway; 'four kronen for a blood-sausage!'

'You cannot get them any cheaper on this train,' said the woman, with relentless logic, 'because there aren't any others to get. In Agram you can buy them cheaper, and in Paradise no doubt they will be given to us for nothing, but here they cost four kronen each. I have a small piece of Emmenthaler cheese and a honey-cake and a piece of bread that I can let you have. That will be another three kronen, eleven kronen in all. There is a piece of ham, but that I cannot let you have on my name-day.'

Abbleway wondered to himself what price she would have put on the ham, and hurried to pay her the eleven kronen before her emergency tariff expanded into a famine tariff. As he was taking possession of his modest store of eatables he suddenly heard a noise which set his heart thumping in a miserable fever of fear. There was a scraping and shuffling as of some animal or animals trying to climb up to the footboard. In another moment, through the snow-encrusted glass of the carriage window, he saw a gaunt prick-eared head, with gaping jaw and lolling tongue and gleaming teeth; a second later another head shot up.

'There are hundreds of them,' whispered Abbleway; 'they have scented us. They will tear the carriage to pieces. We shall be devoured.'

'Not me, on my name-day. The holy Mariä Kleophä would not permit it,' said the woman with provoking calm.

The heads dropped down from the window and an uncanny silence fell on the beleaguered carriage. Abbleway neither moved nor spoke. Perhaps the brutes had not clearly seen or winded the human occupants of the carriage, and had prowled away on some other errand of rapine.

The long torture-laden minutes passed slowly away.

'It grows cold,' said the woman suddenly, crossing over to the far end of the carriage, where the heads had appeared. 'The heating apparatus does not work any longer. See, over there beyond the trees, there is a chimney with smoke coming from it. It is not far, and the snow has nearly stopped. I shall find a path through the forest to that house with the chimney.'

'But the wolves!' exclaimed Abbleway; 'they may——'

'Not on my name-day,' said the woman obstinately, and before he could stop her she had opened the door and climbed down into the snow. A moment later he hid his face in his hands; two gaunt lean figures rushed upon her from the forest. No doubt she had courted her fate, but Abbleway had no wish to see a human being torn to pieces and devoured before his eyes.

When he looked at last a new sensation of scandalized astonishment took possession of him. He had been straitly brought up in a small English town, and he was not prepared to be the witness of a miracle. The wolves were not doing anything worse to the woman than drench her with snow as they gambolled round her.

A short, joyous bark revealed the clue to the situation.

'Are those—dogs?' he called weakly.

'My cousin Karl's dogs, yes,' she answered; 'that is his inn, over beyond the trees. I knew it was there, but I did not want to take you there; he is always grasping with strangers. However, it grows too cold to remain in the train. Ah, ah, see what comes!'

A whistle sounded, and a relief engine made its appearance, snorting its way sulkily through the snow. Abbeway did not have the opportunity for finding out whether Karl was really avaricious.

THE LUMBER-ROOM

THE children were to be driven, as a special treat, to the sands at Jagborough. Nicholas was not to be of the party; he was in disgrace. Only that morning he had refused to eat his wholesome bread-and-milk on the seemingly frivolous ground that there was a frog in it. Older and wiser and better people had told him that there could not possibly be a frog in his bread-and-milk and that he was not to talk nonsense; he continued, nevertheless, to talk what seemed the veriest nonsense, and described with much detail the colouration and markings of the alleged frog. The dramatic part of the incident was that there really was a frog in Nicholas' basin of bread-and-milk; he had put it there himself, so he felt entitled to know something about it. The sin of taking a frog from the garden and putting it into a bowl of wholesome bread-and-milk was enlarged on at great length, but the fact that stood out clearest in the whole affair, as it presented itself to the mind of Nicholas, was that the older, wiser and better people had been proved to be profoundly in error in matters about which they had expressed the utmost assurance.

'You said there couldn't possibly be a frog in my bread-and-milk; there *was* a frog in my bread-and-milk,' he repeated, with the insistence of a skilled tactician who does not intend to shift from favourable ground.

So his boy-cousin and girl-cousin and his quite uninteresting younger brother were to be taken to Jagborough sands that afternoon and he was to stay at home. His cousins' aunt, who insisted, by an unwarranted stretch of imagination, in styling herself his aunt also, had hastily invented the Jagborough expedition in order to impress on Nicholas the delights that he had justly forfeited by his disgraceful conduct at the breakfast-table. It was her habit, whenever one of the children fell from grace, to improvise something of a festival nature from which the offender would be rigorously debarred; if all the children sinned collectively they were suddenly informed of a circus in a neighbouring town, a circus of unrivalled merit and uncounted elephants, to which, but for their depravity, they would have been taken that very day.

A few decent tears were looked for on the part of Nicholas when the moment for the departure of the expedition arrived. As a matter of fact, however, all the crying was done by his girl-cousin, who scraped her knee rather painfully against the step of the carriage as she was scrambling in.

'How she did howl,' said Nicholas cheerfully, as the party drove off without any of the elation of high spirits that should have characterized it.

'She'll soon get over that,' said the *soi-disant* aunt; 'it will be a glorious afternoon for racing about over those beautiful sands. How they will enjoy themselves!'

'Bobby won't enjoy himself much, and he won't race much either,' said Nicholas with a grim chuckle; 'his boots are hurting him. They're too tight.'

'Why didn't he tell me they were hurting?' asked the aunt with some asperity.

'He told you twice, but you weren't listening. You often don't listen when we tell you important things.'

'You are not to go into the gooseberry garden,' said the aunt, changing the subject.

'Why not?' demanded Nicholas.

'Because you are in disgrace,' said the aunt loftily.

Nicholas did not admit the flawlessness of the reasoning; he felt perfectly capable of being in disgrace and in a gooseberry garden at the same moment. His face took on an expression of considerable obstinacy. It was clear to his aunt that he was determined to get into the gooseberry garden, 'only,' as she remarked to herself, 'because I have told him he is not to.'

Now the gooseberry garden had two doors by which it might be entered, and once a small person like Nicholas could slip in there he could effectually disappear from view amid the masking growth of artichokes, raspberry canes, and fruit bushes. The aunt had many other things to do that afternoon, but she spent an hour or two in trivial gardening operations among flower beds and shrubberies, whence she could keep a watchful eye on the two doors that led to the forbidden paradise. She was a woman of few ideas, with immense powers of concentration.

Nicholas made one or two sorties into the front garden, wriggling his way with obvious stealth of purpose towards one or other of the doors, but never able for a moment to evade the aunt's watchful eye. As a matter of fact, he had no intention of trying to get into the gooseberry garden, but it was extremely convenient for him that his aunt should believe that he had; it was a belief that would keep her on self-imposed sentry-duty for the greater part of the afternoon. Having thoroughly confirmed and fortified her suspicions, Nicholas slipped back into the house and rapidly put into execution a plan of action that had long germinated in his brain. By standing on a chair in the library one could reach a shelf on which reposed a fat, important-looking key. The key was as important as it looked; it was the instrument which kept the mysteries of the lumber-room secure from unauthorized intrusion, which opened a way only for aunts and such-like privileged persons. Nicholas had not much experience of the art of fitting keys into keyholes and turning locks, but for some days past he had practised with the key of the school-room door; he did not believe in trusting too much to luck and accident. The key turned stiffly in the lock, but it turned. The door opened, and Nicholas was in an unknown land, compared with which the gooseberry garden was a stale delight, a mere material pleasure.

Often and often Nicholas had pictured to himself what the lumber-room might be like, that region that was so carefully sealed from youthful eyes and concerning which no questions were ever answered. It came up to his expectations. In the first place it was large and dimly lit, one high window opening on to the forbidden garden being its only source of illumination. In the second place it was a storehouse of unimagined treasures. The aunt-by-assertion was one of those people who think that things spoil by use and consign them to dust and damp by way of preserving them. Such parts of the house as Nicholas knew best were rather bare and cheerless, but here there were wonderful things for the eye to feast on. First and foremost there was a piece of framed tapestry that was evidently meant to be a fire-screen. To Nicholas it was a living, breathing story; he sat down on a roll of Indian hangings, glowing in wonderful colours beneath a layer of dust, and took in all the details of the tapestry picture. A man, dressed in the hunting costume of some remote period, had just trans-fixed a stag with an arrow; it could not have been a difficult shot because the stag was only one or two paces away from him; in the thickly growing vegetation that the picture sug-gested it would not have been difficult to creep up to a feeding stag, and the two spotted dogs that were springing forward to join in the chase had evidently been trained to keep to heel till the arrow was discharged. That part of the picture was simple, if interesting, but did the huntsman see, what Nicholas saw, that four galloping wolves were coming in his direction through the wood? There might be more than four of them hidden behind the trees, and in any case would the man and his dogs be able to cope with the four wolves if they made an attack? The man had only two arrows left in his quiver, and he might miss with one or both of them; all one knew about his skill in shooting was that he could hit a large stag at a ridiculously short range. Nicholas sat for many golden min-utes revolving the possibilities of the scene; he was inclined to think that there were more than four wolves and that the man and his dogs were in a tight corner.

But there were other objects of delight and interest claiming his instant attention: here were quaint twisted candlesticks in the shape of snakes, and a teapot fashioned like a china duck, out of whose open beak the tea was supposed to come. How dull and shapeless the nursery teapot seemed in comparison! And there was a carved sandal-wood box packed tight with aromatic cotton-wool, and between the layers of cotton-wool were little brass figures, hump-necked bulls, and peacocks and goblins, delightful to see and to handle. Less promising in appearance was a large square book with plain black covers; Nicholas peeped into it, and, behold, it was full of coloured pictures of birds. And such birds! In the garden, and in the lanes when he went for a walk, Nicholas came across a few birds, of which the largest were an occasional magpie or wood-pigeon; here were herons and bustards, kites, toucans, tiger-bitterns, brush turkeys, ibises, golden pheasants, a whole portrait gallery of undreamed-of creatures. And as he was admiring the colouring of the mandarin duck and assigning a life-history to it, the voice of his aunt in shrill vociferation of his name came from the gooseberry garden without. She had grown suspicious at his long disappearance, and had leapt to the conclusion that he had climbed over the wall behind the sheltering screen of the lilac bushes; she was now engaged in energetic and rather hopeless search for him among the artichokes and raspberry canes.

'Nicholas, Nicholas!' she screamed, 'you are to come out of this at once. It's no use trying to hide there; I can see you all the time.'

It was probably the first time for twenty years that any one had smiled in that lumber-room.

Presently the angry repetitions of Nicholas' name gave way to a shriek, and a cry for somebody to come quickly. Nicholas shut the book, restored it carefully to its place in a corner, and shook some dust from a neighbouring pile of newspapers over it. Then he crept from the room, locked the door, and replaced the key exactly where he had found it. His aunt was still calling his name when he sauntered into the front garden.

'Who's calling?' he asked.

'Me,' came the answer from the other side of the wall, 'didn't you hear me? I've been looking for you in the gooseberry garden, and I've slipped into the rain-water tank. Luckily there's no water in it, but the sides are slippery and I can't get out. Fetch the little ladder from under the cherry tree—'

'I was told I wasn't to go into the gooseberry garden,' said Nicholas promptly.

'I told you not to, and now I tell you that you may,' came the voice from the rain-water tank, rather impatiently.

'Your voice doesn't sound like aunt's,' objected Nicholas; 'you may be the Evil One tempting me to be disobedient. Aunt often tells me that the Evil One tempts me and that I always yield. This time I'm not going to yield.'

'Don't talk nonsense,' said the prisoner in the tank; 'go and fetch the ladder.'

'Will there be strawberry jam for tea?' asked Nicholas innocently.

'Certainly there will be,' said the aunt, privately resolving that Nicholas should have none of it.

'Now I know that you are the Evil One and not aunt,' shouted Nicholas gleefully; 'when we asked aunt for strawberry jam yesterday she said there wasn't any. I know there are four jars of it in the store cupboard, because I looked, and of course you know it's there, but *she* doesn't, because she said there wasn't any. Oh, Devil, you *have* sold yourself!'

There was an unusual sense of luxury in being able to talk to an aunt as though one was talking to the Evil One, but Nicholas knew, with childish discernment, that such luxuries were not to be overindulged in. He walked noisily away, and it was a kitchenmaid, in search of parsley, who eventually rescued the aunt from the rain-water tank.

Tea that evening was partaken of in a fearsome silence. The tide had been at its highest when the children had arrived at Jagborough Cove, so there had been no sands to play on—a circumstance that the aunt had overlooked in the haste of organizing her punitive expedition. The tightness of Bobby's boots had had disastrous effect on his temper the whole of the afternoon, and altogether the children could not have been said to have enjoyed themselves. The aunt maintained the frozen muteness of one who has suffered undignified and unmerited detention in a rain-water tank for thirty-five minutes. As for Nicholas, he, too, was silent, in the absorption of one who has much to think about; it was just possible, he considered, that the huntsman would escape with his hounds while the wolves feasted on the stricken stag.

ON APPROVAL

OF all the genuine Bohemians who strayed from time to time into the would-be-Bohemian circle of the Restaurant Nuremberg, Owl Street, Soho, none was more interesting and more elusive than Gebhard Knopfschrank. He had no friends, and though he treated all the restaurant frequenters as acquaintances he never seemed to wish to carry the acquaintanceship beyond the door that led into Owl Street and the outer world. He dealt with them all rather as a market woman might deal with chance passers-by, exhibiting her wares and chattering about the weather and the slackness of business, occasionally about rheumatism, but never showing a desire to penetrate into their daily lives or to dissect their ambitions.

He was understood to belong to a family of peasant farmers, somewhere in Pomerania; some two years ago, according to all that was known of him, he had abandoned the labours and responsibilities of swine tending and goose rearing to try his fortune as an artist in London.

'Why London and not Paris or Munich?' he had been asked by the curious.

Well, there was a ship that left Stolpmünde for London twice a month, that carried few passengers, but carried them cheaply; the railway fares to Munich or Paris were not cheap. Thus it was that he came to select London as the scene of his great adventure.

The question that had long and seriously agitated the frequenters of the Nuremberg was whether this goose-boy migrant was really a soul-driven genius, spreading his wings to the light, or merely an enterprising young man who fancied he could paint and was pardonably anxious to escape from the monotony of rye bread diet and the sandy, swine-bestrewn plains of Pomerania. There was reasonable ground for doubt and caution; the artistic groups that foregathered at the little restaurant contained so many young women with short hair and so many young men with long hair, who supposed themselves to be abnormally gifted in the domain of music, poetry, painting, or stagecraft, with little or nothing to support the supposition, that a self-announced genius of any sort in their midst was inevitably suspect. On the other hand, there was the ever-imminent danger of entertaining, and snubbing, an angel unawares. There had been the lamentable case of Sledonti, the dramatic poet, who had been belittled and cold-shouldered in the Owl Street hall of judgment, and had been afterwards hailed as a master singer by the Grand Duke Constantine Constantinovitch—'the most educated of the Romanoffs', according to Sylvia Strubble, who spoke rather as one who knew every individual member of the Russian imperial family; as a matter of fact, she knew a newspaper correspondent, a young man who ate borsch with the air of having invented it. Sledonti's *Poems of Death and Passion* were now being sold by the thousand in seven European languages, and were about to be translated into Syrian, a circumstance which made the discerning critics of the Nuremberg rather shy of maturing their future judgments too rapidly and too irrevocably.

As regards Knopfschrank's work, they did not lack opportunity for inspecting and appraising it. However resolutely he might hold himself aloof from the social life of his restaurant acquaintances, he was not minded to hide his artistic performances from their inquiring gaze. Every evening, or nearly every evening, at about seven o'clock, he would make his appearance, sit himself down at his accustomed table, throw a bulky black portfolio on to the chair opposite him, nod round indiscriminately at his fellow-guests, and commence the serious business of eating and drinking. When the coffee stage was reached he would light a cigarette, draw the portfolio over to him, and begin to rummage among its contents. With slow deliberation he would select a few of his more recent studies and sketches, and silently pass them round from table to table, paying especial attention to any new diners who might be present. On the back of each sketch was marked in plain figures the announcement 'Price ten shillings'.

If his work was not obviously stamped with the hall-mark of genius, at any rate it was remarkable for its choice of an unusual and unvarying theme. His pictures always represented some well-known street or public place in London, fallen into decay and denuded of its human population, in the place of which there roamed a wild fauna, which, from its wealth of exotic species, must have originally escaped from Zoological Gardens and travelling beast shows. 'Giraffes drinking at the fountain pools, Trafalgar Square', was one of the most notable and characteristic of his studies, while even more sensational was the gruesome picture of 'Vultures attacking dying camel in Upper Berkeley Street'. There were also photographs of the large canvas on which he had been engaged for some months, and which he was now endeavouring to sell to some enterprising dealer or adventurous amateur. The subject was 'Hyaenas asleep in Euston Station', a composition that left nothing to be desired in the way of suggesting unfathomed depths of desolation.

'Of course it may be immensely clever, it may be something epoch-making in the realm of art,' said Sylvia Strubble to her own particular circle of listeners, 'but, on the other hand, it may be merely mad. One mustn't pay too much attention to the commercial aspect of the case, of course, but still, if some dealer would make a bid for that hyaena picture, or even for some of the sketches, we should know better how to place the man and his work.'

'We may all be cursing ourselves one of these days,' said Mrs Nougat-Jones, 'for not having bought up his entire portfolio of sketches. At the same time, when there is so much real talent going about, one does not feel like planking down ten shillings for what looks like a bit of whimsical oddity. Now that picture that he showed us last week, "Sand-grouse roosting on the Albert Memorial", was very impressive, and of course I could see there was good workmanship in it and breadth of treatment; but it didn't in the least convey the Albert Memorial to me, and Sir James Beanquest tells me that sand-grouse don't roost, they sleep on the ground.'

Whatever talent or genius the Pomeranian artist might possess, it certainly failed to receive commercial sanction. The portfolio remained bulky with unsold sketches, and the 'Euston Siesta', as the wits of the Nuremberg nicknamed the large canvas, was still in the market. The outward and visible signs of financial embarrassment began to be noticeable; the half-bottle of cheap claret at dinner-time gave way to a small glass of lager, and this in turn was displaced by water. The one-and-sixpenny set dinner receded from an everyday event to a Sunday extravagance; on ordinary days the artist contented himself with a sevenpenny omelette and some bread and cheese, and there were evenings when he did not put in an appearance at all. On the rare occasions when he spoke of his own affairs it was observed that he began to talk more about Pomerania and less about the great world of art.

'It is a busy time there now with us,' he said wistfully; 'the schwines are driven out into the fields after harvest, and must be looked after. I could be helping to look after if I was there. Here it is difficult to live; art is not appreciate.'

'Why don't you go home on a visit?' some one asked tactfully.

'Ah, it cost money! There is the ship passage to Stolpmünde, and there is money that I owe at my lodgings. Even here I owe a few schillings. If I could sell some of my sketches—'

'Perhaps,' suggested Mrs Nougat-Jones, 'if you were to offer them for a little less, some of us would be glad to buy a few. Ten shillings is always a consideration, you know, to people who are not over well off. Perhaps if you were to ask six or seven shillings—'

Once a peasant, always a peasant. The mere suggestion of a bargain to be struck brought a twinkle of awakened alertness into the artist's eyes, and hardened the lines of his mouth.

'Nine schilling, nine pence each,' he snapped, and seemed disappointed that Mrs Nougat-Jones did not pursue the subject further. He had evidently expected her to offer seven-and-fourpence.

The weeks sped by, and Knopfschrank came more rarely to the restaurant in Owl Street, while his meals on those occasions became more and more meagre. And then came a triumphal day, when he appeared early in the evening in a high state of elation, and ordered an elaborate meal that scarcely stopped short of being a banquet. The ordinary resources of the kitchen were supplemented by an imported dish of smoked goosebreast, a Pomeranian delicacy that was luckily procurable at a firm of *delikatessen* merchants in Coventry Street, while a long-necked bottle of Rhine wine gave a finishing touch of festivity and good cheer to the crowded table.

'He has evidently sold his masterpiece,' whispered Sylvia Strubble to Mrs Nougat-Jones, who had come in late.

'Who has bought it?' she whispered back.

'Don't know; he hasn't said anything yet, but it must be some American. Do you see, he has got a little American flag on the dessert dish, and he has put pennies in the music box three times, once to play the "Star-spangled Banner", then a

Sousa march, and then the "Star-spangled Banner" again. It must be an American millionaire, and he's evidently got a big price for it; he's just beaming and chuckling with satisfaction.'

'We must ask him who has bought it,' said Mrs Nougat-Jones.

'Hush! no, don't. Let's buy some of his sketches, quick, before we are supposed to know that he's famous; otherwise he'll be doubling the prices. I *am* so glad he's had a success at last. I always believed in him, you know.'

For the sum of ten shillings each Miss Strubble acquired the drawings of the camel dying in Upper Berkeley Street and of the giraffes quenching their thirst in Trafalgar Square; at the same price Mrs Nougat-Jones secured the study of roosting sand-grouse. A more ambitious picture. 'Wolves and wapiti fighting on the steps of the Athenaeum Club', found a purchaser at fifteen shillings.

'And now what are your plans?' asked a young man who contributed occasional paragraphs to an artistic weekly.

'I go back to Stolpmünde as soon as the ship sails,' said the artist, 'and I do not return. Never.'

'But your work? Your career as painter?'

'Ah, there is nossing in it. One starves. Till today I have sold not one of my sketches. Tonight you have bought a few, because I am going away from you, but at other times, not one.'

'But has not some American—?'

'Ah, the rich American,' chuckled the artist. 'God be thanked. He dash his car right into our herd of schwines as they were being driven out to the fields. Many of our best schwines he killed, but he paid all damages. He paid perhaps more than they were worth, many times more than they would have fetched in the market after a month of fattening, but he was in a hurry to get on to Danzig. When one is in a hurry one must pay what one is asked. God be thanked for rich Americans, who are always in a hurry to get somewhere else. My father and mother, they have now so plenty of money; they send me some to pay me debts and come home. I start on Monday for Stolpmünde and I do not come back. Never.'

'But your picture, the hyaenas?'

'No good. It is too big to carry to Stolpmünde. I burn it.'

In time he will be forgotten, but at present Knopfschrank is almost as sore a subject as Sledonti with some of the frequenters of the Nuremberg Restaurant, Owl Street, Soho.

THE WOLVES OF CERNOGRATZ

'ARE there any old legends attached to the castle?' asked Conrad of his sister. Conrad was a prosperous Hamburg merchant, but he was the one poetically-dispositioned member of an eminently practical family.

The Baroness Gruebel shrugged her plump shoulders.

'There are always legends hanging about these old places. They are not difficult to invent and they cost nothing. In this case there is a story that when any one dies in the castle all the dogs in the village and the wild beasts in the forest howl the night long. It would not be pleasant to listen to, would it?'

'It would be weird and romantic,' said the Hamburg merchant.

'Anyhow, it isn't true,' said the Baroness complacently; 'since we bought the place we have had proof that nothing of the sort happens. When the old mother-in-law died last spring-time we all listened, but there was no howling. It is just a story that lends dignity to the place without costing anything.'

'The story is not as you have told it,' said Amalie, the grey old governess. Every one turned and looked at her in astonishment. She was wont to sit silent and prim and faded in her place at table, never speaking unless some one spoke to her, and there were few who troubled themselves to make conversation with her. Today a sudden volubility had descended on her; she continued to talk, rapidly and nervously, looking straight in front of her and seeming to address no one in particular.

'It is not when *any one* dies in the castle that the howling is heard. It was when one of the Cernogratz family died here

that the wolves came from far and near and howled at the
edge of the forest just before the death hour. There were only
a few couple of wolves that had their lairs in this part of the
forest, but at such a time the keepers say there would be scores
of them, gliding about in the shadows and howling in chorus,
and the dogs of the castle and the village and all the farms
round would bay and howl in fear and anger at the wolf
chorus, and as the soul of the dying one left its body a tree
would crash down in the park. That is what happened when
a Cernogratz died in his family castle. But for a stranger dying
here, of course no wolf would howl and no tree would fall.
Oh, no.'

There was a note of defiance, almost of contempt, in her
voice as she said the last words. The well-fed, much-too-well-
dressed Baroness stared angrily at the dowdy old woman who
had come forth from her usual and seemly position of efface-
ment to speak so disrespectfully.

'You seem to know quite a lot about the von Cernogratz
legends, Fräulein Schmidt,' she said sharply; 'I did not know
that family histories were among the subjects you are supposed to be proficient in.'

The answer to her taunt was even more unexpected and
astonishing than the conversational outbreak which had
provoked it.

'I am a von Cernogratz myself,' said the old woman, 'that is
why I know the family history.'

'You a von Cernogratz? You!' came in an incredulous
chorus.

'When we became very poor,' she explained, 'and I had to
go out and give teaching lessons, I took another name; I
thought it would be more in keeping. But my grandfather
spent much of his time as a boy in this castle, and my father
used to tell me many stories about it, and, of course, I knew all
the family legends and stories. When one has nothing left to
one but memories, one guards and dusts them with especial
care. I little thought when I took service with you that I should
one day come with you to the old home of my family. I could
wish it had been anywhere else.'

There was silence when she finished speaking, and then the
Baroness turned the conversation to a less embarrassing topic

than family histories. But afterwards, when the old governess had slipped away quietly to her duties, there arose a clamour of derision and disbelief.

'It was an impertinence,' snapped out the Baron, his protruding eyes taking on a scandalized expression; 'fancy the woman talking like that at our table. She almost told us we were nobodies, and I don't believe a word of it. She is just Schmidt and nothing more. She has been talking to some of the peasants about the old Cernogratz family, and raked up their history and their stories.'

'She wants to make herself out of some consequence,' said the Baroness; 'she knows she will soon be past work and she wants to appeal to our sympathies. Her grandfather, indeed!'

The Baroness had the usual number of grandfathers, but she never, never boasted about them.

'I dare say her grandfather was a pantry boy or something of the sort in the castle,' sniggered the Baron; 'that part of the story may be true.'

The merchant from Hamburg said nothing; he had seen tears in the old woman's eyes when she spoke of guarding her memories—or, being of an imaginative dispositions, he thought he had.

'I shall give her notice to go as soon as the New Year festivities are over,' said the Baroness; 'till then I shall be too busy to manage without her.'

But she had to manage without her all the same, for in the cold biting weather after Christmas, the old governess fell ill and kept to her room.

'It is most provoking,' said the Baroness, as her guests sat round the fire on one of the last evenings of the dying year; 'all the time that she has been with us I cannot remember that she was ever seriously ill, too ill to go about and do her work, I mean. And now, when I have the house full, and she could be useful in so many ways, she goes and breaks down. One is sorry for her, of course, she looks so withered and shrunken, but it is intensely annoying all the same.'

'Most annoying,' agreed the banker's wife sympathetically; 'it is the intense cold, I expect, it breaks the old people up. It has been unusually cold this year.'

'The frost is the sharpest that has been known in December for many years,' said the Baron.

'And, of course, she is quite old,' said the Baroness; 'I wish I had given her notice some weeks ago, then she would have left before this happened to her. Why, Wappi, what is the matter with you?'

The small, woolly lapdog had leapt suddenly down from its cushion and crept shivering under the sofa. At the same moment an outburst of angry barking came from the dogs in the castle-yard, and other dogs could be heard yapping and barking in the distance.

'What is disturbing the animals?' asked the Baron.

And then the humans, listening intently, heard the sound that had roused the dogs to their demonstrations of fear and rage; heard a long-drawn whining howl, rising and falling, seeming at one moment leagues away, at others sweeping across the snow until it appeared to come from the foot of the castle walls. All the starved, cold misery of a frozen world, all the relentless hunger-fury of the wild, blended with other forlorn and haunting melodies to which one could give no name, seemed concentrated in that wailing cry.

'Wolves!' cried the Baron.

Their music broke forth in one raging burst, seeming to come from everywhere.

'Hundreds of wolves,' said the Hamburg merchant, who was a man of strong imagination.

Moved by some impulse which she could not have explained, the Baroness left her guests and made her way to the narrow, cheerless room where the old governess lay watching the hours of the dying year slip by. In spite of the biting cold of the winter night, the window stood open. With a scandalized exclamation on her lips, the Baroness rushed forward to close it.

'Leave it open,' said the old woman in a voice that for all its weakness carried an air of command such as the Baroness had never heard before from her lips.

'But you will die of cold!' she expostulated.

'I am dying in any case,' said the voice, 'and I want to hear their music. They have come from far and wide to sing the death-music of my family. It is beautiful that they have come; I am the last von Cernogratz that will die in our old castle, and they have come to sing to me. Hark, how loud they are calling!'

The cry of the wolves rose on the still winter air and floated round the castle walls in long-drawn piercing wails; the old woman lay back on her couch with a look of long-delayed happiness on her face.

'Go away,' she said to the Baroness; 'I am not lonely any more. I am one of a great old family. . . .'

'I think she is dying,' said the Baroness when she had rejoined her guests; 'I suppose we must send for a doctor. And that terrible howling! Not for much money would I have such death-music.'

'That music is not to be bought for any amount of money,' said Conrad.

'Hark! What is that other sound?' asked the Baron, as a noise of splitting and crashing was heard.

It was a tree falling in the park.

There was a moment of constrained silence, and then the banker's wife spoke.

'It is the intense cold that is splitting the trees. It is also the cold that has brought the wolves out in such numbers. It is many years since we have had such a cold winter.'

The Baroness eagerly agreed that the cold was responsible for these things. It was the cold of the open window, too, which caused the heart failure that made the doctor's ministrations unnecessary for the old Fräulein. But the notice in the newspapers looked very well—

'On December 29th, at Schloss Cernogratz, Amalie von Cernogratz, for many years the valued friend of Baron and Baroness Gruebel.'

THE PENANCE

OCTAVIAN RUTTLE was one of those lively cheerful individuals on whom amiability had set its unmistakable stamp, and, like most of his kind, his soul's peace depended in large

measure on the unstinted approval of his fellows. In hunting
to death a small tabby cat he had done a thing of which he
scarcely approved himself, and he was glad when the gardener
had hidden the body in its hastily dug grave under a lone
oak tree in the meadow, the same tree that the hunted quarry
had climbed as a last effort towards safety. It had been a
distasteful and seemingly ruthless deed, but circumstances had
demanded the doing of it. Octavian kept chickens; at least he
kept some of them; others vanished from his keeping, leaving
only a few bloodstained feathers to mark the manner of their
going. The tabby cat from the large grey house that stood with
its back to the meadow had been detected in many furtive
visits to the hen-coops, and after due negotiation with those in
authority at the grey house a sentence of death had been
agreed on: 'The children will mind, but they need not know,'
had been the last word on the matter.

The children in question were a standing puzzle to
Octavian; in the course of a few months he considered that he
should have known their names, ages, the dates of their birthdays, and have been introduced to their favourite toys. They
remained, however, as non-committal as the long blank wall
that shut them off from the meadow, a wall over which their
three heads sometimes appeared at odd moments. They had
parents in India—that much Octavian had learned in the
neighbourhood; the children, beyond grouping themselves
garmentwise into sexes, a girl and two boys, carried their life-
story no further on his behoof. And now it seemed he was
engaged in something which touched them closely, but must
be hidden from their knowledge.

The poor helpless chickens had gone one by one to their
doom, so it was meet that their destroyer should come to a
violent end, yet Octavian felt some qualms when his share of
the violence was ended. The little cat, headed off from its
wonted tracks of safety, had raced unfriended from shelter to
shelter, and its end had been rather piteous. Octavian walked
through the long grass of the meadow with a step less jaunty
than usual. And as he passed beneath the shadow of the high
blank wall he glanced up and became aware that his hunting
had had undesired witnesses. Three white set faces were look-

ing down at him, and if ever an artist wanted a threefold study of cold human hate, impotent yet unyielding, raging yet masked in stillness, he would have found it in the triple gaze that met Octavian's eye.

'I'm sorry, but it had to be done,' said Octavian, with genuine apology in his voice.

'Beast!'

The answer came from three throats with startling intensity.

Octavian felt that the blank wall would not be more impervious to his explanations than the bunch of human hostility that peered over its coping; he wisely decided to withhold his peace overtures till a more hopeful occasion.

Two days later he ransacked the best sweet-shop in the neighbouring market town for a box of chocolates that by its size and contents should fitly atone for the dismal deed done under the oak tree in the meadow. The two first specimens that were shown him he hastily rejected; one had a group of chickens pictured on its lid, the other bore the portrait of a tabby kitten. A third sample was more simply bedecked with a spray of painted poppies, and Octavian hailed the flowers of forgetfulness as a happy omen. He felt distinctly more at ease with his surroundings when the imposing package had been sent across to the grey house, and a message returned to say that it had been duly given to the children. The next morning he sauntered with purposeful steps past the long blank wall on his way to the chicken-run and piggery that stood at the bottom of the meadow. The three children were perched at their accustomed look-out, and their range of sight did not seem to concern itself with Octavian's presence. As he became depressingly aware of the aloofness of their gaze he also noted a strange variegation in the herbage at his feet; the greensward for a considerable space around was strewn and speckled with a chocolate-coloured hail, enlivened here and there with gay tinsel-like wrappings or the glistening mauve of crystallized violets. It was as though the fairy paradise of a greedy-minded child had taken shape and substance in the vegetation of the meadow. Octavian's blood-money had been flung back at him in scorn.

To increase his discomfiture the march of events tended to

shift the blame of ravaged chicken-coops from the supposed culprit who had already paid full forfeit; the young chicks were still carried off, and it seemed highly probable that the cat had only haunted the chicken-run to prey on the rats which harboured there. Through the flowing channels of servant talk the children learned of this belated revision of verdict, and Octavian one day picked up a sheet of copy-book paper on which was painstakingly written: 'Beast. Rats eated your chickens.' More ardently than ever did he wish for an opportunity for sloughing off the disgrace that enwrapped him, and earning some happier nickname from his three unsparing judges.

And one day a chance inspiration came to him. Olivia, his two-year-old daughter, was accustomed to spend the hour from high noon till one o'clock with her father while the nursemaid gobbled and digested her dinner and novelette. About the same time the blank wall was usually enlivened by the presence of its three small wardens. Octavian, with seeming carelessness of purpose, brought Olivia well within hail of the watchers and noted with hidden delight the growing interest that dawned in that hitherto sternly hostile quarter. His little Olivia, with her sleepy placid ways, was going to succeed where he, with his anxious well-meant overtures, had so signally failed. He brought her a large yellow dahlia, which she grasped tightly in one hand and regarded with a stare of benevolent boredom, such as one might bestow on amateur classical dancing performed in aid of a deserving charity. Then he turned shyly to the group perched on the wall and asked with affected carelessness, 'Do you like flowers?' Three solemn nods rewarded his venture.

'Which sorts do you like best?' he asked, this time with a distinct betrayal of eagerness in his voice.

'Those with all the colours, over there.' Three chubby arms pointed to a distant tangle of sweet-pea. Child-like, they had asked for what lay farthest from hand, but Octavian trotted off gleefully to obey their welcome behest. He pulled and plucked with unsparing hand, and brought every variety of tint that he could see into his bunch that was rapidly becoming a bundle. Then he turned to retrace his steps, and found the blank wall blanker and more deserted than ever, while the foreground was void of all trace of Olivia. Far down the meadow three children were pushing a go-cart at the utmost speed they could muster in the direction of the piggeries; it was Olivia's go-cart and Olivia sat in it, somewhat bumped and shaken by the pace at which she was being driven, but apparently retaining her wonted composure of mind. Octavian stared for a moment at the rapidly moving group, and then started in hot pursuit, shedding as he ran sprays of blossom from the mass of sweet-pea that he still clutched in his hands. Fast as he ran the children had reached the piggery before he could overtake them, and he arrived just in time to see Olivia, wondering but unprotesting, hauled and pushed up to the roof of the nearest sty. They were old buildings in some need of repair, and the rickety roof would certainly not have borne Octavian's weight if he had attempted to follow his daughter and her captors on their new vantage ground.

'What are you going to do with her?' he panted. There was no mistaking the grim trend of mischief in those flushed but sternly composed young faces.

'Hang her in chains over a slow fire,' said one of the boys. Evidently they had been reading English history.

'Frow her down and the pigs will d'vour her, every bit 'cept the palms of her hands,' said the other boy. It was also evident that they had studied Biblical history.

The last proposal was the one which most alarmed Octavian, since it might be carried into effect at a moment's notice; there had been cases, he remembered, of pigs eating babies.

'You surely wouldn't treat my poor little Olivia in that way?' he pleaded.

'You killed our little cat,' came in stern reminder from three throats.

'I'm very sorry I did,' said Octavian, and if there is a standard of measurement in truths Octavian's statement was assuredly a large nine.

'We shall be very sorry when we've killed Olivia,' said the girl, 'but we can't be sorry till we've done it.'

The inexorable child-logic rose like an unyielding rampart

before Octavian's scared pleadings. Before he could think of any fresh line of appeal his energies were called out in another direction. Olivia had slid off the roof and fallen with a soft, unctuous splash into a morass of muck and decaying straw. Octavian scrambled hastily over the pigsty wall to her rescue, and at once found himself in a quagmire that engulfed his feet. Olivia, after the first shock of surprise at her sudden drop through the air, had been mildly pleased at finding herself in close and unstinted contact with the sticky element that oozed around her, but as she began to sink gently into the bed of slime a feeling dawned on her that she was not after all very happy, and she began to cry in the tentative fashion of the normally good child. Octavian, battling with the quagmire, which seemed to have learned the rare art of giving way at all points without yielding an inch, saw his daughter slowly disappearing in the engulfing slush, her smeared face further distorted with the contortions of whimpering wonder, while from their perch on the pigsty roof the three children looked down with the cold unpitying detachment of the Parcae Sisters.

'I can't reach her in time,' gasped Octavian, 'she'll be choked in the muck. Won't you help her?'

'No one helped our cat,' came the inevitable reminder.

'I'll do anything to show you how sorry I am about that,' cried Octavian, with a further desperate flounder, which carried him scarcely two inches forward.

'Will you stand in a white sheet by the grave?'

'Yes,' screamed Octavian.

'Holding a candle?'

'An' saying, "I'm a miserable Beast"?'

Octavian agreed to both suggestions.

'For a long, long time?'

'For half an hour,' said Octavian. There was an anxious ring in his voice as he named the time-limit; was there not the precedent of a German king who did open-air penance for several days and nights at Christmas-time clad only in his shirt? Fortunately the children did not appear to have read German history, and half an hour seemed long and goodly in their eyes.

'All right,' came with threefold solemnity from the roof, and a moment later a short ladder had been laboriously pushed across to Octavian, who lost no time in propping it against the low pigsty wall. Scrambling gingerly along its rungs he was able to lean across the morass that separated him from his slowly foundering offspring and extract her like an unwilling cork from its slushy embrace. A few minutes later he was listening to the shrill and repeated assurances of the nursemaid that her previous experience of filthy spectacles had been on a notably smaller scale.

That same evening when twilight was deepening into darkness Octavian took up his position as penitent under the lone oak tree, having first carefully undressed the part. Clad in a zephyr shirt, which on this occasion thoroughly merited its name, he held in one hand a lighted candle and in the other a watch, into which the soul of a dead plumber seemed to have passed. A box of matches lay at his feet and was resorted to on the fairly frequent occasions when the candle succumbed to the night breezes. The house loomed inscrutable in the middle distance, but as Octavian conscientiously repeated the formula of his penance he felt certain that three pairs of solemn eyes were watching his moth-shared vigil.

And the next morning his eyes were gladdened by a sheet of copy-book paper lying beside the blank wall, on which was written the message 'Un-Beast'.

THE MAPPINED LIFE

'THESE Mappin Terraces at the Zoological Gardens are a great improvement on the old style of wild-beast cage,' said Mrs James Gurtleberry, putting down an illustrated paper; 'they give one the illusion of seeing the animals in their natural surroundings. I wonder how much of the illusion is passed on to the animals?'

'That would depend on the animal,' said her niece; 'a jungle-fowl, for instance, would no doubt think its lawful jungle surroundings were faithfully reproduced if you gave it a sufficiency of wives, a goodly variety of seed food and ants' eggs, a commodious bank of loose earth to dust itself in, a convenient roosting tree, and a rival or two to make matters interesting. Of course there ought to be jungle-cats and birds of prey and other agencies of sudden death to add to the illusion of liberty, but the bird's own imagination is capable of inventing those—look how a domestic fowl will squawk an alarm note if a rook or wood-pigeon passes over its run when it has chickens.'

'You think, then, they really do have a sort of illusion, if you give them space enough—'

'In a few cases only. Nothing will make me believe that an acre or so of concrete enclosure will make up to a wolf or a tiger-cat for the range of night prowling that would belong to it in a wild state. Think of the dictionary of sound and scent and recollection that unfolds before a real wild beast as it comes out from its lair every evening, with the knowledge that in a few minutes it will be hieing along to some distant hunting ground where all the joy and fury of the chase awaits it; think of the crowded sensations of the brain when every rustle, every cry, every bent twig, and every whiff across the nostrils means something, something to do with life and death and dinner. Imagine the satisfaction of stealing down to your own particular drinking spot, choosing your own particular tree to scrape your claws on, finding your own particular bed of dried grass to roll on. Then, in the place of all that, put a concrete promenade, which will be of exactly the same dimensions whether you race or crawl across it, coated with stale, unvarying scents and surrounded with cries and noises that have ceased to have the least meaning or interest. As a substitute for a narrow cage the new enclosures are excellent, but I should think they are a poor imitation of a life of liberty.'

'It's rather depressing to think that,' said Mrs Gurtleberry; 'they look so spacious and so natural, but I suppose a good deal of what seems natural to us would be meaningless to a wild animal.'

'That is where our superior powers of self-deception come in,' said the niece; 'we are able to live our unreal, stupid little lives on our particular Mappin terrace, and persuade ourselves that we really are untrammelled men and women leading a reasonable existence in a reasonable sphere.'

'But good gracious,' exclaimed the aunt, bouncing into an attitude of scandalized defence, 'we are leading reasonable existences! What on earth do you mean by trammels? We are merely trammelled by the ordinary decent conventions of civilized society.'

'We are trammelled,' said the niece, calmly and pitilessly, 'by restrictions of income and opportunity, and above all by lack of initiative. To some people a restricted income doesn't matter a bit, in fact it often seems to help as a means for getting a lot of reality out of life; I am sure there are men and women who do their shopping in little back streets of Paris, buying four carrots and a shred of beef for their daily sustenance, who lead a perfectly real and eventful existence. Lack of initiative is the thing that really cripples one, and that is where you and I and Uncle James are so hopelessly shut in. We are just so many animals stuck down on a Mappin terrace, with this difference in our disfavour, that the animals are there to be looked at, while nobody wants to look at us. As a matter of fact there would be nothing to look at. We get colds in winter and hay-fever in summer, and if a wasp happens to sting one of us, well, that is the wasp's initiative, not ours; all we do is to wait for the swelling to go down. Whenever we do climb into local fame and notice, it is by indirect methods; if it happens to be a good flowering year for magnolias the neighbourhood observes, "Have you seen the Gurtleberrys' magnolia? It is a perfect mass of flowers", and we go about telling people that there are fifty-seven blossoms as against thirty-nine the previous year.'

'In Coronation year there were as many as sixty,' put in the aunt; 'your uncle has kept a record for the last eight years.'

'Doesn't it ever strike you,' continued the niece relentlessly, 'that if we moved away from here or were blotted out of existence our local claim to fame would pass on automatically to whoever happened to take the house and garden? People would say to one another, "Have you seen the Smith-Jenkins' magnolia? It is a perfect mass of flowers," or else, "Smith-Jenkins tells me there won't be a single blossom on their magnolia this year; the east winds have turned all the buds black." Now if, when we had gone, people still associated our names with the magnolia tree, no matter who temporarily possessed it, if they said, "Ah, that's the tree on which the Gurtleberrys hung their cook because she sent up the wrong kind of sauce with the asparagus," that would be something really due to our own initiative, apart from anything east winds or magnolia vitality might have to say in the matter.'

'We should never do such a thing,' said the aunt. The niece gave a reluctant sigh.

'I can't imagine it,' she admitted. 'Of course,' she continued, 'there are heaps of ways of leading a real existence without committing sensational deeds of violence. It's the dreadful little everyday acts of pretended importance that give the Mappin stamp to our life. It would be entertaining, if it wasn't so pathetically tragic, to hear Uncle James fuss in here in the morning and announce, "I must just go down into the town and find out what the men there are saying about Mexico. Matters are beginning to look serious there." Then he patters away into the town, and talks in a highly serious voice to the tobacconist, incidentally buying an ounce of tobacco; perhaps he meets one or two others of the world's thinkers and talks to them in a highly serious voice, then he patters back here and announces with increased importance, "I've just been talking to some men in the town about the condition of affairs in Mexico. They agree with the view that I have formed, that things there will have to get worse before they get better." Of course nobody in the town cared in the least little bit what his views about Mexico were or whether he had any. The tobacconist wasn't even fluttered at his buying the ounce of tobacco; he knows that he purchases the same quantity of the same sort of tobacco every week. Uncle James might just as well have lain on his back in the garden and chattered to the lilac tree about the habits of caterpillars.'

'I really will not listen to such things about your uncle,' protested Mrs James Gurtleberry angrily.

'My own case is just as bad and just as tragic,' said the niece dispassionately: 'nearly everything about me is conventional make-believe. I'm not a good dancer, and no one could honestly call me good-looking, but when I go to one of our dull little local dances I'm conventionally supposed to "have a heavenly time", to attract the ardent homage of the local cavaliers, and to go home with my head awhirl with pleasurable recollections. As a matter of fact, I've merely put in some hours of indifferent dancing, drunk some badly made claret cup, and listened to an enormous amount of laborious light conversation. A moonlight hen-stealing raid with the merry-eyed curate would be infinitely more exciting; imagine the pleasure of carrying off all those white Minorcas that the Chibfords are always bragging about. When we had disposed of them we could give the proceeds to a charity, so there would be nothing really wrong about it. But nothing of that sort lies within the Mappined limits of my life. One of these days somebody dull and decorous and undistinguished will "make himself agreeable" to me at a tennis party, as the saying is, and all the dull old gossips of the neighbourhood will begin to ask when we are to be engaged, and at last we shall be engaged, and people will give us butter-dishes and blotting-cases and framed pictures of young women feeding swans. Hullo, Uncle, are you going out?'

'I'm just going down to the town,' announced Mr James Gurtleberry, with an air of some importance: 'I want to hear what people are saying about Albania. Affairs there are beginning to take on a very serious look. It's my opinion that we haven't seen the worst of things yet.'

In this he was probably right, but there was nothing in the immediate or prospective condition of Albania to warrant Mrs Gurtleberry in bursting into tears.

THE SHEEP

THE enemy had declared 'no trumps'. Rupert played out his ace and king of clubs and cleared the adversary of that suit; then the Sheep, whom the Fates had inflicted on him for a partner, took the third round with the queen of clubs, and, having no other club to lead back, opened another suit. The enemy won the remainder of the tricks—and the rubber.

'I had four more clubs to play; we only wanted the odd trick to win the rubber,' said Rupert.

'But I hadn't another club to lead you,' exclaimed the Sheep, with his ready, defensive smile.

'It didn't occur to you to throw your queen away on my king and leave me with the command of the suit,' said Rupert, with polite bitterness.

'I suppose I ought to have—I wasn't certain what to do. I'm awfully sorry,' said the Sheep.

Being awfully and uselessly sorry formed a large part of his occupation in life. If a similar situation had arisen in a subsequent hand he would have blundered just as certainly, and he would have been just as irritatingly apologetic.

Rupert stared gloomily across at him as he sat smiling and fumbling with his cards. Many men who have good brains for business do not possess the rudiments of a card-brain, and Rupert would not have judged and condemned his prospective brother-in-law on the evidence of his bridge play alone. The tragic part of it was that he smiled and fumbled through life just as fatuously and apologetically as he did at the card-table. And behind the defensive smile and the well-worn expressions of regret there shone a scarcely believable but quite obvious self-satisfaction. Every sheep of the pasture probably imagines that in an emergency it could become terrible as an army with banners—one has only to watch how they stamp their feet and stiffen their necks when a minor object of suspicion comes into view and behaves meekly. And probably the majority of human sheep see themselves in imagination taking great parts in the world's more impressive dramas, forming swift, unerring decisions in moments of crisis, cowing mutinies, allaying panics, brave, strong, simple, but, in spite of their natural modesty, always slightly spectacular.

'Why in the name of all that is unnecessary and perverse should Kathleen choose this man for her future husband?' was the question that Rupert asked himself ruefully. There was young Malcolm Athling, as nice-looking, decent, level-headed a fellow as any one could wish to meet, obviously her very devoted admirer, and yet she must throw herself away on this pale-eyed, weak-mouthed embodiment of self-approving ineptitude. If it had been merely Kathleen's own affair Rupert would have shrugged his shoulders and philosophically hoped that she might make the best of an undeniably bad bargain. But Rupert had no heir; his own boy lay underground somewhere on the Indian frontier, in goodly company. And the property would pass in due course to Kathleen and Kathleen's husband. The Sheep would live there in the beloved old home, rearing up other little Sheep, fatuous and rabbit-faced and self-satisfied like himself, to dwell in the land and possess it. It was not a soothing prospect.

Towards dusk on the afternoon following the bridge experience Rupert and the Sheep made their way homeward after a day's mixed shooting. The Sheep's cartridge bag was nearly empty, but his game bag showed no signs of overcrowding. The birds he had shot at had seemed for the most part as impervious to death or damage as the hero of a melodrama. And for each failure to drop his bird he had some explanation or apology ready on his lips. Now he was striding along in front of his host, chattering happily over his shoulder, but obviously on the look-out for some belated rabbit or wood-pigeon that might haply be secured as an eleventh-hour addition to his bag. As they passed the edge of a small copse a large bird rose from the ground and flew slowly towards the trees, offering an easy shot to the oncoming sportsmen. The Sheep banged forth with both barrels, and gave an exultant cry.

'Hooray! I've shot a thundering big hawk.'

'To be exact, you've shot a honey-buzzard. That is the hen bird of one of the few pairs of honey-buzzards breeding in the United Kingdom. We've kept them under the strictest preservation for the last four years; every gamekeeper and village gun loafer for twenty miles round has been warned and bribed and threatened to respect their sanctity, and egg-snatching agents have been carefully guarded against during the breeding season. Hundreds of lovers of rare birds have delighted in seeing their snap-shotted portraits in *Country*

Life, and now you've reduced the hen bird to a lump of broken feathers.'

Rupert spoke quietly and evenly, but for a moment or two a gleam of positive hatred shone in his eyes.

'I say, I'm so sorry,' said the Sheep, with his apologetic smile. 'Of course I remember hearing about the buzzards, but somehow I didn't connect this bird with them. And it was such an easy shot—'

'Yes,' said Rupert; 'that was the trouble.'

Kathleen found him in the gun-room smoothing out the feathers of the dead bird. She had already been told of the catastrophe.

'What a horrid misfortune,' she said sympathetically.

'It was my dear Robbie who first discovered them the last time he was home on leave. Don't you remember how excited he was about them? Let's go and have some tea.'

Both bridge and shooting were given a rest for the next two or three weeks. Death, who enters into no compacts with party whips, had forced a Parliamentary vacancy on the neighbourhood at the least convenient season, and the local partisans on either side found themselves immersed in the discomforts of a mid-winter election. Rupert took his politics seriously and keenly. He belonged to that type of strangely but rather happily constituted individuals which these islands seem to produce in a fair plenty; men and women who for no personal profit or gain go forth from their comfortable fire-sides or club card-rooms to hunt to and fro in the mud and rain and wind for the capture or tracking of a stray vote here and there on their party's behalf—not because they think they ought to, but because they want to. And his energies were welcome enough on this occasion, for the seat was a closely disputed possession, and its loss or retention would count for much in the present position of the Parliamentary game. With Kathleen to help him, he had worked his corner of the con-stituency with tireless, well-directed zeal, taking his share of the dull routine work as well as of the livelier episodes. The talking part of the campaign wound up on the eve of the poll with a meeting in a certre where more undecided votes were supposed to be concentrated than anywhere else in the division. A good final meeting here would mean everything. And the speakers, local and imported, left nothing undone to improve the occasion. Rupert was down for the unimportant task of moving the complimentary vote to the chairman which should close the proceedings.

'I'm so hoarse,' he protested, when the moment arrived; 'I don't believe I can make my voice heard beyond the platform.'

'Let me do it,' said the Sheep; 'I'm rather good at that sort of thing.'

The chairman was popular with all parties, and the Sheep's opening words of complimentary recognition received a round of applause. The orator smiled expansively on his listeners and seized the opportunity to add a few words of political wisdom on his own account. People looked at the clock or began to grope for umbrellas and discarded neck-wraps. Then, in the midst of a string of meaningless platitudes, the Sheep delivered himself of one of those blundering remarks which travel from one end of a constituency to the other in half an hour, and are seized on by the other side as being more potent on their behalf than a ton of election literature. There was a general shuffling and muttering across the length and breadth of the hall, and a few hisses made themselves heard. The Sheep tried to whittle down his remark, and the chairman unhesitatingly threw him over in his speech of thanks, but the damage was done.

'I'm afraid I lost touch with the audience rather over that remark,' said the Sheep afterwards, with his apologetic smile abnormally developed.

'You lost us the election,' said the chairman, and he proved a true prophet.

A month or so of winter sport seemed a desirable pick-me-up after the strenuous work and crowning discomfiture of the election. Rupert and Kathleen hied them away to a small Alpine resort that was just coming into prominence, and thither the Sheep followed them in due course, in his role of husband-elect. The wedding had been fixed for the end of March.

It was a winter of early and unseasonable thaws, and the far end of the local lake, at a spot where swift currents flowed into it, was decorated with notices, written in three languages, warning skaters not to venture over certain unsafe patches. The folly of approaching too near these danger spots seemed to have a natural fascination for the Sheep.

'I don't see what possible danger there can be,' he protested, with his inevitable smile, when Rupert beckoned him away from the proscribed area; 'the milk that I put out on my window-sill last night was frozen an inch deep.'

'It hadn't got a strong current flowing through it,' said Rupert; 'in any case, there is not much sense in hovering round a doubtful piece of ice when there are acres of good ice to skate over. The secretary of the ice-committee has warned you once already.'

A few minutes later Rupert heard a loud squeal of fear, and saw a dark spot blotting the smoothness of the lake's frozen surface. The Sheep was struggling helplessly in an ice-hole of his own making. Rupert gave one loud curse, and then dashed full tilt for the shore; outside a low stable building on the lake's edge he remembered having seen a ladder. If he could slide it across the ice-hole before the Sheep went under the rescue would be comparatively simple work. Other skaters were dashing up from a distance, and, with the ladder's help, they could get him out of his death-trap without having to trust themselves on the margin of rotten ice. Rupert sprang on to the surface of lumpy, frozen snow, and staggered to where the ladder lay. He had already lifted it when the rattle of a chain and a furious outburst of growls burst on his hearing, and he was dashed to the ground by a mass of white and tawny fur. A sturdy young yard-dog, frantic with the pleasure of performing his first piece of active guardian service, was ramping and snarling over him, rendering the task of regaining his feet or securing the ladder a matter of considerable difficulty. When he had at last succeeded in both efforts he was just by a hair's-breadth too late to be of any use. The Sheep had definitely disappeared under the ice-rift.

Kathleen Athling and her husband stay the greater part of the year with Rupert, and a small Robbie stands in some danger of being idolized by a devoted uncle. But for twelve months of the year Rupert's most inseparable and valued companion is a sturdy tawny and white yard-dog.

HYACINTH

'THE new fashion of introducing the candidate's children into an election contest is a pretty one,' said Mrs Panstreppon; 'it takes away something from the acerbity of party warfare, and it makes an interesting experience for the children to look back on in after years. Still, if you will listen to my advice, Matilda, you will not take Hyacinth with you down to Luffbridge on election day.'

'Not take Hyacinth!' exclaimed his mother; 'but why not? Jutterly is bringing his three children, and they are going to drive a pair of Nubian donkeys about the town, to emphasize the fact that their father has been appointed Colonial Secretary. We are making the demand for a strong Navy a special feature in *our* campaign, and it will be particularly appropriate to have Hyacinth dressed in his sailor suit. He'll look heavenly.'

'The question is, not how he'll look, but how he'll behave. He's a delightful child, of course, but there is a strain of unbridled pugnacity in him that breaks out at times in a really alarming fashion. You may have forgotten the affair of the little Gaffin children; I haven't.'

'I was in India at the time, and I've only a vague recollection of what happened; he was very naughty, I know.'

'He was in his goat-carriage, and met the Gaffins in their perambulator, and he drove the goat full tilt at them and sent the perambulator spinning. Little Jacky Gaffin was pinned down under the wreckage, and while the nurse had her hands full with the goat Hyacinth was laying into Jacky's legs with his belt like a small fury.'

'I'm not defending him,' said Matilda, 'but they must have done something to annoy him.'

'Nothing intentionally, but some one had unfortunately told him that they were half French—their mother was a

Duboc, you know—and he had been having a history lesson that morning, and had just heard of the final loss of Calais by the English, and was furious about it. He said he'd teach the little toads to go snatching towns from us, but we didn't know at the time that he was referring to the Gaffins. I told him afterwards that all bad feeling between the two nations had died out long ago, and that anyhow the Gaffins were only half French, and he said that it was only the French half of Jacky that he had been hitting; the rest had been buried under the perambulator. If the loss of Calais unloosed such fury in him, I tremble to think what the possible loss of the election might entail.'

'All that happened when he was eight; he's older now and knows better.'

'Children with Hyacinth's temperament don't know better as they grow older; they merely know more.'

'Nonsense. He will enjoy the fun of the election, and in any case he'll be tired out by the time the poll is declared, and the new sailor suit that I've had made for him is just in the right shade of blue for our election colours, and it will exactly match the blue of his eyes. He will be a perfectly charming note of colour.'

'There is such a thing as letting one's aesthetic sense override one's moral sense,' said Mrs Panstreppon. 'I believe you would have condoned the South Sea Bubble and the persecution of the Albigenses if they had been carried out in effective colour schemes. However, if anything unfortunate should happen down at Luffbridge, don't say it wasn't foreseen by one member of the family.'

The election was keenly but decorously contested. The newly appointed Colonial Secretary was personally popular, while the Government to which he adhered was distinctly unpopular, and there was some expectancy that the majority of four hundred, obtained at the last election, would be altogether wiped out. Both sides were hopeful, but neither could feel confident. The children were a great success; the little Jutterlys drove their chubby donkeys solemnly up and down the main streets, displaying posters which advocated the claims of their father on the broad general grounds that he was their father, while as for Hyacinth, his conduct might have served as a model for any seraph-child that had strayed unwittingly on to the scene of an electoral contest. Of his own accord, and under the delighted eyes of half a dozen camera operators, he had gone up to the Jutterly children and presented them with a packet of butterscotch; 'we needn't be enemies because we're wearing the opposite colours,' he said with engaging friendliness, and the occupants of the donkey-cart accepted his offering with polite solemnity. The grown-up members of both political camps were delighted at the incident—with the exception of Mrs Panstreppon, who shuddered.

'Never was Clytemnestra's kiss sweeter than on the night she slew me,' she quoted, but made the quotation to herself.

The last hour of the poll was a period of unremitting labour for both parties; it was generally estimated that not more than a dozen votes separated the candidates, and every effort was made to bring up obstinately wavering electors. It was with a feeling of relaxation and relief that every one heard the clocks strike the hour for the close of the poll. Exclamations broke out from the tired workers, and corks flew out from bottles.

'Well, if we haven't won, we've done our level best.' 'It has been a clean, straight fight, with no rancour.' 'The children were quite a charming feature, weren't they?'

The children? It suddenly occurred to everybody that they had seen nothing of the children for the last hour. What had become of the three little Jutterlys and their donkey-cart, and, for the matter of that, what had become of Hyacinth? Hurried, anxious embassies went backwards and forwards between the respective party headquarters and the various committee-rooms, but there was blank ignorance everywhere as to the whereabouts of the children. Every one had been too busy in the closing moments of the poll to bestow a thought on them. Then there came a telephone call at the Unionist Women's Committee-rooms, and the voice of Hyacinth was heard demanding when the poll would be declared.

'Where are you, and where are the Jutterly children?' asked his mother.

'I've just finished having high-tea at a pastry-cook's,' came the answer; 'and they let me telephone. I've had a poached egg and a sausage roll and four meringues.'

'You'll be ill. Are the little Jutterlys with you?'

'Rather not. They're in a pigsty.'

'A pigsty? Why? What pigsty?'

'Near the Crawleigh Road. I met them driving about a back road, and told them they were to have tea with me, and put their donkeys in a yard that I knew of. Then I took them to see an old sow that had got ten little pigs. I got the sow into the outer sty by giving her bits of bread, while the Jutterlys went in to look at the litter, then I bolted the door and left them there.'

'You wicked boy, do you mean to say you've left those poor children there alone in the pigsty?'

'They're not alone, they've got ten little pigs in with them; they're jolly well crowded. They were pretty mad at being shut in, but not half as mad as the old sow is at being shut out from her young ones. If she gets in while they're there she'll bite them into mincemeat. I can get them out by letting a short ladder down through the top window, and that's what I'm going to do *if we win*. If their blighted father gets in, I'm just going to open the door for the sow, and let her do what she dashed well likes to them. That's why I want to know when the poll will be declared.'

Here the narrator rang off. A wild stampede and a frantic sending-off of messengers took place at the other end of the telephone. Nearly all the workers on either side had disappeared to their various club-rooms and public-house bars to await the declaration of the poll, but enough local information could be secured to determine the scene of Hyacinth's exploit. Mr John Ball had a stable yard down near the Crawleigh Road, up a short lane, and his sow was known to have a litter of ten young ones. Thither went in headlong haste both the candidates, Hyacinth's mother, his aunt (Mrs Panstreppon), and two or three hurriedly summoned friends. The two Nubian donkeys, contentedly munching at bundles of hay, met their gaze as they entered the yard. The hoarse savage grunting of an enraged animal and the shriller note of thirteen young voices, three of them human, guided them to the sty, in the outer yard of which a huge Yorkshire sow kept up a ceaseless raging patrol before a closed door. Reclining on the broad ledge of an open window, from which point of vantage he could reach down and shoot the bolt of the door, was Hyacinth, his blue sailor-suit somewhat the worse for wear, and his angel smile exchanged for a look of demoniacal determination.

'If any of you come a step nearer,' he shouted, 'the sow will be inside in half a jiffy.'

A storm of threatening, arguing, entreating expostulation broke from the baffled rescue party, but it made no more impression on Hyacinth than the squealing tempest that raged within the sty.

'If Jutterly heads the poll I'm going to let the sow in. I'll teach the blighters to win elections from us.'

'He means it,' said Mrs Panstreppon; 'I feared the worst when I saw that butterscotch incident.'

'It's all right, my little man,' said Jutterly, with the duplicity to which even a Colonial Secretary can sometimes stoop, 'your father has been elected by a large majority.'

'Liar!' retorted Hyacinth, with the directness of speech that is not merely excusable, but almost obligatory, in the political profession; 'the votes aren't counted yet. You won't gammon me as to the result, either. A boy that I've palled with is going to fire a gun when the poll is declared; two shots if we've won, one shot if we haven't.'

The situation began to look critical. 'Drug the sow,' whispered Hyacinth's father.

Some one went off in the motor to the nearest chemist's shop and returned presently with two large pieces of bread, liberally dosed with narcotic. The bread was thrown deftly and unostentatiously into the sty, but Hyacinth saw through the manœuvre. He set up a piercing imitation of a small pig in Purgatory, and the infuriated mother ramped round and round the sty; the pieces of bread were trampled into slush.

At any moment now the poll might be declared. Jutterly flew back to the Town Hall, where the votes were being counted. His agent met him with a smile of hope.

'You're eleven ahead at present, and only about eighty more to be counted; you're just going to squeak through.'

'I mustn't squeak through,' exclaimed Jutterly hoarsely.

'You must object to every doubtful vote on our side that can possibly be disallowed. I must *not* have the majority.'

Then was seen the unprecedented sight of a party agent challenging the votes on his own side with a captiousness that his opponents would have hesitated to display. One or two votes that would have certainly passed muster under ordinary circumstances were disallowed, but even so Jutterly was six ahead with only thirty more to be counted.

To the watchers by the sty the moments seemed intolerable. As a last resort some one had been sent for a gun with which to shoot the sow, though Hyacinth would probably draw the bolt the moment such a weapon was brought into the yard. Nearly all the men were away from their homes, however, on election night, and the messenger had evidently gone far afield in his search. It must be a matter of minutes now to the declaration of the poll.

A sudden roar of shouting and cheering was heard from the direction of the Town Hall. Hyacinth's father clutched a pitchfork and prepared to dash into the sty in the forlorn hope of being in time.

A shot rang out in the evening air. Hyacinth stooped down from his perch and put his finger on the bolt. The sow pressed furiously against the door.

'Bang!' came another shot.

Hyacinth wriggled back, and sent a short ladder down through the window of the inner sty.

'Now you can come up, you unclean little blighters,' he sang out; 'my daddy's got in, not yours. Hurry up, I can't keep the sow waiting much longer. And don't you jolly well come butting into any election again where I'm on the job.'

In the reaction that set in after the deliverance furious recriminations were indulged in by the lately opposed candidates, their women folk, agents, and party helpers. A recount was demanded, but failed to establish the fact that the Colonial Secretary had obtained a majority. Altogether the election left a legacy of soreness behind it, apart from any that was experienced by Hyacinth in person.

'It is the last time I shall let him go to an election,' exclaimed his mother.

'There I think you are going to extremes,' said Mrs Panstreppon; 'if there should be a general election in Mexico I think you might safely let him go there, but I doubt whether our English politics are suited to the rough and tumble of an angel-child.'

THE GALA PROGRAMME
AN UNRECORDED EPISODE IN ROMAN HISTORY

IT was an auspicious day in the Roman Calendar, the birthday of the popular and gifted young Emperor Placidus Superbus. Every one in Rome was bent on keeping high festival, the weather was at its best, and naturally the Imperial Circus was crowded to its fullest capacity. A few minutes before the hour fixed for the commencement of the spectacle a loud fanfare of trumpets proclaimed the arrival of Caesar, and amid the vociferous acclamations of the multitude the Emperor took his seat in the Imperial Box. As the shouting of the crowd died away an even more thrilling salutation could be heard in the near distance, the angry, impatient roaring and howling of the beasts caged in the Imperial menagerie.

'Explain the programme to me,' commanded the Emperor, having beckoned the Master of the Ceremonies to his side.

That eminent official wore a troubled look.

'Gracious Caesar,' he announced, 'a most promising and entertaining programme has been devised and prepared for your august approval. In the first place there is to be a chariot contest of unusual brilliancy and interest; three teams that have never hitherto suffered defeat are to contend for the Herculaneum Trophy, together with the purse which your Imperial generosity has been pleased to add. The chances of the competing teams are accounted to be as nearly as possible equal, and there is much wagering among the populace. The black Thracians are perhaps the favourites—'

'I know, I know,' interrupted Caesar, who had listened to exhaustive talk on the same subject all the morning; 'what else is there on the programme?'

'The second part of the programme,' said the Imperial Official, 'consists of a grand combat of wild beasts, specially selected for their strength, ferocity, and fighting qualities. There will appear simultaneously in the arena fourteen Nubian lions and lionesses, five tigers, six Syrian bears, eight Persian panthers, and three North African ditto, a number of wolves and lynxes from the Teutonic forests, and seven gigantic wild bulls from the same region. There will also be wild swine of unexampled savageness, a rhinoceros from the Barbary coast, some ferocious man-apes, and a hyaena, reputed to be mad.'

'It promises well,' said the Emperor.

'It *promised* well, O Caesar,' said the official dolorously, 'it promised marvellously well; but between the promise and the performance a cloud has arisen.'

'A cloud? What cloud?' queried Caesar, with a frown.

'The Suffragetae,' explained the official; 'they threaten to interfere with the chariot race.'

'I'd like to see them do it!' exclaimed the Emperor indignantly.

'I fear your Imperial wish may be unpleasantly gratified,' said the Master of the Ceremonies; 'we are taking, of course, every possible precaution, and guarding all the entrances to the arena and the stables with a triple guard; but it is rumoured that at the signal for the entry of the chariots five hundred women will let themselves down with ropes from the public seats and swarm all over the course. Naturally no race could be run under such circumstances; the programme will be ruined.'

'On my birthday,' said Placidus Superbus, 'they would not dare to do such an outrageous thing.'

'The more august the occasion, the more desirous they will be to advertise themselves and their cause,' said the harassed official; 'they do not scruple to make riotous interference even with the ceremonies in the temples.'

'Who *are* these Suffragetae?' asked the Emperor. 'Since I came back from my Pannonian expedition I have heard of nothing else but their excesses and demonstrations.'

'They are a political sect of very recent origin, and their aim seems to be to get a big share of political authority into their hands. The means they are taking to convince us of their fitness to help in making and administering the laws consist of wild indulgence in tumult, destruction, and defiance of all authority. They have already damaged some of the most historically valuable of our public treasures, which can never be replaced.'

'Is it possible that the sex which we hold in such honour and for which we feel such admiration can produce such hordes of Furies?' asked the Emperor.

'It takes all sorts to make a sex,' observed the Master of the Ceremonies, who possessed a certain amount of worldly wisdom; 'also,' he continued anxiously, 'it takes very little to upset a gala programme.'

'Perhaps the disturbance that you anticipate will turn out to be an idle threat,' said the Emperor consolingly.

'But if they should carry out their intention,' said the official, 'the programme will be utterly ruined.'

The Emperor said nothing.

Five minutes later the trumpets rang out for the commencement of the entertainment. A hum of excited anticipation ran through the ranks of the spectators, and final bets on the issue of the great race were hurriedly shouted. The gates leading from the stables were slowly swung open, and a troop of mounted attendants rode round the track to ascertain that everything was clear for the momentous contest. Again the trumpets rang out, and then, before the foremost chariot had appeared, there arose a wild tumult of shouting, laughing, angry protests, and shrill screams of defiance. Hundreds of women were being lowered by their accomplices into the arena. A moment later they were running and dancing in frenzied troops across the track where the chariots were supposed to compete. No team of arena-trained horses would have faced such a frantic mob; the race was clearly an impossibility. Howls of disappointment and rage rose from the spectators, howls of triumph echoed back from the women in possession. The vain efforts of the circus attendants to drive out the invading horde merely added to the uproar and confusion; as fast as the Suffragetae were thrust away from one portion of the track they swarmed on to another.

The Master of the Ceremonies was nearly delirious from rage and mortification. Placidus Superbus, who remained calm and unruffled as ever, beckoned to him and spoke a word or two in his ear. For the first time that afternoon the sorely tried official was seen to smile.

A trumpet rang out from the Imperial Box; an instant hush fell over the excited throng. Perhaps the Emperor, as a last resort, was going to announce some concession to the Suffragetae.

'Close the stable gates,' commanded the Master of the Ceremonies, 'and open all the menagerie dens. It is the Imperial pleasure that the second portion of the programme be taken first.'

It turned out that the Master of the Ceremonies had in no wise exaggerated the probable brilliancy of this portion of the spectacle. The wild bulls were really wild, and the hyaena reputed to be mad thoroughly lived up to its reputation.

THE UNBEARABLE
BASSINGTON

CHAPTER 1

FRANCESCA BASSINGTON sat in the drawing-room of her house in Blue Street, W., regaling herself and her estimable brother Henry with China tea and small cress sandwiches. The meal was of that elegant proportion which, while ministering sympathetically to the desires of the moment, is happily reminiscent of a satisfactory luncheon and blessedly expectant of an elaborate dinner to come.

In her younger days Francesca had been known as the beautiful Miss Greech; at forty, although much of the original beauty remained, she was just dear Francesca Bassington. No one would have dreamed of calling her sweet, but a good many people who scarcely knew her were punctilious about putting in the 'dear'.

Her enemies, in their honester moments, would have admitted that she was svelte and knew how to dress, but they would have agreed with her friends in asserting that she had no soul. When one's friends and enemies agree on any particular point they are usually wrong. Francesca herself, if pressed in an unguarded moment to describe her soul, would probably have described her drawing-room. Not that she would have considered that the one had stamped the impress of its character on the other, so that close scrutiny might reveal its outstanding features, and even suggest its hidden places, but because she might have dimly recognized that her drawing-room was her soul.

Francesca was one of those women towards whom Fate appears to have the best intentions and never to carry them into practice. With the advantages put at her disposal she might have been expected to command a more than average share of feminine happiness. So many of the things that make for fretfulness, disappointment and discouragement in a woman's life were removed from her path that she might well have been considered the fortunate Miss Greech, or later, lucky Francesca Bassington. And she was not of the perverse band of those who make a rock-garden of their souls by dragging into them all the stony griefs and unclaimed troubles they can find lying around them. Francesca loved the smooth ways and pleasant places of life; she liked not merely to look on the bright side of things, but to live there and stay there. And the fact that things had, at one time and another, gone badly with her and cheated her of some of her early illusions made her cling the closer to such good fortune as remained to her now that she seemed to have reached a calmer period of her life. To undiscriminating friends she appeared in the guise of a rather selfish woman, but it was merely the selfishness of one who had seen the happy and unhappy sides of life and wished to enjoy to the utmost what was left to her of the former. The vicissitudes of fortune had not soured her, but they had perhaps narrowed her in the sense of making her concentrate much of her sympathies on things that immediately pleased and amused her, or that recalled and perpetuated the pleasing and successful incidents of other days. And it was her drawing-room in particular that enshrined the memorials or tokens of past and present happiness.

Into that comfortable quaint-shaped room of angles and bays and alcoves had sailed, as into a harbour, those precious personal possessions and trophies that had survived the buffetings and storms of a not very tranquil married life. Wherever her eyes might turn she saw the embodied results of her successes, economies, good luck, good management or good taste. The battle had more than once gone against her, but she had somehow always contrived to save her baggage train, and her complacent gaze could roam over object after object that represented the spoils of victory or the salvage of honourable defeat. The delicious bronze Fremiet on the mantelpiece had been the outcome of a Grand Prix sweepstake of many years ago; a group of Dresden figures of some considerable value had been bequeathed to her by a discreet admirer, who had added death to his other kindnesses; another group had been a self-bestowed present, purchased in blessed and unfading memory of a wonderful nine-days' bridge winnings at a country-house party. There were old Persian and Bokharan rugs and Worcester tea-services of glowing colour, and little treasures of antique silver that each enshrined a history or a memory in addition to its own intrinsic value. It amused her at times to think of the bygone craftsmen and artificers who had hammered and wrought and woven in far distant countries and ages, to produce the wonderful and beautiful things that had come, one way and another, into her possession. Workers in the studios of medieval Italian towns and of later Paris, in the bazaars of Bagdad and of Central Asia, in old-time English workshops and German factories, in all manner of queer hidden corners where craft secrets were jealously guarded, nameless unremembered men and men whose names were worldrenowned and deathless.

And above all her other treasures, dominating in her estimation every other object that the room contained, was the great Van der Meulen that had come from her father's home as part of her wedding dowry. It fitted exactly into the central wall panel above the narrow buhl cabinet, and filled exactly its right space in the composition and balance of the room. From wherever you sat it seemed to confront you as the dominating feature of its surroundings. There was a pleasing serenity about the great pompous battle scene with its solemn courtly warriors bestriding their heavily prancing steeds, grey or skewbald or dun, all gravely in earnest, and yet somehow conveying the impression that their campaigns were but vast serious picnics arranged in the grand manner. Francesca could not imagine the drawing-room without the crowning complement of the stately well-hung picture, just as she could not imagine herself in any other setting than this house in Blue Street with its crowded Pantheon of cherished household gods.

And herein sprouted one of the thorns that obtruded through the rose-leaf damask of what might otherwise have been Francesca's peace of mind. One's happiness always lies in the future rather than in the past. With due deference to an esteemed lyrical authority one may safely say that a sorrow's crown of sorrow is anticipating unhappier things. The house in Blue Street had been left to her by her old friend Sophie Chetrof, but only until such time as her niece Emmeline Chetrof should marry, when it was to pass to her as a wedding present. Emmeline was now seventeen and passably good-looking, and four or five years were all that could be safely allotted to the span of her continued spinsterhood. Beyond that period lay chaos, the wrenching asunder of Francesca from the sheltering habitation that had grown to be her soul. It is true that in imagination she had built herself a bridge across the chasm, a bridge of a single span. The bridge in question was her schoolboy son Comus, now being educated somewhere in the southern counties, or rather one should say the bridge consisted of the possibility of his eventual marriage with Emmeline, in which case Francesca saw herself still reigning, a trifle squeezed and incommoded perhaps, but still reigning in the house in Blue Street. The Van der Meulen would still catch its requisite afternoon light in its place of honour, the Fremiet and the Dresden and Old Worcester would continue undisturbed in their accustomed niches. Emmeline could have the Japanese snuggery, where Francesca sometimes drank her after-dinner coffee, as a separate drawing-room, where she could put her own things. The details of the bridge structure had all been carefully thought out. Only—it was an unfortunate circumstance that Comus should have been the span on which everything balanced.

Francesca's husband had insisted on giving the boy that strange Pagan name, and had not lived long enough to judge as to the appropriateness, or otherwise, of its significance. In seventeen years and some odd months Francesca had had ample opportunity for forming an opinion concerning her son's characteristics. The spirit of mirthfulness which one associates with the name certainly ran riot in the boy, but it was a twisted wayward sort of mirth of which Francesca herself could seldom see the humorous side. In her brother Henry, who sat eating small cress sandwiches as solemnly as though they had been ordained in some immemorial Book of Observances, fate had been undisguisedly kind to her. He might so easily have married some pretty helpless little woman, and lived at Notting Hill Gate, and been the father of a long string of pale, clever, useless children, who would have had birthdays and the sort of illnesses that one is expected to send grapes to, and who would have painted fatuous objects in a South Kensington manner as Christmas offerings to an aunt whose cubic space for lumber was limited. Instead of committing these unbrotherly actions, which are so frequent in family life that they might almost be called brotherly, Henry had married a woman who had both money and a sense of repose, and their one child had the brilliant virtue of never saying anything which even its parents could consider worth repeating. Then he had gone into Parliament, possibly with the idea of making his home life seem less dull; at any rate it redeemed his career from insignificance, for no man whose death can produce the item 'another by-election' on the news posters can be wholly a nonentity. Henry, in short, who might have been an embarrassment and a handicap, had chosen rather to be a friend and counsellor, at times even an emergency bank balance; Francesca on her part, with partiality which a clever and lazily-inclined woman often feels for a reliable fool, not only sought his counsel but frequently followed it. When convenient, moreover, she repaid his loans.

Against this good service on the part of Fate in providing her with Henry for a brother, Francesca could well set the plaguy malice of the destiny that had given her Comus for a son. The boy was one of those untamable young lords of misrule that frolic and chafe themselves through nursery and preparatory and public-school days with the utmost allowance of storm and dust and dislocation and the least possible amount of collar-work, and come somehow with a laugh through a series of catastrophes that has reduced every one else concerned to tears or Cassandra-like forebodings. Sometimes they sober down in after-life and become uninteresting, forgetting that they were ever lords of anything; sometimes Fate plays royally into their hands, and they do great things in a spacious manner, and are thanked by Parliaments and the Press and acclaimed by gala-day crowds. But in most cases their tragedy begins when they leave school and turn themselves loose in a world that has grown too civilized and too crowded and too empty to have any place for them. And they are very many.

Henry Greech had made an end of biting small sandwiches, and settled down like a dust-storm refreshed, to discuss one of the fashionably prevalent topics of the moment, the prevention of destitution.

'It is a question that is only being nibbled at, smelt at, one might say, at the present moment,' he observed, 'but it is one that will have to engage our serious attention and consideration before long. The first thing that we shall have to do is to get out of the dilettante and academic way of approaching it. We must collect and assimilate hard facts. It is a subject that ought to appeal to all thinking minds, and yet, you know, I find it surprisingly difficult to interest people in it.'

Francesca made some monosyllabic response, a sort of sympathetic grunt which was meant to indicate that she was, to a certain extent, listening and appreciating. In reality she was reflecting that Henry possibly found it difficult to interest people in any topic that he enlarged on. His talents lay so thoroughly in the direction of being uninteresting, that even as an eye-witness of the massacre of St Bartholomew he would probably have infused a flavour of boredom into his descriptions of the event.

'I was speaking down in Leicestershire the other day on this subject,' continued Henry, 'and I pointed out at some length a thing that few people ever stop to consider—'

Francesca went over immediately but decorously to the majority that will not stop to consider.

'Did you come across any of the Barnets when you were down there?' she interrupted; 'Eliza Barnet is rather taken up with all those subjects.'

In the propagandist movements of Sociology, as in other arenas of life and struggle, the fiercest competition and rivalry is frequently to be found between closely allied types and species. Eliza Barnet shared many of Henry Greech's political and social views, but she also shared his fondness for pointing things out at some length; there had been occasions when she had extensively occupied the strictly limited span allotted to the platform oratory of a group of speakers of whom Henry Greech had been an impatient unit. He might see eye to eye with her on the leading questions of the day, but he persistently wore mental blinkers as far as her estimable qualities were concerned, and the mention of her name was a skilful lure drawn across the trail of his discourse; if Francesca had to listen to his eloquence on any subject she much preferred that it should be a disparagement of Eliza Barnet rather than the prevention of destitution.

'I've no doubt she means well,' said Henry, 'but it would be a good thing if she could be induced to keep her own personality a little more in the background, and not to imagine that she is the necessary mouthpiece of all the progressive thought in the countryside. I fancy Canon Besomley must have had her in his mind when he said that some people came into the world to shake empires and others to move amendments.'

Francesca laughed with genuine amusement.

'I suppose she is really wonderfully well up in all the subjects she talks about,' was her provocative comment.

Henry grew possibly conscious of the fact that he was being drawn out on the subject of Eliza Barnet, and he presently turned on to a more personal topic.

'From the general air of tranquillity about the house I presume Comus has gone back to Thaleby,' he observed.

'Yes,' said Francesca, 'he went back yesterday. Of course, I'm very fond of him, but I bear the separation well. When he's here it's rather like having a live volcano in the house, a volcano that in its quietest moments asks incessant questions and uses strong scent.'

'It is only a temporary respite,' said Henry; 'in a year or two he will be leaving school, and then what?'

Francesca closed her eyes with the air of one who seeks to shut out a distressing vision. She was not fond of looking intimately at the future in the presence of another person, especially when the future was draped in doubtfully auspicious colours.

'And then what?' persisted Henry.

'Then I suppose he will be upon my hands.'

'Exactly.'

'Don't sit there looking judicial. I'm quite ready to listen to suggestions if you've any to make.'

'In the case of any ordinary boy,' said Henry, 'I might make lots of suggestions as to the finding of suitable employment. From what we know of Comus it would be rather a waste of time for either of us to look for jobs which he wouldn't look at when we'd got them for him.'

'He must do something,' said Francesca.

'I know he must; but he never will. At least, he'll never stick to anything. The most hopeful thing to do with him will be to marry him to an heiress. That would solve the financial side of his problem. If he had unlimited money at his disposal, he might go into the wilds somewhere and shoot big game. I never know what the big game have done to deserve it, but they do help to deflect the destructive energies of some of our social misfits.'

Henry, who never killed anything larger or fiercer than a trout, was scornfully superior on the subject of big game shooting.

Francesca brightened at the matrimonial suggestion. 'I don't know about an heiress,' she said reflectively. 'There's Emmeline Chetrof, of course. One could hardly call her an heiress, but she's got a comfortable little income of her own, and I suppose something more will come to her from her grandmother. Then, of course, you know this house goes to her when she marries.'

'That would be very convenient,' said Henry, probably following a line of thought that his sister had trodden many hundreds of times before him. 'Do she and Comus hit it off at all well together?'

'Oh, well enough in boy and girl fashion,' said Francesca. 'I must arrange for them to see more of each other in future. By the way, that little brother of hers that she dotes on, Lancelot, goes to Thaleby this term. I'll write and tell Comus to be specially kind to him; that will be a sure way to Emmeline's heart. Comus has been made a prefect, you know. Heaven knows why.'

'It can only be for prominence in games,' sniffed Henry; 'I think we may safely leave work and conduct out of the question.'

Comus was not a favourite with his uncle.

Francesca had turned to her writing cabinet and was scribbling a letter to her son in which the delicate health, timid disposition and other inevitable attributes of the new boy were brought to his notice, and commended to his care. When she had sealed and stamped the envelope Henry uttered a belated caution.

'Perhaps on the whole it would be wiser to say nothing about the boy to Comus. He doesn't always respond to directions, you know.'

Francesca did know, and already was more than half of her brother's opinion; but the woman who can sacrifice a clean unspoiled penny stamp is probably yet unborn.

CHAPTER 2

LANCELOT CHETROF stood at the end of a long bare passage, restlessly consulting his watch and fervently wishing himself half an hour older with a certain painful experience already registered in the past; unfortunately it still belonged to the future, and what was still more horrible, to the immediate future. Like many boys new to a school he had cultivated an unhealthy passion for obeying rules and requirements, and his zeal in this direction had proved his undoing. In his hurry to be doing two or three estimable things at once he had omitted to study the notice-board in more than a perfunctory fashion and had thereby missed a football practice specially ordained for newly-joined boys. His fellow-juniors of a term's longer standing had graphically enlightened him as to the inevitable consequences of his lapse; the dread which attaches to the unknown was, at any rate, deleted from his approaching doom, though at the moment he felt scarcely grateful for the knowledge placed at his disposal with such lavish solicitude.

'You'll get six of the very best, over the back of a chair,' said one.

'They'll draw a chalk line across you, of course, you know,' said another.

'A chalk line?'

'Rather. So that every cut can be aimed exactly at the same spot. It hurts much more that way.'

Lancelot tried to nourish a wan hope that there might be

an element of exaggeration in this uncomfortably realistic description.

Meanwhile in the prefects' room at the other end of the passage, Comus Bassington and a fellow-prefect sat also waiting on time, but in a mood of far more pleasurable expectancy. Comus was one of the most junior of the prefect caste, but by no means the least well known, and outside the masters' common-room he enjoyed a certain fitful popularity, or at any rate admiration. At football he was too erratic to be a really brilliant player, but he tackled as if that act of bringing his man headlong to the ground was in itself a sensuous pleasure, and his weird swear-words whenever he got hurt were eagerly treasured by those who were fortunate enough to hear them. At athletics in general he was a showy performer, and although new to the functions of a prefect he had already established a reputation as an effective and artistic caner. In appearance he exactly fitted his fanciful Pagan name. His large green-grey eyes seemed for ever asparkle with goblin mischief and the joy of revelry, and the curved lips might have been those of some wickedly-laughing faun; one almost expected to see embryo horns fretting the smoothness of his sleek dark hair. The chin was firm, but one looked in vain for a redeeming touch of ill-temper in the handsome, half-mocking, half-petulant face. With a strain of sourness in him Comus might have been leavened into something creative and masterful; fate had fashioned him with a certain whimsical charm, and left him all unequipped for the greater purposes of life. Perhaps no one would have called him a lovable character, but in many respects he was adorable; in all respects he was certainly damned.

Rutley, his companion of the moment, sat watching him and wondering, from the depths of a very ordinary brain, whether he liked or hated him; it was easy to do either.

'It's not really your turn to cane,' he said.

'I know it's not,' said Comus, fingering a very serviceable-looking cane as lovingly as a pious violinist might handle his Strad. 'I gave Greyson some mint-chocolate to let me toss whether I caned or him, and I won. He was rather decent over it and let me have half the chocolate back.'

The droll lightheartedness which won Comus Bassington such measures of popularity as he enjoyed among his fellows did not materially help to endear him to the succession of masters with whom he came in contact during the course of his schooldays. He amused and interested such of them as had the saving grace of humour at their disposal, but if they sighed when he passed from their immediate responsibility it was a sigh of relief rather than of regret. The more enlightened and experienced of them realized that he was something outside the scope of the things that they were called upon to deal with. A man who has been trained to cope with storms, to foresee their coming, and to minimize their consequences, may be pardoned if he feels a certain reluctance to measure himself against a tornado.

Men of more limited outlook and with a correspondingly larger belief in their own powers were ready to tackle the tornado had time permitted.

'I think I could tame young Bassington if I had your opportunities,' a form-master once remarked to a colleague whose House had the embarrassing distinction of numbering Comus among its inmates.

'Heaven forbid that I should try,' replied the housemaster.

'But why?' asked the reformer.

'Because Nature hates any interference with her own arrangements, and if you start in to tame the obviously untamable you are taking a fearful responsibility on yourself.'

'Nonsense; boys are Nature's raw material.'

'Millions of boys are. There are just a few, and Bassington is one of them, who are Nature's highly finished product when they are in the schoolboy stage, and we, who are supposed to be moulding raw material, are quite helpless when we come in contact with them.'

'But what happens to them when they grow up?'

'They never do grow up,' said the housemaster; 'that is their tragedy. Bassington will certainly never grow out of his present stage.'

'Now you are talking in the language of Peter Pan,' said the form-master.

'I am not thinking in the manner of Peter Pan,' said the

other. 'With all reverence for the author of that masterpiece I should say he had a wonderful and tender insight into the child mind and knew nothing whatever about boys. To make only one criticism on that particular work, can you imagine a lot of British boys, or boys of any country that one knows of, who would stay contentedly playing children's games in an underground cave when there were wolves and pirates and Red Indians to be had for the asking on the other side of the trap door?'

The form-master laughed. 'You evidently think that the "Boy who would not grow up" must have been written by a "grown-up who could never have been a boy". Perhaps that is the meaning of the "Never-never land". I daresay you're right in your criticism, but I don't agree with you about Bassington. He's a handful to deal with, as any one knows who has come in contact with him, but if one's hands weren't full with a thousand and one other things I hold to my opinion that he could be tamed.'

And he went his way, having maintained a form-master's inalienable privilege of being in the right.

In the prefects' room, Comus busied himself with the exact position of a chair planted out in the middle of the floor.

'I think everything's ready,' he said.

Rutley glanced at the clock with the air of a Roman elegant in the Circus, languidly awaiting the introduction of an expected Christian to an expectant tiger.

'The kid is due in two minutes,' he said.

'He'd jolly well better not be late,' said Comus.

Comus had gone through the mill of many scorching castigations in his earlier schooldays, and was able to appreciate to the last ounce the panic that must be now possessing his foredoomed victim, probably at this moment hovering miserably outside the door. After all, that was part of the fun of the thing, and most things had their amusing side if one knows where to look for it.

There was a knock at the door, and Lancelot entered in response to a hearty friendly summons to 'come in'.

'I've come to be caned,' he said breathlessly; adding by way of identification, 'my name's Chetrof.'

'That's quite bad enough in itself,' said Comus, 'but there is probably worse to follow. You are evidently keeping something back from us.'

'I missed a footer practice,' said Lancelot.

'Six,' said Comus briefly, picking up his cane.

'I didn't see the notice on the board,' hazarded Lancelot as a forlorn hope.

'We are always pleased to listen to excuses, and our charge is two extra cuts. That will be eight. Get over.'

And Comus indicated the chair that stood in sinister isolation in the middle of the room. Never had an article of furniture seemed more hateful in Lancelot's eyes. Comus could well remember the time when a chair stuck in the middle of a room had seemed to him the most horrible of manufactured things.

'Lend me a piece of chalk,' he said to his brother prefect. Lancelot ruefully recognized the truth of the chalk-line story.

Comus drew the desired line with an anxious exactitude which he would have scorned to apply to a diagram of Euclid or a map of the Russo-Persian frontier.

'Bend a little more forward,' he said to the victim, 'and much tighter. Don't trouble to look pleasant, because I can't see your face anyway. It may sound unorthodox to say so, but this is going to hurt you much more than it will hurt me.'

There was a carefully measured pause, and then Lancelot was made vividly aware of what a good cane can be made to do in really efficient hands. At the second cut he projected himself hurriedly off the chair.

'Now I've lost count,' said Comus; 'we shall have to begin all over again. Kindly get back into the same position. If you get down again before I've finished Rutley will hold you over and you'll get a dozen.'

Lancelot got back on to the chair, and was re-arranged to the taste of his executioner. He stayed there somehow or other while Comus made eight accurate and agonizingly effective shots at the chalk line.

'By the way,' he said to his gasping and gulping victim when the infliction was over, 'you said Chetrof, didn't you? I believe I've been asked to be kind to you. As a beginning you can clean out my study this afternoon. Be awfully careful how you dust the old china. If you break any don't come and tell me, but just go and drown yourself somewhere; it will save you from a worse fate.'

'I don't know where your study is,' said Lancelot between his chokes.

'You'd better find it or I shall have to beat you, really hard this time. Here, you'd better keep this chalk in your pocket, it's sure to come in handy later on. Don't stop to thank me for all I've done, it only embarrasses me.'

As Comus hadn't got a study Lancelot spent a feverish half-hour in looking for it, incidentally missing another footer practice.

'Everything is very jolly here,' wrote Lancelot to his sister Emmeline. 'The prefects can give you an awful hot time if they like, but most of them are rather decent. Some are Beasts. Bassington is a prefect, though only a junior one. He is the Limit as Beasts go. At least, I think so.'

Schoolboy reticence went no further, but Emmeline filled in the gaps for herself with the lavish splendour of feminine imagination. Francesca's bridge went crashing into the abyss.

CHAPTER 3

ON the evening of a certain November day, two years after the events heretofore chronicled, Francesca Bassington steered her way through the crowd that filled the rooms of her friend Serena Golackly, bestowing nods of vague recognition as she went, but with eyes that were obviously intent on focusing one particular figure. Parliament had pulled its energies together for an Autumn Session, and both political Parties were fairly well represented in the throng. Serena had a harmless way of inviting a number of more or less public men and women to her house, and hoping that if you left them together long enough they would constitute a *salon*. In pursuance of the same instinct she planted the flower borders at her weekend cottage retreat in Surrey with a large mixture of bulbs, and called the result a Dutch garden. Unfortunately, though you may bring brilliant talkers into your home, you cannot always make them talk brilliantly, or even talk at all; what is worse you cannot restrict the output of those starling-voiced dullards who seem to have, on all subjects, so much to say that was well worth leaving unsaid. One group that Francesca passed was discussing a Spanish painter, who was forty-three, and had painted thousands of square yards of canvas in his time, but of whom no one in London had heard till a few months ago; now the starling-voices seemed determined that one should hear of very little else. Three women knew how his name was pronounced, another always felt that she must go into a forest and pray whenever she saw his pictures, another had noticed that there were always pomegranates in his later compositions, and a man with an indefensible collar knew what the pomegranates 'meant'. 'What I think so splendid about him,' said a stout lady in a loud challenging voice, 'is the way he defies all the conventions of art while retaining all that the conventions stand for.' 'Ah, but have you noticed—' put in the man with the atrocious collar, and Francesca pushed desperately on, wondering dimly as she went what people found so unsupportable in the affliction of deafness. Her progress was impeded for a moment by a couple engaged in earnest and voluble discussion of some smouldering question of the day; a thin spectacled young man with the receding forehead that so often denotes advanced opinions, was talking to a spectacled young woman with a similar type of forehead, and exceedingly untidy hair. It was her ambition in life to be taken for a Russian girl-student, and she had spent weeks of patient research in trying to find out exactly where you put the tea-leaves in a samovar. She had once been introduced to a young Jewess from Odessa, who had died of pneumonia the following week; the experience, slight as it was, constituted the spectacled young lady an authority on all things Russian in the eyes of her immediate set.

'Talk is helpful, talk is needful,' the young man was saying, 'but what we have got to do is to lift the subject out of the furrow of indisciplined talk and place it on the threshing-floor of practical discussion.'

The young woman took advantage of the rhetorical full-stop to dash in with the remark which was already marshalled on the tip of her tongue.

'In emancipating the serfs of poverty we must be careful to avoid the mistakes which Russian bureaucracy stumbled into when liberating the serfs of the soil.'

She paused in her turn for the sake of declamatory effect, but recovered her breath quickly enough to start afresh on level terms with the young man, who had jumped into the stride of his next sentence.

'They got off to a good start that time,' said Francesca to herself; 'I suppose it's the Prevention of Destitution they're hammering at. What on earth would become of these dear good people if any one started a crusade for the prevention of mediocrity?'

Midway through one of the smaller rooms, still questing for an elusive presence, she caught sight of some one that she knew, and the shadow of a frown passed across her face. The object of her faintly signalled displeasure was Courtenay Youghal, a political spur-winner who seemed absurdly youthful to a generation that had never heard of Pitt. It was Youghal's ambition—or perhaps his hobby—to infuse into the greyness of modern political life some of the colour of Disraelian dandyism, tempered with the correctness of Anglo-Saxon taste, and supplemented by the flashes of wit that were inherent from the Celtic strain in him. His success was only a half-measure. The public missed in him that touch of blatancy which it looks for in its rising public men; the decorative smoothness of his chestnut-golden hair, and the lively sparkle of his epigrams were counted to him for good, but the restrained sumptuousness of his waistcoats and cravats were as wasted efforts. If he had habitually smoked cigarettes in a pink coral mouthpiece, or worn spats of Mackenzie tartan, the great heart of the voting-man, and the gush of the paragraph-makers might have been unreservedly his. The art of public life consists to a great extent of knowing exactly where to stop and going a bit farther.

It was not Youghal's lack of political sagacity that had brought the momentary look of disapproval into Francesca's face. The fact was that Comus, who had left off being a schoolboy and was now a social problem, had lately enrolled himself among the young politician's associates and admirers, and as the boy knew and cared nothing about politics, and merely copied Youghal's waistcoats, and, less successfully, his conversation, Francesca felt herself justified in deploring the intimacy. To a woman who dressed well on comparatively nothing a year it was an anxious experience to have a son who dressed sumptuously on absolutely nothing.

The cloud that had passed over her face when she caught sight of the offending Youghal was presently succeeded by a smile of gratified achievement, as she encountered a bow of recognition and welcome from a portly middle-aged gentleman, who seemed genuinely anxious to include her in the rather meagre group that he had gathered about him.

'We were just talking about my new charge,' he observed genially, including in the 'we' his somewhat depressed-looking listeners, who in all human probability had done none of the talking. 'I was just telling them, and you may be interested to hear this—'

Francesca, with Spartan stoicism, continued to wear an ingratiating smile, though the character of the deaf adder that stoppeth her ear and will not hearken, seemed to her at that moment a beautiful one.

Sir Julian Jull had been a member of a House of Commons distinguished for its high standard of well-informed mediocrity, and had harmonized so thoroughly with his surroundings that the most attentive observer of Parliamentary proceedings could scarcely have told even on which side of the House he sat. A baronetcy bestowed on him by the Party in power had at least removed that doubt; some weeks later he had been made Governor of some West Indian dependency, whether as a reward for having accepted the baronetcy, or as an application of a theory that West Indian islands get the Governors they deserve, it would have been hard to say. To Sir Julian the appointment was, doubtless, one of some importance; during the span of his Governorship the island might possibly be visited by a member of the Royal Family, or at the least by an earthquake, and in either case his name would get into the papers. To the public the matter was one of absolute indifference; 'who is he and where is it?' would have correctly epitomized the sum total of general information on the personal and geographical aspects of the case.

Francesca, however, from the moment she had heard of the likelihood of the appointment, had taken a deep and lively interest in Sir Julian. As a Member of Parliament he had not filled any very pressing social want in her life, and on the rare occasions when she took tea on the Terrace of the House she was wont to lapse into rapt contemplation of St Thomas's Hospital whenever she saw him within bowing distance. But as Governor of an island he would, of course, want a private secretary, and as a friend and colleague of Henry Greech, to whom he was indebted for many little acts of political support (they had once jointly drafted an amendment which had been ruled out of order), what was more natural and proper than that he should let his choice fall on Henry's nephew Comus? While privately doubting whether the boy would make the sort of secretary that any public man would esteem as a treasure, Henry was thoroughly in agreement with Francesca as to the excellence and desirability of an arrangement which would transplant that troublesome young animal from the too restricted and conspicuous area that centres in the parish of St James's to some misty corner of the British dominion overseas. Brother and sister had conspired to give an elaborate and at the same time cozy little luncheon to Sir Julian on the very day that his appointment was officially announced, and the question of the secretaryship had been mooted and sedulously fostered as occasion permitted, until all that was now needed to clinch the matter was a formal interview between His Excellency and Comus. The boy had from the first shown very little gratification at the prospect of his deportation. To live on a remote shark-girt island, as he expressed it, with the Jull family as his chief social mainstay, and Sir Julian's conversation as a daily item of his existence, did not inspire him with the same degree of enthusiasm as was displayed by his mother and uncle, who, after all, were not making the experiment. Even the necessity for an entirely new outfit did not appeal to his imagination with the force that might have been expected. But, however lukewarm his adhesion to the project might be, Francesca and her brother were clearly determined that no lack of deft persistence on their part should endanger its success. It was for the purpose of reminding Sir Julian of his promise to meet Comus at lunch on the following day, and definitely settle the matter of the secretaryship, that Francesca was now enduring the ordeal of a long harangue of the value of the West Indian group as an Imperial asset. Other listeners dexterously detached themselves one by one, but Francesca's patience outlasted even Sir Julian's flow of commonplaces, and her devotion was duly rewarded by a renewed acknowledgment of the lunch engagement and its purpose. She pushed her way back through the throng of starling-voiced chatterers fortified by a sense of well-earned victory. Dear Serena's absurd *salons* served some good purpose after all.

Francesca was not an early riser, and her breakfast was only just beginning to mobilize on the breakfast-table next morning when a copy of *The Times*, sent by special messenger from her brother's house, was brought up to her room. A heavy margin of blue pencilling drew her attention to a prominently-printed letter which bore the ironical heading: 'Julian Jull, Proconsul.' The matter of the letter was a cruel disinterment of some fatuous and forgotten speeches made by Sir Julian to his constituents not many years ago, in which the value of some of our Colonial possessions, particularly certain West Indian islands, was decried in a medley of pomposity, ignorance and amazingly cheap humour. The extracts given sounded weak and foolish enough, taken by themselves, but the writer of the letter had interlarded them with comments of his own, which sparkled with an ironical brilliance that was Cervantes-like in its polished cruelty. Remembering her ordeal of the previous evening Francesca permitted herself a certain feeling of amusement as she read the merciless stabs inflicted on the newly-appointed Governor; then she came to the signature at the foot of the letter, and the laughter died out of her eyes. 'Comus Bassington' stared at her from above a thick layer of blue pencil lines marked by Henry Greech's shaking hand.

Comus could no more have devised such a letter than he could have written an Episcopal charge to the clergy of any given diocese. It was obviously the work of Courtenay Youghal, and Comus, for a palpable purpose of his own, had wheedled him into forgoing for once the pride of authorship in a clever piece of political raillery, and letting his young friend stand sponsor instead. It was a daring stroke, and there could be no question as to its success; the secretaryship and the distant shark-girt island faded away into the horizon of impossible things. Francesca, forgetting the golden rule of strategy which enjoins a careful choosing of ground and opportunity before entering on hostilities, made straight for the bathroom door, behind which a lively din of splashing betokened that Comus had at least begun his toilet.

'You wicked boy, what have you done?' she cried reproachfully.

'Me washee,' came a cheerful shout; 'me washee from the neck all the way down to the merrythought, and now washee down from the merrythought to—'

'You have ruined your future. *The Times* has printed that miserable letter with your signature.'

A loud squeal of joy came from the bath. 'Oh, Mummy! Let me see!'

There were sounds as of a sprawling dripping body clambering hastily out of the bath. Francesca fled. One cannot effectively scold a moist nineteen-year-old boy clad only in a bath-towel and a cloud of steam.

Another messenger arrived before Francesca's breakfast was over. This one brought a letter from Sir Julian Jull, excusing himself from fulfilment of the luncheon engagement.

CHAPTER 4

FRANCESCA prided herself on being able to see things from other people's points of view, which meant, as it usually does, that she could see her own point of view from various aspects.

As regards Comus, whose doings and non-doings bulked largely in her thoughts at the present moment, she had mapped out in her mind so clearly what his outlook in life ought to be, that she was peculiarly unfitted to understand the drift of his feelings or the impulses that governed them. Fate had endowed her with a son; in limiting the endowment to a solitary offspring Fate had certainly shown a moderation which Francesca was perfectly willing to acknowledge and be thankful for; but then, as she pointed out to a certain complacent friend of hers who cheerfully sustained an endowment of half a dozen male offsprings and a girl or two, her one child was Comus. Moderation in numbers was more than counter-balanced in his case by extravagance in characteristics.

Francesca mentally compared her son with hundreds of other young men whom she saw around her, steadily, and no doubt happily, engaged in the process of transforming themselves from nice boys into useful citizens. Most of them had occupations, or were industriously engaged in qualifying for such; in their leisure moments they smoked reasonably-priced cigarettes, went to the cheaper seats at music-halls, watched an occasional cricket match at Lord's with apparent interest, saw most of the world's spectacular events through the medium of the cinematograph, and were wont to exchange at parting seemingly superfluous injunctions to 'be good'. The whole of Bond Street and many of the tributary throughfares of Piccadilly might have been swept off the face of modern London without in any way interfering with the supply of their daily wants. They were doubtless dull as acquaintances, but as sons they would have been eminently restful. With a growing sense of irritation Francesca compared these deserving young men with her own intractable offspring, and wondered why Fate should have singled her out to be the parent of such a vexatious variant from a comfortable and desirable type. As far as remunerative achievement was concerned, Comus copied the insouciance of the field lily with a dangerous fidelity. Like his mother he looked round with wistful irritation at the example afforded by contemporary youth, but he concentrated his attention exclusively on the richer circles of his acquaintance, young men who bought cars and polo ponies as unconcernedly as he might purchase a

carnation for his buttonhole, and went for trips to Cairo or
the Tigris valley with less difficulty and finance-stretching
than he encountered in contriving a week-end at Brighton.

Gaiety and good looks had carried Comus successfully and,
on the whole, pleasantly, through schooldays and a recurring
succession of holidays; the same desirable assets were still at
his service to advance him along his road, but it was a disconcerting experience to find that they could not be relied on
to go all distances at all times. In an animal world, and a
fiercely competitive animal world at that, something more was
needed than the decorative *abandon* of the field lily, and it was
just that something more which Comus seemed unable or
unwilling to provide on his own account; it was just the lack
of that something more which left him sulking with Fate over
the numerous breakdowns and stumbling-blocks that held
him up on what he expected to be a triumphal or, at any rate,
unimpeded progress.

Francesca was, in her own way, fonder of Comus than of
any one else in the world, and if he had been browning his
skin somewhere east of Suez she would probably have kissed
his photograph with genuine fervour every night before going
to bed; the appearance of a cholera scare or rumour of native
rising in the columns of her daily news-sheet would have
caused her a flutter of anxiety, and she would have mentally
likened herself to a Spartan mother sacrificing her best-
beloved on the altar of State necessities. But with the best-
beloved installed under her roof, occupying an unreasonable
amount of cubic space, and demanding daily sacrifices instead
of providing the raw material for one, her feelings were tinged
with irritation rather than affection. She might have forgiven
Comus generously for misdeeds of some gravity committed in
another continent, but she could never overlook the fact that
out of a dish of five plovers' eggs he was certain to take three.
The absent may be always wrong, but they are seldom in a
position to be inconsiderate.

Thus a wall of ice had grown up gradually between mother
and son, a barrier across which they could hold converse, but
which gave a wintry chill even to the sparkle of their lightest
words. The boy had the gift of being irresistibly amusing when

he chose to exert himself in that direction, and after a long series of moody or jangling meal-sittings he would break forth into a torrential flow of small talk, scandal and malicious anecdote, true or more generally invented, to which Francesca listened with a relish and appreciation that was all the more flattering from being so unwillingly bestowed.

'If you chose your friends from a rather more reputable set you would be doubtless less amusing, but there would be compensating advantages.'

Francesca snapped the remark out at lunch one day when she had been betrayed into a broader smile than she considered the circumstances of her attitude towards Comus warranted.

'I'm going to move in quite decent society tonight,' replied Comus with a pleased chuckle; 'I'm going to meet you and Uncle Henry and heaps of nice dull God-fearing people at dinner.'

Francesca gave a little gasp of surprise and annoyance.

'You don't mean to say Caroline has asked you to dinner tonight?' she said; 'and of course without telling me. How exceedingly like her!'

Lady Caroline Benaresq had reached that age when you can say and do what you like in defiance of people's most sensitive feelings and most cherished antipathies. Not that she had waited to attain her present age before pursuing that line of conduct; she came of a family whose individual members went through life, from the nursery to the grave, with as much tact and consideration as a cactus-hedge might show in going through a crowded bathing tent. It was a compensating mercy that they disagreed rather more among themselves than they did with the outside world; every known variety and shade of religion and politics had been pressed into the family service to avoid the possibility of any agreement on the larger essentials of life, and such unlooked-for happenings as the Home Rule schism, the Tariff-Reform upheaval and the Suffragette crusade were thankfully seized on as furnishing occasion for further differences and subdivisions. Lady Caroline's favourite scheme of entertaining was to bring jarring and antagonistic elements into close contact and play them remorselessly one against the other. 'One gets much better results under those circumstances,' she used to observe, 'than by asking people who wish to meet each other. Few people talk as brilliantly to impress a friend as they do to depress an enemy.'

She admitted that her theory broke down rather badly if you applied it to Parliamentary debates. At her own dinner table its success was usually triumphantly vindicated.

'Who else is to be there?' Francesca asked, with some pardonable misgiving.

'Courtenay Youghal. He'll probably sit next to you, so you'd better think out a lot of annihilating remarks in readiness. And Elaine de Frey.'

'I don't think I've heard of her. Who is she?'

'Nobody in particular, but rather nice looking in a solemn sort of way, and almost indecently rich.'

'Marry her' was the advice which sprang to Francesca's lips but she choked it back with a salted almond, having a rare perception of the fact that words are sometimes given to us to defeat our purposes.

'Caroline has probably marked her down for Toby or one of the grand-nephews,' she said carelessly; 'a little money would be rather useful in that quarter, I imagine.'

Comus tucked in his underlip with just the shade of pugnacity that she wanted to see.

An advantageous marriage was so obviously the most sensible course for him to embark on that she scarcely dared to hope that he would seriously entertain it; yet there was just a chance that if he got as far as the flirtation stage with an attractive (and attracted) girl who was also an heiress, the sheer perversity of his nature might carry him on to more definite courtship, if only from the desire to thrust other more genuinely enamoured suitors into the background. It was a forlorn hope; so forlorn that the idea even crossed her mind of throwing herself on the mercy of her *bête noire*, Courtenay Youghal, and trying to enlist the influence which he seemed to possess over Comus for the purpose of furthering her hurriedly conceived project. Anyhow, the dinner promised to be more interesting than she had originally anticipated.

Lady Caroline was a professed Socialist in politics, chiefly, it was believed, because she was thus enabled to disagree with most of the Liberals and Conservatives, and all the Socialists of the day. She did not permit her Socialism, however, to penetrate below stairs; her cook and butler had every encouragement to be Individualists. Francesca, who was a keen and intelligent food critic, harboured no misgivings as to her hostess's kitchen and cellar departments; some of the human side-dishes at the feast gave her more ground for uneasiness. Courtenay Youghal, for instance, would probably be brilliantly silent; her brother Henry would almost certainly be the reverse.

The dinner party was a large one, and Francesca arrived late with little time to take preliminary stock of the guests; a card with the name 'Miss de Frey', immediately opposite her own place at the other side of the table, indicated, however, the whereabouts of the heiress. It was characteristic of Francesca that she first carefully read the menu from end to end, and then indulged in an equally careful, though less open, scrutiny of the girl who sat opposite her, the girl who was nobody in particular, but whose income was everything that could be desired. She was pretty in a restrained nut-brown fashion, and had a look of grave reflective calm that probably masked a speculative unsettled temperament. Her pose, if one wished to be critical, was just a little too elaborately careless. She wore such excellently set rubies with that indefinable air of having more at home that is so difficult to improvise. Francesca was distinctly pleased with her survey.

'You seem interested in your *vis-à-vis*,' said Courtenay Youghal.

'I almost think I've seen her before,' said Francesca; 'her face seems familiar to me.'

'The narrow gallery at the Louvre: attributed to Leonardo da Vinci,' said Youghal.

'Of course,' said Francesca, her feelings divided between satisfaction at capturing an elusive impression and annoyance that Youghal should have been her helper. A stronger tinge of annoyance possessed her when she heard the voice of Henry Greech raised in painful prominence at Lady Caroline's end of the table.

'I called on the Trudhams yesterday,' he announced; 'it was their Silver Wedding, you know, at least the day before was. Such lots of silver presents, quite a show. Of course there were a great many duplicates, but still, very nice to have. I think they were very pleased to get so many.'

'We must not grudge them their show of presents after their twenty-five years of married life,' said Lady Caroline gently; 'it is the silver lining to their cloud.'

A third of the guests present were related to the Trudhams.

'Lady Caroline is beginning well,' murmured Courtenay Youghal.

'I should hardly call twenty-five years of married life a cloud,' said Henry Greech lamely.

'Don't let's talk about married life,' said a tall handsome woman, who looked like some modern painter's conception of the goddess Bellona; 'it's my misfortune to write eternally about husbands and wives and their variants. My public expects it of me. I do so envy journalists who can write about plagues and strikes and Anarchist plots, and other pleasing things, instead of being tied down to one stale old topic.'

'Who is that woman and what has she written?' Francesca asked Youghal; she dimly remembered having seen her at one of Serena Golackly's gatherings, surrounded by a little court of admirers.

'I forget her name; she has a villa at San Remo or Mentone, or somewhere where one does have villas, and plays an extraordinary good game of bridge. Also she has the reputation, rather rare in your sex, of being a wonderfully sound judge of wine.'

'But what has she written?'

'Oh, several novels of the thinnish ice order. Her last one, *The Woman who wished it was Wednesday*, has been banned at all the libraries. I expect you've read it.'

'I don't see why you should think so,' said Francesca coldly.

'Only because Comus lent me your copy yesterday,' said Youghal. He threw back his handsome head and gave her a sidelong glance of quizzical amusement. He knew that she hated his intimacy with Comus, and he was secretly rather proud of his influence over the boy, shallow and negative though he knew it to be. It had been, on his part, an unsought intimacy, and it would probably fall to pieces the moment he tried seriously to take up the role of mentor. The fact that Comus's mother openly disapproved of the friendship gave it perhaps its chief interest in the young politician's eyes.

Francesca turned her attention to her brother's end of the table. Henry Greech had willingly availed himself of the invitation to leave the subject of married life, and had launched forthwith into the equally well-worn theme of current politics. He was not a person who was in much demand for public meetings, and the House showed no great impatience to hear his views on the topics of the moment; its impatience, indeed, was manifested rather in the opposite direction. Hence he was prone to unburden himself of accumulated political wisdom as occasion presented itself—sometimes, indeed, to assume an occasion that was hardly visible to the naked intelligence.

'Our opponents are engaged in a hopelessly uphill struggle, and they know it,' he chirruped defiantly; 'they've become possessed, like the Gadarene swine, with a whole legion of—'

'Surely the Gadarene swine went downhill?' put in Lady Caroline in a gently inquiring voice.

Henry Greech hastily abandoned simile and fell back on platitude and the safer kinds of fact.

Francesca did not regard her brother's views of statecraft either in the light of gospel or revelation; as Comus once remarked, they more usually suggested exodus. In the present instance she found distraction in a renewed scrutiny of the girl opposite her, who seemed to be only moderately interested in the conversational efforts of the diners on either side of her. Comus, who was looking and talking his best, was sitting at the farther end of the table, and Francesca was quick to notice in which direction the girl's glances were continually straying. Once or twice the eyes of the young people met and a swift flush of pleasure and a half-smile that spoke of good understanding came to the heiress's face. It did not need the gift of the traditional intuition of her sex to enable Francesca to guess that the girl with the desirable banking account was already considerably attracted by the lively young Pagan who had, when he cared to practise it, such an art of winning admiration. For the first time for many, many months Francesca saw her son's prospects in a rose-coloured setting, and she began, unconsciously, to wonder exactly how much wealth was summed up in the expressive label 'almost indecently rich'. A wife with a really large fortune and a correspondingly big dower of character and ambition, might, perhaps, succeed in turning Comus's latent energies into a groove which would provide him, if not with a career, at least with an occupation, and the young serious face opposite looked as if its owner lacked neither character nor ambition. Francesca's speculations took a more personal turn. Out of the well-filled coffers with which her imagination was toying, an inconsiderable sum might eventually be devoted to the leasing, or even perhaps the purchase of, the house in Blue Street when the present convenient arrangement should have come to an end, and Francesca and the Van der Meulen would not be obliged to seek fresh quarters.

A woman's voice, talking in a discreet undertone on the other side of Courtenay Youghal, broke in on her bridge-building.

'Tons of money and really very presentable. Just the wife for a rising young politician. Go in and win her before she's snapped up by some fortune hunter.'

Youghal and his instructress in worldly wisdom were looking straight across the table at the Leonardo da Vinci girl with the grave reflective eyes and the over-emphasized air of repose. Francesca felt a quick throb of anger against her matchmaking neighbour; why, she asked herself, must some women, with no end or purpose of their own to serve, except the sheer love of meddling in the affairs of others, plunge their hands into plots and schemings of this sort, in which the happiness of more than one person was concerned? And more clearly than ever she realized how thoroughly she detested Courtenay Youghal. She had disliked him as an evil influence, setting before her son an example of showy ambition that he was not in the least likely to follow, and providing him with a model of extravagant dandyism that he was only too certain to copy. In her heart she knew that Comus would have embarked just as surely on his present course of idle self-indulgence if he had never known of the existence of Youghal, but she chose to regard that young man as her son's evil genius, and now he seemed likely to justify more than ever the character she had fastened on to him. For once in his life Comus appeared to have an idea of behaving sensibly and making some use of his opportunities, and almost at the same moment Courtenay Youghal arrived on the scene as a possible and very dangerous rival. Against the good looks and fitful powers of fascination that Comus could bring into the field, the young politican could match half a dozen dazzling qualities which would go far to recommend him in the eyes of a woman of the world, still more in those of a young girl in search of an ideal. Good-looking in his own way, if not on such showy lines as Comus, always well turned-out, witty, self-confident without being bumptious, with a conspicuous Parliamentary career alongside him, and Heaven knew what else in front of him, Courtenay Youghal certainly was not a rival whose chances could be held very lightly. Francesca laughed bitterly to herself as she remembered that a few hours ago she had entertained the idea of begging for his good offices in helping on Comus's wooing. One consolation, at least, she found for herself: if Youghal really meant to step in and try and cut out his young friend, the latter at any rate had snatched a useful start. Comus had mentioned Miss de Frey at luncheon that day, casually and dispassionately; if the subject of the dinner guests had not come up he would probably not have mentioned her at all. But they were obviously already very good friends. It was part and parcel of the state of domestic tension at Blue Street that Francesca should only have come to know of this highly interesting heiress by an accidental sorting of guests at a dinner party.

Lady Caroline's voice broke in on her reflections; it was a gentle purring voice, that possessed an uncanny quality of being able to make itself heard down the longest dinner table.

'The dear Archdeacon is getting *so* absent-minded. He read a list of box-holders for the opera as the First Lesson the other Sunday, instead of the families and lots of the tribes of Israel that entered Canaan. Fortunately no one noticed the mistake.'

CHAPTER 5

ON a conveniently secluded bench facing the Northern
Pheasantry in the Zoological Society's Gardens, Regent's
Park, Courtenay Youghal sat immersed in mature flirtation
with a lady, who, though certainly young in fact and appearance, was some four or five years his senior. When he was a
schoolboy of sixteen, Molly McQuade had personally con-
ducted him to the Zoo and stood him dinner afterwards at
Kettner's, and whenever the two of them happened to be in
town on the anniversary of that bygone festivity they reli-
giously repeated the programme in its entirety. Even the menu
of the dinner was adhered to as nearly as possible; the original
selection of food and wine that schoolboy exuberance, tempered by schoolboy shyness, had pitched on those many years
ago, confronted Youghal on those occasions, as a drowning
man's past life is said to rise up and parade itself in his last
moment of consciousness.

The flirtation which was thus perennially restored to its
old-time footing owed its longevity more to the enterprising
solicitude of Miss McQuade than to any conscious sentimental effort on the part of Youghal himself. Molly McQuade
was known to her neighbours in a minor hunting shire as
a hard-riding conventionally unconventional type of young
woman, who came naturally into the classification, 'a good
sort'. She was just sufficiently good-looking, sufficiently reticent about her own illnesses, when she had any, and sufficiently appreciative of her neighbours' gardens, children and
hunters to be generally popular. Most men liked her, and the
percentage of women who disliked her was not inconveniently
high. One of these days, it was assumed, she would marry
a brewer or a Master of Otter Hounds, and, after a brief
interval, be known to the world as the mother of a boy or two
at Malvern or some similar seat of learning. The romantic side
of her nature was altogether unguessed by the countryside.

Her romances were mostly in serial form, and suffered
perhaps in fervour from their disconnected course what they
gained in length of days. Her affectionate interest in the

several young men who figured in her affairs of the heart was perfectly honest, and certainly made no attempt either to conceal their separate existences, or to play them off one against the other. Neither could it be said that she was a husband hunter; she had made up her mind what sort of man she was likely to marry, and her forecast did not differ very widely from that formed by her local acquaintances. If her married life were eventually to turn out a failure, at least she looked forward to it with very moderate expectations. Her love affairs she put on a very different footing, and apparently they were the all-absorbing element in her life. She possessed the happily constituted temperament which enables a man or woman to be a 'pluralist', and to observe the sage precaution of not putting all one's eggs into one basket. Her demands were not exacting; she required of her affinity that he should be young, good-looking, and at least moderately amusing; she would have preferred him to be invariably faithful, but, with her own example before her, she was prepared for the probability, bordering on certainty, that he would be nothing of the sort. The philosophy of the 'Garden of Kama' was the compass by which she steered her barque, and thus far, if she had encountered some storms and buffeting, she had at least escaped being either ship-wrecked or becalmed.

Courtenay Youghal had not been designed by Nature to fulfil the role of an ardent or devoted lover, and he scrupulously respected the limits which Nature had laid down. For Molly, however, he had a certain responsive affection. She had always obviously admired him, and at the same time she never beset him with crude flattery; the principal reason why the flirtation had stood the test of so many years was the fact that it only flared into active existence at convenient intervals. In an age when the telephone has undermined almost every fastness of human privacy, and the sanctity of one's seclusion depends often on the ability for tactful falsehood shown by a club page-boy, Youghal was duly appreciative of the circumstance that his lady fair spent a large part of the year pursuing foxes, in lieu of pursuing him. Also the honestly admitted fact that, in her human hunting, she rode after more than one quarry, made the inevitable break-up of the affair a matter to which both could look forward without a sense of coming embarrassment and recrimination. When the time for gathering ye rosebuds should be over, neither of them could accuse the other of having wrecked his or her entire life. At the most they would only have disorganized a week-end.

On this particular afternoon, when old reminiscences had been gone through, and the intervening gossip of past months duly recounted, a lull in the conversation made itself rather obstinately felt. Molly had already guessed that matters were about to slip into a new phase; the affair had reached maturity long ago, and a new phase must be in the nature of a wane.

'You're a clever brute,' she said suddenly, with an air of affectionate regret; 'I always knew you'd get on in the House, but I hardly expected you to come to the front so soon.'

'I'm coming to the front,' admitted Youghal judicially; 'the problem is, shall I be able to stay there? Unless something happens in the financial line before long, I don't see how I'm to stay in Parliament at all. Economy is out of the question. It would open people's eyes, I fancy, if they knew how little I exist on as it is. And I'm living so far beyond my income that we may almost be said to be living apart.'

'It will have to be a rich wife, I suppose,' said Molly slowly; 'that's the worst of success, it imposes so many conditions. I rather knew, from something in your manner, that you were drifting that way.'

Youghal said nothing in the way of contradiction; he gazed steadfastly at the aviary in front of him as though exotic pheasants were for the moment the most absorbing study in the world. As a matter of fact, his mind was centred on the image of Elaine de Frey, with her clear untroubled eyes and her Leonardo da Vinci air. He was wondering whether he was likely to fall into a frame of mind concerning her which would be in the least like falling in love.

'I shall mind horribly,' continued Molly, after a pause, 'but, of course, I have always known that something of the sort would have to happen one of these days. When a man goes into politics he can't call his soul his own, and I suppose his heart becomes an impersonal possession in the same way.'

'Most people who know me would tell you that I haven't got a heart,' said Youghal.

'I've often felt inclined to agree with them,' said Molly; 'and then, now and again, I think you have a heart tucked away somewhere.'

'I hope I have,' said Youghal, 'because I'm trying to break to you the fact the I think I'm falling in love with somebody.'

Molly McQuade turned sharply to look at her companion, who still fixed his gaze on the pheasant run in front of him.

'Don't tell me you're losing your head over somebody useless, some one without money,' she said; 'I don't think I could stand that.'

For the moment she feared that Courtenay's selfishness might have taken an unexpected turn, in which ambition had given way to the fancy of the hour; he might be going to sacrifice his Parliamentary career for a life of stupid lounging in momentarily attractive company. He quickly undeceived her.

'She's got heaps of money.'

Molly gave a grunt of relief. Her affection for Courtenay had produced the anxiety which underlay her first question; a natural jealousy prompted the next one.

'Is she young and pretty and all that sort of thing, or is she just a good sort with a sympathetic manner and nice eyes? As a rule that's the kind that goes with a lot of money.'

'Young and quite good-looking in her way, and a distinct style of her own. Some people would call her beautiful. As a political hostess I should think she'd be splendid. I imagine I'm rather in love with her.'

'And is she in love with you?'

Youghal threw back his head with the slight assertive movement that Molly knew and liked.

'She's a girl who I fancy would let judgment influence her a lot. And without being stupidly conceited I think I may say she might do worse than throw herself away on me. I'm young and quite good-looking, and I'm making a name for myself in the House; she'll be able to read all sorts of nice and horrid things about me in the papers at breakfast-time. I can be brilliantly amusing at times, and I understand the value of silence; there is no fear that I shall ever degenerate into that fearsome thing—a cheerful talkative husband. For a girl with money and social ambitions I should think I was rather a good thing.'

'You are certainly in love, Courtenay,' said Molly, 'but it's the old love and not a new one. I'm rather glad. I should have hated to have you head-over-heels in love with a pretty woman, even for a short time. You'll be much happier as it is. And I'm going to put all my feelings in the background, and tell you to go in and win. You've got to marry a rich woman, and if she's nice and will make a good hostess, so much the better for everybody. You'll be happier in your married life than I shall be in mine, when it comes; you'll have other interests to absorb you. I shall just have the garden and dairy and nursery and lending library, as like as two peas to all the gardens and dairies and nurseries for hundreds of miles round. You won't care for your wife enough to be worried every time she has a finger-ache, and you'll like her well enough to be pleased to meet her sometimes at your own house. I shouldn't wonder if you were quite happy. She will probably be miserable, but any woman who married you would be.'

There was a short pause; they were both staring at the pheasant cages. Then Molly spoke again, with the swift nervous tone of a general who is hurriedly altering the disposition of his forces for a strategic retreat.

'When you are safely married and honeymooned and all that sort of thing, and have put your wife through her paces as a political hostess, some time, when the House isn't sitting, you must come down by yourself, and do a little hunting with us. Will you? It won't be quite the same as old times, but it will be something to look forward to when I'm reading the endless paragraphs about your fashionable political wedding.'

'You're looking forward pretty far,' laughed Youghal; 'the lady may take your view as to the probable unhappiness of a future shared with me, and I may have to content myself with penurious political bachelorhood. Anyhow, the present is still with us. We dine at Kettner's tonight, don't we?'

'Rather,' said Molly, 'though it will be more or less a throat-lumpy feast as far as I am concerned. We shall have to drink to the health of the future Mrs Youghal. By the way, it's rather characteristic of you that you haven't told me who she is, and of me that I haven't asked. And now, like a dear boy, trot away and leave me. I haven't got to say good-bye to you yet, but I'm going to take a quiet farewell of the Pheasantry. We've had some jolly good talks, you and I, sitting on this seat, haven't we? And I know, as well as I know anything, that this is the last of them. Eight o'clock tonight, as punctually as possible.'

She watched his retreating figure with eyes that grew slowly misty; he had been such a jolly comely boy-friend, and they had had such good times together. The mist deepened on her lashes as she looked round at the familiar rendezvous where they had so often kept tryst since the day when they had first come there together, he a schoolboy and she but lately out of her teens. For the moment she felt herself in the thrall of a very real sorrow.

Then, with the admirable energy of one who is only in town for a fleeting fortnight, she raced away to have tea with a world-faring naval admirer at his club. Pluralism is a merciful narcotic.

CHAPTER 6

ELAINE DE FREY sat at ease—at bodily ease, at any rate—in a low wicker chair placed under the shade of a group of cedars in the heart of a stately spacious garden that had almost made up its mind to be a park. The shallow stone basin of an old fountain, on whose wide ledge a leaden-moulded otter for ever preyed on a leaden salmon, filled a conspicuous place in the immediate foreground. Around its rim ran an inscription in Latin, warning mortal man that time flows as swiftly as water and exhorting him to make the most of his hours; after which piece of Jacobean moralizing it set itself shamelessly to beguile all who might pass that way into an abandonment of contemplative repose. On all sides of it a stretch of smooth turf spread away, broken up here and there by groups of dwarfish chestnut and mulberry trees, whose leaves and branches cast a laced pattern of shade beneath them. On one side the lawn sloped gently down to a small lake, whereon floated a quartet of swans, their movements suggestive of a certain mournful listlessness, as though a weary dignity of caste held them back from the joyous bustling life of the lesser waterfowl. Elaine liked to imagine that they re-embodied the souls of unhappy boys who had been forced by family interests to become high ecclesiastical dignitaries and had grown prematurely Right Reverend. A low stone balustrade fenced part of the shore of the lake, making a miniature terrace above its level, and here roses grew in a rich multitude. Other rose bushes, carefully pruned and tended, formed little oases of colour and perfume amid the restful green of the sward, and in the distance the eye caught the variegated blaze of a many-hued hedge of rhododendron. With these favoured exceptions flowers were hard to find in this well-ordered garden; the misguided tyranny of staring geranium beds and beflowered archways leading to nowhere, so dear to the sub-urban gardener, found no expression here. Magnificent Amherst pheasants, whose plumage challenged and almost shamed the peacock on his own ground, stepped to and fro over the emerald turf with the assured self-conscious pride of reigning sultans. It was a garden where summer seemed a part-proprietor rather than a hurried visitor.

By the side of Elaine's chair under the shadow of the cedars a wicker table was set out with the paraphernalia of after-noon tea. On some cushions at her feet reclined Courtenay Youghal, smoothly preened and youthfully elegant, the per-sonification of decorative repose; equally decorative, but with the showy restlessness of a dragonfly, Comus disported his flannelled person over a considerable span of the available foreground.

The intimacy existing between the two young men had suffered no immediate dislocation from the circumstance that they were tacitly paying court to the same lady. It was an intimacy founded not in the least on friendship or community of tastes and ideas, but owed its existence to the fact that each was amused and interested by the other. Youghal found

Comus, for the time being at any rate, just as amusing and interesting as a rival for Elaine's favour as he had been in the role of scapegrace boy-about-town; Comus for his part did not wish to lose touch with Youghal, who among other attractions possessed the recommendation of being under the ban of Comus's mother. She disapproved, it is true, of a great many of her son's friends and associates, but this particular one was a special and persistent source of irritation to her from the fact that he figured prominently and more or less successfully in the public life of the day. There was something peculiarly exasperating in reading a brilliant and incisive attack on the Government's rash handling of public expenditure delivered by a young man who encouraged her son in every imaginable extravagance. The actual extent of Youghal's influence over the boy was of the slightest; Comus was quite capable of deriving encouragement to rash outlay and frivolous conversation from an anchorite or an East End parson if he had been thrown into close companionship with such an individual. Francesca, however, exercised a mother's privilege in assuming her son's bachelor associates to be industrious in labouring to achieve his undoing. Therefore the young politician was a source of unconcealed annoyance to her, and in the same degree as she expressed her disapproval of him Comus was careful to maintain and parade the intimacy. Its existence, or rather its continued existence, was one of the things that faintly puzzled the young lady whose sought-for favour might have been expected to furnish an occasion for its rapid dissolution.

With two suitors, one of whom at least she found markedly attractive, courting her at the same moment, Elaine should have had reasonable cause for being on good terms with the world, and with herself in particular. Happiness was not, however, at this auspicious moment, her dominant mood. The grave calm of her face masked as usual a certain degree of grave perturbation. A succession of well-meaning governesses and a plentiful supply of moralizing aunts on both sides of her family, had impressed on her young mind the theoretical fact that wealth is a great responsibility. The consciousness of her responsibility set her continually wondering, not as to her own fitness to discharge her 'stewardship', but as to the motives and merits of people with whom she came in contact. The knowledge that there was so much in the world that she could buy, invited speculation as to how much there was that was worth buying. Gradually she had come to regard her mind as a sort of appeal court before whose secret sittings were examined and judged the motives and actions, the motives especially, of the world in general. In her schoolroom days she had sat in conscientious judgment on the motives that guided or misguided Charles and Cromwell and Monck, Wallenstein and Savonarola. In her present stage she was equally occupied in examining the political sincerity of the Secretary for Foreign Affairs, the good-faith of a honey-tongued but possibly loyal-hearted waiting-maid, and the disinterestedness of a whole circle of indulgent and flattering acquaintants. Even more absorbing, and, in her eyes, more urgently necessary, was the task of dissecting and appraising the characters of the two young men who were favouring her with their attentions. And herein lay cause for much thinking and some perturbation. Youghal, for example, might have baffled a more experienced observer of human nature. Elaine was too clever to confound his dandyism with foppishness or self-advertisement. He admired his own toilet effect in a mirror from a genuine sense of pleasure in a thing good to look upon, just as he would feel a sensuous appreciation of the sight of a well-bred, well-matched, well-turned-out pair of horses. Behind his careful political flippancy and cynicism one might also detect a certain careless sincerity, which would probably in the long run save him from moderate success, and turn him into one of the brilliant failures of his day. Beyond this it was difficult to form an exact appreciation of Courtenay Youghal, and Elaine, who liked to have her impressions distinctly labelled and pigeon-holed, was perpetually scrutinizing the outer surface of his characteristics and utterances, like a baffled art critic vainly searching beneath the varnish and scratches of a doubtfully assigned picture for an enlightening signature. The young man added to her perplexities by his deliberate policy of never trying to show himself in a favourable light even when most anxious to impart a favourable impression. He preferred that people should hunt for his good qualities, and merely took very good care that as far as possible they should never draw blank; even in the matter of selfishness, which was the anchor-sheet of his existence, he contrived to be noted, and justly noted, for doing remarkably unselfish things. As a ruler he would have been reasonably popular; as a husband he would probably be unendurable.

Comus was to a certain extent as great a mystification as Youghal, but here Elaine was herself responsible for some of the perplexity which enshrouded his character in her eyes. She had taken more than a passing fancy for the boy—for the boy as he might be, that was to say—and she was desperately unwilling to see him and appraise him as he really was. Thus the mental court of appeal was constantly engaged in examining witnesses as to character, most of whom signally failed to give any testimony which would support the favourable judgment which the tribunal was so anxious to arrive at. A woman with wider experience of the world's ways and shortcomings would probably have contented herself with an endeavour to find out whether her liking for the boy outweighed her dislike of his characteristics; Elaine took her judgments too seriously to approach the matter from such a simple and convenient standpoint. The fact that she was much more than half in love with Comus made it dreadfully important that she should discover him to have a lovable soul, and Comus, it must be confessed, did little to help forward the discovery.

'At any rate he is honest,' she would observe to herself, after some outspoken admission of unprincipled conduct on his part, and then she would ruefully recall certain episodes in which he had figured, from which honesty had been conspicuously absent. What she tried to label honesty in his candour was probably only a cynical defiance of the laws of right and wrong.

'You look more than usually thoughtful this afternoon,' said Comus to her, 'as if you had invented this summer day and were trying to think out improvements.'

'If I had the power to create improvements anywhere I think I should begin with you,' retorted Elaine.

'I'm sure it's much better to leave me as I am,' protested Comus; 'you're like a relative of mine up in Argyllshire, who spends his time producing improved breeds of sheep and pigs and chickens. So patronizing and irritating to the Almighty, I should think, to go about putting superior finishing touches to Creation.'

Elaine frowned, and then laughed, and finally gave a little sigh.

'It's not easy to talk sense to you,' she said.

'Whatever else you take in hand,' said Youghal, 'you must never improve this garden. It's what our idea of heaven might be like if the Jews hadn't invented one for us on totally different lines. It's dreadful that we should accept them as the impresarios of our religious dreamland instead of the Greeks.'

'You are not very fond of the Jews,' said Elaine.

'I've travelled and lived a good deal in Eastern Europe,' said Youghal.

'It seems largely a question of geography,' said Elaine; 'in England no one really is anti-Semitic.'

Youghal shook his head. 'I know a great many Jews who are.'

Servants had quietly, almost reverently, placed tea and its accessories on the wicker table, and quietly receded from the landscape. Elaine sat like a grave young goddess about to dispense some mysterious potion to her devotees. Her mind was still sitting in judgment on the Jewish question.

Comus scrambled to his feet.

'It's too hot for tea,' he said; 'I shall go and feed the swans.' And he walked off with a little silver basket-dish containing brown bread-and-butter.

Elaine laughed quietly.

'It's so like Comus,' she said, 'to go off with our one dish of bread-and-butter.'

Youghal chuckled responsively. It was an undoubted opportunity for him to put in some disparaging criticism of Comus, and Elaine sat alert in readiness to judge the critic and reserve judgment on the criticized.

'His selfishness is splendid but absolutely futile,' said Youghal; 'now my selfishness is commonplace, but always thoroughly practical and calculated. He will have great difficulty in getting the swans to accept his offering, and he incurs the odium of reducing us to a bread-and-butterless condition. Incidentally, he will get very hot.'

Elaine again had the sense of being thoroughly baffled. If Youghal had said anything unkind it was about himself.

'If my cousin Suzette had been here,' she observed, with the shadow of a malicious smile on her lips, 'I believe she would have gone into a flood of tears at the loss of her bread-and-butter, and Comus would have figured ever after in her mind as something black and destroying and hateful. In fact, I don't really know why we took our loss so unprotestingly.'

'For two reasons,' said Youghal; 'you are rather fond of Comus. And I—am not very fond of bread-and-butter.'

The jesting remark brought a throb of pleasure to Elaine's heart. She had known full well that she cared for Comus, but now that Courtenay Youghal had openly proclaimed the fact as something unchallenged and understood matters seemed placed at once on a more advanced footing. The warm sunlit garden grew suddenly into a heaven that held the secret of eternal happiness. Youth and comeliness would always walk here, under the low-boughed mulberry trees, as unchanging as the leaden otter that for ever preyed on the leaden salmon on the edge of the old fountain, and somehow the lovers would always wear the aspect of herself and the boy who was talking to the four white swans by the water steps. Youghal was right; this was the real heaven of one's dreams and longings, immeasurably removed from that Rue de la Paix Paradise about which one professed utterly insincere hankerings in places of public worship. Elaine drank her tea in a happy silence; besides being a brilliant talker Youghal understood the rarer art of being a non-talker on occasion.

Comus came back across the grass swinging the empty basket-dish in his hand.

'Swans were very pleased,' he cried gaily, 'and said they hoped I would keep the bread-and-butter dish as a souvenir of a happy tea-party. I may really have it, mayn't I?' he continued in an anxious voice; 'it will do to keep studs and things in. You don't want it.'

'It's got the family crest on it,' said Elaine. Some of the happiness had died out of her eyes.

'I'll have that scratched off and my own put on,' said Comus.

'It's been in the family for generations,' protested Elaine, who did not share Comus's view that because you were rich your lesser possessions could have no value in your eyes.

'I want it dreadfully,' said Comus sulkily, 'and you've heaps of other things to put bread-and-butter in.'

For the moment he was possessed by an overmastering desire to keep the dish at all costs; a look of greedy determination dominated his face, and he had not for an instant relaxed his grip of the coveted object.

Elaine was genuinely angry by this time, and was busily telling herself that it was absurd to be put out over such a trifle; at the same moment a sense of justice was telling her that Comus was displaying a good deal of rather shabby selfishness. And somehow her chief anxiety at the moment was to keep Courtenay Youghal from seeing that she was angry.

'I know you don't really want it, so I'm going to keep it,' persisted Comus.

'It's too hot to argue,' said Elaine.

'Happy mistress of your destinies,' laughed Youghal; 'you can suit your disputations to the desired time and temperature. I have to go and argue, or what is worse, listen to other people's arguments, in a hot and doctored atmosphere suitable to an invalid lizard.'

'You haven't got to argue about a bread-and-butter dish,' said Elaine.

'Chiefly about bread-and-butter,' said Youghal; 'our great preoccupation is other people's bread-and-butter. They earn or produce the material, but we busy ourselves with making rules how it shall be cut up, and the size of the slices, and how much butter shall go on how much bread. That is what is called legislation. If we could only make rules as to how the bread-and-butter should be digested we should be quite happy.'

Elaine had been brought up to regard Parliaments as

something to be treated with cheerful solemnity, like illness or family reunions. Youghal's flippant disparagement of the career in which he was involved did not, however, jar on her susceptibilities. She knew him to be not only a lively and effective debater but an industrious worker on committees. If he made light of his labours, at least he afforded no one else a loophole for doing so. And certainly the Parliamentary atmosphere was not uninviting on this hot afternoon.

'When must you go?' she asked sympathetically.

Youghal looked ruefully at his watch. Before he could answer, a cheerful hoot came through the air, as of an owl joyously challenging the sunlight with a foreboding of the coming night. He sprang laughing to his feet.

'Listen! My summons back to my galley,' he cried. 'The Gods have given me an hour in this enchanted garden, so I must not complain.'

Then in a lower voice he almost whispered, 'It's the Persian debate tonight.'

It was the one hint he had given in the midst of his talking and laughing that he was really keenly enthralled in the work that lay before him. It was the one little intimate touch that gave Elaine the knowledge that he cared for her opinion of his work.

Comus, who had emptied his cigarette-case, became suddenly clamorous at the prospect of being temporarily stranded without a smoke. Youghal took the last remaining cigarette from his own case and gravely bisected it.

'Friendship could go no farther,' he observed, as he gave one-half to the doubtfully appeased Comus, and lit the other himself.

'There are heaps more in the hall,' said Elaine.

'It was only done for the Saint Martin of Tours effect,' said Youghal; 'I hate smoking when I'm rushing through the air. Good-bye.'

The departing galley-slave stepped forth into the sunlight, radiant and confident. A few minutes later Elaine could see glimpses of his white car as it rushed past the rhododendron bushes. He woos best who leaves first, particularly if he goes forth to battle or the semblance of battle.

Somehow Elaine's garden of Eternal Youth had already become clouded in its imagery. The girl-figure who walked in it was still distinctly and unchangingly herself, but her companion was more blurred and undefined, as a picture that has been superimposed on another.

Youghal sped townward well satisfied with himself. Tomorrow, he reflected, Elaine would read his speech in her morning paper, and he knew in advance that it was not going to be one of his worst efforts. He knew almost exactly where the punctuations of laughter and applause would burst in, he knew that nimble fingers in the Press Gallery would be taking down each gibe and argument as he flung it at the impassive Minister confronting him, and that the fair lady of his desire would be able to judge what manner of young man this was who spent his afternoon in her garden, lazily chaffing himself and his world.

And he further reflected, with an amused chuckle, that she would be vividly reminded of Comus for days to come, when she took her afternoon tea, and saw the bread-and-butter reposing in an unaccustomed dish.

CHAPTER 7

TOWARDS four o'clock on a hot afternoon Francesca stepped out from a shop entrance near the Piccadilly end of Bond Street and ran almost into the arms of Merla Blathlington. The afternoon seemed to get instantly hotter. Merla was one of those human flies that buzz; in crowded streets, at bazaars and in warm weather, she attained to the proportions of a human bluebottle. Lady Caroline Benaresq had openly predicted that a special fly-paper was being reserved for her accommodation in another world; others, however, held the opinion that she would be miraculously multiplied in a future state, and that four or more Merla Blathlingtons, according to deserts, would be in perpetual and unremitting attendance on each lost soul.

'Here we are,' she cried, with a glad eager buzz, 'popping in and out of shops like rabbits; not that rabbits do pop in and out of shops very extensively.'

It was evidently one of her bluebottle days.

'Don't you love Bond Street?' she gabbled on. 'There's something so unusual and distinctive about it; no other street anywhere else is quite like it. Don't you know those ikons and images and things scattered up and down Europe, that are supposed to have been painted or carved, as the case may be, by St Luke or Zaccheus, or somebody of that sort; I always like to think that some notable person of those times designed Bond Street. St Paul, perhaps. He travelled about a lot.'

'Not in Middlesex, though,' said Francesca.

'One can't be sure,' persisted Merla; 'when one wanders about as much as he did one gets mixed up and forgets where one *has* been. I can never remember whether I've been to the Tyrol twice and St Moritz once, or the other way about; I always have to ask my maid. And there's something about the name Bond that suggests St Paul; didn't he write a lot about the bond and the free?'

'I fancy he wrote in Hebrew or Greek,' objected Francesca; 'the word wouldn't have the least resemblance.'

'So dreadfully non-committal to go about pamphleteering in those bizarre languages,' complained Merla; 'that's what makes all those people so elusive. As soon as you try to pin them down to a definite statement about anything you're told that some vitally important word has fifteen other meanings in the original. I wonder our Cabinet Ministers and politicians don't adopt a sort of dog-Latin or Esperanto jargon to deliver their speeches in; what a lot of subsequent explaining away would be saved! But to go back to Bond Street—not that we've left it—'

'I'm afraid I must leave it now,' said Francesca, preparing to turn up Grafton Street. 'Good-bye.'

'Must you be going? Come and have tea somewhere. I know of a cozy little place where one can talk undisturbed.'

Francesca repressed a shudder and pleaded an urgent engagement.

'I know where you're going,' said Merla, with the resentful buzz of a bluebottle that finds itself thwarted by the cold unreasoning resistance of a windowpane. 'You're going to play bridge at Serena Golackly's. She never asks me to her bridge parties.'

Francesca shuddered openly this time; the prospect of having to play bridge anywhere in the near neighbourhood of Merla's voice was not one that could be contemplated with ordinary calmness.

'Good-bye,' she said again firmly, and passed out of ear-shot; it was rather like leaving the machinery section of an exhibition. Merla's diagnosis of her destination had been a correct one; Francesca made her way slowly through the hot streets in the direction of Serena Golackly's house on the far side of Berkeley Square. To the blessed certainty of finding a game of bridge, she hopefully added the possibility of hearing some fragments of news which might prove interesting and enlightening. And of enlightenment on a particular subject, in which she was acutely and personally interested, she stood in some need. Comus of late had been provokingly reticent as to his movements and doings; partly, perhaps, because it was his nature to be provoking, partly because the daily bickerings over money matters were gradually choking other forms of conversation. Francesca had seen him once or twice in the Park in the desirable company of Elaine de Frey, and from time to time she heard of the young people as having danced together at various houses; on the other hand, she had seen and heard quite as much evidence to connect the heiress's name with that of Courtenay Youghal. Beyond this meagre and conflicting and altogether tantalizing information, her knowledge of the present position of affairs did not go. If either of the young men was seriously 'making the running', it was probable that she would hear some sly hint or open comment about it from one of Serena's gossip-laden friends, without having to go out of her way to introduce the subject and unduly disclose her own state of ignorance. And a game of bridge, played for moderately high points, gave ample excuse for convenient lapses into reticence; if questions took an embarrassingly inquisitive turn, one could always find refuge in a defensive spade.

The afternoon was too warm to make bridge a generally

popular diversion, and Serena's party was a comparatively small one. Only one table was incomplete when Francesca made her appearance on the scene; at it was seated Serena herself, confronted by Ada Spelvexit, whom every one was wont to explain as 'one of the Cheshire Spelvexits', as though any other variety would have been intolerable. Ada Spelvexit was one of those naturally stagnant souls who take infinite pleasure in what are called 'movements'. 'Most of the really great lessons I have learned have been taught me by the Poor,' was one of her favourite statements. The one great lesson that the Poor in general would have liked to have taught her, that their kitchens and sickrooms were not unreservedly at her disposal as private lecture halls, she had never been able to assimilate. She was ready to give them unlimited advice as to how they should keep the wolf from their doors, but in return she claimed and enforced for herself the penetrating powers of an east wind or a dust-storm. Her visits among her wealthier acquaintances were equally extensive and enterprising, and hardly more welcome; in country-house parties, while partaking to the fullest extent of the hospitality offered her, she made a practice of unburdening herself of homilies on the evils of leisure and luxury, which did not particularly endear her to her fellow-guests. Hostesses regarded her philosophically as a form of social measles which every one had to have once.

The third prospective player, Francesca noted without any special enthusiasm, was Lady Caroline Benaresq. Lady Caroline was far from being a remarkably good bridge player, but she always managed to domineer mercilessly over any table that was favoured with her presence, and generally managed to win. A domineering player usually inflicts the chief damage and demoralization on his partner; Lady Caroline's special achievement was to harass and demoralize partner and opponents alike.

'Weak and weak,' she announced in her gentle voice, as she cut her hostess for a partner; 'I suppose we had better play only five shillings a hundred.'

Francesca wondered at the old woman's moderate assessment of the stake, knowing her fondness for highish play and her usual luck in card holding.

'I don't mind what we play,' said Ada Spelvexit, with an incautious parade of elegant indifference; as a matter of fact she was inwardly relieved and rejoicing at the reasonable figure proposed by Lady Caroline, and she would certainly have demurred if a higher stake had been suggested. She was not as a rule a successful player, and money lost at cards was always a poignant bereavement to her.

'Then as you don't mind we'll make it ten shillings a hundred,' said Lady Caroline, with the pleased chuckle of one who has spread a net in the sight of a bird and disproved the vanity of the proceeding.

It proved a tiresome ding-dong rubber, with the strength of the cards slightly on Francesca's side, and the luck of the table going mostly the other way. She was too keen a player not to feel a certain absorption in the game once it had started, but she was conscious today of a distracting interest that competed with the momentary importance of leads and discards and declarations. The little accumulations of talk that were unpent during the dealing of the hands became as noteworthy to her alert attention as the play of the hands themselves.

'Yes, quite a small party this afternoon,' said Serena, in reply to a seemingly casual remark on Francesca's part; 'and two or three non-players, which is unusual on a Wednesday. Canon Besomley was here just before you came; you know, the big preaching man.'

'I've been to hear him scold the human race once or twice,' said Francesca.

'A strong man with a wonderfully strong message,' said Ada Spelvexit, in an impressive and assertive tone.

'The sort of popular pulpiteer who spanks the vices of his age and lunches with them afterwards,' said Lady Caroline.

'Hardly a fair summary of the man and his work,' protested Ada. 'I've been to hear him many times when I've been depressed or discouraged, and I simply can't tell you the impression his words leave—'

'At least you can tell us what you intend to make trumps,' broke in Lady Caroline gently.

'Diamonds,' pronounced Ada, after a rather flurried survey of her hand.

'Doubled,' said Lady Caroline, with increased gentleness, and a few minutes later she was pencilling an addition of twenty-four to her score.

'I stayed with his people down here in Herefordshire last May,' said Ada, returning to the unfinished theme of the Canon; 'such an exquisite rural retreat, and so restful and healing to the nerves. Real country scenery; apple blossom everywhere.'

'Surely only on the apple trees!' said Lady Caroline.

Ada Spelvexit gave up the attempt to reproduce the decorative setting of the Canon's home-life, and fell back on the small but practical consolation of scoring the odd trick in her opponent's declaration of hearts.

'If you had led your highest club to start with, instead of the nine, we should have saved the trick,' remarked Lady Caroline to her partner in a tone of coldly gentle reproof; 'it's no use, my dear,' she continued, as Serena flustered out a halting apology, 'no earthly use to attempt to play bridge at one table and try to see and hear what's going on at two or three other tables.'

'I can generally manage to attend to more than one thing at a time,' said Serena rashly; 'I think I must have a sort of double brain.'

'Much better to economize and have one really good one,' observed Lady Caroline.

'*La belle dame sans merci* scoring a verbal trick or two as usual,' said a player at another table in a discreet undertone.

'Did I tell you Sir Edward Roan is coming to my next big evening?' said Serena hurriedly, by way, perhaps, of restoring herself a little in her own esteem.

'Poor dear good Sir Edward! What have you made trumps?' asked Lady Caroline, in one breath.

'Clubs,' said Francesca; 'and pray, why these adjectives of commiseration?'

Francesca was a Ministerialist by family interest and allegiance, and was inclined to take up the cudgels at the suggested disparagement aimed at the Foreign Secretary.

'He amuses me so much,' purred Lady Caroline. Her amusement was usually of the sort that a sporting cat derives from watching the Swedish exercises of a well-spent and care-fully thought-out mouse.

'Really? He has been rather a brilliant success at the Foreign Office, you know,' said Francesca.

'He reminds one so of a circus elephant—infinitely more intelligent than the people who direct him, but quite content to go on putting his foot down or taking it up as may be required, quite unconcerned whether he steps on a meringue or a hornet's nest in the process of going where he's expected to go.'

'How can you say such things!' protested Francesca.

'I can't,' said Lady Caroline; 'Courtenay Youghal said it in the House last night. Didn't you read the debate? He was really rather in form. I disagree entirely with his point of view, of course, but some of the things he says have just enough truth behind them to redeem them from being merely smart; for instance, his summing up of the Government's attitude towards our embarrassing Colonial Empire in the wistful phrase "Happy is the country that has no geography".'

'What an absurdly unjust thing to say!' put in Francesca; 'I daresay some of our Party at some time have taken up that attitude, but every one knows that Sir Edward is a sound Imperialist at heart.'

'Most politicians are something or other at heart, but no one would be rash enough to insure a politician against heart failure. Particularly when he happens to be in office.'

'Anyhow, I don't see that the Opposition leaders would have acted any differently in the present case,' said Francesca.

'One should always speak guardedly of the Opposition leaders,' said Lady Caroline, in her gentlest voice; 'one never knows what a turn in the situation may do for them.'

'You mean they may one day be at the head of affairs?' asked Serena briskly.

'I mean they may one day lead the Opposition. One never knows.'

Lady Caroline had just remembered that her hostess was on the Opposition side in politics.

Francesca and her partner scored four tricks in clubs; the game stood irresolutely at twenty-four all.

'If you had followed the excellent lyrical advice given to the Maid of Athens and returned my heart we should have made two more tricks and gone game,' said Lady Caroline to her partner.

'Mr Youghal seems pushing himself to the fore of late,' remarked Francesca, as Serena took up the cards to deal. Since the young politician's name had been introduced into their conversation the opportunity for turning the talk more directly on him and his affairs was too good to be missed.

'I think he's got a career before him,' said Serena; 'the House always fills when he's speaking, and that's a good sign. And then he's young and got rather an attractive personality, which is always something in the political world.'

'His lack of money will handicap him, unless he can find himself a rich wife or persuade some one to die and leave him a fat legacy,' said Francesca; 'since MPs have become the recipients of a salary rather more is expected and demanded of them in the expenditure line than before.'

'Yes, the House of Commons still remains rather at the opposite pole to the Kingdom of Heaven as regards entrance qualifications,' observed Lady Caroline.

'There ought to be no difficulty about Youghal picking up a girl with money,' said Serena; 'with his prospects he would make an excellent husband for any woman with social ambitions.'

And she half sighed, as though she almost regretted that a previous matrimonial arrangement precluded her from entering into the competition on her own account.

Francesca, under an assumption of languid interest, was watching Lady Caroline narrowly for some hint of suppressed knowledge of Youghal's courtship of Miss de Frey.

'Whom are you marrying and giving in marriage?'

The question came from George St Michael, who had strayed over from a neighbouring table, attracted by the fragments of small-talk that had reached his ears.

St Michael was one of those dapper, bird-like, illusorily-active men, who seem to have been in a certain stage of middle-age for as long as human memory can recall them. A close-cut peaked beard lent a certain dignity to his appearance—a loan which the rest of his features and mannerisms were continually and successfully repudiating. His profession, if he had one, was submerged in his hobby, which consisted of being an advance-agent for small happenings or possible happenings that were or seemed imminent in the social world around him; he found a perpetual and unflagging satisfaction in acquiring and retailing any stray items of gossip or information, particularly of a matrimonial nature, that chanced to come his way. Given the bare outline of an officially announced engagement, he would immediately fill it in with all manner of details, true or, at any rate, probable, drawn from his own imagination or from some equally exclusive source. The *Morning Post* might content itself with the mere statement of the arrangement which would shortly take place, but it was St Michael's breathless little voice that proclaimed how the contracting parties had originally met over a salmon-fishing incident, why the Guards' Chapel would not be used, why her Aunt Mary had at first opposed the match, how the question of the children's religious upbringing had been compromised, etc., etc., to all whom it might interest and to many whom it might not. Beyond his industriously-earned pre-eminence in this special branch of intelligence, he was chiefly noteworthy for having a wife reputed to be the tallest and thinnest woman in the Home Counties. The two were sometimes seen together in Society, where they passed under the collective name of St Michael and All Angles.

'We are trying to find a rich wife for Courtenay Youghal,' said Serena, in answer to St Michael's question.

'Ah, there I'm afraid you're a little late,' he observed, glowing with the importance of pending revelation; 'I'm afraid you're a little late,' he repeated, watching the effect of his words as a gardener might watch the development of a bed of carefully tended asparagus. 'I think the young gentleman has been before you and already found himself a rich mate in prospect.'

He lowered his voice as he spoke, not with a view to imparting impressive mystery to his statement, but because there were other table groups within hearing to whom he hoped presently to have the privilege of re-disclosing his revelation.

'Do you mean—?' began Serena.

'Miss de Frey,' broke in St Michael hurriedly, fearful lest his revelation should be forestalled, even in guesswork; 'quite an ideal choice, the very wife for a man who means to make his mark in politics. Twenty-four thousand a year, with prospects of more to come, and a charming place of her own not too far from town. Quite the type of girl, too, who will make a good political hostess, brains without being brainy, you know. Just the right thing. Of course, it would be premature to make any definite announcement at present—'

'It would hardly be premature for my partner to announce what she means to make trumps,' interrupted Lady Caroline, in a voice of such sinister gentleness that St Michael fled headlong back to his own table.

'Oh, is it me? I beg your pardon. I leave it,' said Serena.

'Thank you. No trumps,' declared Lady Caroline. The hand was successful, and the rubber ultimately fell to her with a comfortable margin of honours. The same partners cut together again, and this time the cards went distinctly against Francesca and Ada Spelvexit, and a heavily piled-up score confronted them at the close of the rubber. Francesca was conscious that a certain amount of rather erratic play on her part had at least contributed to the result. St Michael's incursion into the conversation had proved rather a powerful distraction to her ordinarily sound bridge-craft.

Ada Spelvexit emptied her purse of several gold pieces, and infused a corresponding degree of superiority into her manner.

'I must be going now,' she announced; 'I'm dining early. I have to give an address to some charwomen afterwards.'

'Why?' asked Lady Caroline, with a disconcerting directness that was one of her most formidable characteristics.

'Oh, well, I have some things to say to them that I daresay they will like to hear,' said Ada, with a thin laugh.

Her statement was received with a silence that betokened profound unbelief in any such probability.

'I go about a good deal among working-class women,' she added.

'No one has ever said it,' observed Lady Caroline, 'but

how painfully true it is that the poor have us always with them!'

Ada Spelvexit hastened her departure; the marred impressiveness of her retreat came as a culminating discomfiture on the top of her ill-fortune at the card-table. Possibly, however, the multiplication of her own annoyances enabled her to survey charwomen's troubles with increased cheerfulness. None of them, at any rate, had spent an afternoon with Lady Caroline.

Francesca cut in at another table, and with better fortune attending on her, succeeded in winning back most of her losses. A sense of satisfaction was distinctly dominant as she took leave of her hostess. St Michael's gossip, or rather the manner in which it had been received, had given her a clue to the real state of affairs, which, however slender and conjectural, at least pointed in the desired direction. At first she had been horribly afraid lest she should be listening to a definite announcement which would have been the death-blow to her hopes, but as the recitation went on without any of those assured little minor details which St Michael so loved to supply, she had come to the conclusion that it was merely a piece of intelligent guesswork. And if Lady Caroline had really believed in the story of Elaine de Frey's virtual engagement to Courtenay Youghal she would have taken a malicious pleasure in encouraging St Michael in his confidences, and in watching Francesca's discomfiture under the recital. The irritated manner in which she had cut short the discussion betrayed the fact that, as far as the old woman's information went, it was Comus, and not Courtenay Youghal, who held the field. And in this particular case Lady Caroline's information was likely to be nearer the truth than St Michael's confident gossip.

Francesca always gave a penny to the first crossing-sweeper or match-seller she chanced across after a successful sitting at bridge. This afternoon she had come out of the fray some fifteen shillings to the bad, but she gave two pennies to a crossing-sweeper at the north-west corner of Berkeley Square as a sort of thank-offering to the gods.

CHAPTER 8

IT was a fresh rain-repentant afternoon, following a morning that had been sultry and torrentially wet by turns: the sort of afternoon that impels people to talk graciously of the rain as having done a lot of good, its chief merit in their eyes probably having been its recognition of the art of moderation. Also it was an afternoon that invited bodily activity after the convalescent languor of the earlier part of the day. Elaine had instinctively found her way into her riding-habit and sent an order down to the stables—a blessed oasis that still smelt sweetly of horse and hay and cleanliness in a world that reeked of petrol, and now she set her mare at a smart pace through a succession of long-stretching country lanes. She was due some time that afternoon at a garden-party, but she rode with determination in an opposite direction. In the first place, neither Comus nor Courtenay would be at the party, which fact seemed to remove any valid reason that could be thought of for inviting her attendance thereat; in the second place about a hundred human beings would be gathered there, and human gatherings were not her most crying need at the present moment. Since her last encounter with her wooers, under the cedars in her own garden, Elaine realized that she was either very happy or cruelly unhappy, she could not quite determine which. She seemed to have what she most wanted in the world lying at her feet, and she was dreadfully uncertain in her more reflective moments whether she really wanted to stretch out her hand and take it. It was all very like some situation in an *Arabian Nights* tale or a story of Pagan Hellas, and consequently the more puzzling and disconcerting to a girl brought up on the methodical lines of Victorian Christianity. Her appeal court was in permanent session these last few days, but it gave no decisions, at least none that she would listen to. And the ride on her fast light-stepping little mare, alone and unattended, through the fresh-smelling leafy lanes into unexplored country, seemed just what she wanted at the moment. The mare made some small delicate pretence of being road-shy, not the staring dolt-like kind of nervousness that shows itself in an irritating hanging-back as each conspicuous wayside object presents itself, but the nerve-flutter of an imaginative animal that merely results in a quick whisk of the head and a swifter bound forward. She might have paraphrased the mental attitude of the immortalized Peter Bell into

> A basket underneath a tree
> A yellow tiger is to me,
> If it is nothing more.

The more really alarming episodes of the road, the hoot and whir of a passing motor-car or the loud vibrating hum of a wayside threshing-machine, were treated with indifference.

On turning a corner out of a narrow coppice-bordered lane into a wider road that sloped steadily upward in a long stretch of hill, Elaine saw, coming toward her at no great distance, a string of yellow-painted vans, drawn for the most part by skewbald or speckled horses. A certain rakish air about these oncoming road-craft proclaimed them as belonging to a travelling wild-beast show, decked out in the rich primitive colouring that one's taste in childhood would have insisted on before it had been schooled in the artistic value of dulness. It was an unlooked-for and distinctly unwelcome encounter. The mare had already commenced a sixfold scrutiny with nostrils, eyes, and daintily-pricked ears; one ear made hurried little backward movements to hear what Elaine was saying about the eminent niceness and respectability of the approach-ing caravan, but even Elaine felt that she would be unable satisfactorily to explain the elephants and camels that could certainly form part of the procession. To turn back would seem rather craven, and the mare might take fright at the manœuvre and try to bolt; a gate standing ajar at the entrance to a farmyard lane provided a convenient way out of the difficulty.

As Elaine pushed her way through she became aware of a man standing just inside the lane, who made a movement forward to open the gate for her.

'Thank you. I'm just getting out of the way of a wild-beast

show,' she explained; 'my mare is tolerant of motors and traction-engines, but I expect camels—hallo!' she broke off, recognizing the man as an old acquaintance, 'I heard you had taken rooms in a farm-house somewhere. Fancy meeting you in this way!'

In the not very distant days of her little-girlhood, Tom Keriway had been a man to be looked upon with a certain awe and envy; indeed the glamour of his roving career would have fired the imagination, and wistful desire to do likewise, of many young Englishmen. It seemed to be the grown-up realization of the games played in dark rooms in winter firelit evenings, and the dreams dreamed over favourite books of adventure. Making Vienna his headquarters, almost his home, he had rambled where he listed through the lands of the Near and Middle East as leisurely and thoroughly as tamer souls might explore Paris. He had wandered through Hungarian horse-fairs, hunted shy crafty beasts on lonely Balkan hill-sides, dropped himself pebble-wise into the stagnant human pool of some Bulgarian monastery, threaded his way through the strange racial mosaic of Salonika, listened with amused politeness to the shallow ultra-modern opinions of a voluble editor or lawyer in some wayside Russian town, or learned wisdom from a chance tavern companion, one of the atoms of the busy ant-stream of men and merchandise that moves untiringly round the shores of the Black Sea. And far and wide as he might roam, he always managed to turn up at frequent intervals, at ball and supper and theatre, in the gay Hauptstadt of the Habsburgs, haunting his favourite cafés and wine-vaults, skimming through his favourite news-sheets, greeting old acquaintances and friends, from ambassadors down to cobblers in the social scale. He seldom talked of his travels, but it might be said that his travels talked of him; there was an air about him that a German diplomat once summed up in a phrase: 'a man that wolves have sniffed at.'

And then two things happened, which he had not mapped out in his route; a severe illness shook half the life and all the energy out of him, and a heavy money loss brought him almost to the door of destitution. With something, perhaps, of the impulse which drives a stricken animal away from its kind,

Tom Keriway left the haunts where he had known so much happiness, and withdrew into the shelter of a secluded farm-house lodging; more than ever he became to Elaine a hearsay personality. And now the chance meeting with the caravan had flung her across the threshold of his retreat.

'What a charming little nook you've got hold of!' she exclaimed with instinctive politeness, and then looked searchingly round, and discovered that she had spoken the truth; it really was charming. The farm-house had that intensely English look that one seldom sees out of Normandy. Over the whole scene of rickyard, garden, outbuildings, horsepond and orchard, brooded that air which seems rightfully to belong to out-of-the-way farm-yards, an air of wakeful dreaminess which suggests that here man and beast and bird have got up so early that the rest of the world has never caught them up and never will.

Elaine dismounted, and Keriway led the mare round to a little paddock by the side of a great grey barn. At the end of the lane they could see the show go past, a string of lumbering vans and great striding beasts that seemed to link the vast silences of the desert with the noises and sights and smells, the naphtha-flares and advertisement hoardings and trampled orange-peel, of an endless succession of towns.

'You had better let the caravan pass well on its way before you get on the road again,' said Keriway; 'the smell of the beasts may make your mare nervous and restive going home.'

Then he called to a boy, who was busy with a hoe among some defiantly prosperous weeds, to fetch the lady a glass of milk and a piece of currant loaf.

'I don't know when I've seen anything so utterly charming and peaceful,' said Elaine, propping herself on a seat that a pear-tree had obligingly designed in the fantastic curve of its trunk.

'Charming, certainly,' said Keriway, 'but too full of the stress of its own little life struggle to be peaceful. Since I have lived here I've learnt, what I've always suspected, that a country farm-house, set away in a world of its own, is one of the most wonderful studies of interwoven happenings and tragedies that can be imagined. It is like the old chronicles of mediaeval Europe in the days when there was a sort of ordered anarchy between feudal lords and overlords, and burg-grafs, and mitred abbots, and prince-bishops, robber barons and merchant guilds, and Electors and so forth, all striving and contending and counter-plotting, and interfering with each other under some vague code of loosely-applied rules. Here one sees it reproduced under one's eyes, like a musty page of black-letter come to life. Look at one little section of it, the poultry-life on the farm. Villa poultry, dull egg-machines, with records kept of how many ounces of food they eat, and how many pennyworths of eggs they lay, give you no idea of the wonder-life of these farm-birds; their feuds and jealousies, and carefully maintained prerogatives, their unsparing tyrannies and persecutions, their calculated courage and bravado or sedulously hidden cowardice, it might all be some human chapter from the annals of the old Rhineland or mediaeval Italy. And then, outside their own bickering wars and hates, the grim enemies that come up against them from the woodlands; the hawk that dashes among the coops like a moss-trooper raiding the border, knowing well that a charge of shot may tear him to bits at any moment. And the stoat, a creeping slip of brown fur a few inches long, intently and unstayably out for blood. And the hunger-taught master of craft, the red fox, who has waited perhaps half the afternoon for his chance while the fowls were dusting themselves under the hedge, and just as they were turning supper-ward to the yard one has stopped a moment to give her feathers a final shake and found death springing upon her. Do you know,' he continued, as Elaine fed herself and the mare with morsels of currant-loaf, 'I don't think any tragedy in literature that I have ever come across impressed me so much as the first one that I spelled out slowly for myself in words of three letters: the bad fox has got the red hen. There was something so dramatically complete about it; the badness of the fox, added to all the traditional guile of his race, seemed to heighten the horror of the hen's fate, and there was such a suggestion of masterful malice about the word "got". One felt that a countryside in arms would not get that hen away from the bad fox. They used to think me a slow dull reader for not getting on with my lesson, but I used to sit and picture to myself the red hen, with its wings beating helplessly, screeching in terrified protest, or perhaps, if he had got it by the neck, with beak wide agape and silent, and eyes staring, as it left the farmyard for ever. I have seen blood-spilling and down-crushings and abject defeat here and there in my time, but the red hen has remained in my mind as the type of helpless tragedy.' He was silent for a moment as if he were again musing over the three-letter drama that had so dwelt in his childhood's imagination.

'Tell me some of the things you have seen in your time,' was the request that was nearly on Elaine's lips, but she hastily checked herself and substituted another.

'Tell me more about the farm, please.'

And he told her of a whole world, or rather of several intermingled worlds, set apart in this sleepy hollow in the hills, of beast lore and wood lore and farm craft, at times touching almost the border of witchcraft—passing lightly here, not with the probing eagerness of those who know nothing, but with the averted glance of those who fear to see too much. He told her of those things that slept and those that prowled when the dusk fell, of strange hunting cats, of the yard swine and the stalled cattle, of the farm folk themselves, as curious and remote in their way, in their ideas and fears and wants and tragedies, as the brutes and feathered stock that they tended. It seemed to Elaine as if a musty store of old-world children's books had been fetched down from some cob-webbed lumber-room and brought to life. Sitting there in the little paddock, grown thickly with tall weeds and rank grasses, and shadowed by the weather-beaten old grey barn, listening to this chronicle of wonderful things, half fanciful, half very real, she could scarcely believe that a few miles away there was a garden-party in full swing, with smart frocks and smart conversation, fashionable refreshments and fashion-able music, and a fevered undercurrent of social strivings and snubbings. Did Vienna and the Balkan Mountains and the Black Sea seem as remote and hard to believe in, she wondered, to the man sitting by her side, who had dis-covered or invented this wonderful fairyland? Was it a true and merciful arrangement of fate and life that the things of the moment thrust out the after-taste of the things that had been? Here was one who had held much that was priceless in the hollow of his hand and lost it all, and he was happy and absorbed and well content with the little wayside corner of the world into which he had crept. And Elaine, who held so many desirable things in the hollow of her hand, could not make up her mind to be even moderately happy. She did not even know whether to take this hero of her childhood down from his pedestal, or to place him on a higher one; on the whole she was inclined to resent rather than approve the idea that ill-health and misfortune could so completely subdue and tame an erstwhile bold and roving spirit.

The mare was showing signs of delicately-hinted impatience; the paddock, with its teasing insects and very indifferent grazing, had not thrust out the image of her own comfortable well-foddered loose-box. Elaine divested her habit of some remaining crumbs of bun-loaf and jumped lightly on to her saddle. As she rode slowly down the lane, with Keriway escorting her as far as its gate, she looked round at what had seemed to her, a short while ago, just a picturesque old farmstead, a place of bee-hives and hollyhocks and gabled cart-sheds; now it was in her eyes a magic city, with an undercurrent of reality beneath its magic.

'You are a person to be envied,' she said to Keriway; 'you have created a fairyland, and you are living in it yourself.'

'Envied?'

He shot the question out with sudden bitterness. She looked down and saw the wistful misery that had come into his face.

'Once,' he said to her, 'in a German paper I read a short story about a tame crippled crane that lived in the park of some small town. I forget what happened in the story, but there was one line that I shall always remember: "it was lame, that is why it was tame." '

He had created a fairyland, but assuredly he was not living in it.

CHAPTER 9

In the warmth of a late June morning the long shaded stretch
of raked earth, gravel-walk and rhododendron bush that is
known affectionately as the Row was alive with the monoto-
nous movement and alert stagnation appropriate to the time
and place. The seekers after health, the seekers after notoriety
and recognition, and the lovers of good exercise were all well
represented on the galloping ground; the gravel-walk and
chairs and long seats held a population whose varied instincts
and motives would have baffled a social catalogue-maker. The
children, handled or in perambulators, might be excused from
instinct or motive; they were brought.

Pleasingly conspicuous among a bunch of indifferent riders
pacing along by the rails where the onlookers were thickest was
Courtenay Youghal, on his handsome plum-roan gelding Anne
de Joyeuse. That delicately stepping animal had taken a prize
at Islington and nearly taken the life of a stable-boy of whom
he disapproved, but his strongest claims to distinction were
his good looks and his high opinion of himself. Youghal evidently believed in thorough accord between horse and rider.

'Please stop and talk to me,' said a quiet beckoning voice
from the other side of the rails, and Youghal drew rein and
greeted Lady Veula Croot. Lady Veula had married into a
family of commercial solidity and enterprising political nonentity. She had a devoted husband, some blond teachable
children, and a look of unutterable weariness in her eyes. To
see her standing at the top of an expensively horticultured
staircase receiving her husband's guests was rather like watching an animal performing on a music-hall stage. One always
tells oneself that the animal likes it, and one always knows
that it doesn't.

'Lady Veula is an ardent Free Trader, isn't she?' some one
once remarked to Lady Caroline.

'I wonder,' said Lady Caroline, in her gently questioning
voice; 'a woman whose dresses are made in Paris and whose
marriage has been made in heaven might be equally biased for
and against free imports.'

Lady Veula looked at Youghal and his mount with slow critical appraisement, and there was a note of blended raillery and wistfulness in her voice.

'You two dear things, I should love to stroke you both, but I'm not sure how Joyeuse would take it. So I'll stroke you down verbally instead. I admired your attack on Sir Edward immensely, though of course I don't agree with a word of it. Your description of him building a hedge round the German cuckoo and hoping he was isolating it was rather sweet. Seriously though, I regard him as one of the pillars of the Administration.'

'So do I,' said Youghal; 'the misfortune is that he is merely propping up a canvas roof. It's just his regrettable solidity and integrity that makes him so expensively dangerous. The average Briton arrives at the same judgment about Roan's handling of foreign affairs as Omar does of the Supreme Being in his dealings with the world: "He's a good fellow and 'twill all be well."'

Lady Veula laughed lightly. 'My Party is in power, so I may exercise the privilege of being optimistic. Who is that who bowed to you?' she continued, as a dark young man with an inclination to stoutness passed by them on foot; 'I've seen him about a good deal lately. He's been to one or two of my dances.'

'Andrei Drakoloff,' said Youghal; 'he's just produced a play that has had a big success in Moscow and is certain to be extremely popular all over Russia. In the first three acts the heroine is supposed to be dying of consumption; in the last act they find she is really dying of cancer.'

'Are the Russians really such a gloomy people?'

'Gloom-loving, but not in the least gloomy. They merely take their sadness pleasurably, just as we are accused of taking our pleasures sadly. Have you noticed that dreadful Klopstock youth has been pounding past us at shortening intervals? He'll come up and talk if he half catches your eye.'

'I only just know him. Isn't he at an agricultural college or something of the sort?'

'Yes, studying to be a gentleman farmer, he told me. I didn't ask if both subjects were compulsory.'

'You're really rather dreadful,' said Lady Veula, trying to look as if she thought so; 'remember, we are all equal in the sight of Heaven.'

For a preacher of wholesome truths her voice rather lacked conviction.

'If I and Ernest Klopstock are really equal in the sight of Heaven,' said Youghal, with intense complacency, 'I should recommend Heaven to consult an eye specialist.'

There was a heavy spattering of loose earth, and a squelching of saddle-leather, as the Klopstock youth lumbered up to the rails and delivered himself of loud, cheerful greetings. Joyeuse laid his ears well back as the ungainly bay cob and his appropriately matched rider drew up beside him; his verdict was reflected and endorsed by the cold stare of Youghal's eyes.

'I've been having a nailing fine time,' recounted the newcomer with clamorous enthusiasm; 'I was over in Paris last month and had lots of strawberries there, then I had a lot more in London, and now I've been having a late crop of them in Herefordshire, so I've had quite a lot this year.' And he laughed as one who had deserved well and received well of Fate.

'The charm of that story,' said Youghal, 'is that it can be told in any drawing-room.' And with a sweep of his wide-brimmed hat to Lady Veula he turned the impatient Joyeuse into the moving stream of horses and horsemen.

'That woman reminds me of some verse I've read and liked,' thought Youghal, as Joyeuse sprang into a light showy canter that gave full recognition to the existence of observant human beings along the side-walk. 'Ah, I have it.'

And he quoted almost aloud, as one does in the exhilaration of a canter:

> 'How much I loved that way you had
> Of smiling most, when very sad,
> A smile which carried tender hints
> Of sun and spring,
> And yet, more than all other thing,
> Of weariness beyond all words.'

And having satisfactorily fitted Lady Veula on to a quotation he dismissed her from his mind. With the constancy of her sex she thought about him, his good looks and his youth and his railing tongue, till late in the afternoon.

While Youghal was putting Joyeuse through his paces under the elm trees of the Row a little drama in which he was directly interested was being played out not many hundred yards away. Elaine and Comus were indulging themselves in two pennyworths of Park chair, drawn aside just a little from the serried rows of sitters who were set out like bedded plants over an acre or so of turf. Comus was, for the moment, in a mood of pugnacious gaiety, disbursing a fund of pointed criticism and unsparing anecdote concerning those of the promenaders or loungers whom he knew personally or by sight. Elaine was rather quieter than usual, and the grave serenity of the Leonardo da Vinci portrait seemed intensified in her face this morning. In his leisurely courtship Comus had relied almost exclusively on his physical attraction and the fitful drollery of his wit and high spirits, and these graces had gone far to make him seem a very desirable and rather lovable thing in Elaine's eyes. But he had left out of account the disfavour which he constantly risked and sometimes incurred from his frank and undisguised indifference to other people's interests and wishes, including, at times, Elaine's. And the more that she felt that she liked him the more she was irritated by his lack of consideration for her. Without expecting that her every wish should become a law to him, she would at least have liked it to reach the formality of a Second Reading. Another important factor he had also left out of his reckoning, namely the presence on the scene of another suitor, who also had youth and wit to recommend him, and who certainly did not lack physical attractions. Comus, marching carelessly through unknown country to effect what seemed already an assured victory, made the mistake of disregarding the existence of an unbeaten army on his flank.

Today Elaine felt that, without having actually quarrelled, she and Comus had drifted a little bit out of sympathy with one another. The fault she knew was scarcely hers, in fact

from the most good-natured point of view it could hardly be
denied that it was almost entirely his. The incident of the silver
dish had lacked even the attraction of novelty; it had been
one of a series, all bearing a strong connecting likeness. There
had been small unrepaid loans which Elaine would not
have grudged in themselves, though the application for them
brought a certain qualm of distaste; with the perversity which
seemed inseparable from his doings, Comus had always flung
away a portion of his borrowings in some ostentatious piece
of glaring and utterly profitless extravagance, which outraged
all the canons of her upbringing without bringing him an
atom of understandable satisfaction. Under these repeated
discouragements it was not surprising that some small part of
her affection should have slipped away, but she had come to
the Park that morning with an unconfessed expectation of
being gently wooed back to the mood of gracious forgetfulness that she was only too eager to assume. It was almost
worth while being angry with Comus for the sake of experi-
encing the pleasure of being coaxed into friendliness again
with the charm which he knew so well how to exert. It was
delicious here under the trees on this perfect June morning,
and Elaine had the blessed assurance that most of the women
within range were envying her the companionship of the
handsome merry-hearted youth who sat by her side. With
special complacence she contemplated her cousin Suzette,
who was self-consciously but not very elatedly basking in
the attentions of her fiancé, an earnest-looking young man
who was superintendent of a People's something-or-other on
the south side of the river, and whose clothes Comus had
described as having been made in Southwark rather than in
anger.

Most of the pleasures in life must be paid for, and the chair-
ticket vendor in due time made his appearance in quest of
pennies. Comus paid him from out of a varied assortment of
coins and then balanced the remainder in the palm of his
hand. Elaine felt a sudden foreknowledge of something disagreeable about to happen, and a red spot deepened in her
cheeks.

'Four shillings and fivepence and a halfpenny,' said Comus

reflectively. 'It's a ridiculous sum to last me for the next three days, and I owe a card debt of over two pounds.'

'Yes?' commented Elaine dryly and with an apparent lack of interest in his exchequer statement. Surely, she was thinking hurriedly to herself, he could not be foolish enough to broach the matter of another loan.

'The card debt is rather a nuisance,' pursued Comus, with fatalistic persistency.

'You won seven pounds last week, didn't you?' asked Elaine; 'don't you put any of your winnings to balance losses?'

'The four shillings and the fivepence and the halfpenny represent the rearguard of the seven pounds,' said Comus; 'the rest have fallen by the way. If I can pay the two pounds today I daresay I shall win something more to go on with; I'm holding rather good cards just now. But if I can't pay it, of course I shan't show up at the club. So you see the fix I am in.'

Elaine took no notice of this indirect application. The Appeal Court was assembling in haste to consider new evidence, and this time there was the rapidity of sudden determination about its movement.

The conversation strayed away from the fateful topic for a few moments, and then Comus brought it deliberately back to the danger zone.

'It would be awfully nice if you would let me have a fiver for a few days, Elaine,' he said quickly; 'if you don't I really don't know what I shall do.'

'If you are really bothered about your card debt I will send you the two pounds by messenger boy early this afternoon.' She spoke quietly and with great decision. 'And I shall not be at the Connors' dance tonight,' she continued; 'it's too hot for dancing. I'm going home now; please don't bother to accompany me, I particularly wish to go alone.'

Comus saw that he had overstepped the mark of her good nature. Wisely he made no immediate attempt to force himself back into her good graces. He would wait till her indignation had cooled.

His tactics would have been excellent if he had not forgotten that unbeaten army on his flank.

Elaine de Frey had known very clearly what qualities she had wanted in Comus, and she had known, against all efforts at self-deception, that he fell far short of those qualities. She had been willing to lower her standard of moral requirements in proportion as she was fond of the boy, but there was a point beyond which she would not go. He had hurt her pride, besides alarming her sense of caution. Suzette, on whom she felt a thoroughly justified tendency to look down, had at any rate an attentive and considerate lover. Elaine walked towards the Park gates feeling that in one essential Suzette possessed something that had been denied to her, and at the gates she met Joyeuse and his spruce young rider preparing to turn homeward.

'Get rid of Joyeuse and come and take me out to lunch somewhere,' demanded Elaine.

'How jolly!' said Youghal. 'Let's go to the Corridor Restaurant. The head-waiter there is an old Viennese friend of mine and looks after me beautifully. I've never been there with a lady before, and he's sure to ask me afterwards, in his fatherly way, if we're engaged.'

The lunch was a success in every way. There was just enough orchestral effort to immerse the conversation without drowning it, and Youghal was an attentive and inspired host. Through an open doorway Elaine could see the café reading-room, with its imposing array of *Neue Freie Presse, Berliner Tageblatt*, and other exotic newspapers hanging on the wall. She looked across at the young man seated opposite her, who gave one the impression of having centred the most serious efforts of his brain on his toilet and his food, and recalled some of the flattering remarks that the Press had bestowed on his recent speeches.

'Doesn't it make you conceited, Courtenay,' she asked, 'to look at all those foreign newspapers hanging there and know that most of them have got paragraphs and articles about your Persian speech?'

Youghal laughed.

'There's always a chastening corrective in the thought that some of them may have printed your portrait. When once you've seen your features hurriedly reproduced in the *Matin*, for instance, you feel you would like to be a veiled Turkish woman for the rest of your life.'

And Youghal gazed long and lovingly at his reflection in the nearest mirror, as an antidote against possible incitements to humility in the portrait gallery of fame.

Elaine felt a certain soothed satisfaction in the fact that this young man, whose knowledge of the Middle East was an embarrassment to Ministers at question time and in debate, was showing himself equally well informed on the subject of her culinary likes and dislikes. If Suzette could have been forced to attend as a witness at a neighbouring table she would have felt even happier.

'Did the head-waiter ask if we were engaged?' asked Elaine, when Courtenay had settled the bill, and she had finished collecting her sunshade and gloves and other impedimenta from the hands of obsequious attendants.

'Yes,' said Youghal, 'and he seemed quite crestfallen when I had to say "No".'

'It would be horrid to disappoint him when he's looked after us so charmingly,' said Elaine; 'tell him that we are.'

CHAPTER 10

THE Rutland Galleries were crowded, especially in the neighbourhood of the tea-buffet, by a fashionable throng of art-patrons which had gathered to inspect Mervyn Quentock's collection of Society portraits. Quentock was a young artist whose abilities were just receiving due recognition from the critics; that the recognition was not overdue he owed largely to his perception of the fact that if one hides one's talent under a bushel one must be careful to point out to every one the exact bushel under which it is hidden. There are two manners of receiving recognition: one is to be discovered so long after one's death that one's grandchildren have to write to the papers to establish their relationship; the other is to be discovered, like the infant Moses, at the very outset of one's career. Mervyn Quentock had chosen the latter and happier manner. In an age when many aspiring young men strive to advertise their wares by imparting to them a freakish imbecility, Quentock turned out work that was characterized by a pleasing delicate restraint, but he contrived to herald his output with a certain fanfare of personal eccentricity, thereby compelling an attention which might otherwise have strayed past his studio. In appearance he was the ordinary cleanly young Englishman, except, perhaps, that his eyes rather suggested a library edition of the *Arabian Nights*; his clothes matched his appearance and showed no taint of the sartorial disorder by which the bourgeois of the garden-city and the Latin Quarter anxiously seeks to proclaim his kinship with art and thought. His eccentricity took the form of flying in the face of some of the prevailing social currents of the day, but as a reactionary, never as a reformer. He produced a gasp of admiring astonishment in fashionable circles by refusing to paint actresses—except, of course, those who had left the legitimate drama to appear between the boards of Debrett. He absolutely declined to execute portraits of Americans unless they hailed from certain favoured States. His 'water-colour line', as a New York paper phrased it, earned for him a crop of angry criticism and a shoal of Transatlantic commissions, and criticism and commissions were the things that Quentock most wanted.

'Of course he is perfectly right,' said Lady Caroline Benaresq, calmly rescuing a piled-up plate of caviare sandwiches from the neighbourhood of a trio of young ladies who had established themselves hopefully within easy reach of it. 'Art,' she continued, addressing herself to the Rev. Poltimore Vardon, 'has always been geographically exclusive. London may be more important from most points of view than Venice, but the art of portrait painting, which would never concern itself with a Lord Mayor, simply grovels at the feet of the Doges. As a Socialist I'm bound to recognize the right of Ealing to compare itself with Avignon, but one cannot expect the Muses to put the two on a level.'

'Exclusiveness,' said the Reverend Poltimore, 'has been the salvation of Art, just as the lack of it is proving the downfall of religion. My colleagues of the cloth go about zealously proclaiming the fact that Christianity, in some form or other, is attracting shoals of converts among all sorts of races and tribes that one had scarcely ever heard of, except in reviews of books of travel that one never read. That sort of thing was all very well when the world was more sparsely populated, but nowadays, when it simply teems with human beings, no one is particularly impressed by the fact that a few million, more or less, of converts, of a low stage of mental development, have accepted the teachings of some particular religion. It not only chills one's enthusiasm, it positively shakes one's convictions when one hears that the things one has been brought up to believe as true are being very favourably spoken of by Buriats and Samoyeds and Kanakas.'

The Rev. Poltimore Vardon had once seen a resemblance in himself to Voltaire, and had lived alongside the comparison ever since.

'No modern cult or fashion,' he continued, 'would be favourably influenced by considerations based on statistics; fancy adopting a certain style of hat or cut of coat, because it was being largely worn in Lancashire and the Midlands; fancy favouring a certain brand of champagne because it was being extensively patronized in German summer resorts! No wonder that religion is falling into disuse in this country under such ill-directed methods.'

'You can't prevent the heathen being converted if they choose to be,' said Lady Caroline; 'this is an age of toleration.'

'You could always deny it,' said the Reverend Poltimore, 'like the Belgians do with regrettable occurrences in the Congo. But I would go further than that. I would stimulate the waning enthusiasm for Christianity in this country by labelling it as the exclusive possession of a privileged few. If one could induce the Duchess of Pelm, for instance, to assert that the Kingdom of Heaven, as far as the British Isles are concerned, is strictly limited to herself, two of the under-gardeners at Pelmby, and, possibly, but not certainly, the Dean of Dunster, there would be an instant reshaping of the popular attitude towards religious convictions and observances. Once let the idea get about that the Christian Church is rather more exclusive than the Lawn at Ascot, and you would have a quickening of religious life such as this generation has never witnessed. But as long as the clergy and the religious organizations advertise their creed on the lines of "Everybody ought to believe in us: millions do," one can expect nothing but indifference and waning faith.'

'Time is just as exclusive in its way as Art,' said Lady Caroline.

'In what way?' said the Reverend Poltimore.

'Your pleasantries about religion would have sounded quite clever and advanced in the early 'nineties. Today they have a dreadfully warmed-up flavour. That is the great delusion of you would-be advanced satirists; you imagine you can sit down comfortably for a couple of decades saying daring and startling things about the age you live in, which, whatever other defects it may have, is certainly not standing still. The whole of the Sherard Blaw school of discursive drama suggests, to my mind, Early Victorian furniture in a travelling circus. However, you will always have relays of people from the suburbs to listen to the Mocking Bird of yesterday, and sincerely imagine it is the harbinger of something new and revolutionizing.'

'*Would* you mind passing that plate of sandwiches?' asked one of the trio of young ladies, emboldened by famine.

'With pleasure,' said Lady Caroline, deftly passing her a nearly empty plate of bread-and-butter.

'I meant the plate of caviare sandwiches. So sorry to trouble you,' persisted the young lady.

Her sorrow was misapplied; Lady Caroline had turned her attention to a new-comer.

'A very interesting exhibition,' Ada Spelvexit was saying; 'faultless technique, as far as I am a judge of technique, and quite a master-touch in the way of poses. But have you noticed how very animal his art is? He seems to shut out the soul from his portraits. I nearly cried when I saw dear Winifred depicted simply as a good-looking healthy blonde.'

'I wish you had,' said Lady Caroline; 'the spectacle of a strong, brave woman weeping at a private view in the Rutland Galleries would have been so sensational. It would certainly have been reproduced in the next Drury Lane drama. And I'm so unlucky; I never see these sensational events. I was ill with appendicitis, you know, when Lulu Braminguard dramatically forgave her husband, after seventeen years of estrangement, during a State luncheon party at Windsor. The old Queen was furious about it. She said it was so disrespectful to the cook to be thinking of such a thing at such a time.'

Lady Caroline's recollections of things that hadn't happened at the court of Queen Victoria were notoriously vivid; it was the very widespread fear that she might one day write a book of reminiscences that made her so universally respected.

'As for his full-length picture of Lady Brickfield,' continued Ada, ignoring Lady Caroline's commentary as far as possible, 'all the expression seems to have been deliberately concentrated in the feet; beautiful feet, no doubt, but still, hardly the most distinctive part of a human being.'

'To paint the right people at the wrong end may be an eccentricity, but it is scarcely an indiscretion,' pronounced Lady Caroline.

One of the portraits which attracted more than a passing flutter of attention was a costume study of Francesca Bassington. Francesca had secured some highly desirable patronage for the young artist, and in return he had enriched her pantheon of personal possessions with a clever piece of work into which he had thrown an unusual amount of imaginative detail. He had painted her in a costume of the Great Louis's brightest period, seated in front of a tapestry that was so prominent in the composition that it could scarcely be said to form part of the background. Flowers and fruit, in exotic profusion, were its dominant note; quinces, pomegranates, passion-flowers, giant convolvulus, great mauve-pink roses, and grapes that were already being pressed by gleeful cupids in a riotous Arcadian vintage, stood out on its woven texture. The same note was struck in the beflowered satin of the lady's kirtle, and in the pomegranate pattern of the brocade that draped the couch on which she was seated. The artist had called his picture 'Recolte'. And after one had taken in all the details of fruit and flower and foliage that earned the composition its name, one noted the landscape that showed through a broad casement in the left-hand corner. It was a landscape clutched in the grip of winter, naked, bleak, black-frozen; a winter in which things died and knew no rewakening. If the picture typified harvest, it was a harvest of artificial growth.

'It leaves a great deal to the imagination, doesn't it?' said Ada Spelvexit, who had edged away from the range of Lady Caroline's tongue.

'At any rate one can tell who it's meant for,' said Serena Golackly.

'Oh, yes, it's a good likeness of dear Francesca,' admitted Ada; 'of course, it flatters her.'

'That, too, is a fault on the right side in portrait painting,' said Serena; 'after all, if posterity is going to stare at one for centuries it's only kind and reasonable to be looking just a little better than one's best.'

'What a curiously unequal style the artist has!' continued Ada, almost as if she felt a personal grievance against him. 'I was just noticing what a lack of soul there was in most of his portraits. Dear Winifred, you know, who speaks so beautifully and feelingly at my gatherings for old women, he's made her look just an ordinary dairy-maidish blonde; and Francesca, who is quite the most soulless woman I've ever met, well, he's given her quite—'

'Hush!' said Serena, 'the Bassington boy is just behind you.'

Comus stood looking at the portrait of his mother with the feeling of one who comes suddenly across a once-familiar, half-forgotten acquaintance in unfamiliar surroundings. The likeness was undoubtedly a good one, but the artist had caught an expression in Francesca's eyes which few people had ever seen there. It was the expression of a woman who had forgotten for one short moment to be absorbed in the small cares and excitements of her life, the money worries and little social plannings, and had found time to send a look of half-wistful friendliness to some sympathetic companion. Comus could recall that look, fitful and fleeting, in his mother's eyes when she had been a few years younger, before her world had grown to be such a committee-room of ways and means. Almost as a re-discovery, he remembered that she had once figured in his boyish mind as a 'rather good sort', more ready to see the laughable side of a piece of mischief than to labour forth a reproof. That the by-gone feeling of good-fellowship had been stamped out was, he knew, probably in great part his own doing, and it was possible that the old friendliness was still there under the surface of things, ready to show itself again if he willed it, and friends were becoming scarcer with him than enemies in these days. Looking at the picture with its wistful hint of a long-ago comradeship, Comus made up his mind that he very much wanted things to be back on their earlier footing, and to see again on his mother's face the look that the artist had caught and perpetuated in its momentary flitting. If the projected Elaine marriage came off, and in spite of recent maladroit behaviour on his part he still counted it an assured thing, much of the immediate cause for estrangement between himself and his mother would be removed, or at any rate easily removable. With the influence of Elaine's money behind him, he promised himself that he would find some occupation that would remove from himself the reproach of being a waster and idler. There were lots of careers, he told himself, that were open to a man with solid financial backing and good connexions. There might yet be jolly times ahead, in which his mother would have her share of the good things that were going, and carking thin-lipped Henry Greech and other of Comus's detractors could take their sour looks and words out of sight and hearing. Thus, staring at the picture as though he were studying its every detail, and seeing really only that wistful friendly smile, Comus made his plans and dispositions for a battle that was already fought and lost.

The crowd grew thicker in the galleries, cheerfully enduring an amount of overcrowding that would have been fiercely resented in a railway carriage. Near the entrance Mervyn Quentock was talking to a Serene Highness, a lady who led a life of obtrusive usefulness largely imposed on her by a good-natured inability to say 'No'. 'That woman creates a positive draught with the number of bazaars she opens,' a frivolously-spoken ex-Cabinet Minister had once remarked. At the present moment she was being whimsically apologetic.

'When I think of the legions of well-meaning young men and women to whom I've given away prizes for proficiency in art-school curriculum, I feel that I ought not to show my face inside a picture gallery. I always imagine that my punishment in another world will be perpetually sharpening pencils and cleaning palettes for unending relays of misguided young people whom I deliberately encouraged in their artistic delusions.'

'Do you suppose we shall all get appropriate punishments in another world for our sins in this?' asked Quentock.

'Not so much for our sins as for our indiscretions; they are the things which do the most harm and cause the greatest trouble. I feel certain that Christopher Columbus will undergo the endless torment of being discovered by parties of American tourists. You see I am quite old-fashioned in my ideas about the terrors and inconveniences of the next world. And now I must be running away; I've got to open a Free Library somewhere. You know the sort of thing that happens—one unveils a bust of Carlyle and makes a speech about Ruskin, and then people come in their thousands and read *Rabid Ralph, or Should He Have Bitten Her?* Don't forget, please, I'm going to have the medallion with the fat cupid sitting on a sun-dial. And just one thing more—perhaps I ought not to ask you, but you have such nice kind eyes, you embolden one to make daring requests, *would* you send me the recipe for those lovely chestnut-and-chicken-liver sandwiches? I know the ingredients, of course, but it's the proportions that make such a difference—just how much liver to how much chestnut, and what amount of red pepper and other things. Thank you so much. I really am going now.'

Staring round with a vague half-smile at everybody within nodding distance, Her Serene Highness made one of her characteristic exits, which Lady Caroline declared always reminded her of a scrambled egg slipping off a piece of toast. At the entrance she stopped for a moment to exchange a word or two with a young man who had just arrived. From a corner where he was momentarily hemmed in by a group of tea-consuming dowagers, Comus recognized the new-comer as Courtenay Youghal, and began slowly to labour his way towards him. Youghal was not at the moment the person whose society he most craved for in the world, but there was at least the possibility that he might provide an opportunity for a game of bridge, which was the dominant desire of the moment. The young politician was already surrounded by a group of friends and acquaintances, and was evidently being made the recipient of a salvo of congratulation— presumably on his recent performances in the Foreign Office debate, Comus concluded. But Youghal himself seemed to be announcing the event with which the congratulations were connected. Had some dramatic catastrophe overtaken the Government? Comus wondered. And then, as he pressed nearer, a chance word, the coupling of two names, told him the news.

CHAPTER 11

AFTER the momentous lunch at the Corridor Restaurant, Elaine had returned to Manchester Square (where she was staying with one of her numerous aunts) in a frame of mind that embraced a tangle of competing emotions. In the first place she was conscious of a dominant feeling of relief; in a moment of impetuosity, not wholly influenced by pique, she had settled the problem which hours of hard thinking and serious heart-searching had brought no nearer to solution, and, although she felt just a little inclined to be scared at the head-long manner of her final decision, she had now very little doubt in her own mind that the decision had been the right one. In fact, the wonder seemed rather that she should have been so long in doubt as to which of her wooers really enjoyed her honest approval. She had been in love these many weeks past with an imaginary Comus, but now that she had definitely walked out of her dreamland she saw that nearly all the qualities that had appealed to her on his behalf had been absent from, or only fitfully present in, the character of the real Comus. And now that she had installed Youghal in the first place of her affections he had rapidly acquired in her eyes some of the qualities which ranked highest in her estimation. Like the proverbial buyer she had the happy feminine tendency of magnifying the worth of her possession as soon as she had acquired it. And Courtenay Youghal gave Elaine some justification for her sense of having chosen wisely. Above all other things, selfish and cynical though he might appear at times, he was unfailingly courteous and considerate towards her. That was a circumstance which would always have carried weight with her in judging any man; in this case its value was enormously heightened by contrast with the behaviour of her other wooer. And Youghal had in her eyes the advantage which the glamour of combat, even the combat of words and wire-pulling, throws over the fighter. He stood well in the forefront of a battle which however carefully stage-managed, however honeycombed with personal insincerities and overlaid with calculated mock-heroics, really meant something, really counted for good or wrong in the nation's development and the world's history. Shrewd parliamentary observers might have warned her that Youghal would never stand much higher in the political world than he did at present, as a brilliant Opposition free-lance, leading lively and rather meaningless forays against the dull and rather purposeless foreign policy of a Government that was scarcely either to be blamed for or congratulated on its handling of foreign affairs. The young politician had not the strength of character or convictions that keeps a man naturally in the forefront of affairs and gives his counsels a sterling value, and on the other hand his insincerity was not deep enough to allow him to pose artificially and successfully as a leader of men and shaper of movements. For the moment, however, his place in public life was sufficiently marked out to give him a secure footing in that world where people are counted individually and not in herds. The woman whom he would make his wife would have the chance, too, if she had the will and the skill, to become an individual who counted.

There was balm to Elaine in this reflection, yet it did not wholly suffice to drive out the feeling of pique which Comus had called into being by his slighting view of her as a convenient cash supply in moments of emergency. She found a certain satisfaction in scrupulously observing her promise, made earlier on that eventful day, and sent off a messenger with the stipulated loan. Then a reaction of compunction set in, and she reminded herself that in fairness she ought to write and tell her news in as friendly a fashion as possible to her dismissed suitor before it burst upon him from some other quarter. They parted on more or less quarrelling terms, it was true, but neither of them had foreseen the finality of the parting nor the permanence of the breach between them; Comus might even now be thinking himself half-forgiven, and the awakening would be rather cruel. The letter, however, did not prove an easy one to write; not only did it present difficulties of its own, but it suffered from the competing urgency of a desire to be doing something far pleasanter than writing explanatory and valedictory phrases. Elaine was possessed with an unusual but quite overmastering hankering to visit her cousin Suzette Brankley. They met but rarely at each other's houses and very seldom anywhere else, and Elaine for her part was never conscious of feeling that their opportunities for intercourse lacked anything in the way of adequacy. Suzette accorded her just that touch of patronage which a moderately well-off and immoderately dull girl will usually try to mete out to an acquaintance who is known to be wealthy and suspected of possessing brains. In return Elaine armed herself with that particular brand of mock humility which can be so terribly disconcerting if properly wielded. No quarrel of any description stood between them and one could not legitimately have described them as enemies, but they never disarmed in one another's presence. A misfortune of any magnitude falling on one of them would have been sincerely regretted by the other, but any minor discomfiture would have produced a feeling very much akin to satisfaction. Human nature knows millions of these inconsequent little feuds, springing up and flourishing apart from any basis of racial, political, religious or economic causes, as a hint perhaps to crass unseeing altruists that enmity has its place and purpose in the world as well as benevolence.

Elaine had not personally congratulated Suzette since the formal announcement of her engagement to the young man with the dissentient tailoring effects. The impulse to go and do so now over-mastered her sense of what was due to Comus in the way of explanation. The letter was still in its blank unwritten stage, an unmarshalled sequence of sentences forming in her brain, when she ordered her car and made a hurried but well-thought-out change into her most sumptuously sober afternoon toilette. Suzette, she felt tolerably sure, would still be in the costume that she had worn in the Park that morning, a costume that aimed at elaboration of detail, and was damned with overmuch success.

Suzette's mother welcomed her unexpected visitor with obvious satisfaction. Her daughter's engagement, she explained, was not so brilliant from the social point of view as a girl of Suzette's attractions and advantages might have legitimately aspired to, but Egbert was a thoroughly commendable and dependable young man, who would very probably win his way before long to membership of the County Council.

'From there, of course, the road would be open to him to higher things.'

'Yes,' said Elaine, 'he might become an alderman.'

'Have you seen their photographs, taken together?' asked Mrs Brankley, abandoning the subject of Egbert's prospective career.

'No; do show me,' said Elaine, with a flattering show of interest; 'I've never seen that sort of thing before. It used to be the fashion once for engaged couples to be photographed together, didn't it?'

'It's *very* much the fashion now,' said Mrs Brankley assertively, but some of the complacency had filtered out of her voice.

Suzette came into the room, wearing the dress that she had worn in the Park that morning.

'Of course, you've been hearing all about *the* engagement from mother,' she cried, and then set to work conscientiously to cover the same ground.

'We met at Grindelwald, you know. He always calls me his Ice Maiden because we first got to know each other on the skating-rink. Quite romantic, wasn't it? Then we asked him to tea one day, and we got to be quite friendly. Then he proposed.'

'He wasn't the only one who was smitten with Suzette,' Mrs Brankley hastened to put in, fearful lest Elaine might suppose that Egbert had had things all his own way. 'There was an American millionaire who was quite taken with her, and a Polish count of a very old family. I assure you I felt quite nervous at some of our tea-parties.'

Mrs Brankley had given Grindelwald a sinister but rather alluring reputation among a large circle of untravelled friends as a place where the insolence of birth and wealth was held in precarious check from breaking forth into scenes of savage violence.

'My marriage with Egbert will, of course, enlarge the sphere of my life enormously,' pursued Suzette.

'Yes,' said Elaine; her eyes were rather remorselessly taking in the details of her cousin's toilette. It is said that nothing is sadder than victory except defeat. Suzette began to feel that the tragedy of both was concentrated in the creation which had given her such unalloyed gratification till Elaine had come on the scene.

'A woman can be so immensely helpful in the social way to a man who is making a career for himself. And I'm so glad to find that we've a great many ideas in common. We each made out a list of our idea of the hundred best books, and quite a number of them were the same.'

'He looks bookish,' said Elaine, with a critical glance at the photograph.

'Oh, he's not at all a bookworm,' said Suzette quickly, 'though he's tremendously well-read. He's quite the man of action.'

'Does he hunt?' asked Elaine.

'No, he doesn't get much time or opportunity for riding.'

'What a pity!' commented Elaine. 'I don't think I could marry a man who wasn't fond of riding.'

'Of course that's a matter of taste,' said Suzette stiffly; 'horsey men are not usually gifted with overmuch brains, are they?'

'There is as much difference between a horseman and a

horsey man as there is between a well-dressed man and a dressy one,' said Elaine judicially; 'and you may have noticed how seldom a dressy woman really knows how to dress. As an old lady of my acquaintance observed the other day, some people are born with a sense of how to clothe themselves, others acquire it, others look as if their clothes had been thrust upon them.'

She gave Lady Caroline her due quotation marks, but the sudden tactfulness with which she looked away from her cousin's frock was entirely her own idea.

A young man entering the room at this moment caused a diversion that was rather welcome to Suzette.

'Here comes Egbert,' she announced, with an air of subdued triumph; it was at least a satisfaction to be able to produce the captive of her charms, alive and in good condition, on the scene. Elaine might be as critical as she pleased, but a live lover outweighed any number of well-dressed straight-riding cavaliers who existed only as a distant vision of the delectable husband.

Egbert was one of those men who have no small talk, but possess an inexhaustible supply of the larger variety. In whatever society he happened to be, and particularly in the immediate neighbourhood of an afternoon-tea table, with a limited audience of womenfolk, he gave the impression of some one who was addressing a public meeting, and would be happy to answer questions afterwards. A suggestion of gaslit mission-halls, wet umbrellas, and discreet applause seemed to accompany him everywhere. He was an exponent, among other things, of what he called New Thought, which seemed to lend itself conveniently to the employment of a good deal of rather stale phraseology. Probably in the course of some thirty odd years of existence he had never been of any notable use to man, woman, child, or animal, but it was his firmly-announced intention to leave the world a better, happier, purer place than he had found it; against the danger of any relapse to earlier conditions after his disappearance from the scene, he was, of course, powerless to guard. 'Tis not in mortals to ensure succession, and Egbert was admittedly mortal.

Elaine found him immensely entertaining, and would

certainly have exerted herself to draw him out if such a proceeding had been at all necessary. She listened to his conversation with the complacent appreciation that one bestows on a stage tragedy, from whose calamities one can escape at any moment by the simple process of leaving one's seat. When at last he checked the flow of his opinions by a hurried reference to his watch, and declared that he must be moving on elsewhere, Elaine almost expected a vote of thanks to be accorded him, or to be asked to signify herself in favour of some resolution by holding up her hand.

When the young man had bidden the company a rapid businesslike farewell, tempered in Suzette's case by the exact degree of tender intimacy that it would have been considered improper to omit or overstep, Elaine turned to her expectant cousin with an air of cordial congratulation.

'He is exactly the husband I should have chosen for you, Suzette.'

For the second time that afternoon Suzette felt a sense of waning enthusiasm for one of her possessions.

Mrs Brankley detected the note of ironical congratulation in her visitor's verdict.

'I suppose she means he's not her idea of a husband, but he's good enough for Suzette,' she observed to herself, with a snort that expressed itself somewhere in the nostrils of the brain. Then with a smiling air of heavy patronage she delivered herself of her one idea of a damaging counterstroke.

'And when are we to hear of your engagement, my dear?'

'Now,' said Elaine quietly, but with electrical effect; 'I came to announce it to you but I wanted to hear all about Suzette first. It will be formally announced in the papers in a day or two.'

'But who is it? Is it the young man who was with you in the Park this morning?' asked Suzette.

'Let me see, who was I with in the Park this morning? A very good-looking dark boy? Oh, no, not Comus Bassington. Some one you know by name, anyway, and I expect you've seen his portrait in the papers.'

'A flying-man?' asked Mrs Brankley.

'Courtenay Youghal,' said Elaine.

Mrs Brankley and Suzette had often rehearsed in the privacy of their minds the occasion when Elaine should come to pay her personal congratulations to her engaged cousin. It had never been in the least like this.

On her return from her enjoyable afternoon visit Elaine found an express messenger letter waiting for her. It was from Comus, thanking her for her loan—and returning it.

'I suppose I ought never to have asked you for it,' he wrote, 'but you are always so deliciously solemn about money matters that I couldn't resist. Just heard the news of your engagement to Courtenay. Congrats to you both. I'm far too stony broke to buy you a wedding present so I'm going to give you back the bread-and-butter dish. Luckily it still has your crest on it. I shall love to think of you and Courtenay eating bread-and-butter out of it for the rest of your lives.'

That was all he had to say on the matter about which Elaine had been preparing to write a long and kindly-expressed letter, closing a rather momentous chapter in her life and his. There was not a trace of regret or upbraiding in his note; he had walked out of their mutual fairyland as abruptly as she had, and to all appearances far more unconcernedly. Reading the letter again and again, Elaine could come to no decision as to whether this was merely a courageous gibe at defeat, or whether it represented the real value that Comus set on the thing that he had lost.

And she would never know. If Comus possessed one useless gift to perfection it was the gift of laughing at Fate even when it had struck him hardest. One day, perhaps, the laughter and mockery would be silent on his lips, and Fate would have the advantage of laughing last.

CHAPTER 12

A DOOR closed and Francesca Bassington sat alone in her well-beloved drawing-room. The visitor who had been enjoying the hospitality of her afternoon-tea table had just taken his departure. The *tête-à-tête* had not been a pleasant one, at any rate as far as Francesca was concerned, but at least it had brought her the information for which she had been seeking. Her role of looker-on from a tactful distance had necessarily left her much in the dark concernimg the progress of the all-important wooing, but during the last few hours she had, on slender though significant evidence, exchanged her complacent expectancy for a conviction that something had gone wrong. She had spent the previous evening at her brother's house, and had naturally seen nothing of Comus in that uncongenial quarter; neither had he put in an appearance at the breakfast table the following morning. She had met him in the hall at eleven o'clock, and he had hurried past her, merely imparting the information that he would not be in till dinner that evening. He spoke in his sulkiest tone, and his face wore a look of defeat, thinly masked by an air of defiance; it was not the defiance of a man who is losing, but of one who has already lost.

Francesca's conviction that things had gone wrong between Comus and Elaine de Frey grew in strength as the day wore on. She lunched at a friend's house, but it was not a quarter where special social information of any importance was likely to come early to hand. Instead of the news she was hankering for, she had to listen to trivial gossip and speculation on the flirtations and 'cases' and 'affairs' of a string of acquaintances whose matrimonial projects interested her about as much as the nesting arrangements of the wildfowl in St James's Park.

'Of course,' said her hostess, with the duly impressive emphasis of a privileged chronicler, 'we've always regarded Claire as the marrying one of the family, so when Emily came to us and said, "I've got some news for you," we all said, "Claire's engaged!" "Oh, no," said Emily, "it's not Claire this time, it's me." So then we had to guess who the lucky man was. "It can't be Captain Parminter," we all said, "because he's always been sweet on Joan." And then Emily said—'

The recording voice reeled off the catalogue of inane remarks with a comfortable purring complacency that held out no hope of an early abandoning of the topic. Francesca sat and wondered why the innocent acceptance of a cutlet and a glass of indifferent claret should lay one open to such unsparing punishment.

A stroll homeward through the Park after lunch brought no further enlightenment on the subject that was uppermost in her mind; what was worse, it brought her, without possibility of escape, within hailing distance of Merla Blathlington, who fastened on to her with the enthusiasm of a lonely tsetse fly encountering an outpost of civilization.

'Just think,' she buzzed inconsequently, 'my sister in Cambridgeshire has hatched out thirty-three White Orpington chickens in her incubator!'

'What eggs did she put in it?' asked Francesca.

'Oh, some very special strain of White Orpington.'

'Then I don't see anything remarkable in the result. If she had put in crocodiles' eggs and hatched out White Orpingtons, there might have been something to write to *Country Life* about.'

'What funny fascinating things these little green park-chairs are,' said Merla, starting off on a fresh topic; 'they always look so quaint and knowing when they're stuck away in pairs by themselves under the trees, as if they were having a heart-to-heart talk or discussing a piece of very private scandal. If they could only speak, what tragedies and comedies they could tell us of, what flirtations and proposals!'

'Let us be devoutly thankful that they can't,' said Francesca, with a shuddering recollection of the luncheon-table conversation.

'Of course, it would make one very careful what one said before them—or above them rather,' Merla rattled on, and then, to Francesca's infinite relief, she espied another acquaintance sitting in unprotected solitude, who promised to supply a more durable audience than her present rapidly moving companion. Francesca was free to return to her drawing-room in Blue Street to await with such patience as she could command the coming of some visitor who might be able to throw light on the subject that was puzzling and disquieting her. The arrival of George St Michael boded bad news, but at any rate news, and she gave him an almost cordial welcome.

'Well, you see I wasn't far wrong about Miss de Frey and Courtenay Youghal, was I?' he chirruped, almost before he had seated himself. Francesca was to be spared any further spinning-out of her period of uncertainty. 'Yes, it's officially given out,' he went on, 'and it's to appear in the *Morning Post* tomorrow. I heard it from Colonel Deel this morning, and he had it direct from Youghal himself. Yes, please, one lump; I'm not fashionable, you see.' He had made the same remark about the sugar in his tea with unfailing regularity for at least thirty years. Fashions in sugar are apparently stationary. 'They say,' he continued hurriedly, 'that he proposed to her on the Terrace of the House, and a division bell rang and he had to hurry off before she had time to give her answer, and when he got back she simply said, "The Ayes have it."' St Michael paused in his narrative to give an appreciative giggle.

'Just the sort of inanity that would go the rounds,' remarked Francesca, with the satisfaction of knowing that she was making the criticism direct to the author and begetter of the inanity in question. Now that the blow had fallen and she knew the full extent of its weight, her feeling towards the bringer of bad news, who sat complacently nibbling at her tea-cakes and scattering crumbs of tiresome small-talk at her feet, was one of whole-hearted dislike. She could sympathize with, or at any rate understand, the tendency of Oriental despots to inflict death or ignominious chastisement on messengers bearing tidings of misfortune and defeat, and St Michael, she perfectly well knew, was thoroughly aware of the fact that her hopes and wishes had been centred on the possibility of having Elaine for a daughter-in-law; every purring remark that his mean little soul prompted him to contribute to the conversation had an easily recognizable undercurrent of malice. Fortunately for her powers of polite endurance, which had been put to such searching and repeated tests that day, St Michael had planned out for himself a busy little time-table of afternoon visits, at each of which his self-appointed task of forestalling and embellishing the newspaper announcements of the Youghal—de Frey engagement would be hurriedly but thoroughly performed.

'They'll be quite one of the best-looking and most interesting couples of the season, won't they?' he cried, by way of farewell. The door closed, and Francesca Bassington sat alone in her drawing-room.

Before she could give way to the bitter luxury of reflection on the downfall of her hopes, it was prudent to take precautionary measures against unwelcome intrusion. Summoning the maid who had just speeded the departing St Michael, she gave the order: 'I am not at home this afternoon to Lady Caroline Benaresq.' On second thoughts she extended the taboo to all possible callers, and sent a telephone message to catch Comus at his club, asking him to come and see her as soon as he could manage before it was time to dress for dinner. Then she sat down to think, and her thinking was beyond the relief of tears.

She had built herself a castle of hopes, and it had not been a castle in Spain, but a structure well on the probable side of the Pyrenees. There had been a solid foundation on which to build. Miss de Frey's fortune was an assured and unhampered one, her liking for Comus had been an obvious fact; his courtship of her a serious reality. The young people had been much together in public, and their names had naturally been coupled in the match-making gossip of the day. The only serious shadow cast over the scene had been the persistent presence, in foreground or background, of Courtenay Youghal. And now the shadow suddenly stood forth as the reality, and the castle of hopes was a ruin, a hideous mortification of dust and debris, with the skeleton outlines of its chambers till standing to make mockery of its discomfited architect. The daily anxiety about Comus and his extravagant ways and intractable disposition had been gradually lulled by the prospect of his making an advantageous marriage, which would have transformed him from a ne'er-do-well and adventurer into a wealthy idler. He might even have been moulded, by the resourceful influence of an ambitious wife, into a man with some definite purpose in life. The prospect had vanished with cruel suddenness, and the anxieties were crowding back again, more insistent than ever. The boy had had his one good chance in the matrimonial market and missed it; if he were to transfer his attentions to some other well-dowered girl he would be marked down at once as a fortune-hunter, and that would constitute a heavy handicap to the most plausible of wooers. His liking for Elaine had evidently been genuine in its way, though perhaps it would have been rash to read any deeper sentiment into it, but even with the spur of his own inclination to assist him he had failed to win the prize that had seemed so temptingly within his reach. And in the dashing of his prospects, Francesca saw the threatening of her own. The old anxiety as to her precarious tenure of her present quarters put on again all its familiar terrors. One day, she foresaw, in the horribly near future, George St Michael would come pattering up her stairs with the breathless intelligence that Emmeline Chetrof was going to marry somebody or other in the Guards or the Record Office, as the case might be, and then there would be an uprooting of her life from its home and haven in Blue Street and a wandering forth to some cheap unhappy far-off dwelling, where the stately Van der Meulen and its companion host of beautiful and desirable things would be stuffed and stowed away in soulless surroundings, like courtly *émigrés* fallen on evil days. It was unthinkable, but the trouble was that it had to be thought about. And if Comus had played his cards well and transformed himself from an encumbrance into a son with wealth at his command, the tragedy which she saw looming in front of her might have been avoided, or at the worst whittled down to easily bearable proportions. With money behind one, the problem of where to live approaches more nearly to the simple question of where do you wish to live, and a rich daughter-in-law would have surely seen to it that she did not have to leave her square mile of Mecca and go out into the wilderness of bricks and mortar. If the house in Blue Street could not have been compounded for there were other desirable residences which would have been capable of consoling Francesca for her lost Eden. And now the detested Courtenay Youghal, with his mocking eyes and air of youthful cynicism, had stepped in and overthrown those golden hopes and plans whose non-fulfilment would make such a world of change in her future. Assuredly she had reason to feel bitter against that young man, and she was not disposed to take a very lenient view of Comus's own mismanagement of the affair; her greeting when he at last arrived was not couched in a sympathetic strain.

'So you have lost your chance with the heiress,' she remarked abruptly.

'Yes,' said Comus coolly; 'Courtenay Youghal has added her to his other successes.'

'And you have added her to your other failures,' pursued Francesca relentlessly; her temper had been tried that day beyond ordinary limits.

'I thought you seemed getting along so well with her,' she continued, as Comus remained uncommunicative.

'We hit it off rather well together,' said Comus, and added with deliberate bluntness, 'I suppose she got rather sick at my borrowing money from her. She thought it was all I was after.'

'You borrowed money from her!' said Francesca; 'you were fool enough to borrow money from a girl who was favourably disposed towards you, and with Courtenay Youghal in the background waiting to step in and oust you!'

Francesca's voice trembled with misery and rage. This great stroke of good luck that had seemed about to fall into their laps had been thrust aside by an act or series of acts of wanton paltry folly. The good ship had been lost for the sake of the traditional ha'p'orth of tar. Comus had paid some pressing tailor's or tobacconist's bill with a loan unwillingly put at his disposal by the girl he was courting, and had flung away his chances of securing a wealthy and in every way desirable bride. Elaine de Frey and her fortune might have been the making of Comus, but he had hurried in as usual to effect his own undoing. Calmness did not in this case come with reflection; the more Francesca thought about the matter, the more exasperated she grew. Comus threw himself down in a low chair and watched her without a trace of embarrassment or concern at her mortification. He had come to her feeling rather sorry for himself, and bitterly conscious of his defeat, and she had met him with a taunt and without the least hint of sympathy; he determined that she should be tantalized with the knowledge of how small and stupid a thing had stood between the realization and ruin of her hopes for him.

'And to think she should be captured by Courtenay Youghal,' said Francesca bitterly: 'I've always deplored your intimacy with that young man.'

'It's hardly my intimacy with him that's made Elaine accept him,' said Comus.

Francesca realized the futility of further upbraiding. Through the tears of vexation that stood in her eyes she looked across at the handsome boy who sat opposite her, mocking at his own misfortune, perversely indifferent to his folly, seemingly almost indifferent to its consequences.

'Comus,' she said quietly and wearily, 'you are an exact reversal of the legend of Pandora's Box. You have all the charm and advantages that a boy could want to help him on in the world, and behind it all there is the fatal damning gift of utter hopelessness.'

'I think,' said Comus, 'that is the best description that any one has ever given of me.'

For the moment there was a flush of sympathy and something like outspoken affection between mother and son. They seemed very much alone in the world just now, and in the general overturn of hopes and plans there flickered a chance that each might stretch out a hand to the other, and summon back to their lives an old dead love that was the best and strongest feeling either of them had known. But the sting of disappointment was too keen, and the flood of resentment mounted too high on either side to allow the chance more than a moment in which to flicker away into nothingness. The old fatal topic of estrangement came to the fore, the question of immediate ways and means, and mother and son faced themselves again as antagonists on a well-disputed field.

'What is done is done,' said Francesca, with a movement of tragic impatience that belied the philosophy of her words; 'there is nothing to be gained by crying over spilt milk. There is the present and the future to be thought about, though. One can't go on indefinitely as a tenant-for-life in a fools' paradise.' Then she pulled herself together and proceeded to deliver an ultimatum which the force of circumstances no longer permitted her to hold in reserve.

'It's not much use talking to you about money, as I know

from long experience, but I can only tell you this, that in the middle of the season I'm already obliged to be thinking of leaving town. And you, I'm afraid, will have to be thinking of leaving England at equally short notice. Henry told me the other day that he can get you something out in West Africa. You've had your chance of doing something better for yourself from the financial point of view, and you've thrown it away for the sake of borrowing a little ready money for your luxuries, so now you must take what you can get. The pay won't be very good at first, but living is not dear out there.'

'West Africa,' said Comus reflectively; 'it's a sort of modern substitute for the old-fashioned *oubliette*, a convenient depository for tiresome people. Dear Uncle Henry may talk lugubriously about the burden of Empire, but he evidently recognizes its uses as a refuse consumer.'

'My dear Comus, you are talking of the West Africa of yesterday. While you have been wasting your time at school, and worse than wasting your time in the West End, other people have been grappling with the study of tropical diseases, and the West African coast country is being rapidly transformed from a lethal chamber into a sanatorium.'

Comus laughed mockingly.

'What a beautiful bit of persuasive prose! It reminds one of the Psalms, and even more of a company prospectus. If you were honest you'd confess that you lifted it straight out of a rubber or railway promotion scheme. Seriously, mother, if I must grub about for a living, why can't I do it in England? I could go into a brewery, for instance.'

Francesca shook her head decisively; she could foresee the sort of steady work Comus was likely to accomplish, with the lodestone of town and the minor attractions of race-meetings and similar festivities always beckoning to him from a conveniently attainable distance, but apart from that aspect of the case there was a financial obstacle in the way of his obtaining any employment at home.

'Breweries and all those sort of things necessitate money to start with; one has to pay premiums or invest capital in the undertaking and so forth. And as we have no money available, and can scarcely pay our debts as it is, it's no use thinking about it.'

'Can't we sell something?' asked Comus.

He made no actual suggestion as to what should be sacrificed, but he was looking straight at the Van der Meulen.

For a moment Francesca felt a stifling sensation of weakness, as though her heart was going to stop beating. Then she sat forward in her chair and spoke with energy, almost fierceness.

'When I am dead my things can be sold and dispersed. As long as I am alive I prefer to keep them by me.'

In her holy place, with all her treasured possessions around her, this dreadful suggestion had been made. Some of her cherished household gods, souvenirs and keepsakes from past days, would, perhaps, not have fetched a very considerable sum in the auction-room, others had a distinct value of their own, but to her they were all precious. And the Van der Meulen, at which Comus had looked with impious appraising eyes, was the most sacred of them all. When Francesca had been away from her town residence or had been confined to her bedroom through illness, the great picture with its stately solemn representation of a long-ago battle-scene, painted to flatter the flattery-loving soul of a warrior-king who was dignified even in his campaigns—this was the first thing she visited on her return to town or convalescence. If an alarm of fire had been raised it would have been the first thing for whose safety she would have troubled. And Comus had almost suggested that it should be parted with, as one sold railway shares and other soulless things.

Scolding, she had long ago realized, was a useless waste of time and energy where Comus was concerned, but this evening she unloosed her tongue for the mere relief that it gave to her surcharged feelings. He sat listening without comment, though she purposely let fall remarks that she hoped might sting him into self-defence or protest. It was an unsparing indictment, the more damaging in that it was so irrefutably true, the more tragic in that it came from perhaps the one person in the world whose opinion he had ever cared for. And he sat through it as silent and seemingly unmoved as though she had been rehearsing a speech for some drawing-room comedy. When she had had her say his method of retort was not the soft answer that turneth away wrath, but the inconsequent one that shelves it.

'Let's go and dress for dinner.'

The meal, like so many that Francesca and Comus had eaten in each other's company of late, was a silent one. Now that the full bearings of the disaster had been discussed in all its aspects, there was nothing more to be said. Any attempt at ignoring the situation and passing on to less controversial topics would have been a mockery and pretence which neither of them would have troubled to sustain. So the meal went forward with its dragged-out dreary intimacy of two people who were separated by a gulf of bitterness, whose hearts were hard with resentment against one another.

Francesca felt a sense of relief when she was able to give the maid the order to serve her coffee upstairs. Comus had a sullen scowl on his face, but he looked up as she rose to leave the room, and gave his half-mocking little laugh.

'You needn't look so tragic,' he said. 'You're going to have your own way. I'll go out to that West African hole.'

CHAPTER 13

COMUS found his way to his seat in the stalls of the Straw Exchange Theatre, and turned to watch the stream of distinguished and distinguishable people who made their appearance as a matter of course at a First Night in the height of the season. Pit and gallery were already packed with a throng, tense, expectant and alert, that waited for the rise of the curtain with the eager patience of a terrier watching a dilatory human prepare for outdoor exercises. Stalls and boxes filled slowly and hesitatingly with a crowd whose component units seemed for the most part to recognize the probability that they were quite as interesting as any play they were likely to see. Those who bore no particular face-value themselves derived a certain amount of social dignity from the near neighbourhood of obvious notabilities; if one could not obtain recognition oneself there was some vague pleasure in being able to recognize notoriety at intimately close quarters.

'Who is that woman with the auburn hair and a rather effective belligerent gleam in her eyes?' asked a man sitting just behind Comus. 'She looks as if she might have created the world in six days and destroyed it on the seventh.'

'I forget her name,' said his neighbour; 'she writes. She's the author of that book, *The Woman Who Wished it was Wednesday*, you know. It used to be the convention that women writers should be plain and dowdy; now we have gone to the other extreme and build them on extravagantly decorative lines.'

A buzz of recognition came from the front rows of the pit, together with a craning of necks on the part of those in less favoured seats. It heralded the arrival of Sherard Blaw, the dramatist who had discovered himself, and who had given so ungrudgingly of his discovery to the world. Lady Caroline, who was already directing little conversational onslaughts from her box, gazed gently for a moment at the new arrival, and then turned to the silver-haired Archdeacon sitting beside her.

'They say the poor man is haunted by the fear that he will die during a general election, and that his obituary notices will be seriously curtailed by the space taken up by the election results. The curse of our party system, from his point of view, is that it takes up so much room in the Press.'

The Archdeacon smiled indulgently. As a man he was so exquisitely worldly that he fully merited the name of the Heavenly Worldling bestowed on him by an admiring duchess, and withal his texture was shot with a pattern of such genuine saintliness that one felt that whoever else might hold the keys of Paradise he, at least, possessed a private latchkey to that abode.

'Is it not significant of the altered grouping of things,' he observed, 'that the Church, as represented by me, sympathizes with the message of Sherard Blaw, while neither the man nor his message find acceptance with unbelievers like you, Lady Caroline?'

Lady Caroline blinked her eyes. 'My dear Archdeacon,' she said, 'no one can be an unbeliever nowadays. The Christian Apologists have left one nothing to disbelieve.'

The Archdeacon rose with a delighted chuckle. 'I must go and tell that to De la Poulett,' he said, indicating a clerical figure sitting in the third row of the stalls; 'he spends his life explaining from his pulpit that the glory of Christianity consists in the fact that though it is not true it has been found necessary to invent it.'

The door of the box opened and Courtenay Youghal entered, bringing with him a subtle suggestion of chaminade and an atmosphere of political tension. The Government had fallen out of the good graces of a section of its supporters, and those who were not in the know were busy predicting a serious crisis over a forthcoming division in the Committee stage of an important Bill. This was Saturday night, and unless some successful cajolery were effected between now and Monday afternoon, Ministers would be, seemingly, in danger of defeat.

'Ah, here is Youghal,' said the Archdeacon; 'he will be able to tell us what is going to happen in the next forty-eight hours. I hear the Prime Minister says it is a matter of conscience, and they will stand or fall by it.'

His hopes and sympathies were notoriously on the Ministerial side.

Youghal greeted Lady Caroline and subsided gracefully into a chair well in the front of the box. A buzz of recognition rippled slowly across the house.

'For the Government to fall on a matter of conscience,' he said, 'would be like a man cutting himself with a safety razor.'

Lady Caroline purred a gentle approval.

'I'm afraid it's true, Archdeacon,' she said.

No one can effectively defend a Government when it's been in office several years. The Archdeacon took refuge in light skirmishing.

'I believe Lady Caroline sees the makings of a great Socialist statesman in you, Youghal,' he observed.

'Great Socialist statesmen aren't made, they're stillborn,' replied Youghal.

'What is the play about tonight?' asked a pale young woman who had taken no part in the talk.

'I don't know,' said Lady Caroline, 'but I hope it's dull. If there is any brilliant conversation in it I shall burst into tears.'

In the front row of the upper circle a woman with a restless starling-voice was discussing the work of a temporarily fashionable composer, chiefly in relation to her own emotions, which she seemed to think might prove generally interesting to those around her.

'Whenever I hear his music I feel that I want to go up into a mountain and pray. Can you understand that feeling?'

The girl to whom she was unburdening herself shook her head.

'You see, I've heard his music chiefly in Switzerland, and we were up among the mountains all the time, so it wouldn't have made any difference.'

'In that case,' said the woman, who seemed to have emergency emotions to suit all geographical conditions, 'I should have wanted to be in a great silent plain by the side of a rushing river.'

'What I think is so splendid about his music—' commenced another starling-voice on the farther side of the girl. Like sheep that feed greedily before the coming of a storm, the starling-voices seemed impelled to extra effort by the knowledge of four imminent intervals of acting during which they would be hushed into constrained silence.

In the back row of the dress circle a late-comer, after a cursory glance at the programme, had settled down into a comfortable narrative, which was evidently the resumed thread of an unfinished taxi-drive monologue.

'We all said, "It can't be Captain Parminter, because he's always been sweet on Joan," and then Emily said—'

The curtain went up, and Emily's contribution to the discussion had to be held over till the entr'acte.

The play promised to be a success. The author, avoiding the pitfall of brilliancy, had aimed at being interesting; and as far as possible, bearing in mind that his play was a comedy, he had striven to be amusing. Above all he had remembered that in the laws of stage proportions it is permissible and generally desirable that the part should be greater than the whole; hence he had been careful to give the leading lady such a clear and commanding lead over the other characters of the play that it was impossible for any of them ever to get on level terms with her. The action of the piece was now and then delayed thereby, but the duration of its run would be materially prolonged.

The curtain came down on the first act amid an encouraging instalment of applause, and the audience turned its back on the stage and began to take a renewed interest in itself. The authoress of *The Woman Who Wished it was Wednesday* had swept like a convalescent whirlwind, subdued but potentially tempestuous, into Lady Caroline's box.

'I've just trodden with all my weight on the foot of an eminent publisher as I was leaving my seat,' she cried, with a peal of delighted laughter. 'He was such a dear about it; I said I hoped I hadn't hurt him, and he said, "I suppose you think, who drives hard bargains should himself be hard." Wasn't it pet lamb of him?'

'I've never trodden on a pet lamb,' said Lady Caroline, 'so I've no idea what its behaviour would be under the circumstances.'

'Tell me,' said the authoress, coming to the front of the box, the better to survey the house, and perhaps also with a charitable desire to make things easy for those who might pardonably wish to survey her, 'tell me, please, where is the girl sitting whom Courtenay Youghal is engaged to?'

Elaine was pointed out to her, sitting in the fourth row of the stalls, on the opposite side of the house to where Comus had his seat. Once during the interval she had turned to give him a friendly nod of recognition as he stood in one of the side gangways, but he was absorbed at the moment in looking at himself in the glass panel. The grave brown eyes and the mocking green-grey ones had looked their last into each other's depths.

For Comus this first-night performance, with its brilliant gathering of spectators, its groups and coteries of lively talkers, even its counterfoil of dull chatterers, its pervading atmosphere of stage and social movement, and its intruding undercurrent of political flutter, all this composed a tragedy in which he was the chief character. It was the life he knew and loved and basked in, and it was the life he was leaving. It would go on reproducing itself again and again, with its stage interest and social interest and intruding outside interests, with the same lively chattering crowd, the people who had done things being pointed out by people who recognized them to people who didn't—it would all go on with unflagging animation and sparkle and enjoyment, and for him it would have stopped utterly. He would be in some unheard-of-sun-blistered wilderness, where natives and pariah dogs and raucous-throated crows fringed round mockingly on one's loneliness, where one rode for sweltering miles for the chance of meeting a collector or police officer, with whom most likely on closer acquaintance one had hardly two ideas in common, where female society was represented at long intervals by some climate-withered woman missionary or official's wife, where food and sickness and veterinary lore became at last the three outstanding subjects on which the mind settled, or rather sank. That was the life he foresaw and dreaded, and that was the life he was going to. For a boy who went out to it from the dullness of some country rectory, from a neighbourhood where a flower show and a cricket match formed the social landmarks of the year, the feeling of exile might not be very crushing, might indeed be lost in the sense of change and adventure. But Comus had lived too thoroughly in the centre of things to regard life in a backwater as anything else than stagnation, and stagnation while one is young he justly regarded as an offence against nature and reason, in keeping with the perverted mockery that sends decrepit invalids touring painfully about the world and shuts panthers up in narrow cages. He was being put aside, as a wine is put aside, but to deteriorate instead of gaining in the process, to lose the best time of his youth and health and good looks in a world where youth and health and good looks count for much and where time never returns lost possessions. And thus, as the curtain swept down on the close of each act, Comus felt a sense of depression and deprivation sweep down on himself; bitterly he watched his last evening of social gaiety slipping away to its end. In less than an hour it would be over; in a few months' time it would be an unreal memory.

In the third interval, as he gazed round at the chattering house, some one touched him on the arm. It was Lady Veula Croot.

'I suppose in a week's time you'll be on the high seas?' she said. 'I'm coming to your farewell dinner, you know; your mother has just asked me. I'm not going to talk the usual rot to you about how much you will like it and so on. I sometimes think that one of the advantages of hell will be that no one will have the impertinence to point out to you that you're really better off than you would be anywhere else. What do you think of the play? Of course one can foresee the end; she will come to her husband with the announcement that their longed-for child is going to be born, and that will smooth over everything. So conveniently effective to wind up a comedy with the commencement of some one else's tragedy. And every one will go away saying, "I'm glad it had a happy ending."'

Lady Veula moved back to her seat, with her pleasant smile on her lips and the look of infinite weariness in her eyes.

The interval, the last interval, was drawing to a close, and the house began to turn with fidgety attention towards the stage for the unfolding of the final phase of the play. Francesca sat in Serena Golackly's box listening to Colonel Springfield's story of what happened to a pigeon-cote in his compound at Poona. Every one who knew the Colonel had to listen to that story a good many times, but Lady Caroline had mitigated the boredom of the infliction, and in fact invested it with a certain sporting interest, by offering a prize to the person who heard it oftenest in the course of the season, the competitors being under an honourable understanding not to lead up to the subject. Ada Spelvexit and a boy in the Foreign Office were at present at the top of the list with five recitals each to their score, but the former was suspected of doubtful adherence to the rules and spirit of the competition.

'And there, dear lady,' concluded the Colonel, 'were the eleven dead pigeons. What had become of the bandicoot no one ever knew.'

Francesca thanked him for his story, and complacently

inscribed the figure 4 on the margin of her theatre programme. Almost at the same moment she heard George St Michael's voice pattering out a breathless piece of intelligence for the edification of Serena Golackly and any one else who might care to listen. Francesca galvanized into sudden attention.

'Emmeline Chetrof to a fellow in the Indian Forest Department. He's got nothing but his pay, and they can't be married for four or five years: an absurdly long engagement, don't you think so? All very well to wait seven years for a wife in patriarchal times when you probably had others to go on with, and you lived long enough to celebrate your own tercentenary, but under modern conditions it seems a foolish arrangement.'

St Michael spoke almost with a sense of grievance. A marriage project that tied up all the small pleasant nuptial gossip items about bridesmaids and honeymoon and recalcitrant aunts and so forth for an indefinite number of years seemed scarcely decent in his eyes, and there was little satisfaction or importance to be derived from early and special knowledge of an event which loomed as far distant as a Presidential Election or a change of Viceroy. But to Francesca, who had listened with startled apprehension at the mention of Emmeline Chetrof's name, the news came in a flood of relief and thankfulness. Short of entering a nunnery and taking celibate vows, Emmeline could hardly have behaved more conveniently than in tying herself up to a lover whose circumstances made it necessary to relegate marriage to the distant future. For four or five years Francesca was assured of undisturbed possession of the house in Blue Street, and after that period who knew what might happen? The engagement might stretch on indefinitely, it might even come to nothing under the weight of its accumulated years, as sometimes happened with these protracted affairs. Emmeline might lose her fancy for her absentee lover, and might never replace him with another. A golden possibility of perpetual tenancy of her present home began to float once more through Francesca's mind. As long as Emmeline had been unbespoken in the marriage market there had always been the haunting likelihood of seeing the dreaded announcement, 'A marriage has been arranged and will shortly take place,' in connexion with her name. And now a marriage had been arranged and would *not* shortly take place, might indeed never take place. St Michael's information was likely to be correct in this instance; he would never have invented a piece of matrimonial intelligence which gave such little scope for supplementary detail of the kind he loved to supply. As Francesca turned to watch the fourth act of the play, her mind was singing a paean of thankfulness and exultation. It was as though some artificer sent by the gods had reinforced with a substantial cord the horsehair thread that held up the sword of Damocles over her head. Her love for her home, for her treasured household possessions and her pleasant social life, was able to expand once more in present security, and feed on future hope. She was still young enough to count four or five years as a long time, and tonight she was optimistic enough to prophesy smooth things of the future that lay beyond that span. Of the fourth act, with its carefully held back but obviously imminent reconciliation between the leading characters, she took in but little, except that she vaguely understood it to have a happy ending. As the lights went up she looked round on the dispersing audience with a feeling of friendliness uppermost in her mind; even the sight of Elaine de Frey and Courtenay Youghal leaving the theatre together did not inspire her with a tenth part of the annoyance that their entrance had caused her. Serena's invitation to go on to the Savoy for supper fitted in exactly with her mood of exhilaration. It would be a fit and appropriate wind-up to an auspicious evening. The cold chicken and modest brand of Chablis waiting for her at home should give way to a banquet of more festive nature.

In the crush of the vestibule, friends and enemies, personal and political, were jostled and locked together in the general effort to rejoin temporarily estranged garments and secure the attendance of elusive vehicles. Lady Caroline found herself at close quarters with the estimable Henry Greech, and experienced some of the joy which comes to the homeward wending sportsman when a chance shot presents itself on which he may expend his remaining cartridges.

'So the Government is going to climb down, after all,' she

said, with a provocative assumption of private information on the subject.

'I assure you the Government will do nothing of the kind,' replied the Member of Parliament with befitting dignity; 'the Prime Minister told me last night that under no circumstances —'

'My dear Mr Greech,' said Lady Caroline, 'we all know that Prime Ministers are wedded to the truth, but like other wedded couples they sometimes live apart.'

For her, at any rate, the comedy had had a happy ending.

Comus made his way slowly and lingeringly from the stalls, so slowly that the lights were already being turned down and great shroud-like dustcloths were being swathed over the ornamental gilt-work. The laughing, chattering, yawning throng had filtered out of the vestibule, and was melting away in final groups from the steps of the theatre. An impatient attendant gave him his coat and locked up the cloak-room. Comus stepped out under the portico; he looked at the posters announcing the play, and in anticipation he could see other posters announcing its 200th performance. Two hundred performances; by that time the Straw Exchange Theatre would be to him something so remote and unreal that it would hardly seem to exist or to have ever existed except in his fancy. And to the laughing, chattering throng that would pass in under that portico to the 200th performance, he would be, to those that had known him, something equally remote and non-existent. 'The good-looking Bassington boy? Oh, dead, or rubber-growing or sheep-farming, or something of that sort.'

CHAPTER 14

THE farewell dinner which Francesca had hurriedly organized in honour of her son's departure threatened from the outset to be a doubtfully successful function. In the first place, as he observed privately, there was very little of Comus and a good deal of farewell in it. His own particular friends were unrepresented. Courtenay Youghal was out of the question; and though Francesca would have stretched a point and welcomed some of his other male associates of whom she scarcely approved, he himself had been opposed to including any of them in the invitations. On the other hand, as Henry Greech had provided Comus with this job that he was going out to, and was, moreover, finding part of the money for the necessary outfit, Francesca had felt it her duty to ask him and his wife to the dinner; the obtuseness that seems to cling to some people like a garment throughout their life had caused Mr Greech to accept the invitation. When Comus heard of the circumstance he laughed long and boisterously; his spirits, Francesca noted, seemed to be rising fast as the hour for departure drew near.

The other guests included Serena Golackly and Lady Veula, the latter having been asked on the inspiration of the moment at the theatrical first night. In the height of the season it was not easy to get together a goodly selection of guests at short notice, and Francesca had gladly fallen in with Serena's suggestion of bringing with her Stephen Thorle, who was alleged, in loose feminine phrasing, to 'know all about' tropical Africa. His travels and experiences in those regions probably did not cover much ground or stretch over any great length of time, but he was one of those individuals who can describe a continent on the strength of a few days' stay in a coast town as intimately and dogmatically as a palaeontologist will reconstruct an extinct mammal from the evidence of a stray shinbone. He had the loud penetrating voice and the prominent penetrating eyes of a man who can do no listening in the ordinary way and whose eyes have to perform the function of listening for him. His vanity did not necessarily make him unbearable, unless one had to spend much time in his society, and his need for a wide field of audience and admiration was mercifully calculated to spread his operations over a considerable human area. Moreover, his craving for attentive listeners forced him to interest himself in a wonderful variety of subjects on which he was able to discourse fluently and with a certain semblance of special knowledge. Politics he avoided; the ground was too well known, and there was a definite No to every definite Yes that could be put forward. Moreover, argument was not congenial to his disposition, which preferred an unchallenged flow of dissertation modified by occasional helpful questions which formed the starting-point for new offshoots of word-spinning. The promotion of cottage industries, the prevention of juvenile street trading, the extension of the Borstal prison system, the furtherance of vague talkative religious movements, the fostering of inter-racial *ententes*, all found in him a tireless exponent, a fluent and entertaining, though perhaps not very convincing, advocate. With the real motive power behind these various causes he was not very closely identified; to the spade-workers who carried on the actual labours of each particular movement he bore the relation of a trowel-worker, delving superficially at the surface, but able to devote a proportionately far greater amount of time to the advertisement of his progress and achievements. Such was Stephen Thorle, a governess in the nursery of Chelsea-bred religions, a skilled window-dresser in the emporium of his own personality, and needless to say, evanescently popular amid a wide but shifting circle of acquaintances. He improved on the record of a socially much-travelled individual whose experience has become classical, and went to most of the best houses—twice.

His inclusion as a guest at this particular dinner-party was not a very happy inspiration. He was inclined to patronize Comus, as well as the African continent, and on even slighter acquaintance. With the exception of Henry Greech, whose feelings towards his nephew had been soured by many years of overt antagonism, there was an uncomfortable feeling among those present that the topic of the black-sheep export trade, as Comus would have himself expressed it, was being given undue prominence in what should have been a festive farewell banquet. And Comus, in whose honour the feast was given, did not contribute much towards its success; though his spirits seemed strung up to a high pitch, his merriment was more the merriment of a cynical and amused onlooker than of one who responds to the gaiety of his companions. Sometimes he laughed quietly to himself at some chance remark of a scarcely mirth-provoking nature, and Lady Veula, watching him narrowly, came to the conclusion that an element of fear was blended with his seemingly buoyant spirits. Once or twice he caught her eye across the table, and a certain sympathy seemed to grow up between them, as though they were both consciously watching some lugubrious comedy that was being played out before them.

An untoward little incident had marked the commencement of the meal. A small still-life picture that hung over the sideboard had snapped its cord and slid down with an alarming clatter on to the crowded board beneath it. The picture itself was scarcely damaged, but its fall had been accompanied by a tinkle of broken glass, and it was found that a liqueur glass, one out of a set of seven that would be impossible to match, had been shivered into fragments. Francesca's almost motherly love for her possessions made her peculiarly sensible to a feeling of annoyance and depression at the accident, but she turned politely to listen to Mrs Greech's account of a misfortune in which four soup-plates were involved. Mrs Henry was not a brilliant conversationalist, and her flank was speedily turned by Stephen Thorle, who recounted a slum experience in which two entire families did all their feeding out of one damaged soup-plate.

'The gratitude of those poor creatures when I presented them with a set of table crockery apiece, the tears in their eyes and in their voices when they thanked me, would be impossible to describe.'

'Thank you all the same for describing it,' said Comus.

The listening eyes went swiftly round the table to gather evidence as to how this rather disconcerting remark had been received, but Thorle's voice continued uninterruptedly to retail stories of East End gratitude, never failing to mention the particular deeds of disinterested charity on his part which had evoked and justified the gratitude. Mrs Greech had to suppress the interesting sequel to her broken crockery narrative, to wit, how she subsequently matched the shattered soup-plates at Harrod's. Like an imported plant species that sometimes flourishes exceedingly, and makes itself at home to the dwarfing and overshadowing of all native species, Thorle dominated the dinner-party and thrust its original purport somewhat into the background. Serena began to look helplessly apologetic. It was altogether rather a relief when the filling of champagne glasses gave Francesca an excuse for bringing matters back to their intended footing.

'We must all drink a health,' she said. 'Comus, my own dear boy, a safe and happy voyage to you, much prosperity in the life you are going out to, and in due time a safe and happy return—'

Her hand gave an involuntary jerk in the act of raising the glass, and the wine went streaming across the tablecloth in a froth of yellow bubbles. It certainly was not turning out a comfortable or auspicious dinner-party.

'My dear mother,' cried Comus, 'you must have been drinking healths all the afternoon to make your hand so unsteady.'

He laughed gaily and with apparent carelessness, but again Lady Veula caught the frightened note in his laughter. Mrs Henry, with practical sympathy, was telling Francesca two good ways for getting wine-stains out of tablecloths. The smaller economies of life were an unnecessary branch of learning for Mrs Greech, but she studied them as carefully and conscientiously as a stay-at-home plain-dwelling English child commits to memory the measurements and altitudes of the world's principal peaks. Some women of her temperament and mentality know by heart the favourite colours, flowers, and hymn-tunes of all the members of the Royal Family; Mrs Greech would possibly have failed in an examination of that nature, but she knew what to do with carrots that have been overlong in storage.

Francesca did not renew her speech-making; a chill seemed to have fallen over all efforts at festivity, and she contented herself with refilling her glass and simply drinking to her boy's good health. The others followed her example, and Comus drained his glass with a brief 'Thank you all very much.' The sense of constraint which hung over the company was not, however, marked by any uncomfortable pause in the conversation. Henry Greech was a fluent thinker, of the kind that prefer to do their thinking aloud; the silence that descended on him as a mantle in the House of Commons was an official livery of which he divested himself as thoroughly as possible in private life. He did not propose to sit through dinner as a mere listener to Mr Thorle's personal narrative of philanthropic movements and experiences, and took the first opportunity of launching himself into a flow of satirical observations on current political affairs. Lady Veula was inured to this sort of thing in her own home circle, and sat listening with the stoical indifference with which an Eskimo might accept the occurrence of one snowstorm the more, in the course of an Arctic winter. Serena Golackly felt a certain relief at the fact that her imported guest was not, after all, monopolizing the conversation. But the latter was too determined a personality to allow himself to be thrust aside for many minutes by the talkative MP. Henry Greech paused for an instant to chuckle at one of his own shafts of satire, and immediately Thorle's penetrating voice swept across the table.

'Oh, you politicians!' he exclaimed, with pleasant superiority; 'you are always fighting about how things should be done, and the consequence is you are never able to do anything. Would you like me to tell you what a Unitarian horse-dealer said to me at Brindisi about politicians?'

A Unitarian horse-dealer at Brindisi had all the allurement of the unexpected. Henry Greech's witticisms at the expense of the Front Opposition bench were destined to remain as unfinished as his wife's history of the broken soup-plates. Thorle was primed with an ample succession of stories and themes, chiefly concerning poverty, thriftlessness, reclamation, reformed characters, and so forth, which carried him in an almost uninterrupted sequence through the remainder of the dinner.

'What I want to do is to make people think,' he said, turning his prominent eyes on to his hostess; 'it's so hard to make people think.'

'At any rate you give them the opportunity,' said Comus cryptically.

As the ladies rose to leave the table Comus crossed over to pick up one of Lady Veula's gloves that had fallen to the floor.

'I did not know you kept a dog,' said Lady Veula.

'We don't,' said Comus, 'there isn't one in the house.'

'I could have sworn I saw one follow you across the hall this evening,' she said.

'A small black dog, something like a schipperke?' asked Comus in a low voice.

'Yes, that was it.'

'I saw it myself tonight; it ran from behind my chair just as I was sitting down. Don't say anything to the others about it; it would frighten my mother.'

'Have you ever seen it before?' Lady Veula asked quickly.

'Once, when I was six years old. It followed my father downstairs.'

Lady Veula said nothing. She knew that Comus had lost his father at the age of six.

In the drawing-room Serena made nervous excuses for her talkative friend.

'Really, rather an interesting man, you know, and up to the eyes in all sorts of movements. Just the sort of person to turn loose at a drawing-room meeting, or to send down to a mission-hall in some unheard-of neighbourhood. Given a sounding-board and a harmonium, and a titled woman of some sort in the chair, and he'll be perfectly happy; I must say I hadn't realized how overpowering he might be at a small dinner-party.'

'I should say he was a very good man,' said Mrs Greech; she had forgiven the mutilation of her soup-plate story.

The party broke up early, as most of the guests had other engagements to keep. With a belated recognition of the farewell nature of the occasion they made pleasant little good-bye remarks to Comus, with the usual predictions of prosperity and anticipations of an ultimate auspicious return. Even Henry Greech sank his personal dislike of the boy for the moment, and made hearty jocular allusions to a home-coming, which, in the elder man's eyes, seemed possibly pleasantly remote. Lady Veula alone made no reference to the future; she simply said, 'Good-bye, Comus,' but her voice was the kindest of all, and he responded with a look of gratitude. The weariness in her eyes was more marked than ever as she lay back against the cushions of her carriage.

'What a tragedy life is!' she said aloud to herself.

Serena and Stephen Thorle were the last to leave, and Francesca stood alone for a moment at the head of the stair-

way watching Comus laughing and chatting as he escorted
the departing guests to the door. The ice-wall was melting
under the influence of coming separation, and never had
he looked more adorably handsome in her eyes, never had
his merry laugh and mischief-loving gaiety seemed more
infectious than on this night of his farewell banquet. She was
glad enough that he was going away from a life of idleness and
extravagance and temptation, but she began to suspect that
she would miss, for a little while at any rate, the high-spirited
boy who could be so attractive in his better moods. Her
impulse, after the guests had gone, was to call him to her and
hold him once more in her arms, and repeat her wishes for his
happiness and good-luck in the land he was going to, and her
promise of his welcome back, some not too distant day, to the
land he was leaving. She wanted to forget, and to make him
forget, the months of irritable jangling and sharp discussions,
the months of cold aloofness and indifference, and to remember only that he was her own dear Comus as in the days of
yore, before he had grown from an unmanageable pickle into
a weariful problem. But she feared lest she should break
down, and she did not wish to cloud his light-hearted gaiety
on the very eve of his departure. She watched him for a
moment as he stood in the hall, settling his tie before a mirror,
and then went quietly back to her drawing-room. It had not
been a very successful dinner-party, and the general effect it
had left on her was one of depression.

Comus, with a lively musical-comedy air on his lips, and a
look of wretchedness in his eyes, went out to visit the haunts
that he was leaving so soon.

CHAPTER 15

ELAINE YOUGHAL sat at lunch in the Speise Saal of one of
Vienna's costlier hotels. The double-headed eagle, with its
'K.u.K.' legend, everywhere met the eye and announced the
imperial favour in which the establishment basked. Some
several square yards of yellow bunting, charged with the

image of another double-headed eagle, floating from the highest flagstaff above the building, betrayed to the initiated the fact that a Russian Grand Duke was concealed somewhere on the premises. Unannounced by heraldic symbolism, but unconcealable by reason of nature's own blazonry, were several citizens and citizenesses of the great republic of the Western world. One or two Cobdenite members of the British Parliament, engaged in the useful task of proving that the cost of living in Vienna was on an exorbitant scale, flitted with restrained importance through a land whose fatness they had come to spy out; every fancied overcharge in their bills was welcome as providing another nail in the coffin of their fiscal opponents. It is the glory of democracies that they may be misled, but never driven. Here and there, like brave deeds in a dust-patterned world, flashed and glittered the sumptuous uniforms of representatives of the Austrian military caste. Also in evidence, at discreet intervals, were stray units of the Semitic tribe that nineteen centuries of European neglect had been unable to mislay.

Elaine, sitting with Courtenay at an elaborately appointed luncheon table, gay with high goblets of Bohemian glassware, was mistress of three discoveries. First, to her disappointment, that if you frequent the more expensive hotels of Europe you must be prepared to find, in whatever country you may chance to be staying, a depressing international likeness between them all. Secondly, to her relief, that one is not expected to be sentimentally amorous during a modern honeymoon. Thirdly, rather to her dismay, that Courtenay Youghal did not necessarily expect her to be markedly affectionate in private. Some one had described him, after their marriage, as one of Nature's bachelors, and she began to see how aptly the description fitted him.

'Will those Germans on our left never stop talking?' she asked, as an undying flow of Teutonic small-talk rattled and jangled across the intervening stretch of carpet. 'Not one of those three women has ceased talking for an instant since we've been sitting here.'

'They will presently, if only for a moment,' said Courtenay; 'when the dish you have ordered comes in there will be a deathly silence at the next table. No German can see a *plat* brought in for some one else without being possessed with a great fear that it represents a more toothsome morsel or a better money's worth than what he has ordered for himself.'

The exuberant Teutonic chatter was balanced on the other side of the room by an even more penetrating conversation unflaggingly maintained by a party of Americans, who were sitting in judgment on the cuisine of the country they were passing through, and finding few extenuating circumstances.

'What Mr Lonkins wants is a real *deep* cherry pie,' announced a lady in a tone of dramatic and honest conviction.

'Why, yes, that is so,' corroborated a gentleman who was apparently the Mr Lonkins in question; 'a real *deep* cherry pie.'

'We had the same trouble way back in Paris,' proclaimed another lady; 'little Jerome and the girls don't want to eat any more *crème renversée*. I'd give anything if they could get some real cherry pie.'

'Real *deep* cherry pie,' assented Mr Lonkins.

'Way down in Ohio we used to have peach pie that was real good,' said Mrs Lonkins, turning on a tap of reminiscence that presently flowed to a cascade. The subject of pies seemed to lend itself to indefinite expansion.

'So those people think of nothing but their food?' asked Elaine, as the virtues of roasted mutton suddenly came to the fore and received emphatic recognition, even the absent and youthful Jerome being quoted in its favour.

'On the contrary,' said Courtenay, 'they are a widely-travelled set, and the man has had a notably interesting career. It is a form of homesickness with them to discuss and lament the cookery and foods that they've never had the leisure to stay at home and digest. The Wandering Jew probably babbled unremittingly about some breakfast dish that took so long to prepare that he had never time to eat it.'

A waiter deposited a dish of Wiener Nierenbraten in front of Elaine. At the same moment a magic hush fell upon the three German ladies at the adjoining table, and the flicker of a great fear passed across their eyes. Then they burst forth again into tumultuous chatter. Courtenay had proved a reliable prophet.

Almost at the same moment as the luncheon-dish appeared on the scene, two ladies arrived at a neighbouring table, and bowed with dignified cordiality to Elaine and Courtenay. They were two of the more worldly and travelled of Elaine's extensive stock of aunts, and they happened to be making a short stay at the same hotel as the young couple. They were far too correct and rationally minded to intrude themselves on their niece, but it was significant of Elaine's altered view as to the sanctity of honeymoon life that she secretly rather welcomed the presence of her two relatives in the hotel, and had found time and occasion to give them more of her society than she would have considered necessary or desirable a few weeks ago. The younger of the two she rather liked, in a restrained fashion, as one likes an unpretentious watering-place or a restaurant that does not try to give one a musical education in addition to one's dinner. One felt instinctively about her that she would never wear rather more valuable diamonds than any other woman in the room, and would never be the only person to be saved in a steamboat disaster or hotel fire. As a child she might have been perfectly well able to recite 'On Linden when the sun was low', but one felt certain that nothing ever induced her to do so. The elder aunt, Mrs Goldbrook, did not share her sister's character as a human rest-cure; most people found her rather disturbing, chiefly, perhaps, from her habit of asking unimportant questions with enormous solemnity. Her manner of inquiring after a trifling ailment gave one the impression that she was more concerned with the fortunes of the malady than with oneself, and when one got rid of a cold one felt that she almost expected to be given its postal address. Probably her manner was merely the defensive outwork of an innate shyness, but she was not a woman who commanded confidences.

'A telephone call for Courtenay,' commented the younger of the two women as Youghal hurriedly flashed through the room; 'the telephone system seems to enter very largely into the young man's life.'

'The telephone has robbed matrimony of most of its sting,'

said the elder; 'so much more discreet than pen and ink communications which get read by the wrong people.'

Elaine's aunts were conscientiously worldly; they were the natural outcome of a stock that had been conscientiously strait-laced for many generations.

Elaine had progressed to the pancake stage before Courtenay returned.

'Sorry to be away so long,' he said, 'but I've arranged something rather nice for tonight. There's rather a jolly masquerade ball on. I've 'phoned about getting a costume for you, and it's all right. It will suit you beautifully, and I've got my harlequin dress with me. Madame Kelnicort, excellent soul, is going to chaperon you, and she'll take you back any time you like; I'm quite unreliable when I get into fancy dress. I shall probably keep going till some unearthly hour of the morning.'

A masquerade ball in a strange city hardly represented Elaine's idea of enjoyment. Carefully to disguise one's identity in a neighbourhood where one was entirely unknown seemed to her rather meaningless. With Courtenay, of course, it was different; he seemed to have friends and acquaintances everywhere. However, the matter had progressed to a point which would have made a refusal to go seem rather ungracious. Elaine finished her pancake and began to take a polite interest in her costume.

'What is your character?' asked Madame Kelnicort that evening, as they uncloaked, preparatory to entering the already crowded ball-room.

'I believe I'm supposed to represent Marjolaine de Montfort, whoever she may have been,' said Elaine. 'Courtenay declares he only wanted to marry me because I'm his ideal of her.'

'But what a mistake to go as a character you know nothing about. To enjoy a masquerade ball you ought to throw away your own self and be the character you represent. Now Courtenay has been Harlequin since half-way through dinner; I could see it dancing in his eyes. At about six o'clock tomorrow morning he will fall asleep and wake up a member of the British House of Parliament on his honeymoon, but tonight he is unrestrainedly Harlequin.'

Elaine stood in the ball-room surrounded by a laughing, jostling throng of pierrots, jockeys, Dresden-china shepherdesses, Rumanian peasant-girls, and all the lively make-believe creatures that form the ingredients of a fancy-dress ball. As she stood watching them she experienced a growing feeling of annoyance, chiefly with herself. She was assisting, as the French say, at one of the gayest scenes of Europe's gayest capital, and she was conscious of being absolutely unaffected by the gaiety around her. The costumes were certainly interesting to look at, and the music good to listen to, and to that extent she was amused, but the *abandon* of the scene made no appeal to her. It was like watching a game of which you did not know the rules, and in the issue of which you were not interested. Elaine began to wonder what was the earliest moment at which she could drag Madame Kelnicort away from the revel without being guilty of sheer cruelty. Then Courtenay wriggled out of the crush and came towards her, a joyous, laughing Courtenay, looking younger and handsomer than she had ever seen him. She could scarcely recognize in him tonight the rising young debater who made embarrassing onslaughts on the Government's foreign policy before a crowded House of Commons. He claimed her for the dance that was just starting, and steered her dexterously into the heart of the waltzing crowd.

'You look more like Marjolaine than I should have thought a mortal woman of these days could look,' he declared, 'only Marjolaine did smile sometimes. You have rather the air of wondering if you'd left out enough tea for the servants' breakfast. Don't mind my teasing; I love you to look like that, and besides, it makes a splendid foil to my Harlequin—my selfishness coming to the fore again, you see. But you really are to go home the moment you're bored; the excellent Kelnicort gets heaps of dances throughout the winter, so don't mind sacrificing her.'

A little later in the evening Elaine found herself standing out a dance with a grave young gentleman from the Russian Embassy.

'Monsieur Courtenay enjoys himself, doesn't he?' he observed, as the youthful-looking harlequin flashed past them, looking like some restless gorgeous-hued dragon-fly. 'Why is it that the good God has given your countrymen the boon of eternal youth? Some of your countrywomen, too, but all of the men.'

Elaine could think of many of her countrymen who were not and never could have been youthful, but as far as Courtenay was concerned she recognized the fitness of the remark. And the recognition carried with it a sense of depression. Would he always remain youthful and keen on gaiety and revelling, while she grew staid and retiring? She had thrust the lively intractable Comus out of her mind, as by his perverseness he had thrust himself out of her heart, and she had chosen the brilliant young man of affairs as her husband. He had honestly let her see the selfish side of his character while he was courting her, but she had been prepared to make due sacrifices to the selfishness of a public man who had his career to consider above all other things. Would she also have to make sacrifices to the harlequin spirit which was now revealing itself as an undercurrent in his nature? When one has inured oneself to the idea of a particular form of victimization it is disconcerting to be confronted with another. Many a man who would patiently undergo martyrdom for religion's sake would be furiously unwilling to be a martyr to neuralgia.

'I think that is why you English love animals so much,' pursued the young diplomat; 'you are such splendid animals yourselves. You are lively because you want to be lively, not because people are looking on at you. Monsieur Courtenay is certainly an animal. I mean it as a high compliment.'

'Am I an animal?' asked Elaine.

'I was going to say you are an angel,' said the Russian, in some embarrassment, 'but I do not think that would do; angels and animals would never get on together. To get on with animals you must have a sense of humour, and I don't suppose angels have any sense of humour; you see it would be no use to them as they never hear any jokes.'

'Perhaps,' said Elaine, with a tinge of bitterness in her voice, 'perhaps I am a vegetable.'

'I think you most remind me of a picture,' said the Russian.

It was not the first time Elaine had heard the simile.

'I know,' she said, 'the Narrow Gallery at the Louvre: attributed to Leonardo da Vinci.'

Evidently the impression she made on people was solely one of externals.

Was that how Courtenay regarded her? Was that to be her function and place in life, a painted background, a decorative setting to other people's triumphs and tragedies? Somehow tonight she had the feeling that a general might have who brought imposing forces into the field and could do nothing with them. She possessed youth and good looks, considerable wealth, and had just made what would be thought by most people a very satisfactory marriage. And already she seemed to be standing aside as an onlooker where she had expected herself to be taking a leading part.

'Does this sort of thing appeal to you?' she asked the young Russian, nodding towards the gay scrimmage of masqueraders and rather prepared to hear an amused negative.

'But yes, of course,' he answered; 'costume balls, fancy fairs, café chantant, casino, anything that is not real life appeals to us Russians. Real life with us is the sort of thing that Maxim Gorki deals in. It interests us immensely, but we like to get away from it sometimes.'

Madame Kelnicort came up with another prospective partner, and Elaine delivered her ukase: one more dance and then back to the hotel. Without any special regret she made her retreat from the revel which Courtenay was enjoying under the impression that it was life and the young Russian under the firm conviction that it was not.

Elaine breakfasted at her aunts' table the next morning at much her usual hour. Courtenay was sleeping the sleep of a happy tired animal. He had given instructions to be called at eleven o'clock, from which time onward the *Neue Freie Presse*, the *Zeit*, and his toilet would occupy his attention till he appeared at the luncheon table. There were not many people breakfasting when Elaine arrived on the scene, but the room seemed to be fuller than it really was by reason of a penetrating voice that was engaged in recounting how far the standard of Viennese breakfast fare fell below the expectations and desires of little Jerome and the girls.

'If ever little Jerome becomes President of the United States,' said Elaine, 'I shall be able to contribute quite an informing article on his gastronomic likes and dislikes to the papers.'

The aunts were discreetly inquisitive as to the previous evening's entertainment.

'If Elaine would flirt mildly with somebody it would be such a good thing,' said Mrs Goldbrook; 'it would remind Courtenay that he's not the only attractive young man in the world.'

Elaine, however, did not gratify their hopes; she referred to the ball with the detachment she would have shown in describing a drawing-room show of cottage industries. It was not difficult to discern in her description of the affair the confession that she had been slightly bored. From Courtenay, later in the day, the aunts received a much livelier impression of the festivities, from which it was abundantly clear that he, at any rate, had managed to amuse himself. Neither did it appear that his good opinion of his own attractions had suffered any serious shock. He was distinctly in a very good temper.

'The secret of enjoying a honeymoon,' said Mrs Goldbrook afterwards to her sister, 'is not to attempt too much.'

'You mean——?'

'Courtenay is content to try and keep one person amused and happy, and he thoroughly succeeds.'

'I certainly don't think Elaine is going to be very happy,' said her sister, 'but at least Courtenay saved her from making the greatest mistake she could have made—marrying that young Bassington.'

'He has also,' said Mrs Goldbrook, 'helped her to make the next biggest mistake of her life—marrying Courtenay Youghal.'

CHAPTER 16

IT was late afternoon by the banks of a swiftly rushing river, a river that gave back a haze of heat from its waters as though it were some stagnant steaming lagoon, and yet seemed to be whirling onward with the determination of a living thing, perpetually eager and remorseless, leaping savagely at any obstacle that attempted to stay its course; an unfriendly river, to whose waters you committed yourself at your peril. Under the hot breathless shade of the trees on its shore arose that acrid all-pervading smell that seems to hang everywhere about the tropics, a smell as of some monstrous musty still-room where herbs and spices have been crushed and distilled and stored for hundreds of years, and where the windows have seldom been opened. In the dazzling heat that still held undisputed sway over the scene, insects and birds seemed preposterously alive and active, flitting their gay colours through the sunbeams, and crawling over the baked dust in the full swing and pursuit of their several businesses; the flies engaged in Heaven knows what, and the fly-catchers busy with the flies. Beasts and humans showed no such indifference to the temperature; the sun would have to slant yet farther downward before the earth would become a fit arena for their revived activities. In the sheltered basement of a wayside rest-house a gang of native hammock-bearers slept or chattered drowsily through the last hours of the long midday halt; wide awake, yet almost motionless in the thrall of a heavy lassitude, their European master sat alone in an upper chamber, staring out through a narrow window-opening at the native village, spreading away in thick clusters of huts girt around with cultivated vegetation. It seemed a vast human ant-hill, which would presently be astir with its teeming human life, as though the Sun God in his last departing stride had roused it with a careless kick. Even as Comus watched he could see the beginnings of the evening's awakening. Women, squatting in front of their huts, began to pound away at the rice or maize that would form the evening meal, girls were collecting their water-pots preparatory to a walk down to the river, and enterprising goats made tentative forays through gaps in the ill-kept fences of neighbouring garden-plots; their hurried retreats showed that here at least some one was keeping alert and wakeful vigil. Behind a hut perched on a steep hill-side, just opposite to the rest-house, two boys were splitting wood with a certain languid industry; farther down the road a group of dogs were leisurely working themselves up to quarrelling pitch. Here and there, bands of evil-looking pigs roamed about, busy with foraging excursions that came unpleasantly athwart the borderline of scavenging. And from the trees that bounded and intersected the village rose the horrible, tireless, spiteful-sounding squawking of the iron-throated crows.

Comus sat and watched it all with a sense of growing aching depression. It was so utterly trivial to his eyes, so devoid of interest, and yet it was so real, so serious, so implacable in its continuity. The brain grew tired with the thought of its unceasing reproduction. It had all gone on, as it was going on now, by the side of the great rushing, swirling river, this tilling and planting and harvesting, marketing and store-keeping, feast-making and fetish-worship and love-making, burying and giving in marriage, child-bearing and child-rearing, all this had been going on, in the shimmering, blistering heat and the warm nights, while he had been a youngster at school, dimly recognizing Africa as a division of the earth's surface that it was advisable to have a certain nodding acquaintance with. It had been going on in all its trifling detail, all its serious intensity, when his father and his grandfather in their day had been little boys at school, it would go on just as intently as ever long after Comus and his generation had passed away, just as the shadows would lengthen and fade under the mulberry trees in that far-away English garden, round the old stone fountain where a leaden otter for ever preyed on a leaden salmon.

Comus rose impatiently from his seat, and walked wearily across the hut to another window-opening which commanded a broad view of the river. There was something which fascinated and then depressed one in its ceaseless hurrying onward sweep, its tons of water rushing on for all time, as long as the face of the earth should remain unchanged. On its farther shore could be seen spread out at intervals other teeming villages, with their cultivated plots and pasture clearings, their moving dots which meant cattle and goats and dogs and children. And far up its course, lost in the forest growth that fringed its banks, were hidden away yet more villages, human herding-grounds where men dwelt and worked and bartered, squabbled and worshipped, sickened and perished, while the river went by with its endless swirl and rush of gleaming waters. One could well understand primitive early races making propitiatory sacrifices to the spirit of a great river on whose shores they dwelt. Time and the river were the two great forces that seemed to matter here.

It was almost a relief to turn back to that other outlook and watch the village life that was now beginning to wake in earnest. The procession of water-fetchers had formed itself in a long chattering line that stretched riverwards. Comus wondered how many tens of thousands of times that procession had been formed since first the village came into existence. They had been doing it while he was playing in the cricket-fields at school, while he was spending Christmas holidays in Paris, while he was going his careless round of theatres, dances, suppers and card-parties, just as they were doing it now; they would be doing it when there was no one alive who remembered Comus Bassington. This thought recurred again and again with painful persistence, a morbid growth arising in part from his loneliness.

Staring dumbly out at the toiling, sweltering human ant-hill, Comus marvelled how missionary enthusiasts could labour hopefully at the work of transplanting their religion, with its home-grown accretions of fatherly parochial benevolence, in this heat-blistered, fever-scourged wilderness, where men lived like groundbait and died like flies. Demons one might believe in, if one did not hold one's imagination in healthy check, but a kindly all-managing God, never. Somewhere in the west country of England Comus had an uncle who lived in a rose-smothered rectory and taught a wholesome gentle-hearted creed that expressed itself in the spirit of 'Little lamb, Who made thee?' and faithfully reflected the beautiful homely Christ-child sentiment of Saxon Europe. What a far-away, unreal fairy-story it all seemed here in this West African land, where the bodies of men were of as little account as the bubbles that floated on the oily froth of the great flowing river, and where it required a stretch of wild profitless imagination to credit them with undying souls! In the life he had come from Comus had been accustomed to think of individuals as definite masterful personalities, making their several marks on the circumstances that revolved around them; they did well or ill, or in most cases indifferently, and were criticized, praised, blamed, thwarted, or tolerated, or given way to. In any case, humdrum or outstanding, they had their spheres of importance, little or big. They dominated a breakfast table or harassed a Government, according to their capabilities or opportunities, or perhaps they merely had irritating mannerisms. At any rate it seemed highly probable that they had souls. Here a man simply made a unit in an unnumbered population, an inconsequent dot in a loosely-compiled death-roll. Even his own position as a white man exalted conspicuously above a horde of black natives did not save Comus from the depressing sense of nothingness which his first experience of fever had thrown over him. He was a lost, soulless body in this great uncaring land; if he died another would take his place, his few effects would be inventoried and sent down to the coast, some one else would finish off any tea or whisky that he left behind—that would be all.

It was nearly time to be starting towards the next halting-place where he would dine, or at any rate eat something. But the lassitude which the fever had bequeathed him made the tedium of travelling through interminable forest-tracks a weariness to be deferred as long as possible. The bearers were nothing loath to let another half-hour or so slip by, and Comus dragged a battered paper-covered novel from the pocket of his coat. It was a story dealing with the elaborately tangled love affairs of a surpassingly uninteresting couple, and even in his almost bookless state Comus had not been able to plough his way through more than two-thirds of its dull length; bound up with the cover, however, were some pages of advertisement, and these the exile scanned with a hungry intentness that the romance itself could never have commanded. The name of a shop, of a street, the address of a restaurant, came to him as a bitter reminder of the world he had lost, a world that ate and drank and flirted, gambled and made merry, a world that debated and intrigued and wire-pulled, fought or compromised political battles—and recked nothing of its outcasts wandering through forest paths and steamy swamps or lying in the grip of fever. Comus read and re-read those few lines of advertisement, just as he treasured a much-crumpled programme of a first-night performance at the Straw Exchange Theatre; they seemed to make a little more real the past that was already too shadowy and so utterly remote. For a moment he could almost capture the sensation of being once again in those haunts that he loved; then he looked round and pushed the book wearily from him. The steaming heat, the forest, the rushing river hemmed him in on all sides.

The two boys who had been splitting wood ceased from their labours and straightened their backs; suddenly the smaller of the two gave the other a resounding whack with a split lath that he still held in his hand, and flew up the hillside with a scream of laughter and simulated terror, the bigger lad following in hot pursuit. Up and down the steep bush-grown slope they raced and twisted and dodged, coming sometimes to close quarters in a hurricane of squeals and smacks, rolling over and over like fighting kittens, and breaking away again to start fresh provocation and fresh pursuit. Now and again they would lie for a time panting in what seemed the last stage of exhaustion, and then they would be off in another wild scamper, their dusky bodies flitting through the bushes, disappearing and reappearing with equal suddenness. Presently two girls of their own age, who had returned from the water-fetching, sprang out on them from ambush, and the four joined in one joyous gambol that lit up the hillside with shrill echoes and glimpses of flying limbs. Comus sat and watched, at first with an amused interest, then with a returning flood of depression and heartache. Those wild young human kittens represented the joy of life, he was the outsider, the lonely alien, watching something in which he could not join, a happiness in which he had no part or lot. He would pass presently out of the village and his bearers' feet would leave their indentations in the dust: that would be his most permanent memorial in this little oasis of teeming life. And that other life, in which he once moved with such confident sense of his own necessary participation in it, how completely he had passed out of it! Amid all its laughing throngs, its card-parties and race-meetings and country-house gatherings, he was just a mere name, remembered or forgotten, Comus Bassington, the boy who went away. He had loved himself very well and never troubled greatly whether any one else really loved him, and now he realized what he had made of his life. And at the same time he knew that if his chance were to come again he would throw it away just as surely, just as perversely. Fate played with him with loaded dice; he would lose always.

One person in the whole world had cared for him, for longer than he could remember, cared for him perhaps more than he knew, cared for him perhaps now. But a wall of ice had mounted up between him and her, and across it there blew that cold breath that chills or kills affection.

The words of a well-known old song, the wistful cry of a lost cause, rang with insistent mockery through his brain:

> Better loved you canna be,
> Will ye ne'er come back again?

If it was love that was to bring him back he must be an exile for ever. His epitaph in the mouths of those that remembered him would be: Comus Bassington, the boy who never came back.

And in his unutterable loneliness he bowed his head on his arms, that he might not see the joyous scrambling frolic on yonder hill-side.

CHAPTER 17

THE bleak rawness of a grey December day held sway over St James's Park, that sanctuary of lawn and tree and pool, into which the bourgeois innovator has rushed ambitiously time and again, to find that he must take the patent leather from off his feet, for the ground on which he stands is hallowed ground.

In the lonely hour of early afternoon, when the workers had gone back to their work, and the loiterers were scarcely yet gathered again, Francesca Bassington made her way restlessly along the stretches of gravelled walk that bordered the ornamental water. The overmastering unhappiness that filled her heart and stifled her thinking powers found answering echo in her surroundings. There is a sorrow that lingers in old parks and gardens that the busy streets have no leisure to keep by them; the dead must bury their dead in Whitehall or the Place de la Concorde, but there are quieter spots where they may still keep tryst with the living and intrude the memory of their bygone selves on generations that have almost forgotten them. Even in tourist-trampled Versailles the desolation of a tragedy that cannot die haunts the terraces and fountains like a bloodstain that will not wash out; in the Saxon Garden at Warsaw there broods the memory of long-dead things, coeval with the stately trees that shade its walks, and with the carp that swim today in its ponds as they doubtless swam there when 'Lieber Augustin' was a living person and not as yet an immortal couplet. And St James's Park, with its lawns and walks and water-fowl, harbours still its associations with a bygone order of men and women, whose happiness and sadness are woven into its history, dim and grey as they were once bright and glowing, like the faded pattern worked into the fabric of an old tapestry. It was here that Francesca had made her way when the intolerable inaction of waiting had driven her forth from her home. She was waiting for that worst news of all, the news which does not kill hope, because there has been none to kill, but merely ends suspense. An early message had said that Comus was ill, which might have meant much or little; then there had come that morning a cablegram which only meant one thing; in a few hours she would get a final message, of which this was the preparatory forerunner. She already knew as much as that awaited message would tell her. She knew that she would never see Comus again, and she knew now that she loved him beyond all things that the world could hold for her. It was no sudden rush of pity or compunction that clouded her judgment or gilded her recollection of him; she saw him as he was, the beautiful wayward laughing boy, with his naughtiness, his exasperating selfishness, his insurmountable folly and perverseness, his cruelty that spared not even himself, and as he was, as he always had been, she knew that he was the one thing that the Fates had willed that she should love. She did not stop to accuse or excuse herself for having sent him forth to what was to prove his death. It was, doubtless, right and reasonable that he should have gone out there, as hundreds of other men went out, in pursuit of careers; the terrible thing was that he would never come back. The old cruel hopelessness that had always chequered her pride and pleasure in his good looks and high spirits and fitfully charming ways had dealt her a last crushing blow; he was dying somewhere thousands of miles away without hope of recovery, without a word of love to comfort him, and without hope or shred of consolation she was waiting to hear of the end. The end; that last dreadful piece of news which would write 'Nevermore' across his life and hers.

The lively bustle in the streets had been a torture that she could not bear. It wanted but two days to Christmas, and the gaiety of the season, forced or genuine, rang out everywhere. Christmas shopping, with its anxious solicitude or self-centred absorption, overspread the West End and made the pavements scarcely passable at certain favoured points. Proud parents, parcel-laden and surrounded by escorts of their young people, compared notes with one another on the looks and qualities of their offspring and exchanged loud hurried confidences on the difficulty or success which each had experienced in getting the right presents for one and all. Shouted directions where to find this or that article at its best mingled with salvos of Christmas good wishes. To Francesca, making her way frantically through the carnival of happiness with that lonely deathbed in her eyes, it had seemed a callous mockery of her pain; could not people remember that there were crucifixions as well as joyous birthdays in the world? Every mother that she passed happy in the company of a fresh-looking, clean-limbed schoolboy son sent a fresh stab at her heart, and the very shops had their bitter memories. There was the tea-shop where he and she had often taken tea together, or, in the days of their estrangement, sat with their separate friends at separate tables. There were other shops where extravagantly-incurred bills had furnished material for those frequently recurring scenes of recrimination, and the Colonial outfitters, where, as he had phrased it in whimsical mockery, he had bought grave-clothes for his burying-alive. The 'oubliette'! She remembered the bitter petulant name he had flung at his destined exile. There at least he had been harder on himself than the Fates were pleased to will; never, as long as Francesca lived and had a brain that served her, would she be able to forget. That narcotic would never be given to her. Unrelenting, unsparing memory would be with her always to remind her of those last days of tragedy. Already her mind was dwelling on the details of that ghastly farewell dinner-party and recalling one by one the incidents of ill-omen that had marked it; how they had sat down seven to table and how one liqueur glass in the set of seven had been shivered into fragments, how her glass had slipped from her hand as she raised it to her lips to wish Comus a safe return; and the strange, quiet hopelessness of Lady Veula's 'Good-bye'; she remembered now how it had chilled and frightened her at the moment.

The park was filling again with its floating population of loiterers, and Francesca's footsteps began to take a homeward direction. Something seemed to tell her that the message for which she waited had arrived and was lying there on the hall table. Her brother, who had announced his intention of visiting her early in the afternoon, would have gone by now; he knew nothing of this morning's bad news—the instinct of a wounded animal to creep away by itself had prompted her to keep her sorrow from him as long as possible. His visit did not necessitate her presence; he was bringing an Austrian friend, who was compiling a work on the Franco-Flemish school of painting, to inspect the Van der Meulen, which Henry Greech hoped might perhaps figure as an illustration in the book. They were due to arrive shortly after lunch, and Francesca had left a note of apology, pleading an urgent engagement elsewhere. As she turned to make her way across the Mall into the Green Park a gentle voice hailed her from a carriage that was just drawing up by the sidewalk. Lady Caroline Benaresq had been favouring the Victoria Memorial with a long unfriendly stare.

'In primitive days,' she remarked, 'I believe it was the fashion for great chiefs and rulers to have large numbers of their relatives and dependents killed and buried with them; in these more enlightened times we have invented quite another way of making a great sovereign universally regretted. My dear Francesca,' she broke off suddenly, catching the misery that had settled in the other's eyes, 'what is the matter? Have you had bad news from out there?'

'I am waiting for very bad news,' said Francesca, and Lady Caroline knew what had happened.

'I wish I could say something; I can't.' Lady Caroline spoke in a harsh, grunting voice that few people had ever heard her use.

Francesca crossed the Mall, and the carriage drove on.

'Heaven help that poor woman,' said Lady Caroline, which was, for her, startlingly like a prayer.

As Francesca entered the hall she gave a quick look at the table; several packages, evidently an early batch of Christmas presents, were there, and two or three letters. On a salver by itself was the cablegram for which she had waited. A maid, who had evidently been on the look-out for her, brought her the salver. The servants were well aware of the dreadful thing that was happening, and there was pity on the girl's face and in her voice.

'This came for you ten minutes ago, ma'am, and Mr Greech has been here, ma'am, with another gentleman, and was sorry you weren't at home. Mr Greech said he would call again in about half an hour.'

Francesca carried the cablegram unopened into the drawing-room and sat down for a moment to think. There was no need to read it yet, for she knew what she would find written there. For a few pitiful moments Comus would seem less hopelessly lost to her if she put off the reading of that last terrible message. She rose and crossed over to the windows and pulled down the blinds, shutting out the waning December day, and then re-seated herself. Perhaps in the shadowy half-light her boy would come and sit with her again

for awhile and let h her last upon his loved face; she
could never touch h her last upon his loved face; she
voice, but surely she m or hear his laughing petulant
eyes saw only the hatek on her dead. And her starving
and porcelain that she ess things of bronze and silver
look where she would th up and worshipped as gods
ruling deities of the home te there around her, the col
He had moved in and out d no place for her dead boy
breathing thing that had been g them, the warm, living,
her eyes from that youthful co. igure to love, and she had turned
of painted canvas, a musty relic long-departed craftsman.
And now he was gone from heit, from her touch, from
her hearing for ever, without ev thought to flash between
them for all the dreary years the should live, and these
things of canvas and pigment an rought metal would stay
with her. They were her soul. A hat shall it profit a man
if he save his soul and slay his h in torment?

On a small table by her sid as Mervyn Quentock's
portrait of her——the prophetic syn of her tragedy; the rich
dead harvest of unreal things tha ad never known life, and
the bleak thrall of black unending Vinter, a Winter in which
things died and knew no re-awaking.

Francesca turned to the small er elope lying in her lap; very
slowly she opened it and read the ort message. Then she sat
numb and silent for a long, longtime, or perhaps only for
minutes. The voice of Henry Green in the hall, inquiring for
her, called her to herself. Huriedly she crushed the piece of
paper out of sight; he would lave to be told, of course, but
just yet her pain seemed too dreadful to be laid bare. 'Comus
is dead' was a sentence beyond her power to speak.

'I have bad news for you, Francesca, I'm sorry to say,'
Henry announced. Had he heard, too?

'Henneberg has been here and looked at the picture,' he
continued, seating himself by her side, 'and though he
admired it immensely as a work of art, he gave me a disagreeable surprise by assuring me that it's not a genuine Van der
Meulen. It's a splendid copy, but still, unfortunately, only
a copy.'

Henry paused and glanced at his sister to see how she had

...Even in the dim light he...
...unwelcome...
...some of the an...thingly, laying his hand
...My dear Francesca...that this must be a great
...fectionately on he...ways set such store by this
disappointment to o...too much to heart. These
picture, but you...st...imes to most picture fanciers
disagreeable disco...y per cent of the alleged Old
and owners. Why bo...osed to be wrongly attributed.
Masters in the...re...lar cases in this country. Lady
And there are...the other day that they simply
Dovecourt was...to examine the Van Dykes at
daren't have an...elcome disclosures. And, besides,
Columbey for fe...cellent copy that it's by no means
your picture is...You must get over the disappoint-
without a value o...d take a philosophical view of the
ment you naturall...
matter....'

Francesca sat in st...ilence, crushing the folded morsel
of paper tightly in he...and wondering if the thin, cheerful voice with its pi...ghastly mockery of consolation
would never stop.

THE WORLD'S CLASSICS

A Select List

VIRGIL: The Aeneid
Translated by C. Day Lewis
Edited by Jasper Griffin

HORACE WALPOLE : The Castle of Otranto
Edited by W. S. Lewis

IZAAK WALTON and CHARLES COTTON:
The Compleat Angler
Edited by John Buxton
Introduction by John Buchan

OSCAR WILDE: Complete Shorter Fiction
Edited by Isobel Murray

The Picture of Dorian Gray
Edited by Isobel Murray

VIRGINIA WOOLF: Orlando
Edited by Rachel Bowlby

ÉMILE ZOLA:
The Attack on the Mill and other stories
Translated by Douglas Parmée